THE LANGUAGE OF PARADISE

ALSO BY

BARBARA KLEIN MOSS

———

LITTLE EDENS: STORIES

The

LANGUAGE

of

PARADISE

—

BARBARA

KLEIN MOSS

W. W. NORTON & COMPANY

NEW YORK • LONDON

For information about permission to reproduce
selections from this book, write to Permissions,
W. W. Norton & Company, Inc.,
500 Fifth Avenue, New York, NY 10110

For information about special discounts for bulk
purchases, please contact W. W. Norton Special Sales
at specialsales@wwnorton.com or 800-233-4830

Manufacturing by Courier Westford
Book design by Barbara M. Bachman
Production managers: Devon Zahn and Ruth Toda

LIBRARY OF CONGRESS
CATALOGING-IN-PUBLICATION DATA

Moss, Barbara Klein.
The language of paradise / Barbara Klein Moss. — First Edition.
pages cm
ISBN 978-0-393-05713-3 (hardcover)
1. Young women—History—19th century—Fiction. 2. Artist—Fiction.
3. New England—History—19th century—Fiction. I. Title.
PS3613.O7795L36 2015
813'.6—dc23

2014046223

W. W. Norton & Company, Inc.,
500 Fifth Avenue, New York, N.Y. 10110
www.wwnorton.com

W. W. Norton & Company Ltd., Castle House,
75/76 Wells Street, London W1T 3QT

1 2 3 4 5 6 7 8 9 0

For Stewart and Sara, always,

and in memory of Wendy Weil

and Carol Houck Smith

CONTENTS

Love, it is said, was the inventor of drawing. It might also have invented speech, though less felicitously; Dissatisfied with speech, love disdains it, it has livelier ways of expressing itself. How many things the girl who took such pleasure in tracing her Lover's shadow was telling him! What sounds could she have used to convey what she conveyed with this movement of the twig?

—JEAN-JACQUES ROUSSEAU,
"Essay on the Origin of Languages in Which Something Is Said About Melody and Musical Imitation"
(from *Rousseau: The Discourses and Other Early Political Writings*, ed. and trans. Victor Gourevitch)

Build therefore your own world. As fast as you conform your life to the pure idea in your mind, that will unfold its great proportions.

—RALPH WALDO EMERSON (from *Nature*)

THE LANGUAGE OF PARADISE

PROLOGUE

*BIRDS AND BEASTS FLY OUT OF
OUR MOUTHS LIKE ANGELS*

S O P H I A , July 1838

S UMMER IS THE SEASON OF UNVEILING. THE BED CURTAINS
came down last month, the carpets have been rolled up, straw matting
laid on floors that hold the winter chill. Every door is open. The hall
has been transformed into an airy cloister, a whole other room where
the family sits on humid nights, enjoying the crosswind. It is possible
to walk from the front path straight through the center of the house and
out into the garden. Sophy Birdsall does that now, just because she can.

She is conscious of a certain impropriety. A few weeks along as she
is, she should not be carrying herself like a bride walking down the aisle.
She should not be *sweeping*, even if the infinitesimal weight makes her
feel majestic. She's always been a scanty little thing, a light craft at the
mercy of every current. Now that she will soon have a prow, she feels
for the first time like a vessel of substance, balanced even in unsettled
waters. She believes she has finally grown into her proper name. She
sees it inscribed on the stern of her boat in majestic, undulating cursive:
Sophia.

The hall mirror stops her in mid-stride; these days she can't pass by
without measuring her silhouette. She steps away with a gasp—Mama
draped the glass with muslin to keep fly-spots off! That won't do, the

soon-to-be-ample Sophia will not be reduced to a ghost! Her white dress has faded away, but her face and neck and hands show through the gauzy cotton, ruddy with a life of their own. *Like a nun bathing in her shift.*

She doesn't know where the thought came from, but before she can ponder it, a nun confronts her from the clouded depths of the mirror. Eyes staring straight ahead, hands moving furtively over the wet cloth.

Sophy's mind has always been prone to strange couplings. In her girlhood she would speak what she saw without hesitating, the words darting from her brain to her tongue in a single headlong swoop like birds lighting on the nearest branch. People might laugh or shake their heads—"Sophy," her brothers would say by way of explanation, shrugging, as if her oddity were its own excuse—but at times these unlikely matches were even taken for wit. Then they came like gifts on the wing, quick and airy. Lately they barge in like intruders and harden to images that haunt her for days. Sophy supposes it must be her condition. She wishes she could ask Mama, for all the good it would do. Mama, who is no more troubled by unruly thoughts than she was by morning queasiness.

Gideon would never imagine his little wife could be prey to such unwholesome fancies. He assumes that her inner landscape is as sunny and placid as a baby's. It suits his purposes to think so. An hour ago over breakfast—as avid for the quiet of his study as she was for his company—he gave her a commission. "Why don't you paint me a soothing scene to contemplate while I work?"

"You would do better to look out the window," she told him. She meant only to disparage her own talents, but he is not a man to take words lightly.

"I'm not asking for a view," he said, peevish. "If I wanted a prospect, I would climb a hill. Just paint what you see, as you see it, and for the Lord's sake, don't try to get it right. Remember what Leander told you. Perspective is the Devil's trick."

Leander Solloway, the schoolmaster, is a man of strong opinions, and he is not shy about sharing them.

With effort, Sophy fixes her attention on the rectangle of garden

framed in the back doorway. There's a painting begging to be made
here, if only she had the skill. Her brushwork isn't deft enough to catch
the conversation between sun and shadow, liquid gold and new green.
She would approach it too earnestly, try to catch the movement and
reduce it all to blotches.

On the back stair, she pauses to tent her eyes. The sun is a force
today. Even in summer the Hedge farmhouse is dark, shrouded in old
shade trees that reach above the roof. Her late Reverend Papa, a practical man, was thinking more of warmth than light when he put the
windows in. Since childhood Sophy has moped through the winter—an
eternal night in New England—but today she is grateful for months of
cold and gloom. Contrast is everything, playing with paint has taught
her that. Would the roses and sweet peas seem so bounteous, the foliage
so lush, if it were brighter indoors? She and Gideon echo these contrasts, in their way. Sophy won't go so far as to say that she is spring, he
winter. It would be blasphemy to think so—not with his cornsilk hair.
But his character she thinks of as wintry. Singleness of mind. A gravity
rare in one so young. A stern and probing eye that pierces through the
world's seductions to the greater glory beneath. With these virtues to
gird him, he hides himself in the study on this brilliant Monday morning, snatching a few hours at his desk before going off with Mr. Solloway to finish the house where the three of them will live one day. She is
not permitted to know their intentions. They're preparing a grand surprise for her, Gideon says: a sanctuary where she can paint from nature
all year round.

Today she is glad enough to work outdoors. Her easel is under the
copper beech, but she walks past it to the outbuilding Papa built for his
study. Since the days when she and Gideon were courting, it has been a
little home for them. Sophy can't resist a peek through the window. She
rarely has her husband to herself nowadays; if she can't be at his side, she
must settle for a glimpse of the back of his head.

By his own choice, his desk faces the far wall. The light that trick-
les through the small panes is barely sufficient for the minuscule print
he pores over hour after hour; her beloved astral lamp—a wedding

gift from Papa's congregation—burns all day next to his open book. Its crystal drops hold rainbows she could look at for hours, but the colors are wasted on Gideon. Sophy would love nothing better than to slip in behind him, clasp his temples in her cool hands, ease his poor laden head back to rest against her. She would remove the spectacles that grip his nose like pincers, and rub the clefts they leave, and the ridge between his eyes. But she knows better than to interrupt him at his work.

Gideon is unveiling words, peeling off layers of meaning encrusted over centuries—barnacles, he calls them—to get to the pure image at the core. His interest is more than scholarly, his ambitions infinitely higher than the usual reverend gentleman's. Papa's thick black dictionaries and works of philology line the walls of the study. Mausoleums for language, in Gideon's opinion. Words are alive, they carry the breath of Creation. Is it any wonder they turn to ash in such sepulchers? Sometimes, after supper, he opens one of the tomb-tomes and chooses a word at random—a choice morsel for Mr. Solloway's delectation. Last night he was hilarious over "baboon," pursing his lips and reciting each stage of its etymology in a pinch-nose drone. "*The syllables* ba, pa, *naturally uttered in talking, are used to signify the motion of the lips, or the lips themselves, especially large or movable lips, the lips of a beast.* Arriving at the end, he'd paused and heralded the words with a sputtering fanfare: "*An animal with large ugly lips when compared with those of a man.*" When he clapped the book shut, a puff of dust rose from it. "Pity the poor beast," Gideon said gleefully. "Summed up for all eternity in such an epitaph! I ask you—who is the monkey here?"

Gideon likes to call himself a naturalist of the chairbound variety, who prowls for specimens in the dictionary instead of the forest or jungle. In truth, his aim is so lofty that the thought of it prickles the skin on the back of Sophy's neck. The object of his investigation is nothing less than the language spoken in man's first home. Gideon believes that the world God spoke into being—the tender new world that he trusted Adam to name—is as round and real as their little village of Ormsby,

Massachusetts, but sunk deeper than Atlantis beneath eons of careless speech. The great task, then, is to raise up this fallen garden by the same means as it was created: word by word. "Delving" is his name for this process—an anointed form of digging, it seems. If he can trace even one or two words back to their original source, reclaim a microscopic fragment of that sacred green, he will have done his life's work. The thought of it carries him away. "Imagine the conversations we will have. We'll go Adam one better, Sophy—we won't just name the animals, we'll speak them. Birds and beasts flying out of our mouths like angels!"

It is hard for an ordinary mind like hers to grasp. "What will it be like to live there?" she asks him. "How will it be different?"

Then he paints for her a picture she could never reproduce on any canvas, had she a thousand times the skill she was born with. Colors so radiant that the brightest hues appear sickly gray in comparison. A preternatural clarity of light: each man and beast and tree cut cleanly against a sky of purest crystal; each the ruler of its own small kingdom, inhabiting its allotted space with authority and grace. And yet, a harmony of which man can only dream, all these potent singularities joyfully subservient to the whole—*immersed*, he says, and bids her think of a pastoral landscape reflected in a lake, the forms distinct but liquidly blending into each other.

The present world is only a covering. Gideon often says so, and she knows it must be true. Yet, looking around her now—the garden at its peak, all her roses out at once like suitors contending for her favor, the stone wall giddy with honeysuckle—Sophy thinks this ought to be enough. Is it a shallowness of soul that her longings are so easily satisfied? She can't quite stifle a wish that he might sit beside her on the stone bench as he used to when they were first acquainted, the two of them gazing out at the trellis as if their joined lives were twined there. On a day like this, the troubles that beset them these last months seem like relics of a dark age. The summer has come, Gideon is himself again, and she is as she was meant to be: as filled with life as the rest of creation.

———

SOPHY SETTLES INTO HER CHAIR, the afternoon heat, heavy with fragrance, gathering around her. The painting on the easel has preoccupied her for the last week. She has been trying to capture that section of the garden where the land rises ever so slightly to meet a wall of wild roses and honeysuckle. The illusion of height seems to promise some marvel just beyond the bushes: a still lake or a verdant valley, a meadow rolling in rhythmic curves to a gently lapping sea. She's done well by the foliage—she will grant herself that—and the effect of light and shade is the best she's ever managed. Today, though, the painting doesn't draw her in. There is a flatness to it, a mincing correctness that Gideon and Leander will mock. She can't lift her brush without their voices resounding in her ear. "Imagine you are Mother Eve, gazing at the world for the first time."

She has what they call an *innocent eye*—or so they tell her. It is an affliction she was born with—not so inconvenient as a wandering eye, or so noticeable as crossed, but of particular interest to Gideon and Leander.

"Are you trying to tell me I paint badly?" she asked when they first began to rhapsodize about the phenomenon. "There's no need to mock me. I know that already."

Between the two of them, they've decided that she is a simple, natural creature who can shrug off experience as easily as changing a dress. She feels a sudden sympathy for the maligned ape, doomed to be defined by the terms of others. Who is the monkey here? She thinks she knows. True, she hasn't delved as deeply as Gideon, or explored as much of the world as Leander, but she's seen things. Her eye is more weathered than they realize. That being so, how is she to fool the jaded organ into discovering this scene for the first time when she's been contemplating the same patch of garden for days?

They're right, of course. Exactitude isn't truth. Something more than accuracy must have pulled each name, full-blown, from Adam's throat as the parade of beasts passed before him. An urge to play is pulling at her now—overflow from the beauty of the day. She stares into the painting and introduces, in turn, a small ruined temple; a pillar, behind which a hunter lurks; a fleeing nymph; great bloated clouds hanging placidly above, indifferent to the chase. The drama plays itself out while her hands are still folded in her lap.

When at last she picks up her brush, it is to paint a single figure: a few quick strokes that make a man. She places him at the highest point of the hill, with the roses at his back. He stands alone for almost an hour as Sophy squints at him and makes timid dabs at the angle of his head. By four o'clock his mouth is wide open, and poised on his lower lip, like a diver about to leap into the brink, is the small but scrupulously rendered figure of a baboon.

PART ONE

COME WITH ME

CHAPTER I

GIDEON

G IDEON BIRDSALL—BENT OVER ONE OF THE WEIGHTY black volumes he professes to despise, trying to ignore the doubled radiance of the July day and his wife's bright face at the window—might remove his spectacles to rest his eyes and reflect that he owes his present existence entirely to his gift for Hebrew. It was his facility with that ancient tongue that commended him, a scant two years ago, to the notice of the Reverend Samuel Hedge.

His first sight of the man whose acquaintance would alter the course of his life was not promising. The Reverend Professor Hedge had chosen to welcome the new crop of students to Andover Seminary with a sermon on Divine Election—hardly a theme to mesmerize a group of raw seminarians sweating through their first chapel service on a sultry day in September. The Reverend was sparsely made, sharp-featured, his black coat well brushed but rusty with wear, and when he began to speak, his voice was as meager as his person. "Strive to enter in at the strait gate, for many, I say unto you, will seek to enter in and shall not be able . . ." An exhortation—yet his tone was both flat and hollow, as if the marrow had been scooped out of the words, leaving only brittle casing; his voice rose on the last phrase in a verbal flinging-up-of-hands. It seemed clear that he had little hope for one such as himself, and even less for the sad specimens before him. He paused and sighed, lost in morose contemplation, and the seminarians, Gideon included, shifted in their seats and waited for it to be over. The Reverend looked up then, impaling the lot of them with his pointed gaze. "For STRAIT is the gate, and NARROW is the way, which leadeth unto life, and FEW THERE BE THAT FIND IT!" He drove the words in like nails, and, having secured his listeners, proceeded to transport their rigid forms through a veritable Red Sea of flame, the Chosen marching single file like miners in a shaft, eyes straight ahead, hands locked in prayer, while on either side of them the sizzling multitudes begged for mercy. When he finished, an hour and a half later, more than a few of the young men were shivering as if an early frost had descended.

That evening, sleepless in his narrow bed, Gideon wondered why Reverend Hedge never said a word about where the Redeemed were headed. Toward some vaporous mist, apparently, not unlike the formless matter from which God made the earth. Why had the parson poured all his eloquence into the torments of the damned and saved none for Paradise? Gideon had been asking that question since he was very young. Alone for the first time in his own room, he'd awakened in the night to pure black and cried out that he was blind. His mother had to light a candle to prove to him that he could see. After that, he would burrow under the covers and, in the shelter of a more intimate darkness, try to imagine a paradise of pure light. The preachers at Sunday meeting gave him little to build on. Heaven was only a name to them: the featureless opposite of the other place. The horrors they warned of seemed garish and exaggerated, no more real than the stories boys told about ghosts and bogeymen. Gideon was not frightened of Hell. He was frightened that there was no place as light as the dark was dark.

He had grown up poor, the only son of a widowed schoolmistress. His father had died before he was born—"lost at sea," his mother told him when he was old enough to ask questions. If Gideon pressed her, she gave him more—releasing each fact with a curious reluctance, always defining his father by what he was not. Good-looking, but "his features were not as noble as yours." Intelligent, but "had not your refinement of mind." In time these negative attributes condensed to a comfortable absence in Gideon's thoughts. As he became more conscious of his own place in the world, his curiosity dwindled. Clearly, his father's purpose in life had been achieved in creating him. Other boys might make heroes of their dead fathers, but Gideon was not like other boys. A man so inconsequential wasn't worth mourning, and, as his mother often said, "We make our way well enough, you and I."

When she was done teaching for the day, his mother tutored him herself, but his knowledge of Latin and French soon exceeded hers, and larger schools in neighboring villages had little to offer him. He had few friends—his intensity struck children of his age as strange and his precocity intimidated the local teachers—but he learned early to cultivate the regard of men of influence. A local mill owner, a wealthy and pious man whose daughter had been taught by Gideon's mother, saw to it that he was tutored in the classics, and sent him first to Harvard and then (judging the Divinity School too liberal) to Andover Seminary as a living tithe. Such a scholarly boy must surely be destined for the church.

If, at Harvard, Gideon had been considered too serious, wanting in humor and high spirits, at Andover he was among peers. Yet even in this natural habitat, he held himself aloof from the irreverent joking that lightened the long days of his fellow seminarians. The classroom was more sacred to him than chapel, and the men who presided there, eccentric and fallible as they sometimes appeared, emanated the power of shamans, dispensing knowledge as priests dispensed the host. Of all their teachers, the Reverend Hedge was most often mocked—in part because he was feared—but Gideon couldn't bring himself to call the master of Hebrew and Greek "Hedgehog" and "Prickles," as others did. It might be true that the professor's rare words of praise concealed a stinging quill of reproof; still, Gideon coveted them, and worked hard to merit them. He moved ahead quickly with his translations, from sentences to verses to psalms, English to Hebrew and the reverse, and eventually his papers were returned to him without corrections, and even a "Well Done" in the professor's angular script. Emboldened, he decided to attempt a longer translation from the Hebrew on his own time. He kept hidden from himself his desire to present it to his teacher as an offering—pride, he knew, was his besetting sin—but agonized over which passage to choose as if Hedge's gimlet eyes were already boring holes in the page. After much deliberation, he settled on ten chapters of Isaiah, beginning with God's mockery of the idols of Babylon and ending with 55, a chapter he loved for its exuberance, the mountains singing and the trees clapping their hands.

Gideon began his labor in the middle of a snow-bound February, working late into the night after completing his regular assignments. The room was so cold that his fingers cramped as he wrote. His chambermate, a surveyor's son from Billerica, snored all night, then complained in the mornings that Gideon's candle had kept him awake. But no adversity could quench the revelations he was drawing from the text. His earlier exercises had been shallow compared to this: simple surface transactions, an English word supplied for a Hebrew one. Never before had the Hebrew pulled him in and under, made him swim in the depths beneath the familiar verses. Often he was flailing like a drowning man, grasping at the ready word from the text he knew by rote. But once in a while he would plunge deep enough to glimpse a sunken city: the crystal walls of the New Jerusalem. And beneath this, a place simpler and more brilliant still, a clarity so dazzling that he was filled with awe.

He remembered sitting in his mother's lap when he was very small, staring at the page as she read to him. The lines of letters were as stiff and straight as soldiers, but the story his mother enticed out of them was all movement and color, brighter than the world he walked through every day. It seemed to him then that the elves and giants and dragons must be trapped in the white space behind the letters, waiting to be released, just as the sleeping princess behind the briar hedge waited to be awakened by a kiss. He would have liked to set them free himself, if only he were clever enough, if only he knew the way in.

His expectations diminished when he learned to read. It was too easy for him, his brain effortlessly converting the symbols on the page to meaning. Before Gideon quite knew what was happening, his early wonder had ebbed to a fascination with words: the shape and sound of them, their feel on the tongue. Reading was to him what running or leaping was to other children—a release of energy that was physical, the encounter on the page so vital that he sometimes had to put a book aside to catch his breath. But once he closed the book, the world was what it had always been. The tale that had transported him would live in his mind for a few days and then fade, like a hothouse plant exposed to harsh weather. Not until he was older and beginning to study the classical languages did the magic return. His tutor had given him a Greek Alphabet to master, along with a worn copy of Plato's *Republic* in the original tongue. The letters stirred his sense of mystery: some were close to the ones he knew, but others were tantalizingly strange, as cryptic as hieroglyphs cut in stone. He had an idea that if he discovered their secrets, he would be admitted to the land of gods and heroes. He took to studying them at night, the light of his candle making eerie patterns across the ancient script. Athens eluded him, but one evening, very late, Gideon blinked his weary eyes and saw white marble pillars sprouting like cornstalks from a field of rocks.

SPRING WAS IN FULL BLOOM by the time he finally finished; the term was nearly over. Gideon put down his pen at three in the morning, and heaved himself from his desk to his bed as Handel oratorios resounded from the hills and the campus elms rustled their new leaves in discreet applause. He slept until the middle of the afternoon, missing two of his classes; Osgood, perhaps in revenge, had not bothered to wake him, or had tried and failed. Gideon splashed water on his face and raked his hair back with damp fingers. He stared in the little mirror above the basin, shocked at how pale and thin he'd grown. He had been so absorbed in his work that he'd neglected himself. But at the thought of his accomplishment, the triumph of the night before came back to him, and he turned again to his desk.

His small store of rapture drained out of him as he read. He was struck first by the crudity of his translation. The prophet's words, cadenced and elegant in the King James, had been reduced to lumps that weighed on his tongue like chunks of mutton. All the poetry was gone. There would never be a Birdsall Version of the Scriptures, but perhaps his clumsy efforts would be of use in the mission field. He saw himself capering before a tribe of squatting New Guineans, fleshing out his tortured locutions with pantomime. Had he really been so vain, so foolish, as to think Reverend Hedge might look kindly on this monstrous hybrid?

Self-disgust made his head spin; he'd tumbled too quickly from the heights. He tried to open a window, but the old frame refused to budge. He flung open the door instead, and ran headlong down the stairs and out of the dormitory. The sweetness of the air was a shock to him. He had ignored his surroundings for so many weeks that spring had advanced without his noticing. Gideon stood for a moment taking in the different shades of green, the flowering bushes that softened the gray stone of the chapel like lace trim on a mourning dress. It was a privilege just to breathe, he thought. From now on, he would renounce ambition and seek to live a life of simple purity. He would forsake the seductions of the mind and find his nourishment in Holy Scripture. But even as he imagined feeding his soul on the plain brown bread of the Word, he realized that he was fiercely hungry; he had scarcely eaten these last two days. He headed for the kitchen to beg alms from the cook.

That evening, having dined well and lingered at the table for the first time in weeks ("Now that Lazarus has risen, I might even get some sleep," Osgood had said), Gideon forced himself to look at the translation again. For whatever it was worth, he had completed the task he'd undertaken. It would be an act of cowardice not to submit the result to Reverend Hedge. He was here to learn, not to display his plumage and wait for praise. If the professor chastised him, he would take his stripes like a man, and strive to do better next time. And it was just possible that Hedge might find one or two things of interest: neat little solutions that shone like crystals in a mud puddle. The King James translators, divinely inspired though they were, were only men, and not in possession of the full mind of God. Was it unthinkable that a humble student, made of the same clay, might be granted an insight that eluded others? The light of truth, it was said, could penetrate the densest substance. Gideon sat back, his hands folded over his full stomach, feeling pleasantly dense himself. Now that the decision had been made, the only question was how to approach the professor.

AFTER CLASS THE NEXT DAY, Gideon lingered as Reverend Hedge attended to papers on his desk. Gideon had memorized a graceful little speech, deferential without groveling, but his mouth was so dry that the words stuck in his craw. He cleared his throat. "Sir, you are very busy!" he pronounced, plunging in headfirst when he had meant to tread water. "I mean, I believe—I know—that you have no time. Even so, I've been bold to make this unworthy attempt—" He staggered to a halt, clutching the pages he had inscribed with such care the night before.

The professor regarded him with a long look, fixed and all-seeing like the framed Eye of God that haunted Gideon's bedroom. "You appear to know a great deal about me, Mr. Birdsall," he said. "Since we only meet in class, I wonder how you come by your knowledge. I have the same ration of time allotted to every other creature in our limited sphere, but I don't hoard my hours like miser's gold. I *spend* them, and I hope you do the same, young man, for none of us knows the measure of his days. Now, what have you brought me? The fruit of some precious minutes, I hope." Without waiting for an answer, he snatched the pages from Gideon's hand. "Isaiah! I admire your ambition. The prophets are not easy, I find; they are not straightforward like the Gospel accounts. One doesn't translate prophecy; one *strives* with it. I myself have recently attempted the Lamentations with limited success, but I'll wrestle on. I won't let it go until it blesses me."

"There were moments when I did feel blessed," Gideon ventured, gaining courage. "I struggled, just as you said, and then a word would . . . reveal itself, and it seemed to me that I saw something wonderful. A glimpse of another world." He was certain that he'd gone too far. "It was late. I was probably dreaming."

To his astonishment, the stern features softened. "It is wrong to diminish these experiences. Very likely, what you saw was no shadow, but a greater solidity. Minds more distinguished than my own are persuaded that Hebrew is the language our first parents spoke in the Garden. When we disturb the topsoil, who knows what fragment of the sacred turf we might unearth? I've followed in the footsteps of my betters and done some small research on the subject. A few essays— trivial things from my etymological cabinet of curiosities—and the work that has an enduring claim on my heart, a Philosophical Lexicon of the Hebrew Bible."

"I-I'm not acquainted with *philosophical* lexicons," Gideon stumbled. "I know Gesenius's, of course—"

"And you are wondering how anyone could improve on that great scholar's work. I confess, when my colleague Gibbs produced his translation from the German, I put my own efforts aside. I made a fine copy of the pages I'd completed and laid them in a drawer, feeling—do not judge me, Mr. Birdsall—that I'd buried one of my children." Reverend Hedge bowed his head in brief homage, cocking a watchful eye at Gideon, who might, after all, be caught judging.

"I humbled my ambitions. Went about my duties with a chastened spirit. When I was all but quenched, the Lord gave my vision back to me—doublefold, as He restored Job. It is one thing to anatomize the body of a language—the grammar, the logic of its structure—quite another to apprehend its soul. Yet both make the man, isn't it so? I resolved to compose a monograph on each of the Hebrew letters, drawing out its essential character—its nature, if you will. The purpose that God infused at the dawn of Creation—so far as a mortal mind can discern—with disquisitions on relevant words, by way of illustration."

Hedge leaned across the desk, his dark eyes gleaming. "An enormous undertaking—yet one to which I am called. Our good Mr. Gibbs is a diligent scholar whose modest manner is a credit to him. Perhaps also a limitation. He is not, how shall I say, an *architect*, he does not see the whole. He chisels each stone with a master hand, but the Temple, Mr. Birdsall—the Temple remains unbuilt!"

In the silence that followed this effusion, Gideon realized that the professor was waiting for a response. "It's the work of a lifetime," he said. "Several lifetimes."

The Reverend nodded soberly. "I pray I may be granted the time to pursue it. If not in this world, then the next—though why we will need dictionaries there I cannot imagine. I've sometimes fancied that our Heavenly Father might place those of us who are philologically inclined at tall desks, like the monks of old—purely to keep a record of earthly speech, you see. But it is useless to speculate. We look through a dark glass, and our own selfish needs look back at us." He sighed, looking so wistful that Gideon was alarmed by the unguarded display of emotion, as though a statue had begun to weep. "You have some affinity for Hebrew. Perhaps my jottings would interest you."

"I would be honored to see anything you're willing to show me."

"Then come to our service at Ormsby on Sunday and stay for dinner. You look as if you could do with a good meal. I'll get to your translation on Friday evening. It's my habit to reserve the Jewish Sabbath for the tongue of the Patriarchs."

Gideon stammered his thanks, but the professor had already turned away, busy with the papers on his desk.

CHAPTER 2

HOYDEN

WOODEN TEETH SLICE DOWN THE CENTER OF HER SCALP. In her mind's eye, a ribbon of blood, a furrow of fire. A yank to the left, a yank to the right. Mama anchors the comb in Sophy's hair as she assesses.

"Crooked! If you weren't such a fidget, I could part it straight the first time. Do you want Papa to look down from the pulpit and see you all askew?"

"Oh, can he see through my bonnet?"

"That's enough sauce from you, miss. And on a Sunday, too—if Papa doesn't see, you know who will." Mama takes her revenge with the comb, this time to her satisfaction. She pulls the hair tight on either side, pasting Sophy's ears to her skull, and twists it into a knot behind. "There!" she says, putting in the pins. "Don't go galloping about now. Try and act as if . . . "

As if you were the Reverend's true daughter and not his niece, an errant shoot grafted onto the family tree. No need to finish the sentence when they live out its substance daily. Mama is too kind to say so, and too stoical to complain, but Sophy suspects that she besieges Heaven at times, demanding to know why the Lord took the daughters of her own robust flesh if his only intention was to put such a flimsy excuse of a girl in their place. An alien creature, another woman's blood and bone. There is a baffled affection in her eyes as she looks Sophy over one last time, fluffing the skirt of the blue Sunday dress she stitched with care, flicking a bit of dust off the white stocking. "We'll make a proper lady of you yet," she says.

Vain hope. Sophy has lately discovered that being the family misfit confers a certain freedom. Folks expect more of her than, say, a half-wit, but they make allowances. These last couple of years, as she turned from girl to woman, she has begun to wear her difference as an ornament, a badge of pride. Let her brothers tease and mock her, let Papa frown or Mama despair aloud. A person Sophy has never met lives in her: an animating presence, sometimes quiet, sometimes active, always there.

"Tell me about my mother," she begged Papa when she was younger. "Tell me what she was like." In those days he was her best friend, taking her on long walks in all seasons and pointing out small marvels she might miss on her own, beetles and bird's nests and garish orange fungi that sprouted like Gypsies in their damp New England woods. Papa would sigh and offer words so sparse that Sophy couldn't patch a picture out of them. "She was small like you. Full of life, always happy. A sweet singer." If she pressed him for more, he turned away, a pinched look on his face— miserly, hoarding his memories of his only sister, keeping them to himself. The last time she questioned him, he said, "I was wrong to burden you with your beginnings when your own life is forming. No good can come of it. Don't ask me again, Sophy." That was the end of the confidence between them. He looks at her now with narrowed eyes, always on guard—against what, she isn't sure. Some unseemly thing that's been growing inside her since she was born and might erupt any day.

From the woman she calls Mama, she has gotten even less. A tart look. Hands on hips. "Your mother is the one who did the work of raising you. Be thankful, girl, and don't brood on the dead when you can be useful to the living."

How to conjure the author of one's being from scraps? And yet, her mother will not be subdued. The older Sophy gets, the more boldly she asserts herself—or perhaps it's only that Sophy recognizes her now. The oddities that people have marked in her since she was a child—the likenesses she sees, the way words turn to images in her head—what can these be but her mother trying to escape her unnatural confinement, reminding Sophy she's still here? Some in the congregation might call this possession, but there's nothing dark in it. If a spirit inhabits her, its nature is joyful, verging on the wild. Sophy will be sweeping the kitchen, or sitting quietly in a corner reading, and suddenly she'll feel a shimmer through her body, as if the blood running in her veins has turned to silver. She has to get away then, somewhere she can be alone. A meadow faces the front of their house, a farmer's field abandoned for as long as she can remember; Papa talks of acquiring the land and putting it to good use. Meanwhile, the grasses are tall, the flowers are thick and wild, and sated bees circle crazily, drunk with sweetness. A garden of glorious neglect.

Sophy gazes out the window. Ahead are hours of sitting still in the front pew, her sides compressed in the stays Mama makes her wear at meeting to improve her posture and concentration. Hours of Reverend Papa droning on about sin and salvation and the next world, while spring exults outside. The torment won't end at dinner: Papa is bringing one of his students home, and they'll be theologizing all afternoon, possibly in Hebrew or Greek, and she'll be expected to help Mama serve, and pretend to read her Bible after, and speak when spoken to, if anyone bothers to address her. There will be no time to paint at all.

Mama is upstairs in her usual state of distraction, making Micah presentable as she parleys between James and Reuben, who are having one of their disputes.

"I'm just going out for a bit," Sophy calls.

"The wild asparagus should be up. Pull some if you can, but don't be long. You'll make us late."

IN A MONTH OR TWO, the meadow will be its own seclusion, the grasses higher than her knee. Now the green is new and tender. To be safe from prying eyes, Sophy has to tramp halfway across, crushing violets and dandelions underfoot.

Once the spot is chosen, she plants her feet firmly and raises her face to the sun, letting the stillness fill her. Unhurried, she waits for what will come. The only movement is her breath: her mother defying the laces, buoying her from within. Her arms lift of their own accord. The first steps are decorous, a ballroom twirl in a bell-shaped skirt. But the circles get wider. She spins faster, her feet thrust and kick, her head whips round and round until her soul—that cumbersome catchall she's toted since infancy, subject of endless admonition—sails off her like a hat in the wind. Oh, the lightness! Though the dance is always different, its end is the same: the body exalted, her true and only home. She would keep on forever, but too soon she is still again, her heart hammering, her ribs straining against her stays.

Behind her, a disturbance of the air. If her senses weren't overkeen from her exertions, she wouldn't hear anything at all.

A man in a white shirt is watching her from the road. He is very fair, his light hair swept back from his brow, and even at a distance she can see that he is beautiful. The startling perfection of his face clashes with the hanging shirttail, the loose cravat—as if (she will affect later, musing on him in church) he pulled those coarse garments on in haste to cover telltale wings. His coat is suspended from one hand, held up stiffly like a sign. He lowers his arm, slow and rigid, and Sophy is seized with fear. If the apparition has a message for her, she is in no state to receive it. In a blind panic, she turns and runs for the shelter of the house.

Mama is waiting at the door. "Where have you got to? Look at you, you hoyden! No time to fix you now, you'll have to go as you are and shame us all." She clamps Sophy's bonnet down, hard, and whisks the loose strands underneath.

CHAPTER 3

THE REVEREND'S HOUSE

THE CHURCH WAS FOUR MILES FROM THE SEMINARY—NO great distance, but the day was warm, and after an hour of brisk walking, Gideon's best shirt was soaked through. He had shed garments along the way, tossing his jacket over one arm and stuffing his cravat in his pocket so his shirt gaped at the neck. When the parsonage came into view—a square yellow structure with an off-center chimney, a raffish touch like a feather in a straw hat—Gideon recognized it immediately. Its design and raising, its furnishing and maintenance, its conveniences and solid comforts had been a constant theme in Reverend Hedge's lectures and sermons. He had managed to insinuate its virtues into all manner of topics, from the dangers of breathing stale air while sleeping to the building of Solomon's Temple. Gazing at the house now across a meadow dotted with dandelions, Gideon felt that he knew every jot and cubit of its interior without having ventured inside. He stopped under a tree to mop his face and make himself presentable, and saw that he was not alone.

A girl in a blue dress stood very still in the meadow. She seemed to be gazing intently at the sky; he couldn't see her face, only the back of her head, with its gathered knot of light brown hair at the nape. The scene satisfied his eye in a way he could not explain. It was as though God had arranged the composition just for him: planted the girl in this field of yellow and purple and green, and posed her so Gideon could take pleasure in the sun on her hair, her sloping shoulders, the half-moon of white rising out of the scoop of her neckline. As he watched, hardly breathing for fear of startling her, she spread her arms and brought them slowly into an arc over her head. His first thought was that she must be doing some sort of calisthenics, in the manner of the ancient Greeks. But she began to spin in place, then to whirl in widening circles, lifting her leg so high that he could see her ankle in its white stocking. She raised her skirt with both hands, as if wading through a stream, and executed a series of rapid kicks, whipping the grasses. She arched her back, reached up to the heavens, dropped down into a deep curtsy. Gideon had never seen a dance so stately, yet so abandoned. Her movements were as spacious and flowing as a Maenad's. He had no idea what god she might be invoking, but knew at once that it wasn't the one he worshiped on Sundays.

If the Reverend had not been waiting, armed with sermons about squandered time, Gideon would have been content to lean against the tree for the rest of the morning, lost in the spectacle before him. The dancer spared him that choice. Her gestures grew more circumscribed, and in a moment or two she was as he had first seen her. It seemed that the dance had finished with her and let her go. He kept his eyes on her as he took his cravat from his pocket; a superstition had come over him that if he looked away she would vanish into the ether. He made a dumb show of knotting his tie, stretching out the habitual movements until they felt as ceremonial as her own. With infinite care he lifted his coat from the branch where he'd hung it. The small motion was enough to alert her. She crooked her head like a wren—one long look that took him in whole—and flew off toward the house.

Gideon stood for a moment staring after her, trying to apply his powers of reasoning to the vision he'd just seen. She had fled on her own two feet toward a solid destination: therefore she was neither sprite nor spirit. She was most likely a member of the Hedge household, but in what capacity? A servant? His intuition told him she was not; there was a gentility about her, and besides, she was too free. A daughter, then. For all his awe of his professor, the idea was absurd. He would sooner believe she was a wood nymph! It went against the laws of nature that something so wild and lovely could have sprung from the parson's loins.

ONCE GIDEON CROSSED the meadow, he found that he was part of a procession. The Reverend had no doubt been at church since dawn, but the rest of his flock were straggling in more slowly. Gideon thought he sensed some reluctance in their halting gait—a disinclination to be raked over the coals on such a splendid day. From the looks of them, they were mostly small farmers and farmworkers, perhaps a few trades-men and shopkeepers. Ormsby was a rural town, hardly more than a village. Andover was like Athens compared to it—a seat of culture, a fountain of intellect. He wondered why a man of learning would choose to settle in such a backwater.

The meetinghouse was as expected, all straight lines and white shin-gles, but Gideon was impressed by the height and handsomeness of the steeple. He had a weakness for grandeur, and secretly envied the Catho-lics their stone cathedrals and festooned altars, their ceilings that soared like the dome of Heaven; he had even questioned whether it might be easier to pray in a setting that costumed Divinity in the vestments of earthly glory. The stark Congregational interiors he'd grown up with had turned God into an abstraction, chilly and remote. Even now, com-mitted to a career in the church, Gideon had yet to feel the intimacy that the great preachers spoke of, had never known that unalterable transfor-mation of the heart. From time to time he tried to work up an appropri-ate panic about the state of his soul, but these attempts usually ended in frustration. How could he inspire others when he had no tools but dry Scripture? Would it really be such a sin if the Blessed Assurance were embodied in a statue or mediated through stained glass?

He knew what Hedge would make of such reflections. From his place at the end of the queue, Gideon had plenty of leisure to observe the Reverend as he presided at the door. On the pretense of shaking hands, Hedge immobilized each person's forearm in a wrestler's hold as he bestowed a few words, then propelled the congregant into the sanctuary with a firm pat on the back.

"Welcome, Mr. Birdsall!" he said when Gideon's turn came. His grip was powerful for such a small man. "We are looking forward to your company today. My wife pillaged the garden as though we were having three guests—or one very large one. I made the error of telling her you were on the thin side."

"I'll try to do justice to her expectations," Gideon said, realizing at once that he should have said, "generosity." But even as he amended the word, Hedge was launching him into the church. Passing through the door, he was uncomfortably reminded of the sermon about the strait gate. Here was no magnificence to lift his spirit, only a narrow aisle separating rows of boxlike pews, and an elevated pulpit, from which height the Reverend would look down on his flock, peppering them with wisdom. Unlike the dusky cathedrals of Gideon's dreams, the interior was very bright. Light streamed through the long windows and rebounded from whitewashed walls. If the theater of the Roman church required darkness for its effects, and smoky incense to conjure mystery, here all was exposed—most particularly, the souls of those assembled.

Today the light was Gideon's friend. A quick scan of the aisles revealed his dancer in the front pew—unmistakable in her blue dress, though a straw bonnet eclipsed his view of her face. The church was filling up, but he managed to squeeze into a space only two rows behind her. An older woman sat to her left, nearest the center aisle, and a veritable phalanx of tall young men filled the rest of the pew. It had never been Hedge's habit to speak as freely of his family as of his house. The name of one son or another would surface at times, flotsam in the vast sea of his household innovations. If he mentioned his Consort, as he called her (pronounced with ponderous gravity, as if it were a royal title), it was usually in reference to a task they'd shared, or to illustrate the virtues of a proper helpmate. These comments spawned a flurry of speculation among the students about the true nature of the serviceable

Mrs. Hedge: she was a potted plant, a fruit-bearing tree, an iron cooking pot, a broom. Gideon couldn't recall that Hedge had ever spoken of a daughter.

The parson began in a benevolent mood. He preached briefly on God's bounteous provision—"You who made your way here on foot no doubt beheld the lilies sprouting in our humble fields"—before veering into a rebuke of those misguided Boston preachers who, in addition to offering their parishioners the sop of universal salvation, had departed so far from the fold as to make an idol of nature.

Gideon tried to listen attentively in case Hedge should question him afterward, but his mind wandered. He could not stop thinking of his own view of the field, and of the lily he had seen there. The girl was incidental, he told himself: one element in a charming rural scene. If he hadn't caught her dancing—that extraordinary pagan ballet!—he might have forgotten her by now. One couldn't cling to such beauty, and if she were indeed Hedge's daughter, the illusion might be cruelly fleeting. He'd scarcely glimpsed her face; for all he knew, she might be snaggle-toothed, or sharp-featured like her father. Still, he kept his eyes on the bonnet and remembered the part in her hair—a marvel of geometric straightness, better achieved with a ruler than a comb—and the two perfect wings that followed the curve of her cheekbones and folded back over her ears.

After the service, Gideon waited in the yard while Reverend Hedge took leave of his flock. People came out of meeting and drifted into clusters, greeting each other, gossiping. In this little village, everyone knew everyone else, and knew their places, too. It was as if they stood in trenches that had been dug before they were born. Sooner or later dirt would cover them, the parson would say a few words, a stone would be erected, and a new generation would sprout up in soil fertilized by its elders. Maybe this wasn't such a bad thing, Gideon reflected, feeling like the outsider he was. He had never felt part of a community. From the moment he could think at all, he had seen himself as singular and self-contained, a collection of attributes making its way through the world.

———

HIS MOTHER ENCOURAGED his independence. She had always stood aloof from her surroundings: dutiful and competent, immaculate in the remnants of her beauty, coldly civil to the matrons who condescended to her. She carried herself like a queen, but her pride was in her son. As a boy, he had quickly grasped that his gifts were all she required of him. The only way to thank her for her sacrifices was to forge ahead and leave her behind. Not until her death the year before—a sore throat acquired from a student turned to diphtheria and took her in a fortnight—had Gideon been haunted by a nagging, shapeless suspicion that he shook off before it could congeal into words. During the day he managed to keep it at bay, but at night it materialized like a demon, taunting him and troubling his sleep.

"It is all taken care of," she'd whispered at the end, clutching his fingers with a force she couldn't bring to her voice. After the funeral, Mr. Pilkington, the mill owner, parroted her words. "Taken care of," he told Gideon. "School fees, all of it. See that you make her proud." And then he'd turned away and honked noisily into a kerchief—a bulky, red-faced, pragmatic man who quoted Scripture at every turn and had none of the polish he admired in others. Gideon was ashamed to call him a benefactor, but was eloquent in his gratitude nevertheless, mindful that important men like to be flattered. Only later did Gideon remember Pilkington's periodic visits to his house during his school years—"to discuss your future," his mother had explained—and how, instead of reciting a poem or showing off his Latin, he was always made to leave. He had resented these enforced exiles, especially during the winter, when it was too raw outside to walk, and he was banished to the icy schoolroom with nothing but a book to divert him. Once, when his mother came to get him, he flung his book to the floor in a temper.

"Two hours! What do you talk about with that stupid man? Does he really have that much conversation?"

His mother was always very quiet after the mill owner's visits, but that afternoon there was an iron stillness about her. She folded her white hands and set her lips in a smile.

"I sing your praises," she said.

THE OCCUPANTS OF THE FRONT pew were the last to leave the church. The older woman headed straight for Gideon, followed by the hulking youths and, a few paces behind them, the girl in the blue dress, who appeared to be encased in a dream. No one had deigned to notice the newcomer before, but now every eye went to him, as if he'd just arrived.

"Mr. Birdsall? I am Fanny Hedge, and here are James and Reuben and Micah, and our schoolmaster, Mr. Unsworth, who boards with us. That moony thing there is Sophy, who isn't always so bashful."

So she was the parson's daughter, after all. The fact seemed no less fantastic for having been confirmed by a reliable source. He had read of spirits who took up residence in human form, though he had never expected to meet one. In the old stories, they fell in love with mortals. His fellow students would be gratified to see Mrs. Hedge, Gideon thought: she was as functional as they'd imagined her, a plain woman with a horsy, good-natured face and hands as broad as spades. The boys were clearly hers, but the moon-girl, who stood at a little distance watching two squirrels play hide-and-seek among the gravestones, bore no resemblance to her. Her mother had to call her twice before she came over.

"I think we already met, informally." Gideon spoke softly to prevent her shying like a deer and running away. "On my way to church I saw you in the meadow."

"I was hunting for asparagus, but there weren't any. It's too late, I think." Her voice was barely audible, but she looked up at him. If she was chagrined that he had seen her dance, or fearful of what he might reveal, she did not show it. Her eyes were dark like her father's, but widely spaced and luminous. There was something disconcerting about her glance, at once direct and unfocused; she seemed to be gazing through him toward a distant vista, of which he was a random but interesting feature of the landscape.

"I don't think she looked very hard," said Mrs. Hedge. "I picked some yesterday."

"I must take exception. She was a model of diligence," Gideon said, "so intent on her task that she didn't even notice me."

This earned him a fleeting smile from Sophy—of sufficient duration to prove that her teeth were straight—but Mrs. Hedge was oblivious. She chattered on about her herbarium and what she would plant in the garden, about weather prognostications and last year's yield, about the treacherous nature of lettuce. After listening to the good woman for five minutes, Gideon knew that she would pluck irony and allusion from conversation like so many weeds—not because they offended her, but because they were of no practical use. The Hedge sons and Mr. Unsworth had backed away, perhaps all too familiar with such monologues. Sophy stood by quietly, nodding when her mother mentioned the "smelling garden" she was starting, but never interrupting the flow of words. She wasn't comely in the usual way, Gideon decided; his classmates wouldn't look at her twice. Her forehead was too high and her cheekbones too pronounced to fit the tranquil oval of classic beauty. Except for her eyes, her features were undistinguished, the mouth erring on the generous side. But her face was full of life even when still, and she had a piquant charm that he found appealing. Whether it was a girl's charm or a woman's, he lacked the experience to say. She looked fifteen or sixteen, but her smallness could be deceptive. She was made as neatly and precisely as a doll; he could easily span her wrist with a thumb and forefinger.

Soon no one was left in the churchyard but the Hedges and their boarder. "I see you're already acquainted," the Reverend said, joining them. He seemed relaxed, even jovial.

"You've spoken of your family so often that I felt we had already met," Gideon said.

"I like to remind my students that a well-ordered family is one of the blessings of this life. A prefiguration of Heaven—*ordained* for the benefit of our foreparents in Eden, *sustained* by grace after the Fall, *attained*, alas, by all too few. I'm happy to say that I am fortunate in mine." Reverend Hedge regarded his clan fondly, with a touch of smug approval that Gideon had seen in the classroom. The parson could easily have been expounding on his well-constructed furniture or his well-designed garden. It was clear that he regarded the household as a felicitous collaboration between himself and the Almighty. Gideon wondered how the others felt about being reduced to anonymous—though well-oiled and smoothly meshing—parts in a predestined plan. Mrs. Hedge and Sophy took no notice, but he thought he saw James and Reuben exchange glances.

The eight of them formed another procession going back to the house, and Gideon was flattered to be at its head, keeping up a brisk pace with the Reverend. Unsworth walked alongside them at first, but fell back when the talk turned to Gideon's translation.

"An interesting effort," Hedge said. "Ingenious in its way. You have been so literal that you've wrested a rough poetry from the text. Too rough, I think—though there is a precedent. The Lord made Adam out of clay, and who is to say that our ancestor was the vision of perfection we imagine? A little coarse, a little raw—you can observe it in our masculine natures to this day. If it were not for the civilizing influence of woman, what would we be? When I think of the impulses of my youth—" He cleared his throat. Mrs. Hedge and Sophy were following close behind. "It's perhaps too much to call a field a 'flat place' and to speak of the trees 'clapping their palms.' Such a rendering may be exact—may even give us a glimpse of a world that wrongheaded men call primitive. But it doesn't *sing*, you see."

Gideon did see, though he was aware that Hedge had just jabbed him with another of his quilled compliments. "I'm grateful you found any merit in it at all," he said. He hesitated and went on. "It's true that the primal drew me, but the coarseness you speak of is my lack of skill—not what I saw. It was as though the text were a wall, and, I was on one side of it, peering through tiny cracks at a world I could just glimpse. I would have given anything to breach that wall, sir! Only my ignorance prevented me."

The Reverend stopped in mid-stride. He wheeled around and looked

Gideon full in the face. "Tell me, Mr. Birdsall, what is the purpose of a wall?"

"Why—to contain, I suppose. To mark boundaries."

"And the function of a boundary—its whole reason for being—is to *keep intruders out*." The last words emerged with full stops between them, each a fortification unto itself. Hedge drew nearer as he spoke, stopping so close to Gideon that he seemed to be admonishing his Adam's apple.

"It is one thing to recognize that such wonders exist, quite another to covet them beforetime. I've observed in my ministry, and also among my students, that mysticism is an enticement for certain young men of sensitive disposition. The given world isn't enough for these fragile souls. They confuse their own curiosity with spiritual seeking, their restlessness with the inbuilt longing for Heaven. Too often, when life thwarts them, they turn to drink or opiates. Or worse, a universalism diluted even from its original anemic brew. Think of it—rather than wait for the joys to come, they worship the sun and bow their heads to trees and rocks like pagans! No one loves the natural world more than I, but I do not mistake the Creation for its Author."

He had raised one hand, as was his habit while lecturing, and his forefinger was inches from Gideon's nose. "I pray you will avoid their fate, Mr. Birdsall. Remember, we are caretakers. There is more than enough to occupy us here."

Later, Gideon would reflect that the pastor had timed his exhortation perfectly. The Hedge homestead loomed before them, the yellow house set amid apple orchards and tamed fields: a perfect denouement to the spontaneous sermon. To Gideon, it was a parable come to life. He was reeling from Hedge's unexpected scolding. One moment they had been talking like equals, and the next the thread of sympathy—so palpable in their first conversation—had been severed, and he was once again a lowly student, fit only to be chastised. Worst of all, he had been shamed in front of the family. Although he couldn't look at them, he could feel them at his back, halted in place like a team of yoked oxen. He would never dare to speak to Sophy now, and what did it matter? The meadow was no amphitheater, and she was only a clergyman's dallying daughter, not the ecstatic dancer of his vision. But such fantasies were only to be expected of a fragile soul, prey to every whim of his overworked imagination. How well his teacher knew him!

Mrs. Hedge stepped up and gave her husband a sour look. "If you don't mind, I'll borrow Mr. Birdsall for a few minutes and show him the gardens before you hide him away in your study. I have to cut some rhubarb for dinner and get lamb's ear for Micah's foot."

"As you can see," the Reverend said to Gideon, "the duties of rural life are such that it is difficult for us to rest, even on the Lord's Day." He sounded chastened, even a bit sheepish. It was clear that his Consort knew how to douse his fire.

Though Mrs. Hedge had described the gardens at length, Gideon was unprepared for the sheer variety of plantings that flourished behind the Hedge house. Much of the vegetable garden was still nascent, but Mrs. Hedge pointed out fledgling beans and peas, cucumbers and squash, Indian corn, cabbage and potatoes and carrots. Sophy followed behind with a basket, a dog frisking about her skirts, as her mother culled what she could. There was even a peach tree, a gnarled specimen covered with pale pink blossoms. "Some say they don't thrive in this climate, but ours drops more than we can use," Mrs. Hedge said. "I can only make so many pies and preserves—after a while even the pigs get loose bowels. But the first bites are like heaven. Such sweetness! This year I am being very bold, though some would call it foolish." She glanced at Gideon, one eyebrow raised, assessing where he might stand on the matter. "I won't dissemble with you, Mr. Birdsall. I am contemplating melons."

Her pride in the vegetables was utilitarian; they were servants following orders. But the herbs were her gifted children. She had arranged them in families and planted them in elevated beds, looking down on the crops raised for mere sustenance. The way she spoke of them, Gideon thought, they might as well have magical properties. "Bloodroot, now there's a wonder. It will take down a fever and soothe the rheumatics; nothing else would help my poor father. Lovage and sage do as much good to the stomach as they do for turkey dressing. Here, take a sniff of this . . . lemon balm, a true prodigy. Sophy likes it for the smell, but I call it Mother's Friend, for it lifts the heart and calms the mind."

"Mama is a natural physician," Sophy said. "The folks here trust her more than the doctors. I am grateful she was born in civilized times, or she would surely have been burnt for witchcraft."

Mrs. Hedge's hands flew to her breast. "There's a nice thought to take to Sunday dinner! You had better guard your tongue, girl. Don't let the Reverend hear you talk like that."

Gideon was impressed, and a little startled, that such tartness could issue from a girl so shy. "And where is your garden, Miss Sophy?" he asked, changing the subject like a discreet guest, but in truth, succumbing to an urge to say her name. It filled his mouth pleasantly: the slippery *s*; the round *o*, fat and full like her celestial alter ego; the soft crush of the *ph* giving way, after mild resistance, to the diminutive.

"Not much is coming up at the moment," the girl said. "The lilacs are gone and the roses are just starting."

She led him to a circular plot surrounded by ornamental stones. At its center was a spindly bush with plantings radiating out from it like the spokes of a wheel. "I wanted a statue in the middle, or a little fountain, but Papa said that wasn't practical. Soon I'll have sweet peas and heliotrope and jasmine. Daisies, too—I don't spurn the wildflowers. The rosebush was my birthday present. I call it the queen of the garden. It looks very proud and regal, don't you think? Micah said he would build me a trellis to train the vines on."

"I think it's lovely just as it is," Gideon said.

Shyness overtook her again. She lowered her eyes and gazed at him through the screen of her lashes. "I must get back to the house with these," she said, and ran off with her basket.

Mrs. Hedge was bending over the herbs, but Gideon was certain she'd been attending to every word that passed between him and Sophy.

"You've truly made an Eden here," he said. "I wonder how you manage to find time for anything else."

"We all do our part. The Reverend and the boys prime the soil and put the garden to bed come winter. It's hard work getting them to weed, though. I could use more daughters, but the Lord gave me just the one, and she is mine only because my husband's sister died bearing her. My own girls didn't keep. I had three, and not one lived to see her second birthday."

She spoke with such dispassion that she might have been talking about a bushel of apples gone bad. "It must be a great consolation to have Sophy," Gideon said.

"A consolation, and a trial. She's not easy, my Sophy. She and I have little in common, we are always rubbing each other wrong. Some days I think she hasn't a practical bone in her body, that head of hers is always somewhere else. She has the Hedge temperament. Artistic, like the Reverend, though she lacks his core of granite. Each year I see more of Mary in her—not to speak ill of the dead." She looked at Gideon, uneasy. "Don't mistake me, we are very fond. She's all the daughter I have, and I'm the only mother she knows. I thank God for her every day."

THE HEDGES HAD CREATED a home that fit them as neatly as a shell fits a tortoise. The rooms seemed enormous to Gideon, who was used to cramped quarters. He thought first of a barn, and then of a small factory, for every space was devoted to some kind of industry. The sitting room alone housed a spinning wheel, a loom, and an easel; reeds and half-finished baskets were stacked in one corner. Apart from a few old pieces that had been handed down, the Reverend and his sons had made all the furniture. The style was sturdy rather than elegant, but Gideon was intrigued by the rocking chairs—six of them, arranged in a semicircle around the fireplace. Ornamental carving gave each an individual character. "I've made one for every member of my family," Hedge told him. "A superior form of seating, in my opinion. I find the motion facilitates reflection." Gideon noticed that the headboards bore different Scripture references. He wondered which chapter-and-verse belonged to Sophy.

They gathered around a table almost as long as the room that housed it: a long slab of oak set end-to-end with platters and bowls. In contrast to the Puritan austerity of the surroundings, the spread struck Gideon as a Tudor banquet. He hadn't realized until he sat down how famished he was; a tureen of stewed chicken fragrant with herbs brought water to his eyes as well as his mouth. With as much stoicism as he could muster, he resigned himself to an interminable grace; Hedge's dining-hall sermons were famous. He was startled when the pastor asked him to give thanks.

"Our Father in Heaven," Gideon began, taking a deep breath and shutting his eyes on the bowed heads around him. "I count myself fortunate to be in the bosom of this warm home, where signs of your favor are everywhere, in the abundance of the fields and the peace and plenty within. Never have I felt so much like a . . . a wayfaring stranger who looks with yearning at the lighted windows of a house along the road, and is surprised and gratified to be invited inside. I thank you for the wisdom of Reverend Hedge and the kind hospitality of his family. May you bless this food to our use, and . . . multiply the blessings of those who prepared it." No more words came, so he said, "Amen."

If the Hedges were surprised at the brevity of the grace, they hid it well. Mrs. Hedge smiled and nodded, and the young men were openly relieved at the prospect of eating while the food was hot. The Reverend had not yet raised his eyes. He appeared to be praying silently, holding them all in suspension as he covered the ground that his guest had missed. Color rose in Gideon's cheeks as seconds turned to minutes.

"I fear I lack your eloquence," he said when Hedge finally looked up.

"You have spoken from the heart. Nothing could be more pleasing to the Lord." The parson inclined his head slightly in his guest's direction, and turned to the roast, taking up his carving tools with solemn ceremony—as if, Gideon thought, he had received a command during prayer to shoulder the cross of daily life.

The talk at table began casually enough. James, who was to be married soon, was contemplating buying a parcel of land, and Reuben and the Reverend offered their opinions. The two older sons seemed born to work the soil. Bluff and hardy, long-chinned like their mother, they reminded Gideon of English squires, forking up hunks of meat while discussing the price of real estate and the merits of various fishing holes. If there was a grain of philosophy in them, it wasn't evident from their conversation. The youngest, Micah, was the quiet one, never offering a word, but gazing at each speaker with a lively interest. He seemed no older than Sophy, his skin as soft and rosy as a girl's, but Gideon pegged him as the Reverend's true descendant.

"Do you have plans to follow your father to seminary?" he asked.

Micah, caught with a mouthful, took a second to grasp that the question was directed at him. He blushed and shifted the food to his cheek. "That was f-for S-Sam. My b-b-brother. I'm no s-s-s-stu—" His neck reddened, the sinews bulging with the effort of getting the words out. Gideon was beset with a fear that the boy would choke; he could almost see the unspoken syllables dammed up in his throat. "*I'mnogoodat-studying.*" This last emerged in a single breath, clotted like a German noun. In the ensuing silence, Micah slowly began to chew again.

Gideon was ashamed that his well-meant question had brought the young man's struggles to light. Unsworth was looking at him with reproach—as though he had humiliated Micah out of malice—but Reverend Hedge interceded smoothly. "My son is too modest. He did well with Latin, and his copybooks were the neatest of all my children's. If he is somewhat slow of speech, he's marvelously quick with his hands. He's all but taken over my workshop! One day, I believe, Micah will see his affliction as a special gift. A calling, even, for who can plumb the hidden purposes of our God? When Moses balked at speaking to the Egyptians, did the Lord not respond, 'Who hath made a man's mouth?'"

No one found it necessary to affirm the quotation. Gideon wished that Hedge had simply praised his son without appending a lesson; he was beginning to think that the pastor was that rare man whose private face perfectly matched his public one. He wanted to ask Micah what pieces of furniture he had worked on, but knew now to avoid the interrogative. "I've been admiring the rocking chairs," he ventured, proceeding with caution. "Such fine craftsmanship."

"Micah made my chair," Sophy said suddenly. She had been silent during dinner, up and down with Mrs. Hedge, though Gideon had caught her looking at him once or twice; he was acutely aware of her but had made an effort to focus on the table at large. "Not the verse, of course. Papa does the letters himself to work the blessing in. But the rest is Micah's—the back and seat and base, and the fancy carving. I think it's the most beautiful one of all."

"I'm eager to see it," Gideon said. "Would you be so kind as to point it out after dinner?"

Before she could answer, Unsworth shifted the conversation in a different direction. "Garrison is to speak at a rally in Boston next Saturday. Pritchard and I are going down, and I hope at least one of you will join us. The more voices heard, the better." He turned to Gideon with a tight smile. "What about you, Mr. Birdsall? I know we have many friends at the seminary. What cause could be holier to a praying man? We would welcome some company on the journey."

Gideon was caught off guard. It was true that the slavery question was much spoken of at seminary, but he had paid little attention. Though, in theory, he was in favor of abolition, the issues of the day took up little space in his thoughts. Politics had no appeal for him: worldly affairs were transient, external to his longings. The idea of attending a rally, of merging with others in support of a cause, however noble, was foreign to his nature. From earliest childhood, his instinct had been to shy away from mobs of any sort; groups of rowdy children sent him running for his mother's skirts. He couldn't help suspecting that Unsworth had somehow divined this weakness and extended the invitation only to embarrass him. Gideon sensed that the boarder didn't like him—perhaps saw him as a usurper. When Reverend Hedge singled Gideon out for conversation, Unsworth had withdrawn too quickly, receding with a sullen deference. After the parson's rebuke, he'd abruptly turned affable and talkative, his gratification all too evident. There was something heavy about the man: a calculation that made even his loosest gestures seem contrived.

Gideon was about to plead his studies, but James rescued him. "Well, I can't go. I have enough to do, getting ready for Caroline, and the farm won't run itself. It's not as if I have a moment to spare for the next month."

"We can't just take a day off," Reuben echoed. "Besides, Garrison is a troublemaker, isn't he, Pa?" He leaned back, smirking, an anticipatory glitter in his eye. It was obvious that he was hoping for a tussle.

The Reverend looked sternly at his son. "You never heard me say so, Reuben. I hope I'm kinder than to attach such labels to my fellow creatures. Mr. Garrison is a powerful orator, in thrall to a just cause. I don't question his motives, only his method. His words inflame, but to what end? Any student of history knows what happens when rhetoric overcomes reason. The slave owners must be courted and gradually won over. Liberia held up as the city on a hill. In time they'll see that resettlement is the only logical solution." He made a steeple of his fingers and regarded the construction soberly. "You are all well acquainted with my views; I'm happy to discuss them further any other evening. On this day, it is more profitable to fix our minds on eternal truths. Mr. Birdsall, shall we retreat to my study for a little Hebrew?"

CHAPTER 4

CELESTIAL GUEST

SOPHY WONDERS IF, AMONG THE BOOKS MAMA HAS PASSED
on to her—*The Female Friend, Means and Ends, The Sphere and Duties
of Woman*—there is anywhere a chapter on the etiquette for entertaining an angelic visitor. Reuben plagued her while she was washing the
dishes, making sheep-eyes and talking in a fluting voice. "*Oh, Mr. Birdsall, won't you please sit in my rocker? I do believe it's the nicest one of all!*"
Mama shushed him, but with a smile. "I'm glad you spoke up, Sophy,"
she said. "It's about time you acquired some conversation."

She has at last escaped to her easel, and is trying to lose herself in the
English country scene that she started last week. The charm of the picture was all in her mind: her greenery is muddy, her thatch-roofed cottage is a woodshed wearing a wig. Usually she expends some Christian
zeal on her poorer efforts—ye downtrodden one, I will lift ye up—but
this afternoon her attention strays. The painting's flaws are no match
for the shining countenance of their guest, whose blue eyes have surely
dwelled on celestial vistas.

The day has been filled with revelations. Sophy has read in the Bible
that angels walk among us in the guise of men, but where is it written
that they have surnames and hearty appetites? She'd fled from him this

morning, hardly knowing why, and when he reappeared at church and spoke to her, she was like Micah, words frozen in her throat, thawing finally in humblest form. Asparagus was all she could offer, laying it at his altar like the poor gawking farmers at the Manger, giving what they had. It took all the courage she had to look into those eyes, but once she did, she knew they'd keep each other's secrets: he would never tell about her dancing and she would never tell about his disguise. On the way home, Papa preached at his prize pupil, making a public show of him, and she thought, O foolish mortal, you know not who comes to your door.

The grace he said moved her to tears. Papa's students usually rambled on and on, adding dollops of Scripture to impress the professor, but Mr. Birdsall's words had been simple and sincere. She had been touched by the image of the poor wanderer gazing with longing at lighted windows. Who would imagine that a higher nature could be lonely for the homely comforts of ordinary men? But how poignant—how piercing to the heart—that it should be so!

His appetite at dinner stirred her in another way. He had devoured two plates of stewed chicken and a thick slice of pork, and sampled every dish that Mama offered him with fervent thanks. (Very mannerly, Mama had called him afterward.) Sophy isn't sure why watching him eat was a cause for wonder. The sensible part of her knows that if Mr. Birdsall relishes food, he must have, inside his ethereal casing, innards and organs like other men. Yet, he wears his body as carelessly as he wears his clothes. After years of Sunday sermons, she's learned to distrust words like "spirit"—limp and thin like much-fingered cloth—but if anyone possesses the elusive quality, Mr. Birdsall does. It's as though he *deigns* to hunger, and having been humbled with needs, takes an innocent delight in their satisfaction.

Sophy will never understand what prompted her to speak to him at dinner. Mama seated him directly across from her, and every time he looked her way, she blushed to think that he'd seen her as no one else ever had—as shameless as Salome and, in one sense, nearly as bare. After their awkward exchange in her garden, she'd tried to make herself invisible, but the words were out of her mouth before the thought was in her head. Her rocking chair, of all subjects. He'd asked her to point it out after dinner. A casual gesture, requiring minimal motion on Sophy's part, yet since she's been sitting here, she's contrived at least eight different ways to accomplish it.

Sophy gazes out the window. Over two hours have passed since Papa took him to the study. A half-hour is the usual allotment, measured to the minute by the Reverend's pocket watch, and then the dazed scholar is sent on his way, laden with books and cautions. A sobering thought comes to her. Mr. Birdsall probably left long ago, his head full of Hebrew. He had come to see Papa, after all. Why should he remember a casual politeness to the Reverend's daughter?

Grimly, she returns to her painting. A second look confirms that it's one of the damned, beyond reclaiming. Tomorrow she'll cover the canvas with white and start again. She is about to get up when she hears footsteps behind her.

"Working, are we? Ah, a vernal scene. Very pretty!"

Mr. Unsworth, creeping up on her again. He has an irritating habit of addressing her in the plural, as if she were an infant or a cat. Mr. Unsworth's chief attribute is persistence, a quality native to snails and other creatures that leave traces. She doesn't have to look at him to feel his eyes, heavy-lidded, clinging to her back. In the flush of her disappointment, she swirls her brush in green and attacks the foliage with such vigor that Mr. Unsworth, muttering "Well, I see you're busy," has no choice but to withdraw.

CHAPTER 5

IN THE REVEREND'S STUDY

THE REVEREND HEDGE HAD OFFERED HEBREW AS OTHER men suggested a postprandial dram of brandy. Gideon was surprised when the parson took a bottle down from the shelf. He had been led to expect sustenance, but not in the harder form.

"Do you indulge, Mr. Birdsall? This won't do you harm. It's the last of our blackberry cordial, and there'll be no more once it's gone. My wife and I have been making wine since the first year of our marriage— experimenting, I should say, for we were quite the alchemists in the early days, mixing all manner of fruit with every kind of vegetable and herb. No combination was beyond us. Peaches and parsnips sweetened with syrup. Damsons and rhubarb with a pinch of lavender. Oh, we were sly! Not all of our unions were blessed—some were downright sulfurous— but practice is all, our results refined with time. I don't mind saying I'll regret giving it up. The biblical precedent is substantial, and I have little natural sympathy with the temperance folk. Their rhetoric seems hardly more palatable than Mr. Garrison's!" He measured a couple of inches of dark liquid into two wine glasses. "But I can't deny the abuse—I see enough in my own parish. A preacher and his family must be exemplars. As you will discover, our lives are not our own."

"I'll enjoy the last fruits, then." Gideon knew nothing about wine. The cordial seemed a good place to start, though it looked suspiciously like the tonics he'd been dosed with in his childhood. Excessively sweet going down, it lingered after he swallowed, leaving a rich aftertaste on his tongue. After only a couple of sips he felt pleasantly relaxed. He suspected an infusion of Mrs. Hedge's wily herbs.

The parson had set up his study next to his shop, in an outbuilding a short distance from the house. It was easy to imagine that, having been admitted to his teacher's inner sanctum, Gideon was now privy to the contents of his mind, for in this concentrated space were all the innovations Hedge had trumpeted in class. The three-sided desk: one wing devoted to Latin, the other to Greek, the center reserved for his beloved Hebrew. The wall cabinet with revolving shelves stacked with books instead of crockery or condiments. The famous reversible table designed for engraving.

"I do my drawing and tracing on the flat surface," Hedge explained. "When the time comes to cut, I rotate, and presto! A box to catch the chips! Try it yourself, if you like." He looked on with transparent delight as Gideon flipped the table from one side to the other. "A simple device, but adequate for my purposes. As usual, necessity dictated, and ingenuity followed, limping, in its wake. Do you notice the lock? That did require a bit of thought."

"I believe you mentioned a book for children," Gideon said, hoping to nudge the conversation in a less mechanical direction.

"My Alphabetical Bestiary. Have I spoken of it in class? That was premature of me. I'm only now sketching the Dromedary, but the project is dear to my heart. There'll be an Old Testament animal for each letter, and the letters themselves I am etching in English and Hebrew. My hope is that a sharp-eyed child will look beyond the illustrations and see beasts lurking in the ancient characters. At times, when I'm cutting, I fancy they're coming to life under my hands."

Hedge took a tray from a shelf and set it on the table. It was filled with small woodblocks of the Hebrew letters. "The ox's head in *Aleph* isn't easy to make out, even if you know it's there. I see it best with my thumb." He ran a finger over the raised surface of the letter, tracing its curves. "Here are the ears, and here the patient head. *Nun*'s serpent is not so subtle. See how it arches up? As if a snake charmer were piping at it. In just such a posture the creature must have whispered to Eve."

Gideon was struck by how finely made his teacher's hands were, the fingers tapering like a gentleman's in spite of all his manual work. In class Hedge used them to drive his lessons home: the students were all too familiar with his admonitory forefinger. Who would have thought that he had it in him to touch a thing so tenderly, with such a lingering caress? Gideon knew now that the Reverend wasn't Sophy's father, but for the first time, he could almost imagine him in that role. A man who could show ardor for a bunch of wooden letters might logically have produced the girl in the meadow.

"I love the *heft* of Hebrew," Hedge was saying. "The *shapeliness* of it. The words are as dense in the mouth as earth in the hand—as substantial, in their way, as the objects they name. And why should we be surprised? Isn't Adam's breath still in them?" He came closer and peered into Gideon's eyes. "Tell me, Mr. Birdsall, why did God choose the Jews?"

Gideon had a moment of sinking panic. His mind was a blank. Had he been dozing in class when Hedge lectured on the subject?

"Prophets of matter!" Hedge thundered. "Geniuses of the concrete! The Lord intended the Hebrews to keep His spirit alive in earthen vessels, but that stubborn tribe refused to see beyond the clay. Think of their fabled financial acumen. What is it but a perversion of their great natural gift? Profits of another sort, is it not so? I always say, scratch a sin and you will find a talent suppurating underneath. Ah, the Jews . . ." Hedge inhaled deeply and breathed the Chosen People out like aromatic smoke. "What a subject! Forgive me if I go on, but I have made them my special burden. I pray for them—not, I confess, with much hope. I like to think that reading Scripture in the language of the forefathers is itself a form of prayer."

The parson let loose another sigh and put the tray of lette
the shelf—alongside the perplexing Hebrews, Gideon coul
feeling. "And now we must get to your translation. But fi
show you my Behemoth. I had to consult Berwick's *Quadrupeas* about
the length of the trunk, but once I got the features down, I added a few
touches of my own. I think this big fellow came out rather well, don't
you?"

Only the deepening shadows in the room told Gideon how much
time had passed. He had admired other fauna of Hedge's alphabetical
kingdom, and been introduced to the pastor's great work-in-progress,
the Philosophical Hebrew Lexicon. He had reentered the thicket of his
translation with Hedge as his guide, emerging with the feeling that his
teacher respected the work more than he disliked it. The day had been
very full, and he was looking forward to savoring its best moments on
his long, solitary walk back to seminary. He wasn't used to spending so
much time in company.

"I can't thank you enough," he began, half-rising. But the Reverend
motioned him back into his chair.

"I spoke harshly to you earlier. I would be remiss if I didn't offer a
word of explanation."

Gideon took a second to absorb the astonishing fact that Hedge,
the unshakable pillar of righteousness, was about to justify himself to
a student.

"I assure you, sir, none is required," he said. "Only an ingrate would
have taken offense. It's not easy to speak of such experiences, and I did
so awkwardly. I'm afraid you took me by surprise. Our earlier conversation led me to believe that my discoveries were congenial to you."

"Con-gen-i-al." Hedge lingered so long over each syllable that
Gideon wondered if he was being mocked. "What an apt choice of
word, Mr. Birdsall. Perhaps you know that *genius* is at the heart of it?
And deeper still, the lurking demon: the *genie* who drives us to abuse
our God-given talents. He may not wield a pitchfork, but his jabs are
just as sharp! You remind me of a young man I knew. Another zealous
student whose affinities enticed him to breach walls."

The pastor had been looking into Gideon's eyes, but now his glance turned inward. Gideon thought he might be praying again.

"From boyhood I have had a love for languages. When I was not yet seven, Father began to teach me Latin." He smiled, with a touch of self-satisfaction, and looked up. "He was surprised at how quickly I learned. I had a gift, you see, coupled with an adventurous spirit. Mastering the native tongue was a way to claim places I longed to explore—planting the flag, if you will. Greek and my beloved Hebrew were major excursions, French and Italian amusing day trips. German I left until college because the sounds didn't please me, but soon enough I could make my way through Goethe."

"And did you discover your New Found Land?" Gideon kept his tone light, though the pulse in his neck throbbed so energetically he was sure the parson must notice.

"What I discovered," Hedge said, "was Poetry."

"I'm sorry, I don't understand." Gideon was vaguely disappointed; he wondered if the professor had departed from his usual plain speech to take refuge in metaphor.

Hedge seemed to anticipate his reaction. "I began to write verse around the age of sixteen, and threw myself into it heart and soul. In those days I was the sort of young man who would spend hours gazing at the night sky, questioning the universe and dreaming of other worlds. Maybe all that Hebrew had gotten into my bones—I was forever poking at the ineffable with my pen, trying to trap it on the page."

"To be a poet is a high calling," Gideon said. "It's not an unusual ambition when one is young."

He was starting to feel restless, a state that would have seemed impossible a few hours ago. The narrative had taken a mundane turn, and in any case, how much more of the Reverend could he absorb in one sitting? His attention wandered to a single painting on the wall: a fountain, a baroque affair with an elaborate scalloped base from which geysers spurted up, deluging a small bed of flowers beneath. Some effort had been made to render the plumes of water transparent, but the paint had been laid on too thickly. It was as if the floodgates of heaven had opened to irrigate a daisy.

Hedge did not appear to notice his distraction. "A high calling," he went on, "but only if it comes from above. I left for Harvard convinced I was about to make my mark on the world—a Dante in embryo, or at very least, a Bunyan. My magnum opus was already begun: a long visionary poem transposing the legend of Orpheus to a biblical setting. Night after night I stayed up to work on it, contending so long and hard that the words, when at last I managed to subdue them, seemed to bleed upon the page. Let my classmates spend their evenings carousing. The romance of creation was intoxicant enough for me! I was afloat in my own ether, forever trembling on the edge of revelation. What did it matter that I was putting an intolerable strain on my eyes and mind? If only I had taken a lesson from my subject matter, Mr. Birdsall. Soon enough, I began to fall." His voice had taken on a dismal, ringing tone. He made a fist and tolled the progress of his undoing into the palm of his other hand. "*Primus*, into worship of my own powers. *Secundus*, into a state I called love, with a young woman I knew to be far beyond me. *Tertius*, when she spurned me, into the deepest darkness I've yet known. The fall from grace doesn't happen all at once, you know. That privilege is reserved for the angels."

Gideon suspected that a stately graded descent might be more to the parson's taste than a long tumble; it was difficult to picture him, even in extremity, plummeting heels over head, limbs askew.

"It pains me to think of you sinking so low, sir," he said. "I hope you won't mind my asking how you . . . recovered yourself." He had neatly avoided the word "saved," though the symmetry of the sermon to come was already obvious. The tripartite fall could only mean that the Holy Trinity was waiting on the front line, prepared to retrieve the fallen soldier. But Reverend Hedge surprised him again.

"That, too, came in stages. The first step was making a chest for my father. A small one, to hold his pipes." Hedge reached for the tray and ran his fingers through the Hebrew letters, sifting them. He flipped one into his palm—a *Lamed*, Gideon noted—and palpated it with his thumb. "I'd done nothing for months. The torpor of my mind was such that study was impossible; I'd taken leave from the College and come home, and spent the better part of each day lying on a couch with a cloth over my eyes. My poor mother and father must have plotted between them to contrive some project to divert me. I still remember how timidly they approached me, asking if I felt well enough to consider the *vexing* problem of the stray pipes . . ."

He smiled, his face softening at the recollection. "I doubt that I will ever lift anything heavier than that first piece of wood. The task seemed gargantuan, but it drew me out of myself and back into the world. Reflect on it, Mr. Birdsall—I had thought to stretch my mind to the far reaches of the cosmos, and now my whole being was concentrated on a little box! You will say it is a diminution. Yet I can tell you that this box was the opposite of Pandora's, for all my blessings came out of it. My good wife—perhaps not so fair of form as my first love, but far better suited to the rigors of the clerical life. My family. My calling itself. And this, the humble but useful work of my hands." He swept out both his arms in a gesture meant to encompass not only the study, but the house, the garden, the orchard, the spreading field. "How great is our God, and how infinite His mercies!"

"Indeed," said Gideon. "An inspiring story." The Reverend's cautionary tale had caused his mood to plunge as swiftly as one of Hedge's falling angels. What was a man of vision to aspire to, then? Growing a superior squash? Making a chair? "But I think you will agree, sir," he said, "that the fault is not with language, which was God's gift to us in Eden. I hope you haven't forsaken poetry altogether."

"'Forsaken' is the wrong word. Rather, I've diverted the stream." Hedge sounded suddenly weary. Sharpness had crept into his voice. "I'm told my sermons are more varied and numerous than those produced by any of my colleagues. My lectures you are familiar with. My correspondence alone is of such volume that I often pray to the Lord for patience." He took up his glass and twisted the stem between two fingers. "I do undertake the occasional poem of a sacred nature—eulogies and moral lessons and the like. Only last month, I was moved to commemorate the hanging of a local blacksmith, a drunkard who murdered his wife; I printed copies of the verse for my congregation, with an illustration of the sad event, and the demand was such that I exhausted my supply. But I'm a better man when I confine myself to the practical crafts. There's a purity about them that the higher arts lack. They turn the imagination to wholesome ends. Given your own susceptibilities, you could do worse than follow my example."

"I'm no artist," Gideon said, stung again. "But I can't agree that creating beauty, or seeking it, or contemplating it, leads to sin. If that is so, why do you hang a painting above your desk?"

Hedge regarded him coldly. "You are no artist, Mr. Birdsall, and I hope you'll agree that I am no Philistine. The painting is Sophy's; I saw you looking at it earlier. She has some ability, I think, though this isn't one of her better efforts. The sentiment behind it compensates for its shortcomings. She painted it for my birthday, and I display it to please her."

"I think it's quite good. She's taken such care with the details." Remembering Sophy's wish for a centerpiece for her garden, Gideon felt a sudden surge of tenderness for the fountain's lack of scale. The Reverend would never see, as he did, that she had enhanced it in measure to her longing. "Mrs. Hedge believes Sophy has inherited your talents," he said.

"I haven't discouraged her," the parson said. "Quite the contrary. I've taught her what little I know, though it's never enough for her. It's in the blood, you see. For good or ill, the artistic strain runs in my family, a thin line, but persistent. Her mother was my only sister—a great favorite of mine. Mary was a blithe spirit, the bright star of our sober brood, always making up rhymes and songs and stories. I used to think she must be a changeling—that the midwife had spirited off the true Hedge and left this sunny creature instead." He sighed. "She assumed all men were as open-hearted as she was. Far too fanciful for this hard world, and the world took advantage of her, as is its way. She didn't tarry here for long."

Hedge paused, hand on chin, contemplating the painting. "Mary would have named her daughter for one of the Muses—I believe Calliope had been mentioned." He raised his eyebrows. "When she died, the task fell to us. I never saw such a mite as that infant was! I tell you without exaggeration, my own were giants compared to her. The midwife doubted she would survive, but I sensed a will there, and my Consort, bless her, was untiring in her efforts. It was my idea to call the baby Sophia. I thought wisdom would be a tree of life to her, after such a precarious beginning. If my sister had possessed more of it, she might be among us still." He turned to Gideon, his eyes misted over with an old sorrow. "Next month Sophy turns eighteen. A good girl, but flighty, and willful in her way. Time will tell whether the name has tempered her nature."

THEY WALKED BACK to the house in silence. Though Hedge had exhausted his store of words, he had endowed Gideon with a number of his written works as compensation: A discourse on "The Peculiar Nature of Time and Tense in Ancient Hebrew." An essay roguishly titled "An Eye for an Eye: Some In-sights into the Function of the Letter *Ayin*." And the only remaining copy of "The Blacksmith's Lament: The Last Words of Abner Turnbull Upon the Occasion of his Execution for the Heinous Murder of His Wife (With Illustrations from Life)."

Gideon was glad to be released from the study. This was his favorite time of day. Late-afternoon light glazed the fields and painted the yellow house a rich ochre—the color of blessing, he had always thought. The Hedge homestead looked as natural in this setting as if it had grown from seed, as cozily eternal as a village in a Dutch landscape.

"The day has gotten away from us," Hedge said, "pleasurable as it was. Will you take some supper before you go?"

"I've imposed on your hospitality enough," Gideon said quickly. "But if you can tolerate me a little longer, I'd like to see some of Micah's handiwork. He has a quality that's quite remarkable."

"I'm glad you sense it. Micah has a depth that is missing in his brothers. I wish my firstborn had a tenth of his seriousness. Sam was once handsome to look at, agreeable in company, but a shallow stream. At seminary he lasted less than a year. Instead of attending to his studies, he entangled himself with a clothier's daughter, and now he's locked in a hasty marriage, working in her father's shop in Lowell." The parson took off his hat and fanned at a circling bee. "The education I gave to Sam would have been better spent on Micah, but to what end? He will never preach." Hedge's voice was too flat for bitterness, but his face clenched as if the bee had stung him. "At times I'm weak enough to cry out about his condition. The sins of the fathers, Mr. Birdsall. I know all too well why the Lord hobbled his tongue."

The dog was waiting at the door, and Reverend Hedge took his leave of Gideon there; he had to help his sons with evening chores. "Micah will be out," he said, "but my wife will show you a few of his pieces. Or Sophia. She loves to trumpet her brother's talents."

CHAPTER 6

A SINGLE EYE

GIDEON WALKED THROUGH THE HALL ON THE BALLS OF his feet, trying to keep from pressing too loudly on the floorboards. He hoped Mrs. Hedge was busy elsewhere. She would insist on giving him a complete tour of the house and its contents, and he would never get away before nightfall.

Sophy was in the sitting room, at her easel by the window, blessedly alone. She looked up brightly when he came in, as if she were surprised to see him. "There you are, Mr. Birdsall! I've been waiting all day to show you my chair, but you took so long with Papa that I worked on my picture instead."

"May I see it? I've just been admiring your fountain." He stood at a respectful distance, wary of coming closer with only the two of them in the room. The canvas was clearly visible: a hut under a low-hanging fog of foliage, vaguely suggested in thick strokes of green.

"Please don't look. You mustn't, it's not finished." She stood and blocked the easel with her body: a gesture that struck him as too functional to be coy. "It needs a cow, I think. I'm very fond of cows, but I never can get them right. Mine always look like barrels with tails."

Gideon laughed, relieved that he wouldn't have to conjure up profound remarks about the painting. Her dancing was far superior to her artwork, but he understood that he must make no reference to it. "Then I'll have to settle for Micah's chair," he said.

Sophy wasn't as pristine as she'd appeared that morning: a ribbon of hair had come loose and broken the symmetry of her face, and a smudge of green marred one cheek—a suitable emblem, Gideon thought: the elf in her coming to the surface. But even these flaws were a charm.

She showed him a chest of drawers first, and then a clock that Micah and the Reverend were building—a labor of love, she explained; the intricate works still claimed their evenings, though the case had been completed months ago. Proudly she pointed out fine details in the carving, little flourishes that differentiated her brother's style from the father's. "And they've asked me to decorate the face," she said. "Isn't that trusting of them? I've already made some sketches. I wish my hand were as sure as Micah's. The design is in my head, but what I paint is so far from what I dream."

"I've had the same experience with my translations," Gideon said. "But the important thing is to *have* a dream, don't you think? It's like a compass. It points us in the direction we're meant to go."

The thought seemed to delight her. "I'll think of myself as traveling, then," she said, "and not be so unhappy that I haven't arrived. I can tell that you're a very determined person, Mr. Birdsall. You will surely reach your destination."

Sophy's chair was made of oak like the others, but Micah had managed to infuse some of her airy spirit into the wood. The finials were birds on the wing caught in mid-soar; in their beaks they held the corners of a scroll that stretched between them, forming the back post. "Matthew 6:22" had been carved on the post in an elegant hand.

"I ought to know the verse from the citation, but I don't," Gideon said. "Will you share it with a stranger?"

"Oh, it's very mysterious." She traced the inscription with a finger as if it would open at her touch. "*The light of the body is the eye. If there-*

fore thine eye be single, thy whole body shall be full of light. What do you suppose it means? I haven't any idea what use a single eye would be to anyone. Unless you have the misfortune to be born a Cyclops."

Gideon wasn't about to offer an exegesis. "I wonder why your father chose that passage."

"Even Papa can't tell you. He prays over the chair and a verse comes to him. He has faith that the Lord will tell him what we need to know."

And Hedge had accused *him* of mysticism, Gideon thought. How was Sophy to profit from a verse she couldn't understand? He remembered the passage now, and the even stranger one that followed it. *But if thine eye be evil, thy whole body shall be filled with darkness. If therefore the light that is in thee be darkness, how great is that darkness!* When he first read the verses as a boy, his orderly mind had rebelled at the odd diametric of "single" and "evil." But he had thrilled, too, at the whiff of paganism that the words gave off—incantations and the black arts infiltrating the familiar neighborhood of the Golden Rule. Could the good shepherd that Gideon and his mother prayed to each night really have inflicted such a dire prophecy? The exclamation point at the end had filled him with pleasurable terror: he had imagined a hooded Druid priest poising his long knife over a bound sacrifice. It seemed a travesty that Sophy's slender back should rest against such an enigma night after night, with only her innocence to shield her.

She had left him to his meditations on the chair and was looking out the window. "Mama is coming back from the garden," she reported. "Mr. Unsworth is carrying her basket. He reminds me of an old dog, the way he follows behind."

"I think you mean to say that he is faithful," Gideon said, making no attempt to suppress the lilt in his voice.

"Oh, he is that, I suppose—he's always underfoot. I wish I liked him more. He stares at me when he thinks I'm not watching. I'm sure he means no harm, but he makes me uncomfortable." Sophy turned to Gideon and lifted her chin, swiping with one hand at the errant lock of hair. "It would be quite different if you were boarding with us, Mr. Birdsall. We would have wonderful conversations about deep subjects—art and philosophy and true religion. Do you know, when I saw you in the meadow with the sun glinting on your hair, I thought you were an angel? That was why I ran away. I knew I wasn't fit to meet an angel."

SHE WASN'T THE FIRST GIRL to draw conclusions about his character from the color of his hair. Gideon was reminded of this as he retraced his path through sweet-smelling fields back to the road, the drone of insects making a soothing counterpoint to his thoughts. For as long as he could remember, women had cooed over his blondness, assuming that a boy so fair must be as angelic as he looked. As a child he'd delighted in mocking their effusions, screwing up his face and sticking out his tongue while his mother feigned horror.

When he was not quite fourteen, he began to stir another kind of interest. Gideon had been waiting in the schoolroom one afternoon when the girl who cleaned up after class stopped in front of him. She had never spoken to him before, and on the rare occasions when they'd shared the space, he'd ignored her presence. She was a farmworker's daughter, a vacant, lumbering creature who moved sullenly around the room with her mop and pail, choosing at random the patches of floor she would favor with suds that day; his mother was always complaining about her. The girl gaped at him, her mouth half-open. "It shines like gold!" she said, and before he caught her meaning, she reached out two grubby fingers to touch his hair. Gideon was too startled to recoil. Then, as if to pay him in kind for the liberty she'd taken, she grabbed his hand and thrust it under her bodice. The sudden contact with her flesh shocked him. The spongy fullness overflowed his palm. Until that moment, he had hardly seen her as a person, much less a woman. It seemed to him that she said things, but he couldn't absorb them. He didn't know how long he stood there—long enough for her to mistake his paralysis for pleasure and lift her skirts. Only then did he find the strength to wrench away from her and run out of the room.

His mother wanted to know why he wouldn't stay in the schoolroom anymore. He couldn't tell her. The experience had nothing to do with him; it had happened in an underworld he never planned to visit again. But in spite of his best efforts to lock it away, he would see the girl's face, at once knowing and stupid, the tip of her tongue between her slack lips; he would hear her whisper in his ear—breathy exhalations, a murmurous crooning—and even as his mind revolted, his body would be roused.

After a few weeks, he went again, telling himself he would exorcise her once and for all. The girl laughed lazily, as if she had been waiting for him, and without a word began to unbutton her dress. He pelted her with names to keep her away: "Fat cow! Filthy pig!" For a boy who acquired words easily, he knew few bad ones. Even these weren't so very bad—feathers rather than stones, for they tickled the girl, and the more he flung, the more she showed him, lifting her skirt to display thighs the color of curd, a great puckered rump that she parted with her hands, looking at him coyly over her shoulder. When he could stand it no more, he ran. She hadn't touched him—all the times he would go to her, she never touched him—but as soon as he got home, he touched himself. It was as though they had reached an agreement.

Love wasn't something Gideon felt a need for, nor did he connect it with the eruptions of his body. His college classmates attributed his restraint to an excess of piety. It was simply that whoring had no meaning for him, didn't kindle his desire. Why should he go to some degenerate stranger to slake a momentary urge that he could stifle on his own? This was a sin, he knew, but he was neat and quick about it. In his own mind he was preserving himself for the wife of his destiny, though his notions about that worthy goal were vague. Love, when he thought of it at all, was an exalted enigma, not unlike the Lord Himself: infinitely lofty, conveniently remote. Until this morning, it had never had a face.

Gideon could not say, even now, why that face should be Sophy's. Nothing about her seemed to warrant such an operatic intensity of feeling. She was small and spare—skimpy, his friends would judge her, no ornament for a man's arm—and uncommon to the point of being odd. Her manner was the opposite of artful. Although it was their first meeting, she had not bothered to disguise her admiration for him, and had openly hinted that he should take Unsworth's place in the household. Yet he liked all these things about her: liked her childish looks and the frankness that went with them, which would have seemed audacious in any other girl; liked her solitary dancing, and yes, even the endearing ineptitude of her paintings, which were only clumsy sketches of her dreams. Maybe, Gideon thought, love was nothing more than a series of likings, strung together like beads on a chain. Not pearls or rubies, but humble wooden beads: the sight of a girl in a field, the part in her hair, the feeling of possession that came over him when he entered the room where she sat alone. Had Dante felt more for Beatrice, Petrarch for Laura? Or were they simply more skilled at translating such moments from the vernacular of life into the high language of art?

A rabbit skittered across Gideon's path, startling him. He stopped and looked around, amazed to find himself halfway to the seminary already. Without realizing it, he had been moving along at a fast clip, his feet keeping pace with his thoughts. He had almost outrun the night, but it seemed to be gaining on him; the sky had lost its luster, the air had an edge. He pulled his coat closer. In spite of himself, he felt his old fear of being alone on the road after dark. The sweat he'd worked up was trickling coldly down his sides.

Reality seeped in, along with the chill. What nonsense had he been entertaining? It was all very fine to imagine coming home to Sophy after parish rounds or monklike hours in his study, to open a door and find her waiting for him, as she had waited this afternoon. *His little wife.* But he knew very well that these pleasantries were only the outer layer of marriage, the thin skin over the pulsing heart. Singular and unfathered as he was—hatched from an egg, his mother used to tease him—he was aware that beneath the homely comforts of the hearth, its reassuring rituals, gaped a mystery. He, who had always kept himself to himself, who had looked out at the world from a calculated distance: how would he manage the thorny business of becoming one flesh?

It was not Gideon's habit to open the door of the marital chamber, even in his dreams. He opened it now, but only a crack—just enough to glimpse Sophy in her white nightdress, chastely gathered at the neck.

Against the bank of pillows, her hair in a thick plait over one shoulder, she looked more childlike than ever. He would have spared her the sight of his pale calves in his nightshirt, but it was too late. Her face lifted to him with that bright candor he loved: a flower to the sun. He approached slowly, so as not to overwhelm her, marshaling all the wisdom he had picked up secondhand in the college common room ("A woman must be opened with care, like a bottle of fine wine."); bestowed a reverent kiss on her brow and her temple ("Let the points of the pulse be your guide!") before touching her lips; loosened with one finger the ribbons at her throat; drew up by millimeters the hem of her gown. But beneath the fabric was more gauze: a blur of a body, as nebulous as the trees in her painting. Her intimate particulars would not come clear.

He knew why. For all his care, a pair of ghosts had materialized in the room. His mother, as composed as she had been in her coffin, sealed in perpetuity behind her fixed smile. The schoolroom girl, goading him on with throat sounds and nonsense words. They had stationed themselves on either side of the bed, like attendants at a wedding.

"Go away! Go!"

A flock of birds rose suddenly from a nearby tree, and Gideon realized that he had shouted out loud. Sheepish, he looked around him, but the road was empty except for the persistent rabbit, whose button eyes were trained on him from a safe distance, curiosity having overcome its timidity. The bridal chamber had receded into the vapors, leaving him with a sediment of resolve. If he were lucky enough to be admitted to Sophy's presence again, he would devote himself to creating the garden of her dreams, with a fountain whose spray aspired to heaven, and statues, too. And he would build a wall around it, and set the stones so snugly that no dark influence could pass through, from this world or the next. The Reverend would have no cause to reproach him.

Not that there was much chance. He began to walk again, more slowly, with every step conscious of his life narrowing to the size of his solitary room. The family would be sitting down to their supper about now—a clan with its own rites and customs. They had probably already forgotten the poor student they'd invited into their midst; he was nothing more than a Sunday's good deed, briefly embraced, soon effaced. Even more ominous was the possibility that they were sharing their opinions of him over the remains of the stew. At this very moment Sophy might be amusing Unsworth with remarks about the serious young man who had stolen her precious Sunday afternoon. *He looked at me in the field. He thought I wasn't watching.*

Gideon shifted the packet of papers from one arm to the other. In the grip of his fantasies he had almost forgotten Hedge's parting loan. The essays, wrapped like butcher's paper around the unfortunate blacksmith's cautionary verse, were a tangible reason to return. He would contrive a few clever questions requiring long-winded responses and ask to see the Reverend outside of class. It was obvious that Hedge never needed an excuse to expound.

As for the rest, why should he concern himself? Marriage was a sacrament—or so the church proclaimed. There were vows to be spoken—vows he would soon be empowered to pronounce. If such a one as he, unfinished, imperfect, could bind two souls together for eternity, how could he doubt the efficacy of the promises? Surely, if he and his future wife pledged in the company of the faithful to worship one another with their bodies, their bodies would show them the way. Who knew what marvels lay in wait, what unknown lands they would discover?

The thought was such a revelation that it burned in his head like a lantern, illuminating the road ahead. He began to run again, and was in his room before the dark set in.

ON TUESDAY, THE MORNING of his first Hebrew class of the week, Gideon woke early and took special pains with his clothes. His reflection in the glass mocked him. A couple of days ago he had cared only for Reverend Hedge's opinion of his mind, and here he was, fussing over the whiteness of his collar.

He had always taken his beauty for granted. It was something he had been born with, like hands and feet. He knew that his mother took pride in his looks as an outward token of his general superiority, and was secretly pleased when others fawned, but Gideon had little vanity himself. Such admiration was too easily won. Fair hair and fine features were hardly as worthy of praise as mastering Greek. Now, for the first time, he considered that these attributes might have a practical use. Hadn't Sophy mistaken him for an angel? Absurd, of course, another sign of her innocence—still, it was hard to resist such an exalted vision when, all his life, he had felt set apart, groomed for something higher. He would do his best to live up to her lofty view of him, though he wasn't sure what she would think of his new ambition. Apparently— Gideon adjusted his cravat, squared his shoulders, exchanged a radiant smile with his conspirator in the mirror—he was applying for the position of suitor.

He need not have bothered. The Reverend strode into class with his head down, scowling and preoccupied. The last examination papers had been disappointing. Abysmal, as a matter of fact. Hedge made as if to set the offending papers on the desk, but, appearing to think better of defiling its surface, held them at the end of one stiff arm.

"I have asked myself—nay, interrogated myself—whether my instruction is at fault. Whether I have lingered too long on my little tales of house and home, thinking to sweeten the labor of learning with a bit of honey, as I'm told the Hebrew sages do. I have scoured my conscience, yet I find I cannot take up the cross for such *incompetence*, such *indifference*, such outright *contempt* for the language of Holy Scripture. I must bear down, gentlemen! For the sake of those souls who will one day be in your care, I must wield the rod!"

The arm swung in their direction, the papers came at them like grapeshot.

Gideon was unmoved by these histrionics. He had seen them before, and besides, he had nothing to fear: his own examination was clean, except for a couple of insignificant changes. He could no longer summon up the holy awe he had felt in Hedge's presence; observing the man in his native habitat had taken care of that. Still, he wished the Reverend would acknowledge him in some small way, raise him above his disgraced classmates with a quick glance or a nod. Hedge's baleful eye hadn't settled on him once—seemed, actually, to skim over him with willful disregard.

The class wandered on, interminable. Hedge was at his driest, Hebrew issuing from his mouth in a continuous uninflected line, as from a parchment scroll rolled out by inches. Gideon knew he wasn't the only one who lacked the courage to sneak a look at his pocket watch. Stomachs were grumbling all around him; dinner hour must be long past. The professor's teaching lacked the drama of his preaching. His domestic homilies might be universally mocked, but it was clearer with each passing minute how much they had leavened the tedium. When at last he creaked to a close, the students didn't move for several seconds. Boredom had numbed them into docility.

Hedge busied himself at his desk, taking no notice of them as they straggled out. Gideon considered stopping to ask him one of his rehearsed questions, but thought better of it. He was just about to step into the hall—sun-drenched after the murky classroom—when a thin voice hooked him and reeled him back. "Mr. Birdsall."

Gideon turned, blinking. "Yes, sir?"

"Mrs. Hedge has asked me to inquire whether you will be joining us again this Sunday."

"This Sunday? I didn't know—I hadn't assumed—"

The Reverend went on as if Gideon hadn't spoken. "It occurred to me after our interesting discussion that you might be willing to assist me with my Hebrew Lexicon. Only the most minor tasks, of course—copying, organizing notes, and the like. I would prefer to do it all myself, but you are well acquainted with the demands on my time. Lately, I have been turning over in my mind the possibility—say, rather, the necessity—of employing an aide to speed my project along. An amanuensis, if you will."

"A-man-u-en-sis," he said, lingering for a fraction of a second between each syllable, letting the last glide like syrup off the tip of his tongue.

"Should you have an interest in such a position, I am prepared to compensate you in a modest way. I am not a wealthy man, but what I can't supply in dollars, I have no doubt my Consort will make up for at table." Hedge gave a dry, barking cough that Gideon interpreted, a moment late, as a laugh. "No need to decide right away. You have until the Sabbath to mull over my little offer."

CHAPTER 7

AMANUENSIS

THE FIELD HAD LOOKED SERENE FROM A DISTANCE, DOTTED with wildflowers, tall grasses waving gently in the wind, but as soon as he set foot in it, he began to stumble. Dense, knotty undergrowth had entrenched itself in the soil and was rapidly taking over. Wiry tendrils thick as vines wound about his ankles; it was all he could do to stay upright. He would never make a trail through this midget jungle with only his hands to clear the way. A scythe was what he needed. Across the field he could see Sophy, a basket on her arm, gazing in his direction. It seemed to him that she stood on a placid shore, waiting, while he wrestled a choppy sea to get to her. With all the breath he could muster, he called out her name. Somehow the frail sound reached her: she tented her eyes with one hand and waved. He lifted his arm to wave back, but the distraction broke his concentration. He tripped, falling forward, his arms flung out helplessly, hungry vines arching up to meet him even before he hit the ground. Within seconds he was immobilized, tangled in roots.

Gideon woke in a sweat, the coverlet twisted around his legs. He kicked it aside and fell back against the damp pillow. His eyes were open, but the dream still clasped him—not its drama, which was already fading, but its atmosphere of paralysis and slow dread. He was late for an appointment—that much he remembered. He felt a muffled urgency, yet he could not persuade his limbs to move.

A gust of wind blew the curtains apart; there was a pause like a sucked-in breath, then the hollow boom of thunder. Another wet day, the sixth in a row. After a hot, dry summer, the rain had come all at once and with a vengeance. Osgood groaned in unconscious protest and turned over on his back, discharging a fusillade of snores. The noise jolted Gideon into clarity. It was Sunday. He was due at the Hedges to expedite the momentous transition from *Aleph* to *Beth*. The Lexicon awaited.

HE HAD BEEN ASSISTING the parson for nearly two months. Seven Sundays, and by now he was a fixture: yet another domestic improvement, obediently slipping into the niche that had been prepared for him in a corner of the study. Gideon could imagine the parson pointing him out to a visitor. "And here we have my amanuensis. A simple device, but adequate for my purposes."

His function in the household continued to mystify him. He supposed he was a sort of apprentice scholar, a rung or so higher than a clerk. Reverend Hedge was always hovering, finding his way back to the desk in the midst of whatever activity engrossed him to check on Gideon's progress, assess his efforts, send him scurrying after another source. The primary Hebrew roots—sturdy three-legged stools on which all manner of meaning could be stacked—were only the beginning. Samaritan, Phoenician, Arabic, Syriac—Gideon's head swarmed with ancient alphabets. Scripture references had to be hunted down, derivatives traced to their furthest reaches. His adventures with translation had led him to believe that the quest for a word's essence would be vertical: a clean dive into deep, still waters; the gem, half-buried, gleaming in the silt. The reality was more like the noxious plant of his dream, spreading relentlessly outward in every direction.

Although the work Gideon was doing went far beyond the basic tasks that the parson had described, Hedge was never satisfied with his progress; each week he badgered him to stay a little longer, do a little more. "We are engaged in *sacred studies*, Mr. Birdsall," he would exhort, neatly skirting the command to rest on the Sabbath. "To probe the language of the Lord is to journey into the very heart and bowels of Scripture." Gideon suspected that Hedge, for all his criticism, was willing the Lexicon into being through him. He had not gotten very far with it on his own. Twenty-one letters remained: a whole continent of words still to be plumbed, enough work for an army of secretaries. In Gideon's first flush of excitement after receiving Hedge's offer, he had consulted his dictionary about the word "amanuensis" and found that it derived from a custom of the scribes of old, who signed documents they had been ordered to copy. Its literal meaning was "slave at hand." Flexing his cramped fingers after hours at the desk, Gideon found it all too easy to envision a life spent in lexical servitude, submerged like a galley oarsman in endless repetitive labor.

This morning, as he threw on his clothes, he reminded himself that he was a free man; he could plead the pressure of his studies and leave whenever he wanted. But if he did so, he would lose all connection to Sophy. Gideon had assumed that proximity would increase the intimacy between the two of them; had even contrived some promising remarks that might develop into the philosophical conversations she longed for. Just the opposite proved to be true. He saw her at church and at dinner, always in company. He was Hedge's property now. He barely had time to put down his fork before the Reverend herded him off to the study, discoursing along the way on his errors of the week before. *You have slighted the Arabic, Mr. Birdsall. Do not be seduced by easy solutions!* In Gideon's state of fatigue and frustration, it was easy to see a Machiavellian plot behind it all. Hedge was too sharp not to have sensed a budding attraction between Sophy and his student, and had devised this devilish scheme to smother it in its infancy. Instead of banishing Gideon, which might lead to lovesick pining on Sophy's part, he had installed the admirer as a permanent cog in the household machine, thereby rendering him commonplace.

Or worse, invisible. Sophy hardly ever favored him with her musing glance these days. Their relationship seemed to have regressed to formality. After the service they exchanged a few stiff words; he asked about her garden, and she replied with a precise inventory of the state of her plants, those that were flourishing, those that had faded. Gideon was reduced to mining this unpromising material for hidden meaning; his mother, he remembered, had owned an old French book about the secret language of flowers. In his lowest moments, he doubted they would speak at all once the growing season was over. She seemed different now—not so much changed as muted, her vivid presence watered down to a faded pastel. From Mrs. Hedge he learned that there had been an argument over the design Sophy had planned for the clock face, an elaborate arrangement of the signs of the Zodiac, copied from an almanac. The Reverend had judged the images unsuitable, and he had prevailed. Mrs. Hedge had no idea why Sophy had taken it so hard.

"He was well within his rights," Fanny said. "Can you believe the girl put the constellations in place of numerals? She would have us consult Aries to see whether it is time for dinner and Capricorn for supper. And in the center, the phases of the moon, all in a ring. Even a cathedral clock would have trouble accommodating so many heavenly bodies! She means well, but she can't see past her fancies, and if they are thwarted, she sulks."

Gideon's own theory was that Sophy had run away without leaving. At dinner she sat with downcast eyes, lost in her own thoughts as conversation eddied around her. But as the weeks wore on and her withdrawal persisted, he began to wonder if the exuberant dancer of his imagination had ever existed—if, after all, he had dreamed her.

The talk at table was all of James's autumn nuptials. James had purchased land and was drawing up designs for a house, to be built by the brothers and overseen by the Reverend; until it was finished, he and his bride would live at home. They were likely to be in residence for some time. Each week the plans grew more elaborate, as James, by nature a modest, sensible fellow, added features that had clearly originated with his fiancée.

Gideon was ignored during these discussions, and not displeased to be so. It was sufficient that his mind was in bondage; he had no wish to be conscripted for months of hard labor. Taking advantage of his invisibility, he piled enough food on his plate to carry him through the lean week ahead, and applied himself to it as Micah did, with steady, reverential concentration. He felt justified in his generous helpings. Although the parson muttered about setting his wages, he had paid him nothing yet. Last week, Reuben, whose rough humor bordered on bullying, suddenly took notice of him. Pointing his fork and knife at Gideon like a pair of pistols, he'd said to the company at large, "Look at what this weedy fellow puts away! He has quite an appetite for a man who spends all day in a chair. How do you work off all that beef, little preacher?" Gideon had blushed red. Mrs. Hedge was quick to come to his defense. "You leave Mr. Birdsall alone," she scolded. "Do you suppose he doesn't need his nourishment as much as a great ox like you? Anyone can see how hard he is thinking!" The well-meaning woman seemed puzzled by the hilarity she'd generated. Even Sophy had smiled.

The only one who paid him any real attention was Unsworth, who was moving out at the end of the month to make room for the newly-weds. If the schoolmaster had once shunned Gideon as a rival, he now treated him as a comrade, in need of sage advice from an older and wiser friend. He waylaid Gideon at every opportunity, monopolizing him after church and appearing out of nowhere as he set off for seminary, clinging close to his side for the first mile or two. Gideon had never trusted the man, and took no pleasure in his company. The worst of it was that Unsworth forced him into the position of confidant, a recep-tacle for all his accumulated grievances against the Hedges. The longer Gideon listened to this vitriol, the more ashamed he was of his own festering thoughts.

"I suppose you haven't seen any money yet," Unsworth said late the previous Sunday afternoon, having met him on the road a quarter-mile from the house. "You aren't the first and you won't be the last. The parson likes to pretend he's living on good works and turnips, but it's a sham. He's as well-off as any banker. Interests, you know, properties and the like, and he never spends a penny without putting three back. He depends on free labor—his family, the odd parishioner who's in his debt, bright young fellows like you. I don't see that it's all that different from what's happening in the South, except his slaves aren't fettered and locked up at night."

"That's an odious comparison!" Gideon was genuinely outraged, in part because he'd indulged in similar hyperbole himself. "The Hedges have more than repaid me with their kind attentions. I consider it a privilege to work under a brilliant scholar like the Reverend, who gives me the equal of a private tutorial each week. How can I attach a price to the knowledge I am gaining?"

"No need to take offense," Unsworth said, panting from trying to match Gideon's pace. "My eye for exploitation is perhaps too keen these days—God knows there's enough injustice to hone it on. I was only thinking of your welfare."

Gideon had to bite down on the "None taken" that sprung to his lips—the legacy of a lifetime of training in good manners. They strolled along in silence for a few minutes, Unsworth with his hands behind his back, staring intently at the ground between his feet as if a trail of pebbles had been laid out for him to follow. From the mulish expression on his sallow face, it was clear that he considered himself the injured party. Gideon walked even faster, hoping that his companion would finally turn tail, but the schoolmaster seemed determined to continue their parallel trot until he got some satisfaction out of their conversation.

At last Gideon said, "You have no regrets about leaving, then."

"None at all. I've reached a time in life when I require more private accommodations." Unsworth glanced at Gideon out of the corner of his eye. "Well, there is something I regret, if I'm to be honest. Have you seen the beauteous Miss Mills? James is a lucky fellow, don't you think? I tell you as one bachelor to another, I wouldn't mind gazing at that confection across the table each night. I haven't had anything so fine to feast on for many a month. Meager fare at the parson's. Scrawny, undergrown—but that's only one man's opinion." He winked, showing one thick palm in a facsimile of carefree farewell, and scuttled off in such haste that Gideon could only stare after him, open-mouthed.

GIDEON ARRIVED AT the meetinghouse just as the congregation was rising for the final hymn. The abrupt swish of black-clad backs rebuked him. He stood at attention behind the last row of pews and tried to join in, but his voice was ragged; he had walked all the way in the rain, and was soaked to the skin. The Reverend Hedge looked past him as he processed down the aisle, sanctioning the effect of public shunning.

In the churchyard, Gideon kept to himself, feeling as much the outsider as he had on the first Sunday he had worshiped there. A few of the parishioners nodded to him in passing, but no one stopped to talk. He could not blame them. Whatever they might think of his lateness, the weather was hardly conducive to conversation. By now the rain had thinned to a morose drizzle. The sky had lightened without brightening, casting a sooty monochrome over the churchyard and everyone in it. Gideon could see its effect in the curve of the old people's backs, the way the men crushed their hats down over their foreheads and the women huddled under their cloaks. He thought of his mother's perennial warning: "You'll catch your death in this weather!" "Not me. I'm too fast," he'd taunted her, ashamed even then of her superstitions, but now he had to acknowledge the truth in the old saw. How could you escape something so amorphous? It crept into the bones like damp, and once inside, it made itself at home.

Hedge was in his element. Adversity, be it atmospheric or circumstantial, infused him with resounding good humor. He reached deep in himself and pulled up an extra measure of vigor, to be applied, like liniment, where it was most needed: a revitalizing handshake, a clap upon a sagging shoulder. He inquired about people's health, asked after their families and their crops, offered scraps of Scripture and miniature homilies. "We must not let the weather dampen our spirits," he said again and again. "The Lord is inviting us to turn our gaze inward, to loosen our hold on worldly things. How ingenious are His ways! He arranges that we reap the harvest in our souls as the earth drinks its fill. 'For He watereth the hills from His chambers . . . '"

Gideon heard more than one disgruntled farmer, at a safe distance from the parson's geniality, mutter about mildew and rot. The rain they had prayed for all summer had come too late.

James was the first of the family to emerge from the church, his fiancée on his arm. Caroline Mills was dimpled and buxom, her face framed in yellow ringlets that peeked out from her bonnet with artful symmetry, like an extra ruffle. For her debut in her future husband's parish, she had arrayed herself in a flowery lace-trimmed frock with matching parasol—more suitable for a garden party than a Congregational service on a dank day like this one, Gideon thought. But he had to admit that she shone in this crowd of drab women like a butterfly among moths. He could see why James had courted her; she was all circles to his mother's bony angles, a bed of pillows for a man to rest on. James's face showed his pride as he introduced her around. He was as open and straight as Reuben was sly, and humble enough to be dazzled by his own good fortune. A dutiful son, he had departed from the paternal model only once. He had put aside utility to marry for love.

"No one will blame you for sleeping in on a morning like this," he said to Gideon. "Allow me to present Miss Mills. I don't mind telling you I'm jealous. She's told me she thinks you're good-looking."

"James, I never did! Don't listen to him, Mr. Birdsall." The lady looked up at Gideon with prim coquetry, her small mouth pursed prettily. It was plain that she was used to being admired, and had developed a set of stock airs and attitudes that served her well on most occasions.

"A pleasure. I've heard so much about you. When is the happy day?"

Gideon managed an agreeable smile, although his mind was raging. This was the object of Unsworth's desire? How cheap, how trite, was his idea of beauty! Confection, indeed. In a few years she would be fat, her pert features drowned in blown-out cheeks and extra chins. The schoolmaster had departed earlier in the week, absolving Gideon of the necessity of murdering him, but his insults still stung. It was no surprise that the lout would find this coy creature superior to Sophy. She was miles beyond the likes of him.

Gideon listened with half an ear as the couple, oblivious as only those pledged to each other can be, gave him a detailed summary of their preparations for married life. The merits of stone fireplaces versus brick. The impossibility of finding decent lace. As Caroline prattled on about her epic quest for trim for the gown she was making—"I promise you, there is nothing to be had outside of Boston, nothing!"—his eyes wandered to the church doorway, where Mrs. Hedge chatted with a shopkeeper's wife. Sophy stood nearby, but in the open, her chin upraised to the rain as if each drop on her face were a balm to be savored. She wore a mole-colored cloak that seemed, in its refusal to declare itself either gray or brown, expressly woven to blend with the weather.

She disguises herself in dull feathers, he thought. She believes she is invisible. Free to look where she pleases, but safe from other's eyes.

Gideon was certain of one thing. For all the press of family and her public life as a minister's daughter, Sophy was as solitary as he. Loved, yes, protected and modestly indulged, but a stranger to those who had raised her. Mrs. Hedge was merely uncomprehending—she would do no harm—but the parson's tie to his adopted child was blood-deep; he would never rest until he had tamed her nature as he'd tamed his own. As long as Sophy lived under his roof, she would be expected to conform to the name he had chosen, her every playful impulse doomed to be slain in infancy and laid on the altar of the goddess of wisdom. It was no surprise that the girl had been driven into the field to express herself. What would she think, he wondered, if she knew that he was more than a casual observer? That he could see through her dun-colored layers as clearly as he had seen through the clotted paint of her fountain, to the heart of her and the longings stored there?

"YOU LOOK PEAKY," Mrs. Hedge pronounced. "You had better sit by the fire. But not in those wet things—you will spoil the finish on the chair." Gideon was now clothed neck to ankles in Hedge motley: an old shirt of James's; one of the Reverend's vests, too tight to button; and a pair of Reuben's trousers that bagged on him like pantaloons, the sight of which would surely give Reuben joy. Though the day was humid, Mrs. Hedge took a shawl from a peg by the back door and insisted on swaddling him in its folds. It was one of those homely garments that most likely belonged to no one and anyone, a castoff to be thrown on before going out to the garden. But he was pleased to think that the last shoulders it had warmed might have been Sophy's.

Grateful as he was to be ordered to sit, Gideon hesitated over the rocking chairs. Was there one set apart for guests? It seemed rude, even blasphemous, to occupy the Hedges' designated seats; he would sooner have reclined on the Pope's throne than the parson's straight-backed rocker. Micah came in and, seeing his dilemma, dragged his oldest brother's chair from another corner of the room. Gideon took note of the feckless Sam's Scripture; he had expected a verse about the Prodigal Son, and could not help feeling smug when he saw that it was something bland from Ecclesiastes. So much for the Reverend's gift for prophecy.

"They've made an old woman of me," he told Micah, who had dropped into his own chair and was stretching his damp boot soles to the fire. The boy's feet and hands were enormous, like a half-grown puppy's. He looked at Gideon and laughed softly, shaking his head, as if to say, "What a piece of good fortune that the two of us can be ridiculous together!" There was not an ounce of guile in him; Reuben had gotten it all. Gideon was comfortable in his presence and believed Micah felt the same about him. Since their first awkward encounter, they had managed to communicate without relying on the back-and-forth of ordinary talk, and by now a companionable silence had grown between them. Gideon felt free to wrap the shawl closer about him, fit his back to the admirable contours of the chair and shut his eyes. He needed to rest a little to make up for his fitful sleep the night before.

The dinner bell startled him. He could not have been dozing long, but he had slept deeply, a white sleep unmarked by dreams. His body was stiff, his joints aching. Rising out of the chair was a conscious effort; he had to fight the urge to grab Micah's strong arm. Every muscle ached, and there was a thickness in his throat. When he opened his mouth to speak the blessing (Hedge's revenge on him for missing the sermon), he could manage only a croak.

"Don't tell me you're sickening for something," the parson said. "Not on this day of all days, when we cross the border into a new land. I don't favor one letter over another, any more than I favor one of my children, but *Beth* is a pleasant country. I think you will enjoy your travels there. Rally yourself, Mr. Birdsall! We are moving forward! We are on the march!"

For once, Gideon had little appetite. It was a labor to chew and a painful trial to swallow. He might have been encased in wax for all the connection he felt to the rest of them; still, he was aware of an unusual restraint at the table that had nothing to do with his dulled senses. Although James had been betrothed for some time, he had, perhaps wisely, kept his fiancée to himself. Caroline's first appearance at a family gathering was a rehearsal for the months they were all about to spend together. Gideon knew that beneath the tranquil surface of Sunday dinner, the members of Clan Hedge were nervous, even agitated, trying to assimilate this foreign element introduced into their midst.

Gideon was predisposed to dislike Caroline; yet he couldn't help but feel compassion for her when he saw how hard she was trying. She was an only daughter, a late-life gift to a prosperous farmer who had married in middle age. It was evident from her manner that affection and approval had been bestowed on her from the cradle. She had never had to earn the esteem that she must now court from each member of this peculiar family, so different from her own. Her cheeks were pink from the exertion. Her high, thin voice, intended by nature to burble like a woodland stream, swooped and fell with exaggerated emotion.

"Do please let me help!" she implored Mrs. Hedge. "I will be very distressed if you treat me like a guest!"

The parson's wife was unmoved. "The rule of the house is, no work on the first visit," she said in her flattest tone. "After today you may help all you please." She collected the plates with ruthless efficiency and bore the towering stack off to the kitchen. Her discomfort was evident in the set of her shoulders. Her home was her province, and now she must learn to share it with this frivolous girl whose domestic skills were confined to flower arranging and needlework. Not the wife she would have chosen for her most dependable son, Gideon thought. If she had hoped for a like-minded daughter, Caroline would not suffice.

This afternoon, as if to make amends, Sophy followed in Fanny's footsteps as a novice follows a mother superior, alert to help wherever she could. Gideon suspected that Sophy's industry had a motive: she must be desperate to escape the effusions of her sister-in-law-to-be. Seated next to Caroline, she might be mistaken for a nun in her dark, simply cut dress with her hair drawn over her ears like a wimple. The more Caroline put herself forward, the more Sophy receded, spurring Caroline to ever more strenuous efforts to draw her out. "I think it is *charming* to be so shy and modest. I should be more that way myself. But you must promise not to be shy with *me*. We'll be sisters soon! Think of the good times we'll have, the secrets we'll tell behind the backs of all these men." She looked archly at James, who sat at attention beside her, stiff with discomfort. "Will you promise me that, Sophy dear?"

Gideon did not miss the note of condescension in Caroline's trills. She used the same cajoling tones with Sophy as she did with Micah, rather as if they were children who needed to be fussed over for an obligatory moment before being hidden away in the nursery. She must already have decided that James's quiet mouse of a sister was no threat to her—and, Gideon guessed, no true companion either. He suspected that once her own household was established, Caroline would metamorphose from village belle to society matron, and Sophy would be left behind like a curio on a side table.

By the time dessert was set down—a frosted cake instead of the usual slapdash bruised-fruit tart—he was longing for the refuge of the study. No one would miss him if he slipped away a little early. Caroline was having some luck exercising her charms on Reuben, who—ever competitive with his brother—was teasing her and telling her outlandish stories that made her laugh. "James, he is too comical! Tell him to stop!" she pleaded, but she seemed to be enjoying herself for the first time.

"If you will excuse me, I had better get to work," Gideon said, standing. The close atmosphere in the room had become intolerable. His head felt too heavy for his body. For a second he thought he would topple over; he grabbed the back of the chair, pretending to retrieve the shawl. Rain or no, he needed to get into the open air.

"You'd do better to get to bed," Mrs. Hedge muttered, and Sophy, at her heels, said. "I'll bring you a slice of cake later, and a nice big cup of tea."

The Reverend was unable to repress a look of envy. His face had grown longer and more saturnine as the meal progressed. He had informed Gideon earlier that he would not be available to, as he put it, "plant the flag in fresh earth"; he must take this opportunity, long overdue, to instruct the fledgling couple in the sacred nature and multiple responsibilities of the marital bond, a lecture he gave to all the young people of his parish before agreeing to unite them.

Gideon wondered if Hedge regretted the match. He was fatherly toward Caroline, even courtly in an old-fashioned way—and no doubt mindful of the respected family she came from and the inheritance she would bring with her. But she was a living antithesis to all he valued. How could he not be troubled by her lack of substance?

ALTHOUGH THE RAIN had stopped, sun was just beginning to penetrate the clouds; the sky had taken on a pearly, luminous sheen. The air smelled pungently of grass and herbs. Gideon took deep breaths, drinking in draught after draught, as if he had been deprived of oxygen for weeks. The freshness was intoxicating. It went straight to his stuffed head, clearing out the crusty residue of dinner chatter, odd bits of Hebrew, months of stale thoughts.

He understood, with clarity he'd been incapable of moments before, that what might trouble the parson about Caroline Mills was not too little substance, but too much. In the voluptuousness of her pampered flesh, she embodied all the excess that Hedge had trimmed from his lean and dutiful life. He had loved with ardor once, as James loved now. Romance, with its minions of lust and poetry, had come back to haunt him by way of his son.

Gideon remembered what the parson had confided to him on his first visit to the study: how he and Fanny had made a laboratory of their kitchen, coaxing the liquors from humble garden produce and fermenting them into wine. He'd had to hold back his laughter at the time, and had even thought of gaining some favor with his classmates by embellishing the story at dinner: Hedgehog and his functional Consort infusing a little spirit into their conjugal arrangement. He was glad that he had resisted such meanness. It might be the air, or his strange malaise, but the Hedges' vegetal alchemy no longer seemed amusing. The thought of the couple communing over their pots, measuring and mixing, straining and boiling, made him want to weep. Their long patience, and their zeal to extract from arid virtue a few drops of the elixir of love, struck him as more miraculous by far than Jesus's water trick at the wedding feast in Cana.

CHAPTER 8

THE COUNTRY OF BETH

EVEREND HEDGE HAD SET IT ALL OUT FOR HIM. GIBBS'S translation of Gesenius ("A punctilious scholar in the Germanic tradition, but his work is tainted by the rationalism of his countrymen. On guard, Mr. Birdsall!"). The lexicons: Greek and Latin, Chaldee, Syriaco-Arabic. The parson's notes, which had been jotted on scraps thriftily culled from the bottom halves of lists and the last pages of sermon drafts, and secured under a brimming pot of ink. A cherished hand-hewn pen, laid at an alluring angle atop a stack of paper.

The bounty was lost on Gideon. He lifted the pen and put it down. He opened Gesenius to *B*, but his eyes refused to penetrate the mesh of fine print. The magnifying glass made things worse, the enlarged words leaping up at him like trolls from behind a rock, leering and grotesque. His head was aching again. So many characters so close together, coating each page from top to bottom. So many words. Far too many, it seemed to him now: countless thousands through the ages, chiseled on tablets, contorted in scripts, inscribed on the hides of sheep and goats, set in iron and pounded mercilessly onto paper, ordered and analyzed until the breath of speech was pressed out of them, clapped between covers like dried specimens in a drawer. When did it all start? Where would it end?

He pushed the book to the far corner of the desk, leaving the paper in the cleared space before him. Hedge had meant the blank sheets to entice, but Gideon felt only an irresistible desire to rest his head on top of the stack and go to sleep again. There was something peaceful about these fields of white, an emptiness that soothed his eyes; it seemed a shame to deface such purity with scribbles. The world of letters that had dominated his life seemed absurd to him. He thought how liberating it would be to bypass this arbitrary code—what was it but a go-between, a cumbersome intermediary?—and make pictures like Sophy. To plunder your imagination for forms, or render what you saw as your eye took it in: a man, a tree, a horse, a hill. His infatuation with language had begun early, but as a child he had liked to draw. The instinct must be in him still, atrophied from neglect.

Gideon took a single sheet from the top of the stack. Dipping the nib of his pen in ink, he drew an experimental line across the whiteness, and where it ended, another line straight down. He could feel his wrist loosen with the long strokes. He had created a sort of lean-to, the corner of something afloat in space. Under these he drew a third line, extending it a little behind the first two, as a child might indicate the ground. Now he had an enclosure, open on one side. He remembered well enough what ought to follow. The sealing wall. The triangle of the roof, topped by a crooked chimney and a thin curl of smoke. Inside, three rectangles: a pair of windows and a door. But his hand refused to carry out his orders; it seemed to be telling him that the house, such as it was, was complete.

He stared at the stark lines for a long time, compelled in a way he could not explain. Their very simplicity shimmered with mystery. At last it dawned on him that his half-house was actually the letter *Beth*— or rather, the letter was a house, taking its shape from the most primitive form of shelter. He laughed out loud to think he had missed the obvious; he should have known that more wonders lurked in the Hebrew alphabet than could be contained in Hedge's stable of beasts! *Aleph*, Hedge had explained, was not yet a full-fledged letter, but rather the *intention* to speak: the ox might lift its ponderous head, trying to communicate its bestial will, but such was the order of creation that the brute could produce nothing more coherent than a bellow. The true first letter of the alphabet was *Beth*. It was no accident that the book of Genesis began with a *B. Bereishit*. In the beginning. The words were perhaps the most familiar in the Bible, dulled by repetition, but as evocative in their way as "Once upon a time"—and far more potent. It had never occurred to him that the first lines of the oldest story might refer to a dwelling that could be entered, that the ancient letters might be a code.

His thoughts were coming very fast now, starbursts arranging themselves into orderly constellations as he watched. From a distance he observed the shortness of his breath and the trembling of his hands. Symptoms only—at his core he was perfectly calm, fixed on his task. It was as clear as a mathematical equation. If he could find a way into the House of *Beth*, he would discover its secrets.

His house had no door, but there ought to be a handhold to guide him into the interior; he had neglected to install it. He bore down with his pen to make the dot in the center, inking it over until he had a nice solid knob. He wasn't sure how to grasp it, but this seemed of no consequence, a minor difficulty that would resolve on its own. The solution would be simple, because, at root, the nature of life was simple. For most of his youth he had striven to master one complex system after another: languages ancient and modern; the thousand-and-one theologies by which men parsed God. He had lost sight of the quest he'd set himself before he could even read. To get behind the scrim of print and into the story.

The answer to his problem came to him without effort, as he had known it would. He was to grasp the knob the only way he could—with his eyes.

The dot beckoned. He focused on it with all the concentration he could muster, envisioning his own black dots, his pupils, as a pair of hands, turning, pushing in. There was no movement that he could detect; the knob sat firmly on the surface, where he had placed it. After

a while—how long he had no idea—the throbbing in his head sharpened; it seemed that staring at the dot with such fixation had worked a
dot-sized hole between his brows. His attention started to flag. Worldly
concerns intruded themselves; any minute the parson could come in,
full of anticipatory zeal, and catch him meditating on a blotch of dried
ink. Once, twice, he tried to turn away, only to be brought back.

The change, when it came, was so gradual that Gideon thought his
eyes must be playing tricks on him. The dot seemed to be sinking ever
so slightly into the white background. The white itself had taken on a
subtle shine, like the reflection of light on the surface of a cup of milk.
His heart stopped when he saw it: a little pause, a hyphen between beats,
as his body registered the surprise.

He blinked and rubbed his eyes, shut them tight, opened them to the
bare wall behind his worktable. Hedge had stationed him in a corner of
the study where he would have no distractions, but after weeks of work
Gideon had come to know the wall's every crack, bulge, and stain inti-
mately; he saw as many shapes in the plaster as children saw in clouds.
The lobster was still there, and the hunchbacked bird, and the hot-air
balloon, just as they had been last Sunday, and all the Sundays before.

Although his chest had tightened of its own volition, he refused to
surrender to excitement. He meant to examine the evidence slowly and
deliberately, like a natural philosopher peering through a lens at a specimen on glass. He lowered his eyes. One look was enough to confirm that
the letter had returned to its original state, safely on top of the paper, just
as he had drawn it. What he had seen must have been an optical illusion,
the result of eyestrain and a wretched headache.

He supposed he ought to feel relieved. After a brief holiday, his heart
was ticking again, steady as a Hedge timepiece, and the earth was turning at its usual monotonous pace, while gravity, faithful lackey, kept the
current population securely pinned to its crust—where the lot of them
belonged, the good Reverend would say.

Gravity, whose roots were planted in the grave.

Cosmic etiquette be damned! The drawing enraged him now; he
could hardly stand the sight of it. His day's work. The façade of the

House of *Beth*, as plain and smug as Hedge's white-shingled church, promising mystery but filled with nothing but air. The letter had drawn him in, but only to deceive. And his own curiosity was to blame—his infernal need to dig deeper, see under, know more. He took the pen in one fist, and plunged it into the pool of ink with such force that drops spattered onto the table. His intention was to obliterate the letter with slashes, but first he wanted the satisfaction of stabbing it through the heart. He poised the pen over the black dot.

It was too quick for him, sinking with a sucking sound, so that even as he gave chase he was deluged by a sea of white that poured in on him from the letter's open side. He wanted to cry out that this was all wrong. He had intended to stride through on his own two feet like the Hebrews crossing the Red Sea, shoulders squared and eyes fixed on the Promised Land. Instead he was plunging headfirst, limbs flailing, pen and papers flying, adrift in the deep with the Egyptians, their horses and chariots.

CHAPTER 9

MEANS AND ENDS

"MAY I CONFIDE IN YOU, SOPHY? I BELIEVE IT'S PROVI-dential that poor Mr. Birdsall has been laid up in the bedroom for so long."

The request is moot, for Caroline has been confiding for much of the past hour while reclining on Sophy's bed in a pose that invites intimacy: legs stretched out, petticoats spread around her, stays loosened after Sunday dinner. She hasn't bothered to remove her kid slippers, and is gazing at them now, turning her feet this way and that.

"Providential?" Sophy has discovered that she only needs to parrot one or two words of Caroline's latest revelation to give the appearance of attention. She is sitting in a straight-backed chair, as she has sat for days by their guest's bedside, and imagining how she'll describe the scene to him. *She might have been confiding in her feet, Mr. Birdsall, for she looked at them more than she looked at me. They're small and neat, and she's quite proud of them—with reason, I'm sure. But don't you think it's funny to tell secrets to your feet?* Mr. Birdsall won't answer. He is mostly asleep, but Sophy feels that it's good for him to hear her voice. More than once he's seemed on the verge of floating away and she has pulled him back to earth with her chatter.

"I don't mean that Mr. Birdsall should be sick for my sake," Caroline goes on. "Heaven forbid! But his misfortune has got me to thinking that James and I should wait to marry until our house is finished. Your parents are the souls of generosity to invite me to stay, Sophy, and I would, gladly, if the first months of marriage weren't so precious. Better to start fresh in our own dear little home."

"Have you discussed this with James? It could be months," Sophy says.

Caroline added yet another improvement this afternoon. She must have a piazza. A grand Italian porch to match the Greek columns at the front entrance. None of them has ever heard of such a thing, but she deems it essential, for where else will their future children play?

"Oh, Sophy, he took it very hard. He called me selfish! He said I loved comfort more than I loved him. Can you imagine your brother being so harsh? He drove me to tears, and when I cried, he was shattered and begged me to forgive him." Caroline's chin begins to tremble. She sits up straighter and clutches her knees. "*You're* the one who is being selfish, I said. You'd deny my poor parents a few more months of my company when they're soon to lose me for good. You'd burden your family with another guest when they're worn out with caring for Mr. Birdsall. And what if the poor man doesn't recover, I said. Shall we spend our wedding night in a bed recently occupied by a—well, you know. What kind of omen is that, James Hedge?"

"He will recover," Sophy says. "He is better every day."

Was it her face, or the steel in her words, that betrayed more than she intended? Caroline had been galloping along like a Valkyrie, fire in her eye and blood in her cheek, and she has stopped short; Sophy can hear the snorting of the horse, see its hooves pawing the air.

"Did you and James make peace? I hope so," she says quickly.

"In the most magnificent way. He knelt before me and promised that if I would honor him with my hand, he would work even harder to raise a house fit to receive me. He spoke plainly but from his heart, and it was poetry to my ear. What were a few months, he said, when measured against the years of happiness we would share? I raised him up, Sophy, and we embraced. We are closer than ever!" Caroline sighs, lost in bliss recollected. "And really," she says in a different voice, "it's much nicer to be married in the spring. November is such a drab month."

Caroline reaches for her sewing; she finished her wedding dress long ago, but to fill the time, she is scattering rosebuds across the bodice. Sophy makes a token stitch or two in the pattern of a full-blown rose that Caroline brought her, and wonders whether she will still be required as a confidante, now that her companion is playing Queen of the May. Some of the afternoon might still be salvaged for painting. She takes the pattern out of its ring and puts it in the sewing box.

Caroline raises one eyebrow. "I hope Mr. Birdsall's illness hasn't altered his good looks. He's quite handsome, don't you think?" She makes a knot at the base of a flower and delicately bites off the thread. "I speak as one with no personal interest. I prefer strength to appearance in a man. It wears better."

"He is very thin," Sophy says, "but still handsome." The wrong word, she thinks. Many are handsome, few are beautiful. "He looks even purer now. Mama says that when the flesh fades, the spirit shines through."

"Oh, is that what it is? He seemed a cold sort of man to me. Taken with himself—the opposite of my honest James. You don't find him standoffish?"

"I don't find him any way at all. I hardly know him." Sophy speaks sharply to counter the blush that might be rising.

"I saw him looking at you that day at dinner," Caroline says. "Are you really such a goose that you didn't notice?"

Goose she might be, but if Mr. Birdsall had looked at her that way, Sophy would have noticed. Once or twice—not counting Mr. Unsworth—young men have paid her some attention. Ezra Keene, the shoemaker's son, hung about her last summer, cornering her in the churchyard after meeting and seeking her thoughts on universal salvation, but he was so awkward and pimpled and doggedly earnest that she was tart with him, assuring him she had none. Poor Ezra had mistaken her church face for piety. The truth was, her look of rapt attention had nothing to do with the sermon. No sooner did the Reverend clutch the pulpit and cast a glacial eye on his flock than his pagan daughter flew away to tropical climes.

"I'm sure you're mistaken," she says. "Mr. Birdsall has his mind on higher things. Philosophy. He is far beyond the likes of me."

"Sophy dear, you're an innocent. Men may be philosophical, but they don't want philosophy in a woman, any more than they want a hump on her back or a wart on her nose. They want to be flattered. Looked after. Nursing Mr. Birdsall has given you a great advantage, you know. He'll remember how tenderly you cared for him." A sly smile. "And there is the other thing they want. I suppose Mother Hedge has had a talk with you?"

"She says I have enough ideas in my head. When there's something to tether them to, we'll talk." Mama is frank about animals and female complaints, and will tell Sophy what she needs to know when she needs to know it. Monthly bleeding was briskly dispensed with, but they've made scant progress since.

Caroline nods, commiserating. "Mothers are not always the best to ask. I learned much more from my Cousin Isabel, who married last year." She inches closer, almost to the edge of the bed, and leans toward Sophy. "Izzie told me that the pain is dreadful at first, but we ought not to fear it for it is the *Portal to Bliss*."

Absorbing the awe that Caroline breathes into the phrase, its fantail of seductive sibilants, Sophy pictures a natural wonder on the order of the falls of Niagara. A door in a mountain, perhaps, opening to a cave of sparkling crystal.

"But it's no use dwelling on that now," Caroline says. "If anything is to happen, we have work to do. Stand up, and let's have a look at you."

With a grunt, Caroline swings her legs down from the bed. She stands a few feet from Sophy, folding her arms over her voluminous skirts. Her eyes are a guileless blue and round as a child's, but they penetrate. Sophy is transfixed, rooted to the spot. She has endured plenty of criticism about her character, but no one has ever appraised her outer layer so coolly.

"Your hair is good, nice and thick, but the style is too strict and old-fashioned . . . We must shorten that forehead—such an expanse, it makes you look simple . . . Your eyes are your best feature, though a little far apart . . . I envy you those lashes, we blondes make do with peach fuzz." Sophy's nose and mouth and chin and neck are passed over, apparently unworthy of comment. "Your bosom is not much, but that can be remedied, and you're not straight up and down, I spy a waist!" This last sung out in triumph, with a wag of Caroline's finger, as if Sophy had been concealing the indentation all along.

Caroline steps back for an overall view. "We can make something of you, Sophy, and we will! When Mr. Birdsall opens his eyes, he'll look upon a vision and think he's gone to Heaven after all."

CHAPTER 10

RETURN TO EARTH

GIDEON WAS BACK IN HIS CHILDHOOD BED. THE COMFORTING weight of the quilts over him, the feather pillow under his head. Soon his mother would come in with a tray of something nice to tempt him, melted cheese or a sunburst egg on a slice of toast. She would put her cool hand on his forehead and tell him he must stay home another day.

"Mr. Birdsall, are you awake?"

Sophy sat in a rocking chair near the bed, poking a needle into a piece of embroidery. Sophy, or someone who resembled her—she looked older, but perhaps it was her hair, which had been pulled straight back from her brow and twisted into a topknot. The short strands had been pinched into commas that circled her face, and worst of all, her ears stuck out, a plaited loop of hair draped around each like a garland around a horse's neck. Where were the wings he loved? He wondered if he had traveled from the past to the future, losing the years between. In some netherworld he had finished his studies, courted Sophy and married her, entered into a settled life.

"Where are we?" He tried to sit up, but his neck and shoulders were painfully stiff; he must have been lying in one position for a long time.

"Sam's old room. Lately, Mr. Unsworth's." Sophy rose, letting her sewing fall to the floor. She ran over to plump his pillow, slipping another behind him to support his head. "You have been here for nearly two weeks. We've been terribly worried. Mama believes it's all Papa's fault for working you too hard. She made him feel so guilty that he went and fetched Dr. Craddock. She wouldn't leave you alone with the poor man, though; she watched him like a hawk. In her view physicians are medicine men in frock coats, on no account to be trusted."

"And what did the shaman conclude?" Gideon was still very weak, though he felt well enough. His head no longer hurt, and he had the odd sensation of resting comfortably in his skin, as if he had been exiled from his body and come home.

"He thought it began as influenza and migrated to the brain. You kept crying out. You were very eloquent, Mr. Birdsall! I'm sure I could never think of such wonderful things, even in the best of health. I wanted to write them down, but Papa said it would be disrespectful—that we should let your soul unburden itself in privacy, for you might be conversing with the Lord."

"Maybe one day you will tell me what I said." Gideon's eyes filled with tears. He knew it was unmanly—what indignities must she have seen while tending to him?—but he couldn't help himself. It had been so long since he had been cared for. He had forgotten how it felt. "I owe you all so much. How can I ever repay you for your kindness?"

Sophy put her hand over his. "We were glad to do it. Mama and Papa would tell you so, if they were here." She paused, hesitant. "We would have brought your own parents to comfort you, but you never spoke of them, and the seminary has no record."

"There was only my mother, and she is dead," he said.

"We are both orphans then. I felt that it must be so." She nodded, patting his hand. "It's a strange thing to belong only to oneself, isn't it?"

Until this moment, he hadn't been sure she had been told the circumstances of her birth. "I suppose," he said. "I've never known any other way."

He had only meant to state a fact, but Sophy was all sympathy. "You are a member of this family now—if you want to be. We're awfully odd. I think poor Caroline is intimidated by us. It's too late to break the engagement, and she does love James, so she has decided that her only recourse is to improve us. Improve *me*, that is. Mama and Papa are fixed in their ways, Reuben is too wild, and Micah—well, he is as God made him."

"I see she has started with your hair," Gideon said, more drily than he intended.

"It was very generous of her. She spent hours, and used quantities of her own floral pomade." Sophy touched the topknot gingerly with a forefinger. "It's quite remarkably stiff. Indifferent to weather. A great storm could blow me from one end of the county to the other, and not one hair would stir. If only it didn't itch so."

Her expression was so serious, her tone so full of solemn wonder, that Gideon could not help grinning. Sophy pressed a hand to her mouth, and began to laugh through her fingers. He laughed too, until a fit of coughing overtook him.

When he could speak again, he said, "Let it down."

"What?"

"Your hair. Free it from its bonds. Liberate it."

"I would do anything you asked, Mr. Birdsall, but don't ask me to do that. I'm trying to preserve it until next Sunday, so Caroline won't think her labor was in vain." Sophy knelt and scooped her sewing from the floor. "She gave me this rose pattern so I could practice my needlework. Do you see how far I've gotten? Two miserable petals! It's not in my nature to do stitch after stitch—it makes me feel like a chicken pecking for corn. And tell me, please, what is the use of *sewing* a rose? I would much rather plant one, or paint one." She stopped suddenly, abashed. "You understand why I have to keep the hair. I mustn't seem ungrateful."

"I command you." His voice was firm and even. He had no idea where the sternness was coming from. He wasn't in the habit of giving orders.

Sophy stepped back from the bed, and reached up with both hands.

Gideon could not see what hidden pin or clasp she removed, but its powers of restraint must have been heroic. Her hair sprang out about her head, wavy from long confinement. She ran her fingers through the mass and it fell in a torrent from her shoulders nearly to her waist.

Gideon thought first how lovely it was, and then that there was too much for such a small person. When he called up a mental picture of her, her hair was always swept back in its simple, artless style, inseparable from who she was; even in his dreams, he had not imagined it loose. Certainly he could never have anticipated such a luxuriant crop. There was something feral about the face that peered out at him from the thicket: eyes wide and startled, mouth slightly open. He watched her cheeks fill with color as he stared at her, unable to shift his gaze.

He had done this. He'd *had his way with her*—the leering phrase, wiped clean of smut and swagger and restored to brisk utility. The thrill of the transaction was still with him. And yet, even as Gideon admired what he had wrought, he saw that something had been lost. She was not quite the Sophy he knew, that being who was her own definition. As she relaxed, he could detect signs of the self-delight he had seen in other girls her age, the coquetry that had always provoked scorn in him. It struck him with a pang that even the Unsworths of the world might look upon her now and find her pretty. Her motion of a moment ago came back to him, magnified as if under a glass. The small breasts lifting when she raised her arms, the prim V at her waistline riding up.

Neither of them spoke. He couldn't read her expression. Her eyes were tender, but something hard shone in their depths: a victory she hoarded for herself. At last she said, very quietly, "That is much better. Thank you."

"What have I done to deserve thanks?"

"You made me do what I wanted to do. I wouldn't have had the courage on my own."

Voices could be heard outside, Mrs. Hedge talking to a neighbor. "The young man is holding steady," she was saying. "The worst is past, Lord be praised."

A dubious gift, Gideon thought: to teach selfishness and the primacy of the will. He had chosen a fine way to thank Reverend Hedge and his wife for their attentions. The intoxicating power that had flared in him was souring to shame. He fell back against the pillow and turned away.

Immediately, Sophy was at his side. "What am I thinking, chattering away, tiring you so? Please forgive me, Mr. Birdsall. And I forgot your drink! Mama made it specially and I was to give it to you the moment you woke up. You will find it very refreshing—not medicinal at all."

She removed the cloth that covered a pitcher on the night table and poured a clear liquid into a tumbler. Bending, she held the glass to his lips, her hair falling forward as she stooped, the ends brushing his face. He shut his eyes and breathed in lilac, cool and sweet, and faint beneath the pomade, the warmer animal smell.

CHAPTER II

DECIDING ON A POSE

ROFILE. FULL-FACE. THREE-QUARTER VIEW. SOPHY IS ALWAYS turning Gideon's head this way and that, as if it were a clay bust: observing it godlike from above, gazing upward into the sun of his countenance like a kneeling disciple, tilting it back so she can gauge the precise blue of his eyes and acquaint her fingers with the angle in his cheek. Since his return to seminary more than a month ago, she sees him everywhere—even in her landscapes, where his face has a way of rising to the surface of the canvas and obscuring the scene that is already there. When he appears in the flesh for his Sunday visits, she blushes to think of the liberties she's taken. "Paint him," Caroline urges. "A few sittings and you'll have him for life." Even if she were so shameless, how could she trap the whole of Gideon in a single portrait? She might manage a passable likeness of the serious young man she's getting to know, but could she capture the vision she saw in the meadow?

Caroline was right about one thing: his illness has brought them closer. He seeks her company now. Walking home after church, he falls in step beside her and makes conversation. It is all very proper, with Mama and Papa looking on, but lately he has asked her to walk with him in the garden after dinner. He speaks freely to her then, about his studies and his life at seminary and the work he hopes to do. Sophy says little, for fear of betraying her ignorance, but she listens with her whole being and takes in every word. Last week, in the exuberance of a rare sunny day, he grabbed her hand and swung her arm, and she thought, This is what lovers do, we must be in love, and that night in her room, she said the words aloud to her mirror, by way of experiment: "I love him," and then, "I love you." Her face in the glass looked the same, but speaking the phrase gave it substance, just as talking to God makes Him seem as real and solid as Papa.

Love is a puzzle she will have to solve on her own. Papa must have courted Mama, but Sophy has never seen them caress and can't imagine how they ever made children. If she had to wake Mama at night, she found them always in the same position: lying on their backs like loaves set out to cool, ready for the Reaper. Observing lovers doesn't teach her much. James and Caroline, what do they feel, and do they mean the same thing when they say the word? Or the girls at church, flirting and mincing as they chat with favored boys after the service? Parasols, bonnets, fans—the drama is customarily enacted behind one screen or another, but as in a shadow play, meaning is conveyed.

Sophy isn't brash enough to say, *He loves me*, even to the mirror. Gideon's feet might touch the earth as hers do, but his thoughts soar where hers can't follow, and in those spheres he finds his true home. Majesty, Sophy has discovered, is a cold quality, whether possessed by kings or angels. More than once she's stood inside the doorway of the study, covered dish in hand, waiting in vain for him to look up from his desk. One stormy Sunday she lingered for almost half an hour as the apple dumpling she'd brought him turned cold and soggy, and when she summoned the courage to call his name, the expression on his face— absent, uncomprehending—chilled her to the bone. Now she sets the plate on the nearest surface and tiptoes out.

She knows this much: Loving a man like Gideon will require a special skill. The two sides of him must always be kept in balance, each given an equal weight. Caring for his humblest needs did not diminish the angel in him. She was happy to wipe the dribbles from his chin and carry out his slops, honored to hold the basin as Mama bathed him. His helplessness stirred her—that he should be burdened with a body as vulnerable as other men's, and still cry out messages from another world.

"DO YOU REMEMBER what I said?" He asked her this as soon as he was well enough to speak, and he goes on asking, as if repetition will spur her memory. Sophy always makes a fresh effort. She'd felt that same urgency asking about her mother: the desired object on some distant shore and the questioner in a boat, being borne away by time.

"It's like calling back a dream," she told him one damp September afternoon. "I can feel its atmosphere in my brain, but I can't bring it down to words."

Gideon had only recently been allowed to leave his bed, and was propped in the visitor's chair, swathed in blankets he'd thrown off in his impatience to be well. He was thin to begin with, but the fever had burned flesh off him, and his face against the coverlets reminded her of a desert prophet's, all sharp bones and glittering eyes. Only his hair was untouched: thick because it needed cutting and more abundant than before, as if it had profited from his misfortune.

"Even fragments are valuable," he said. "Dreams can be reconstructed from their traces. Maybe if you would sit and close your eyes . . . ?"

Sophy obliged him, perching gingerly on the edge of the mattress in case Mama came in. She knew from long experience that she had no gift for silent contemplation. As soon as her lids dropped, the world she was trying to shut out elbowed her in the dark. A fly buzzed, sounding like twenty flies, all whirring round her head. Random cries, animal and human, taunted her from outside, and in the sickroom the very air joined the conspiracy, bathing her in an odorous broth of camphor, vinegar, and sweated sheets, the only window having been sealed against drafts. After a few minutes her back began to ache from her unnatural posture—a clerical daughter's compromise, halfway between the propriety of standing and the license of sitting, and the worst half of each. She wished she'd worn her Sunday corset for a bolster. She could feel Gideon's eyes on her. He had framed his request softly, but she'd heard the command in it.

"You were agitated at first," she said, stalling. She had given him all this before. "Thrashing and waving your arms about. The doctor said we must tie you down, but we hated to do it. You cried out in some strange tongue. Papa said your spirit was in travail—that good and evil were contending for you. He made us all kneel round the bed while he chanted a Psalm in Hebrew, loud enough to drown out the Evil One. You'd been panting, but then your breath faltered and sank deep in your chest. I started to cry. I thought you were dying."

The stark words brought Sophy back to that moment, when her sorrow had welled up and spilled over. Her eyes watered, and she squeezed them tighter to hold back the flood. Gideon said nothing, but she could feel the force of his attention. There was something pitiless about it— like a surgeon probing for a bullet, so intent on the object that he pays no heed to the patient's pain. She wanted him to be consoling, to take her hand as the Lord had taken Doubting Thomas's and put it to his beating heart, but he only waited.

"'*The green. It's too sharp, it hurts me!*' You said that!" The fragment came to her when she stopped searching for it. She remembered how his head had tossed from side to side and come suddenly to rest, struck still. "Then you begged for the scales to be removed, that you might look on it with eyes . . . unclothed."

The word he had used was sanctified in the Bible, but ugly in the mouth. Even at this moment of triumph, she hesitated to say it plain. The gaping *na* rubbing right up against the shaming harshness of the *k*—she never could speak it without seeing her child self crouching in the tub, goose bumps all over till Mama poured the water in. And the *ed* stitching her up in her skin, showing her that this was the sum of Sophy, this plucked, shivering thing. No wonder God had made garments for Adam and Eve!

But "unclothed" sounded pompous, and it wasn't what Gideon had said. He had cried out again and again, pleading with a desperate logic, as if he would wear the listeners' hard hearts down.

Sophy waited, hardly daring to breathe, but no more came. She opened her eyes and wiped away the tears. "The rest was like a poem. It washed over me. I can't repeat it word for word."

Gideon was staring at her with a hunger so avid that she was frightened. She felt herself grow small in his sight, all her flaws magnified by the force of his attention. She spoke quickly to hide her unease.

"Green, who would have imagined it? When I think of Heaven, it is always white."

There was a pause. She watched the ardor fade from his eyes.

"*Heaven.*" He displayed the word for mockery. He shrugged his shoulders and laughed: a cool, dry sound, an antidote to fever. "My dear Sophy, I have no idea what color Heaven is, and I don't much care. It's the Garden I was talking of. *Paradeisos!* The common mind confuses the two, but you, with your clear sight—I thought you would understand."

Blood rushed to her cheeks. "I'm sorry to disappoint you," she said. "You estimate me too high, Mr. Birdsall. I may be more common than you think." They had been "Gideon" and "Sophy" to each other since the day he woke, though always correct in public. But now she regressed to formality, coasting right over his endearment. "We simple folk, we leave naming to the scholars. We don't fuss about what the good place is called, so long as we end up there."

"That's it, exactly!" Gideon started toward her, gripping the arms of his chair. "You and I have been lectured since infancy about this glorious destination we're to strive for—always in the future, never in reach. If we're sufficiently righteous, we'll be admitted, but since our character is flawed, we must depend on grace. And if the Emperor should take a dislike to one of us and put his thumb down, we can still be turned away." He seemed to quiver with some pent-up joke, a vein pulsing in his forehead and his mouth twisted in a grin. "Sophy, it's all nonsense! The groveling, the infernal rules, the gatekeeper with his giant key. There are other paths to that good place. I have seen the green for myself, and I can testify—you won't find its like in a forest or park, or a flower bed, or anywhere else in this pale imposter we dignify with the name of Nature. You will never find it on your palette. To call it a color is too weak. Too static. It is growth itself, made visible!" He reached out to her, his thin fingers cupped as if he would grip her from afar. "Come with me. We'll walk there together."

Sophy knew that she ought to quiet him with soothing words, coax him gently back to bed and run to the pantry for one of Mama's anodynes. Fever had roiled his mind, and only sleep would smooth it out again. But she didn't dare stir from her chosen seat, though the crick in her neck had progressed to a zigzag streak between her shoulder blades. She had never imagined such a Paradise as Gideon spoke of—had never thought of Paradise as a place at all, except in a storybook way: more real than Camelot, not quite as substantial as Bethlehem.

Gardens were more familiar. Each spring, since she was old enough to pat seeds into earth, Sophy had been given a square of soil to transform according to her own notions of beauty. Having created so many Edens single-handed, she was strongly tempted to compare her handiwork to the original. She wasn't sure she believed in this good place of Gideon's, but she believed in him who told her of it. The green he described brought it nearer than the Bible ever had. It was as if he offered her a souvenir of his travels: a tuft of grass that would never wither, or a few leaves plucked from the Tree of Life.

Gideon fell back against the cushions. His hands rested on his knees, palms up, fingers extended; he meant to show her that his invitation still stood, though he could not. His languor was at odds with the fervor in his eyes. For all his weakness, a royal will emanated from him: she *must* see what he saw. Sophy had never felt such sureness, even about things readily observed and touched. His faith was different than Papa's, which was heavy and unyielding, a massive stone such as might have plugged the door of the empty tomb. Gideon's truth was all motion. He was asking her to accompany him on a journey, and she had never taken one in her life. She wanted to go, but she was afraid. Already her restless mother was mocking her timidity, making prickles up and down her spine, goading her. If Sophy were to get up now, she would walk to Gideon with arms outstretched. Put her wrists in his bony shackles and let him lead her—where?

All around her stood the house the Hedges had built, its thick walls mortared with good sense and good works, remedies tried and true, devotion and self-denial. The only home she had ever known. She wasn't brave enough to leave it yet. She kept her seat and took what it offered: a set of stays to keep her back straight until she trusted herself to move.

CHAPTER 12

DESTINATIONS

SOPHY IS BEGINNING TO THINK THE CHOICE WAS MADE FOR her—that there never was a choice at all. She doesn't necessarily believe that the Emperor in the Sky has been twiddling his thumbs. Still, it is a remarkable fact that she and Gideon are together more often now, with little meddling from the outside world. This is all so new that she can't help but wonder whether, at the beginning of time, some farseeing deity, matching names on a celestial chart, decreed that this Gideon and this Sophy would be a pair. Whether—to use a phrase of Caroline's—the two of them were meant to be.

In her more realistic moments, she has to acknowledge that predestination may have nothing to do with it. They are being ignored because they're insignificant: a couple of extra parts with no real function in the household. In good times they're made use of, but in crisis they are only in the way. Sophy isn't sure what, exactly, has happened to her family. All she knows is that preoccupation hangs over the Hedge household like smoke. Papa—the fixed point of everyone's world, whose routines regulate their movements as precisely as the works of their new clock—is in Boston for days at a time. Twice he has left early on a Monday morning, sitting straight-backed in the wagon with reins loose in his hand, his old beaver hat set squarely on his head and the scarf Mama knitted for him coiled to his ears. The weather on Mondays seems always to be gray and chill, a brooding cold too miserly to bloom into snow. They assemble outside to watch him go, and as the horse begins its reluctant swaying amble down the road, desolation overtakes them all, as if he were being carried from home for the last time.

Everyone seems lost without his guiding spirit. James is sullen, prone to fits of melancholy. Caretaking the farm steals all his time; he has none left over for the house he is building. He had expected to be married by now, but Caroline's visits grow more widely spaced, and when she bothers to come at all, he clings to her and doesn't hide his misery. Sophy has heard them arguing—Caroline alternately childlike and imperious, James pleading—and the note of supplication in her stalwart brother's voice wrenches her heart.

Reuben does his share: no more, no less, with a drop of bitters added. He seems to look upon their troubles through a spyglass, and to find them a sorry spectacle. With Papa gone, he leaves right after dinner and stays out half the night, never arriving home till the early hours. Lately he has begun to invent outings that take him away during the day. Agricultural fairs, he informs them: if the farm is to thrive, it's important to learn about the latest methods, see the new implements. But everyone knows that the real purpose of the fairs is to race horses. People travel miles to wager on these trials of speed, and a few foolish locals have fallen victim to swindlers and lost all their money. Papa has devoted an entire sermon to the subject, quoting Zechariah on the "plague of the horse." He fears that this new vice, until recently the property of the gentry, might outpace drunkenness in the competition for the laboring man's soul.

In the clutch of these changes, Mama says nothing. Not when Papa sends a letter saying he can't be back for Sunday services—an event as rare and portentous as a celestial eclipse—and instructing her to ask the deacon to take his place in the pulpit. Not when Reuben swaggers to the breakfast table smelling of what he drank the night before, or James shoves his plate aside and rests his head in his hands, as if his thoughts are too heavy to bear. She goes about her tasks in a mute fury, her lips set tightly; Sophy imagines a merciless overseer cracking a whip inside her, but Mama, being Mama, won't give him the satisfaction of crying out. Her silence is the most frightening omen of all. For years now, Sophy has considered Mama's talk a tedium to be borne, an endless commentary on the topmost crust of life, with never a thought going deeper or a fancy rising above. Sophy has made it a habit to store this daily chatter on the same shelf as Papa's sermons, escaping into her own thoughts as she pretends to listen. These days, she wishes she could reach up to that shelf and retrieve a handful of trite sayings, blow the dust off and look at them in the light. *Beans doing poorly, turnips coming up nice this year, that chair needs mending, dog going lame.* All adding up to blessed assurance. This too will pass. Life goes on.

ONLY MICAH IS THE SAME. It isn't just that he's one of them—living on the periphery as she and Gideon do—but that, in some mysterious way, he is theirs. The three of them have become a little family, and Micah, being the youngest, has taken on the role of child. A very agreeable child, hardworking and self-sufficient, quiet to a fault, asking only to be near them. Sophy believes she has always regarded him in a maternal way. Though less than four years separate them, he is the only Hedge born after her, the only one of her brothers that she has seen at the breast and in the cradle. She remembers leading him by the hand when he learned to walk, and deciphering his infant syllables in the early days when his speech came freely. It's a gift that has persisted. She isn't sure where her understanding comes from, or whether the possession of it makes her a translator or a prophet, but even Mama will grant that Sophy knows what Micah means to say before he can get the words out.

At around four on this Sunday in January, Micah knocks on the door of the study. He has been chopping wood since dinner. His hat and shoulders are sugared with white, the sky having finally consented to give up its riches. Cradled in his gloved hands are three apples from the cellar, as ruddy as his cheeks and polished on his sleeve to a high shine. He likes to bring them little presents. She takes his coat and claps the snow off, whispers that she's making tea.

They are careful to be quiet while Gideon is working. The Lexicon is his charge now, since Papa has no time for it, and Gideon is digging deeper than Papa ever dared, using his freedom to pursue his own inquiries. Although he's just a few yards from them, bent over his desk in a corner of the room, he might as well be miles away. Sophy believes he actually is—embarked on a journey they can only guess at, mapping routes for them to follow. She pictures him on the road like Papa, only his destination isn't banks and business in Boston—a city she would paint in shades of gray, though she has never been there—but a place so drenched in color as to dazzle mortal eyes. Colors not to be possessed, but longed for, as Joseph's brothers coveted his dazzling coat: a potent glimpse that lodges in the mind, itching and smarting, until it turns to lust.

One thing Gideon has in common with Papa. He will come home, eventually. The hour of pleasurable anticipation is Sophy's favorite part of the day, and on an afternoon like this, the sky darkening early, the window dashed with snow, she savors it all the more. The cold outside makes their one-room house feel warmer. She puts another log in the woodstove and sets the kettle on top, pondering (as she has seen Mama do a thousand times) what they have to eat. She is scrupulous about what she will take from the pantry. Mostly she steals from her own plate, slipping bread and cheese and a bit of meat into a napkin when no one is looking, contriving to keep it from the dog. Today she's done well by her brood, with oatcakes and cold bacon from breakfast, and Micah's apples for dessert. A modest feast, though they won't be subsisting on it: Mama expects them at the big table for leftovers from Sunday dinner, and they eat to please her, whether they are hungry or not. Still, Sophy cherishes the illusion of self-sufficiency. They could survive here, if necessary. They have warmth and food and each other. All they need.

She circles the room lighting candles, taking pleasure in the corners that leap into vivid life, as if she had applied paint to a pencil sketch. She wishes, not for the first time, that she could bring her easel here and play with her pale excuses for colors while Gideon works. The only lamp, a small one, is on his desk, though he is too absorbed to make use of it. He must be seeing with his inner eye, Sophy thinks. How else can he go on reading fine print in the well of shadow that his desk has become? She bustles about discreetly while making tea, hoping that the clatter of plates on the engraving table and the aroma of cakes warming on the stove will lure him back to earthly comforts.

Micah needs no such tempting. He's sitting cross-legged on the small rug in front of the stove, knife in hand, chipping a piece of wood into another animal. His creatures line the window: a rabbit, a fox, a vole, a squirrel. Common beasts quirked up, a single trait exaggerated so they seem to laugh at themselves as they strike a pose, like characters in their own Aesop's. Sophy prefers them to the august inhabitants of Papa's Bestiary; they have more life and teach no lessons. Every few seconds Micah gazes at the stove, then at the back of Gideon's bright head, which hasn't strayed from regions celestial for the last half-hour. Ravenous as the boy must be after his chores, he would never eat a bite before they do. He is always hungry, but it's a patient hunger.

Sophy mouths, "Soon." She leans over his shoulder to see what he's making—a quizzical sparrow. Once again, she marvels at the sureness of his hand as he cuts; it seems the bird has always lived in this block of wood, and Micah is doing what he must to release it. When they look up, their small world has turned on its axis. Gideon is yawning, rubbing his eyes and asking what's for tea.

"ALL THIS TALK OF WORDS has put our young friend to sleep," Gideon says.

They've moved nearer the stove, pleasantly full after disposing of the oatcakes, lacking only rockers under their straight-backed chairs. Gideon pours the last of the tea and jiggles his cup to settle the leaves. "Do you think he minds? I wonder sometimes if I'm being cruel to jabber on about language when he struggles with a simple sentence. He must see it as a kind of flaunting—like doing an Irish jig in front of a cripple."

The object of their discussion is snoring gently on the hooked rug, in a state of bliss beyond all moral quandaries. His head is pillowed on his hands and his knees are drawn up close to his body, an infant's pose that stirs a wave of tenderness in Sophy. She knows about original sin, but it seems to her that he was born innocent and is likely to remain so. Much as she hates it when Papa extracts a lesson from Micah's affliction, she believes that stuttering has kept him pure, free of the sins of speech that bedevil the rest of them. Slander, lying, mockery, boasting find no home in him: it's as though the hurtful impulses die without words to stoke them. If trapped thoughts churn and boil in him, he hides it well. Nothing disturbs his composure except a direct question.

"I doubt that Micah cares," she tells Gideon. "He admires you so much. Can't you see it? You could read from the Lexicon and he would cherish every word. All he wants is to be in the same room with you."

"With us. He's no less fond of you." Gideon turns Micah's bird in his hands, testing the sharp beak against his forefinger. "I have great respect for Micah—not only for his many gifts, but for the light way he carries them. He's such a modest soul, I'm sure he never considers the service he does us. His natural tact makes him the perfect duenna."

"What are you calling my little brother? One of your Latin names?"

"Just a fancy word for 'chaperone.' Not even accurate in Micah's case. He's no dragon of a Spanish lady. He lends his presence in the humblest way, and vanishes at the right moments. Without him, we wouldn't be free to enjoy each other's company. We would lose all this." He waves his hand as if a vast estate surrounded them, instead of a single cluttered room. "He has been our faithful companion, and we must be his wherever life takes us, always."

Always. Gideon pronounces the word with such solemn finality that Sophy hears *all ways*: not a single straight path to eternity, but roads running riot in every direction, spreading over the earth's face like cracks in ice.

She looks down at her lap before meeting his eyes. Is he offering her the future as if it were a settled fact between them? Her mind can't stretch to cover such a distance—not from here. The study is too warm and snug, its plain comforts too near at hand. She feels a sudden longing to be out in the sharp, clean air, gazing up at the sky as white manna rains on her.

Her mother again, tempting her to dance—a command performance that propels her out of her chair and over to the window.

Gideon follows her. "Sophy, have I assumed too much?" He lowers his voice to a whisper. "Is it Micah? I regard him as you do—a brother in spirit, the first fruit of our new family. I thought you would want him with us. If I'm wrong—"

"You are not wrong."

Sophy continues to look out. The darkness is complete by now. No snow is visible, but she senses it drifting down, mounding in heaps on the ground, abundant as the blessings Papa says flow ever from above. In the glass the points of the candle flames shiver in front of their faces: tremulous little tokens of the make-believe home they've made, the family they pretend to be. The room they stand in is no more substantial than the Garden he assures her is ahead: their true home and ultimate destination, where he spends so many precious hours of their shared time. It seems to her that the only solid thing, in this world or the next, is the snow she can't see. All she wants, at this moment, is to be the first to print a pattern on it.

"What is it, then? Please tell me."

She directs her answer to the window. "How can we talk of family when we don't belong to each other? Not in any way that matters outside this room." Impossible for her to speak such brash truths and meet his eyes. It's easier to sketch swirling arabesques and figure eights on the flawless white, to skim the surface like a skater, never sinking in. "You make me feel I'm part of some grand plan, but I don't know what we're to be. I don't know what we *are*."

Gideon breathes in sharply, but seconds pass before any words come, and when they do, he surrenders them as haltingly as Micah. "I don't—we can't—understand everything now. It's too soon. We have no resources, and my . . . explorations have just begun. There is a bond between us—that much is certain—and we must trust that more will be revealed when we are ready. Meanwhile, we have our sanctuary."

"We have it once a week, and Papa will reclaim it soon. Where will we go then?"

"What is the matter with you today?" He spins on his heels, paces a few steps, turns to her again. "You seem to delight in making difficulties. Must you ruin the few hours we have? It isn't like you, Sophy! You're always so cheerful."

His voice breaks on "cheerful," which is oddly consoling. His reflection in the window is as wraithlike as hers, but the ghost-face reveals how young he appears when discomposed, how temper has quelled the angel in him and brought out the boy. She never thinks of his mother— it still seems an aberration that he had one—but it strikes her now that this is the face his mother must have seen.

"If you looked at me more often, you would know what I'm like," she says evenly. "All day you lose yourself in your work, and when you finally come back to Micah and me, you don't see us—only a couple of ideas you haven't written down yet. I wonder if you've ever really seen me at all."

He doesn't answer, and in the silence, they fix their attention on the glass. The words she spoke might be written there, the two of them rival scholars competing to decipher the text.

"Sophy." Gideon is looking at her now. He clasps her face in his hands and draws her toward him. She is surprised how strong his hands are, how persuasive; the rest of her hangs back like a bashful child. "No one has ever seen you as I do," he whispers. "No one ever will." As if to seal what he has spoken, he bends and kisses the top of her head.

Days later, when she has an hour to call her own, she will wonder whether the awkwardness of his gesture might have made her bold. His lips planted, like an uncle's, where her hair parts: an arid strip where nothing can grow. Whether she might have done as her mother prompted her and lifted her face to his, kissed him on the mouth. She will never know because the thunder at the door came first.

A blow that shakes the sturdy planks. She and Gideon stiffen and fall apart. Micah starts awake and scrambles to his feet, looking wildly around him.

"Snow sliding off the roof," Gideon says, but he doesn't believe it himself for he goes straight to the door.

Reuben stands back from the doorway, his boot poised for another kick. "I tried knocking. Have you all been struck deaf?" His face still registers a rising glee, which wanes as he delivers his news. The Reverend's horse made it all the way back from Boston, intrepid through the storm, then bolted not three miles from home. A wheel came loose and the wagon overturned. If Driscoll hadn't happened to be passing, in search of one of his dogs, Pa would have frozen to death where he lay. As luck would have it, he is alive, though badly hurt. James is off fetching the doctor, and Reuben must go after the horse. Did they think they could leave their studies long enough to give Ma some help?

He stomps in, tracking snow with each step, and seizes Micah by the arm, reclaiming the property they've purloined. Sophy warrants only a brusque swerve of his chin, his eyes shifting to the door. Gideon stands alone as the prodigal Hedges are herded into the storm.

"You come too, little preacher," Reuben says. The scorn he gives off is so pungent that it hangs in the room like a smell. "You can pray."

PART TWO

THE FATAL ROUND

CHAPTER 13

CONSEQUENCES OF THE FALL

THE REVEREND LAY ON HIS BED, LOOKING, FOR ALL THE care taken in arranging him, like an abandoned puppet. His eyes, wide open, fixed their gaze on the ceiling. The left side of his body was rigid, his fingers clutching the sheet as if he would make himself plumb by virtue of grim will, but the opposing limbs were in casual disarray, twisted at odd angles. By the time the three of them entered, Mrs. Hedge had already cut the boot off the swollen foot and was wielding her scissors to free him from his sodden clothes. Without looking up, she dispatched Micah to get brandy from the cupboard, Sophy to gather blankets and set bricks to warming.

Gideon, useless in a corner, tried to perform silently the only office he was trained for, but his appeals for mercy and healing were sabotaged by a fundamental amazement. How could Hedge have splintered so easily? The man was all elastic sinew, springing out of chairs like a jack-in-the-box, stretching his neck to interrogate a student, practicing a stride that a man twice his height would envy. He had disciplined his small body to cover the greatest amount of ground in the least possible time. Such resilience ought to prevail, even in extremity. Gideon could hardly bear to look at the broken figure on the bed, swathed in blankets and packed in flannel-wrapped bricks. Instead, he focused on the beaver hat, deemed by Driscoll an essential part of the Reverend and returned along with its owner. Someone had set it on a child's ladder-back chair that might have been made for it, from whence it emanated a battered dignity. Gideon half-expected to see a Scripture reference inscribed on one of the slats.

With effort, Mrs. Hedge managed to spoon some brandy down her husband's throat; it was necessary, she said, to stimulate his heart. There was such tenderness in the hand she cupped beneath his chin that Gideon felt a quickening in his own chest. Now he understood why Sophy had been angry at him. The devotion he saw in this room was real. Their sham housekeeping in the study was only an elaborate game of pretend: two innocents—each come into the world uninvited—playing at life. What right had he to draw this young girl into his theories, to addle her with words and lure her with promises? Sophy stood at Fanny's elbow, supporting the Reverend's head. Her face was as contained as a grieving Madonna's, her sorrow revealed only in the line between her eyebrows. Gideon wanted to kneel before her and ask forgiveness, but she never looked his way.

James arrived with Dr. Craddock; the snow had finally stopped, leaving a dry, powdery surface good for traveling. Craddock had just presided at the deathbed of a farmer's wife, a mother of many children who had sunk with the strain of birthing the last, but the weeping and wailing hadn't dulled his countenance. He was one of those men who always looked jovial, his cheeks round and gleaming, his red sideburns adding a clownish touch to the dourest proceedings. Though rumor had it that he was a secret drinker, the gossip failed to diminish his status in the community. He was the town's only physician, and revered as such. Fanny alone regarded him as a practitioner of the dark arts, an attitude he didn't appear to hold against her.

"A bad business," he said amiably after taking a quick look at Hedge. "But the Reverend has strength to spare. I never saw a man with more bounce in him. With a little luck we'll have him on his feet again." His benevolent glance swept over the room as if it were a scenic landscape, lighting at last on Gideon. "And look at this flourishing fella, much improved since I last saw him! Very good, sir! You can return the favor by helping with the setting."

Gideon wasn't sure, at first, what sort of assistance would be required of him. The word seemed benign, a coming-to-rest that his frayed nerves magicked into a soothing image of a hen roosting on eggs. Reason took hold soon enough, but before he could protest his lack of experience, he was waved out of the room, along with Sophy and Micah. Mrs. Hedge was about to remove the blankets, and only James, the parson's second-born son and likely surrogate, was permitted to look upon his father's nakedness.

In the kitchen, Sophy took out bread and cold meat to slice in case the doctor was hungry. Her movements were sure, but Gideon thought she was cutting far more than one hungry man could eat. Micah sat on a stool by the fireplace, his shoulders hunched and his big hands dangling between his knees. Gideon was lost in his own misery. Craddock's request had put a fear in him that was larger than his unfitness for the task. The life of the body struck him as a monstrous fraud. No one asked to be born; yet each packet of flesh pulled squalling into the world carried the seeds of its own doom. The nature of that doom—illness or accident, dissipation or decrepitude—was a matter of chance, the only certainty being its outworking in pain and loss.

And what did this make of marriage, the mystical union he'd anticipated for so long? Sophy had begun to weep, tears sliding slowly down her cheeks as her wrists and hands went on performing their rote task. He knew that he should go to her, gently lead her to a chair and speak comfort to her, but he could not. He wanted only to run away—not just from the Hedges, but from the whole fatal round of love and birth and death. He would retreat to some remote hamlet in the mountains, and find a monastic order where the rule of silence was practiced, and live out his days doing bracing physical tasks in the pure air. He saw himself leaning on a tall crook and contemplating the cloud-crowned peaks as sheep munched tender grasses all around him. The impression was so vivid that he could feel the release in his muscles as he sat with the other monks at the end of the day, dipping a hunk of coarse bread into thick soup.

Dr. Craddock intruded on his ruminations. The news was partially good. The Reverend's shoulder was dislocated, not broken as he had feared, and needed only to be worked back into place. But his right leg was fractured in two places; his ankle must have caught in the footrest as he struggled to keep control of the tipping wagon, and that limb had borne the brunt of its weight when it overturned. There was some splintering below the knee, and by rights he should cut, but he knew where the parson would consign him if he didn't do his best to keep him in one piece. Craddock gave a wistful glance at the food on the table, then clapped his hands briskly as though a better meal awaited him. "We are ready for you now," he said to Gideon. "Young man"— he raised his voice for Micah's benefit, apparently assuming that the boy's hearing was as limited as his speech—"I must ask you to be Abraham and sacrifice one of these fine chairs for splints. The legs should be about the right length. And you, miss—if you've an old sheet to spare, we'll be needing linen for bandages."

As he waited in the kitchen, Gideon had hoped—believed even— that Reuben would return and take his place. Surely the Reverend would rather have family with him at such a time. What about Micah, whose hands were steady—did Craddock assume he was incapable because he stuttered? Yet he said nothing as he followed the doctor to the bedroom. Inevitability had brought a kind of calm, a paralysis of feeling that approached numbness. He was aware that his fingers were cold, and wondered in a detached way whether his touch would disturb the patient.

The bedchamber, dim even in full day, had been illuminated by a candle in each corner, lending the small, Spartan room the hushed sanctity of a chapel. Mrs. Hedge stood ready beside the bed with a lamp in one hand, while James, stoical as ever, waited across from her. Both looked up when Gideon and the doctor entered, then returned their attention to the parson, who had been stripped of his clerical authority along with his clothes, and was now simply a damaged body, draped in blankets and awaiting the ministrations of a priest with greater powers. Hedge's eyes had closed; his face was set and pale. Gideon could not banish the sense that he was about to partake in some savage rite: the old leader offered up to the gods for the good of the tribe. The close atmosphere reminded him of the sickroom he'd vacated so recently. He thought he might faint.

Dr. Craddock reached into his bag and brought out a vial and a small bottle of rust-colored liquid.

"What is that you're giving him?" Mrs. Hedge asked, instantly vigilant.

"Only a little something to dull his senses." Craddock tapped a few drops into the vial and raised the Reverend's head. "Here, open up now, this will make you more comfortable," he crooned.

Hedge had come awake. His eyes burned into the doctor's. He turned his head aside with such vehemence that a drop of the offered medicine spilled on his jaw. "I will not be deprived of my chastisement!"

"There'll be enough of that left over, no need to worry." Craddock, speaking in the same light, lulling monotone, dabbed at Hedge's face with his little finger. "Never a shortage of that particular quantity. Not in my experience." When the rigid jaw relaxed, he seized Hedge's hair, forced his head back, and poured the contents of the vial down his throat. The parson, unmanned by the doctor's sleight-of-hand, swallowed. Although the maneuver had taken a mere fraction of a second, its effect was to render the whole company, even Mrs. Hedge, as docile as the patient, who was resting again on his pillow, grimacing at the bitter taste. Shaman indeed, Gideon thought. He had seen in the Reverend's eyes a foreign body that had never lodged there before: the unmistakable glint of fear.

The shoulder was to be dealt with first, because, Craddock said, it was quickly done. "Stability is all," he instructed them. Gideon understood that he and James were to be anchors. Craddock positioned James behind his father and showed him how to lay the flat of one hand on the forehead and grasp the good shoulder with the other. Gideon was to immobilize the legs, holding them firmly above the knee. He tried to fix his eyes on his own chapped knuckles, the familiar shape of his thumb, and avoid the sight of the white bone poking through Hedge's flesh a few inches below.

The doctor began to work the injured joint with a kneading motion, rolling his hands as if molding dough or clay. "Come now," he coaxed. "Come along, you rapscallion, that's the way, that's the way," singing to the bone under his breath, wooing it. Gideon was so mesmerized by the performance that he almost forgot his own unease. When the click came—hollow and dull, a chillingly mechanical sound—his grip loosened and his muscles jumped along with the patient's. Craddock did not seem to notice his weakness. He was already fashioning a sling from the strips of sheet that Sophy had brought in.

But the doctor had seen enough to ask his helpers to change places. James would assist with the crucial positioning of the leg, and Gideon had the lesser task of securing the upper body. He looked down upon the Reverend's face, which was covered with a film of sweat. Hedge breathed shallowly though lips that were dry and cracked. His eyes sought Gideon's with a roving intensity, as if something he'd lost might be found there.

"Talk to him," Craddock said. "Give him a Psalm or a bit of Scripture. It will distract him, and might do you some good, too."

From early childhood, Gideon had been called upon to recite—like a parrot, he'd complained to his mother—but at times his mind rebelled, presenting only a white sheet instead of the text he'd mastered to perfection. This had happened, on rare occasions, in Hedge's presence. It was happening now. The entire Bible fled from him, leaving not one line he could grab hold of and use as a lure to draw others. Everyone seemed to be waiting on him: James with his hands in position, tensed as if for a starting shot; Mrs. Hedge, her lamp at half-mast; even the doctor, who was rummaging in his bag, puncturing the silence with the utilitarian clink of his instruments. Sophy and Micah had come in and were hovering by the door. Gideon took a deep breath, and opened his mouth in the hope of dredging up some embedded singsong from his infancy: *Our Father. Now I lay me down to sleep.* He breathed out Hebrew.

A fountain of it. Effortless, gushing from some well he didn't know was there. At seminary he had been required to learn a few of the Psalms as they were written, but he couldn't stop the flow to identify them now. The words were tactile, spelling out their shapes on his palate as they passed out of him and into Hedge. Gideon remembered what the Reverend had said about the solidity of the language he loved, how it filled the mouth and left a sweetness on the tongue. He was only a conduit—yet he was conscious of an exhilarating force in him whose depths he had only skimmed. This, surely, was a small taste of what he'd stumbled on in his first bungling efforts at translation, what he had sought, laboriously and to so little effect, in his research. Whatever the source, he wasn't meant to hoard its bounty but to dip into the well and offer a healing draught to his teacher. The parson's lips had begun to move along with his. No sound emerged at first, but soon Gideon heard a thin vibrato, a wavering line under his own voice. Hedge was chanting along with him, as best he could.

In what might have been another country, Craddock and James huddled over the fractured leg. Gideon's view of the procedure was obscured, but he could see in the light of the lamp that the doctor's brow shone with sweat. To an outsider's eye, the setting appeared to be an athletic feat—a contest even—arduous enough to tax the strength of two strong men.

"Damn if his muscles don't resist me all on their own," the doctor muttered, "laudanum or no." His orders to James were terse. The broken bones must be pulled apart in order to be made straight.

Each time they shifted the leg, Hedge moaned, a throttled noise wrung from him against his will. For a few seconds Gideon sang alone, but always Hedge's voice rejoined his. His pain seemed woven into the prayer. Gideon had long considered the Psalms a relic of a more credulous age—for who in modern times would expend such urgent emotion on the Ineffable?—but never again would he find it difficult to imagine

David beating his chest or grinding his forehead in the dust, pleading with his God for victory, forgiveness, salvation, revenge.

Craddock mopped his face with one sleeve. "Steady now," he said, and he and James leaned into each other. Hedge let out a cry so piercing that Gideon's Hebrew froze in his throat, cut off in midstream. The lamp shook and slanted downward, casting them all into momentary darkness as Fanny bent to her husband. Gideon had hardly given her a thought since the procedure began. Her face was a mirror of Hedge's pain, alive with it, filled with feeling that had been absent for weeks. "Almost done, my lamb," she said, stroking his cheek. "I am here to bear it with you." But the Reverend was gazing into the eyes of his pupil, and all through the stitching and splinting and binding, he never looked away.

CHAPTER 14

KNIT

ICAH MADE THE CRUTCHES HIMSELF. FORAGING IN THE workshop, he chose some pieces from a pile of white oak set aside for seasoning, and lavished on them all the care he would have devoted to a chest or chair, with a measure of his father's ingenuity mixed in. The usual crude T-shape, an unforgiving bar atop a tapered stick, would have been quick work, but the Reverend's condition gave him time. He constructed models out of chips and scraps, lining them up along the windows—a new species of fauna for his menagerie—and walking them with his fingers up and down the sill until he arrived at an elegantly simple split-stick design that pleased him. Once the sticks were cut and turned, he drove a wedge between them to bend the wood to the S-curves he wanted. His effort was well spent: the cross-pieces fit inside the splits with just the right tension, like Samson braced between the temple pillars. Then he polished them to bring out the pattern of the oak, oiled them until they shone, and covered the arm-cradles with sheepskin.

The crutches had been propped against the bedroom wall for a month, stirring the admiration of all the Reverend's visitors. Dr. Craddock called them "the handsome twins"; he praised their flexibility and said he'd never seen a prettier pair. As days turned to weeks, Gideon began to think of them as sculpture, for Hedge was still in bed and showed no sign of leaving, his leg, trussed now in proper splints, stretched out and elevated on a pillow. The wound from the protruding bone continued red and angry, oozing pus through the stitches. Twice a week Fanny undid the bindings herself to apply a special poultice. Craddock marveled that no fever had developed but refused to credit her potions, attributing the phenomenon to the parson's strong character and innate resistance to corruption. Craddock's optimism had lately been tempered with caution. "I haven't lost hope that he will knit," he told them at the door one afternoon, hat in hand. "But, you understand, I can't guarantee he will knit *straight*." He smiled at Micah. "It's good sense to keep those fine crutches in plain sight. That way he'll get used to 'em before he ever has to lean on 'em."

THE SNOW THAT HAD been slow to come fell in abundance all through February, as if a stopper had been removed in the heavens. Even well-traveled roads were impassable; no sooner was one layer trodden down than a new one smoothed it over, filling in wagon ruts and effacing the prints of intrepid horses and walkers. For nearly a month, Gideon had been unable to trek to Ormsby for his Sunday visits. He missed Sophy, poignantly at times, but was glad to put aside the complications of affection and be a hermit in his room, a simple student once again, devoting all his energy to his last semester in seminary. The Hedges had consumed him for the better part of a year. When he wasn't with them physically, he thought about them. For all practical purposes, it occurred to him one evening over his thesis, he had been living *there* rather than *here*. A strange emotion stole over him, a compound of resentment and regret seasoned with nostalgia. They had ensnared him, these wily Hedges— diverted him from his path! A few short months ago his only allegiance had been to his own brilliant future, a destination to be approached systematically. Now he was attached, and there was nothing to be done, no escape from the fetters that bound him.

The subject of his thesis was the quest for the language of Paradise. He was careful to keep a scholar's skeptical distance, confining his research to a honed selection of those who had plowed the field before him. He jumped nimbly from the Egyptians and Greeks to Philo, from the pre-Socratics to Rousseau and Herder (how familiar their theories of nature seemed, ripe to be vilified from Hedge's pulpit), from John Webb's Chinese-spouting Noah, run aground in Cathay, to von Schlegel's infatuation with Sanskrit. He devoted an entire section to his fellow Harvardian Cotton Mather, whose master's thesis had championed Hebrew origins more than a century before, when plain-spoken America was still the New Eden. In expounding Mather's arguments, Gideon allowed a few of his own doubts to creep in, but so subtly and with such restraint that he was certain the most hidebound reader would find nothing to pick at.

Again and again as he stone-skipped through history, he encountered a strange experiment. There seemed to be a recurrent fascination among the language-obsessed with the tabula rasa of infancy. Herodotus wrote of an Egyptian pharaoh who sequestered two newborns in the mountains, with only a shepherd, sworn to silence, to look after them. Between them, the babies produced a single spontaneous word, which the pharaoh interpreted as Phrygian for bread. The subjects of Frederick II's curiosity had not fared so well. Although the Holy Roman Emperor arranged that their physical needs be met, the children didn't survive long enough to babble primal words, for, as a monk wrote, they "could not live without clappings of the hands, and gestures, and gladness of countenance, and blandishments." Gideon wondered whether such considerations had led the Scottish king James IV to appoint a mute to nurse his tiny prisoners, who, it was reported, eventually burst into flawless Hebrew. How else could the king ensure that endearments would not slip out, or whispered words of comfort; that lullabies would not be crooned low on fretful nights?

Thoughts of the children came to Gideon during his own restless nights, when he lay on his back staring at the ceiling, too agitated from the day's mental exertions to sleep. Before the babies were of talking age, had their cries taken on the nuances of speech? Did they communicate, if only with each other? Or was silence as nourishing to them as bread and milk, sharpening their senses, attuning them to a higher music? And what became of them when the experiment was over? Were they disposed of as coldly as animals, or sacrificed to anonymous labor, forced to haul stones for pyramids or work in the fields until they died? Not one historian had bothered to record their fate.

THE WRITING WENT QUICKLY. His pen skimmed over the paper; page after page piled up in the corner of his desk, the ink barely dry on one before another topped it. What drove him was not the work he was doing but the book he *would* write. An idea was shaping in his mind, vague but numinous. A lexicon of unique character, combining elements of dictionary and diary. An etymology that would function like an ark, carrying the reader back to that primal place where words were indistinguishable from things. However incomplete, his book would be a key to the natural language that was each person's birthright. His own experience would be essential, but he realized that he needed to broaden his research, to subject his curiosity to scientific rigor so that its fruits might enlighten others. It seemed to him that he was racing through a desert littered with the mummified remains of other men's quests to get to his own verdant oasis, where words would stride across the page in full leaf, like the walking trees that the blind man saw. The green!

Since Hedge was unlikely to return before term ended, his reader would likely be Mr. Satterfield, one of the few professors who was not ordained, a specialist in church history who had taken over the Reverend's Hebrew classes—reluctantly, Gideon suspected, to secure his shaky berth at the school. A plump fellow with a lisp that lent itself to parody, Satterfield was not popular with his students or his peers. Perhaps to compensate for the indignities that nature had inflicted, he spoke with excessive formality: Hebrew in his mouth sounded like an obscure branch of Gaelic. He was no less sententious in English. His periodic pronouncements on the condition of "your respected master and my esteemed colleague, the Reverend Hedge" were so lugubrious that he might have been reading from a prepared obituary.

On a Tuesday in early March, Satterfield had just delivered one of these morose reports, filled with details of the Reverend's continuing travails, when he stopped Gideon at the end of class and put a sealed note into his hand. "It came for you this morning, with a bundle of books Mrs. Hedge was kind enough to send me," Satterfield said, raising his eyebrows ominously. "I fear the Reverend may be reaching the end of his mortal struggles. If your presence is requested, you must go, of course. I've had no news since Thursday last."

Gideon stumbled out of the hall and walked blindly across the snow-covered green. The day was mild, patches of earth already showing under the trees. He thought, I will remember all this later: the feel of the air, the look of the sky, how indifferent the world was as Reverend Hedge departed from it. He could not decide where to read the note. The solitude of his cluttered room seemed intolerable, but sharing the news in company would be even worse. Finally he took shelter under a roofed side entrance of the chapel; there were no services today, little danger of being disturbed. As icicles dripped from the eaves, he pulled the letter from his pocket and broke the seal.

"My Dear Mr. Birdsall," he read. The script was forceful, though the lines lurched upward as if written on a vertical surface. "I trust that this finds you Well and Immersed in your Studies. It has been some time since we have had the Pleasure of your Company, Circumstances having Prevented, but a glance out the window today tells me we may anticipate a Thaw. May we also anticipate a Visit? I would not distract you from your Labours, but I believe that you and I have Much to Discuss."

Gideon read almost to the scrawled signature before he fully understood that Lazarus had risen and taken up his pen. The hostile mood that he had nursed for days lifted from him whole. In the fervor of his relief, he could not imagine sitting down and composing a reply. But in the end, he wrote, and was invited to come late on Sunday afternoon.

———

FANNY HEDGE GREETED HIM at the door. She folded both his hands in her own, warm as always, though Gideon sensed a nervousness that was new. There was the usual barrage of words, but her eyes darted away from him as she spoke, and he wondered if she was listening for a signal from her husband.

"I would have given you a proper dinner, but who is here to eat it? The children wander to the four corners, and the Reverend and I live like mice, ferreting bits of cheese from the larder. Reuben is in Boston, seeing to business, and James has gone to Duxbury to look at a horse and taken Micah with him for company. Did you know about our poor Zeke? Lame from gallivanting on the Woeful Night, and had to be released. Not one of us but Reuben had the heart to do it. Where do you stand on the redemption of animals, Mr. Birdsall? I see no reason why a good beast should be less precious to the Lord than a good man, though the Reverend thinks otherwise. Silent servants, they are, and—I'll say to you what I could not to him—Heaven would be a duller place without them."

"My thoughts, exactly." Gideon spoke with as much finality as he could muster. He waited, hoping she would continue the family chronicle, but she only smiled at him in a fixed way, as if he were a stranger come to seek her husband's counsel. "And Sophy?" he said. "Is she at home?"

"Ah, Sophy!" From Mrs. Hedge's tone, Gideon might have concluded that she had a dozen daughters, all scattered to the winds. "Now *she* is with her brother Sam in Lowell. His wife has just produced her fourth girl, and Sophy has gone to help with the other three. A full day's work for most mortals, but she *would* take her paints and easel. With so many little ones to watch over, I only hope she doesn't get lost in a daydream and misplace one." She gave him one of her arch looks. "I oughtn't to keep you from the Reverend. I think you'll be pleased to see how well he's mending."

Walking to the back of the house, Gideon felt a growing unease. Its source was obvious. He was retracing the steps he'd taken on the Woeful Night, as Mrs. Hedge had aptly named it, and the dread he'd suppressed then was having its revenge on him now.

The bedroom door was partly open, but Gideon rapped lightly with his knuckles to announce his presence. "Come in, Mr. Birdsall," he heard. "You are expected. You will forgive me for receiving you like this. *Couchant* is my natural posture these days." Reverend Hedge sounded like himself, and yet not himself. The old crisp authority was still there, but softened to unctuousness, like an apple stewed in its own juices.

"It's good to see you restored, sir," Gideon said. In fact, Hedge's appearance was so startling that the salutation almost died on his lips. The parson sat in state upon his bed, draped in a voluminous purple robe that covered him from neck to ankles. His injured leg had been elevated on a pillow of the same rich velvet. Gideon's first impression was of a gouty king receiving courtiers in his boudoir. Never had a garment been contrived that was more alien to its wearer. Hedge's walnut head, streaked with black hairs across the pate, was an incongruous topping for such royal raiment. His slight frame was enveloped in the very luxury he shunned, his hands lost in the folds of the sleeves. Could he be in costume? The idea was ridiculous; yet the whole visit had a staged quality that made it almost credible. The dramatic summons, Mrs. Hedge's odd manner, the absence of the rest of the clan—all seemed to herald some theatrical event to be performed for his benefit. Gideon's mouth was stretching in an involuntary grin, and only a series of desperate facial contortions kept his features in line.

The Reverend was not a blushing man, but Gideon thought he saw color in the pallid cheeks. "My wife found some draperies in an old chest," he said. "Trousers won't fit over the splints, you see, and she wanted me to be warm and comfortable. The style is perhaps more ostentatious than I am used to, but it performs its function admirably." He wiggled his toes to demonstrate his freedom. "At times, the Lord scourges our proud souls with the kindness of others."

Hedge gestured to a chair by the bed. Gideon recognized it as the one that had held the beaver hat on the day of the accident. "So, bring me some news of seminary. I confess I'm pining for the old halls. He who said habits die hard did not lie. And your thesis—how is that shaping?"

Gideon rambled on for a few minutes, making sure to mention Satterfield's Gaelic Hebrew. Hedge waggled a chastising finger—"Unkind, Mr. Birdsall!"—but his pleasure showed in his eyes. Gideon had just begun to talk about his research when Mrs. Hedge sailed in with a tray of freshly baked gingerbread and tea. She filled their cups, passed the plate, prodded the spitting log on the grate, and was gone before he finished thanking her. Gideon inhaled, savoring the aroma of mingled spices, which warmed the room more thoroughly than the feeble heat from the fireplace. He teased his hunger with a bite of sugared crust, his thoughts benignly blasphemous. The sacrament of Home. What comforts could Heaven offer to exceed this?

The atmosphere in the room changed. Hedge was staring at him, cup gripped in his left hand, his elbow crooked sharply. He pursed his lips, sipped long and loud, and set the cup clattering back into its saucer.

"It has been some time since you came to us, has it not, Mr. Birdsall?"

Gideon agreed that it had. He licked crumbs from his mouth and prepared to launch into the requisite appreciation, but the Reverend didn't pause.

"Mrs. Hedge and I have opened our house to other young men over the years. Most have benefited from our hospitality, and offered some small service in return. You recall Mr. Unsworth? Not a generous nature, nor an agreeable one, but where is it written that we should reserve our better instincts for those who are easy to love? You, on the other hand, made a favorable impression from the beginning."

"I'm happy to hear that," Gideon murmured. After a second's hesitation, he rescued the cup and saucer from the parson's precarious grip, and returned them to the tray.

"Your facility in the classroom did not escape my notice. I won't call it brilliance—that term is used far too loosely these days—but your work showed intellect, and enough discipline and ambition to make use of it. I told you once that I saw in you an incarnation of my younger self. The passion for language, and, yes, the excesses that such passion is disposed to. When I took you on as my amanuensis, I hoped to be an influence for moderation in your life. Who better than one who had passed through the fire before you?"

Hedge cocked his head and glanced at Gideon from beneath drooping lids, his expression improbably coy. "You know my fondness for mixing diverse elements—I believe you sampled the last of our experiments with wine. And I'm not above seasoning my sermons with the odd classical reference, if only to illustrate the fulfillment of pagan wisdom in Scripture. What you may not know is that I sometimes apply these same methods to the human dilemma. In the case of a certain young scholar of my acquaintance, I thought that a dose of wholesome family life, coupled with honest labor in the lexical vineyards, might steady a flighty soul. There's nothing like digging up roots to bring us back to earth, Mr. Birdsall! Reminds us of what we're made of, I always think."

The emotions that Gideon had indulged while working on his thesis came back to him now in force. The pompous old bag of wind! Had Hedge really convinced himself that Gideon's year of solitary drudgery in service of his pet project was an act of benevolence? That the hours he had expended on the Lexicon were some sort of tonic concocted for his spiritual health? He remembered Unsworth's remarks about slavery, and thought of the boarder with new respect. What might he have accomplished had he spent those months pursuing his own work?

"Since you're making such progress, you'll soon be able to return to the Lexicon with renewed vigor," Gideon said. "No doubt I'm much improved for having worked on it, but I will be leaving soon to make my way. Time to put your investment in me to practical use." Sarcasm floated on top of his words like cream; he couldn't help himself.

The Reverend receded into silence. The lively engagement in his face faded, his features stiffened into a mask; he seemed to compose himself around his core. Now he really did look like a king, Gideon thought: a withered mandarin clasping his hands beneath pendant sleeves.

"Please don't think I'm ungrateful, sir." Gideon was instantly repentant. "I've learned so much from you. The Hedges—all of you—will always be with me, wherever life takes me." For the first time since entering the room, he thought of Sophy. "I may not go far," he added. "Who knows, we may be neighbors. If so, I can only hope you won't get weary of an old student knocking at your door."

"I thought you understood," Hedge said, as if he hadn't heard. "Is it possible you have not?"

It was Gideon's turn to be silent. He felt as he had once or twice in class when Hedge fired a question at him—as if the required answer was suspended somewhere in the immediate universe, accessible but perversely out of his reach.

"The night of my accident. The text you chanted."

Hedge was prompting him, but to what end? "I was in such a state, sir. I hardly knew what I was saying, the Hebrew just kept coming. It . . . at the time, it seemed quite miraculous."

"Seemed, Mr. Birdsall? There is no question in my mind that the Lord used you as a vessel to speak to me in the language we both love. How many times have I read Isaiah? A hundred. Two hundred. How many times have I sermonized on the Suffering Servant and the verses that follow? Thirty, maybe more. I thought I knew that text as well as I know my own children's names—yet I never felt its meaning till I heard it from your mouth. It was as if I had no skin—as if the words went directly to my heart. *All we like sheep have gone astray; we have turned every one to his own way . . .* "

As he intoned the verse, bearing down on the last syllables of each line to emphasize the nursery rhythm, Hedge milled his gingerbread between two fingers, filling his napkin with crumbs.

"How was the Lord to deal with a man of the cloth who went his own way, not once, but twice? Who set such a high value on worldly security that he risked his modest income—the sustenance of his family and the future of his sons—for the sole purpose of making more? Who *dabbled*, Mr. Birdsall! He saw the path I was on, and upset the wagon to divert me from it. You see before you a man crippled in body and in business, all earthly prospects destroyed. Yet, in His mercy, He has given me reason to believe that the bones He has broken will rejoice."

The parson's eyes searched Gideon's with the same restless ardor as on the night of the accident. There was no condemnation in his gaze—yet, Gideon thought, Hedge must surely be aware that the wondrous outpouring of Hebrew was a regurgitation of the passages from Isaiah he'd translated all those months ago. The only miracle—if so it could be called—was how deeply the chapters had engraved themselves in his memory, how fluently they'd poured out at a time of stress. Gideon had known the truth, but he hadn't confronted it until Hedge recited the verse to him, reduced in English to rhyming doggerel. He felt a familiar pang of loss. Often, after leaving his own work to return to daily tasks, he'd had to shake off this poignant longing, for which he had no name. It was like homesickness, but for something more primal than his past. For mystery itself. The numinous lurking in the mundane world. He lowered his head, surrendering to his disappointment.

"Why won't you look at me, my boy? Have I overwhelmed you?"

Hedge's voice was so gentle that Gideon did look up, astonished. Was the Reverend playing the part of the fond paterfamilias, addressing him like one of his sons? If there were lines to be learned, Gideon hadn't mastered his. He stared back, dumbly, awaiting a cue.

"You are right to be confused," Hedge went on. "My own pride blinded me to the signs, though I see now that they were posted from our first acquaintance. I don't apologize for this. A man in his full vigor doesn't brood about who will carry on his work. He is too busy doing it. When I thought about the matter at all, I followed the prompting of nature and looked to my own offspring. I have four sons, Mr. Birdsall, and not one has gotten the whole of me. I observe them and see Hedge Dismembered: amiability here, native shrewdness there, a staunch heart here, able hands there. Perhaps that is always the way."

And what of your excellent wife, Gideon thought. Were any of her traits passed down? He felt a twinge of foreboding, but said nothing. His instinct told him to wait for Hedge to reveal himself.

The parson's good leg jerked. He subdued it with pats and vigorous rubbing, as one might calm an obstreperous dog. "Immobility is a trial for an active man," he said. "But I must make peace with doing less. I don't fool myself that I will be what I was. Even with the help of Micah's splendid sticks"—he nodded at the crutches glowing in oiled perfection against the whitewashed walls—"I'll never stand before my flock again, dispensing the Word of Truth, or travel to their humble dwellings to minister to them. It is a hard punishment, to renounce a way of life—the more so if that life is one of service. When I fall into self-pity—and I am human, I succumb—I cling to those words you fed me in my hour of deepest need." Hedge stretched out his hand to Gideon. "Say them with me, dear boy!"

Gideon stumbled over the Hebrew, following the Reverend as best he could. His fluency was gone, but the sluggish pace had one advantage. He could savor the text as he went along: Isaiah 55, his favorite in all the Bible, the reason he had chosen to translate these passages to begin with. He loved the music of it, the way the last verses built to a crescendo of singing hills and applauding trees, myrtles sprouting up in place of briars, the earth transformed. He imagined the prophet on a mountaintop, sending forth King James cadences like clear, bright peals of a trumpet: *For my thoughts are not your thoughts . . . For as the heavens are higher than the earth . . . For as the rain cometh down, and the snow from heaven . . .*

Hedge stopped abruptly, leaving Gideon to straggle on for a few syllables before realizing that nature would not exult today—at least not in Hebrew. The parson began to recite in English, slow and deliberate, giving each word its full value. He might have been instructing a deaf pupil, or an exceptionally dull one.

"*So shall my word be that goeth forth out of my mouth: it shall not return unto me void, but it shall accomplish that which I please, and it shall prosper in the thing whereto I sent it.*"

He paused, letting the words settle, his eyes fixed on Gideon. "Wonderful, is it not? You may think you are not up to the task, that you're too young, too raw to undertake an established ministry. But I assure you, it has all been inscribed from the beginning of time. Think of the precedents! Moses and Joshua, Elijah and Elisha . . . will you judge me arrogant if I suggest that we too share this sacred bond, writ infinitely small?'"

Gideon's lips were stiff, his tongue felt as thick as a cow's. "Are you saying," he said, enunciating with difficulty, "that *I* am to be *you*?"

"Only in a public sense." Hedge gave a light laugh. "I had forgotten your tendency to interpret literally. Some of the more eccentric locutions in your little translation give me pleasure to this day."

And what you ask, Gideon thought, is the crudest kind of translation. Substitution. A word for a word. The hallmark of the amateur.

"No," Hedge went on, "I am not asking you to replace me—as you see, I am still very much present—but to stand in my place, to preach and teach and minister as my emissary. You will not be alone. I will be with you every step of the way. Together we will get the Word out, and I have no doubt that it will prosper." The parson looked down at his legs with some irony and twitched his toes. "There is blessing even in the Lord's punishments, my friend. I despaired that I would ever find time for the Lexicon, though it is the true work of my heart. Now I can entrust my pastoral duties to a younger man, and devote myself to a labor that will outlast me."

Emissary? How had Hedge arrived at that word, Gideon wondered. Wasn't an emissary a kind of spy? Possibly the Reverend expected him to prowl dark corners of the parish, reporting on subversion in the ranks. The title for a new book came to him: *From Amanuensis to Emissary: A Slave's Progress.* It was not the one he intended to write.

"I am sensible of the honor," he said, keeping his voice tight and formal, "but I'm not prepared to make such a commitment. I need time to decide what I will do next. I am considering several options."

"Are you indeed, Mr. Birdsall?" Hedge had easily divined that Gideon's last statement had no substance. "Seems to me that in these hard times, a young man should think twice before refusing a solid offer. There's many a seminary graduate sweeping out churches who would welcome such an opportunity. Your phraseology interests me. You say you are not ready to make a commitment—yet, I think you've recently made one. Perhaps not in so many words. In certain situations, actions speak louder."

"I don't know what you refer to," Gideon said. He was addled by Hedge's sudden switch from celestial destiny to hard-edged pragmatism. But understanding was already creeping into him via his extremities. His hands were cold.

"Reuben saw you with Sophy on the night of my misfortune. He said you were making advances of the most explicit kind. I've observed your fondness for her, but I never expected that you would abuse the trust we placed in you—particularly after I confided the circumstances of her birth. Sophy is not like other girls. She is innocent, but heir to certain . . . influences that run rampant in her blood. My Consort and I have sheltered her from the world, for her own protection." He pointed his forefinger at Gideon. "The past must not repeat itself. I won't allow it."

Reuben. The serpent twisted around Hedge's family tree. Gideon made an attempt to speak past the bile flooding his throat. "I have only the highest feelings for Sophy. You greatly underestimate her, sir, if you treat her like a weak child, easily swayed to one influence or another. Her character is beautiful and pure—in that sense you are right, she is not like other girls. Be assured, nothing wanton passed between us, that night or any other. If Reuben says otherwise, the fault—the filth—is in him."

His voice shook. He could not go on.

Hedge put up a placating hand. "Calm yourself, dear boy, I had to test you. How was I to know the depth of your emotions? My son is no moral exemplar, but he is cunning, he sees what he sees and says what he will. This is a small parish, things get about. I thought it best to send Reuben to the city for the time being. He wants direction, and his energies require a larger scope; he will unravel my poor affairs if anyone can."

The parson looked down at the scattered crumbs in his lap. With an air of serendipity he took a morsel and placed it on his tongue. His expression was bland, his eyes distant and musing, strikingly like Sophy's.

"I would not have chosen you for a son-in-law," he said. "I had in mind a simpler, more practical man who would be an anchor for my daughter. An abiding decency that would keep her safe at home, wherever her fancies take her. Sophy is a dreamer, her thoughts range wide just as yours do. In my experience, minds too alike lack the necessary friction. Such marriages exacerbate each partner's flaws—and rarely do they result in vigorous offspring. But the Lord had larger plans, and who are we to contradict Him? When I see how artfully He has woven the threads of our lives together, I am in awe."

Hedge gathered the fragments of gingerbread in the napkin, tied the ends to make a bundle, and motioned for Gideon to relieve him of it. He brushed a few stray crumbs from his sumptuous robe and gathered it closer around him. "Tea is such a *thin* liquid, I find it goes right through me. It's the idea that warms, not the beverage itself. I wonder if Mrs. Hedge might be persuaded to bring us a wee dram of her medicinal brandy. The occasion warrants something stronger than flavored water, I think. What do you say, Mr. Birdsall? Shall we take a lesson from the Psalmist and turn our mourning into dancing?"

CHAPTER 15

HIDDEN IN PLAIN SIGHT

MAMA WOULD SAY IT'S NO BETTER THAN WITCHCRAFT. That the only art she's practicing is a dark one. But now that she's been sent away, what else can Sophy do?

Life at Sam's is crowded and dull, and, two weeks in, she has little time to call her own. The children are forever tugging at her skirts, getting into the few things she brought with her. They are always *attached*. She wishes she liked them more. She has made sketches of the older girls in the rare moments she can persuade them to sit still, thinking to compose them into a group portrait for the grandparents. A bouquet of tousled heads is what she has in mind, but these little ones don't inspire. They have no faces to speak of—not to paint. It isn't just that they're young and soft-featured. Their parents seem to vanish in the same way, rendered invisible by blandness. The best that could be said of Lucy was that she "looked mild enough," in Mama's words. Given the suddenness of the betrothal, they all understood "mild" to be a euphemism for "easily persuaded." At the hastily arranged wedding, the question in their minds was why Sam had taken up with such an insignificant creature to begin with. He had been handsome then, the only Hedge ever to be called dashing. It seems that the lack of character Papa lamented has spread to his exterior, puffing out his cheeks and blurring his features, coating his bones with a layer of extra flesh. Sophy has no idea whether he is happy. She would like to ask him, but feels she can't. He goes to his father-in-law's shop each day, uncomplaining, and comes home to Lucy's indifferent dinner, and eats in silence, still uncomplaining. Not yet thirty, he has settled like a stone at the bottom of a pond. Sophy hesitates to ripple the surface.

When she first arrived, she tried to act in Mama's stead, attending to the children's needs, straightening the casual disorder, making herself useful. But the strain of being pulled in so many directions gave her headaches. Her sister-in-law's placidity runs deep. She seems content to give over the household to Sophy's keeping, though she never expresses gratitude and has yet to inquire about the rest of the family. After a week of chasing the little ones, and hovering over the baby to make sure it didn't smother at the breast when Lucy dozed, Sophy began to relax. The children had survived before she got here, and would probably thrive whether she danced attendance on them or not. The junior Hedges would not meet untimely ends if, once in a while, she retreated to the attic to paint.

Once in a while has become every day. If Lucy objects, she has not told her so directly—though, yesterday, descending the stairs, Sophy heard her brother ask why dinner was late. "I don't know," Lucy said, genuinely perplexed. "That girl vanishes to the attic whenever it's time to help with the cooking. Lord knows what she does up there."

THE ATTIC WOULD BE a fine place to work, if she were doing any. Sophy goes there late in the afternoon; the days are longer now, and light slants pleasantly through the window. The peace she feels when she is finally alone more than compensates for the cold. She wraps her shawl around her shoulders and settles with care on an abandoned chair.

The eyes that look back at Sophy from the easel are her own— the lone part of the self-portrait that feels true. It is the only work-in-progress she brought with her, in sheer defiance of Mama, who insisted that she'd be too busy to fiddle with paints. She had started the portrait at home, on a poplar board Micah prepared for her. To render herself on wood seemed a utility rather than a vanity, and she liked the idea of putting her image on something that had been alive. At first Sophy used a hand mirror she'd been told belonged to her mother, but this method proved awkward. Propping it at the right angle was a problem, and even when she managed, she couldn't really see herself; her reflection, with its puckered brow and bitten lip, its irritating lack of composure, got in the way. She couldn't begin to paint until she put the mirror aside and dreamed her face as if it were someone else's, or no one's in particular, like the cottages and gardens and sylvan landscapes that pop into her head when she gazes at an empty canvas. Mama cannot grasp that they aren't real. "Is that Bartletts' place?" she asks. "You got the color of the roof wrong, and that shade tree was cut down before you were born."

The Sophy in the picture reminds her of a doll she had when she was little: the same slick cap of painted hair parted in the middle, the same wide eyes over an enameled valentine of a mouth, prim in spite of being puckered for a kiss. She hasn't touched a brush to it since she arrived at Sam's. The flatness of the image proves she has no gift for likeness; yet she can't quite regard the girl as just another exercise. The eyes seem to demand that this thin slice of a self be plumped out, filled fuller with life. Sophy would provide satisfaction, if she were able.

On a rainy Wednesday afternoon, the implacable stare is too much for her. She has had a harried day, having awakened to cramps from her monthly and two of the children sick with colds. Instead of comforting them, she's behaved like an irritable child herself, speaking sharply and ordering Alice, the eldest, to stand in a corner. The worst of it is that Lucy approved of her excesses. "See how wicked you are?" she chided her snuffling daughters. "No wonder Auntie hides herself away!" Even the hard-won solitude of the attic doesn't cheer Sophy after such a display. Her facsimile on the easel is no help; she has as little character as the nieces, and like them, she wants, wants, wants. Sophy has been saying no, no, no all day, and she says it now. She turns the board over to its blank side.

The smooth wood is blessedly mute. As she relaxes, the fist in her stomach unclenches and the sluggish blood flows free. Each month, for a day or two, she goes soft like this, liquid inside. Her body weeps with a sweet need, private and cloistered, not to be dissipated in dancing. Most months the longing is general, but lately she's been dwelling on Gideon. She hasn't seen him since the first weeks after Papa's accident. She wonders what he is doing at this moment, separated from her by nothing more substantial than miles. Is he perhaps thinking of her, too? Of the home they made in the study? The kiss he ventured, barely?

Papa summoned her to his bedside before she left for Sam's. "You and I have always been close," he'd said, reaching for her hand. "If something is weighing on your heart, I would like to know." She would have confided in the man who took her for conversational walks, but it had been too long since he had sought her feelings. She shook her head, not wishing to cast a lie in words, and he had sighed and read her flushed cheeks instead.

Sophy puts a finger to the board and traces Gideon's head, the curve of his jaw, his neck and shoulders. She has rehearsed his body so often that the line comes easily. Caroline said she should paint him, and—putting aside Caroline's meaning—she has been working up to it all these months. During their time in the study she'd thought of asking him to pose, but whenever she gathered courage to broach the subject a reserve came over her—a hesitation, as if a cautioning hand had been laid on her shoulder. To replicate Gideon is a liberty she can't risk. It is one thing to show him her hazy rural views of no place in particular, quite another to subject his features to her lack of skill. He would be kind, and that would be terrible.

But the unmarked surface entices her. She imagines dipping her fingers in paint, feeling the grain of the wood as she works. Why would he ever have to know? She can paint him for herself—or for her other self, that deprived creature who faces the easel like a naughty child. And when she is done for the day, she can turn painted Sophy to the light again, and no one will be the wiser. Gideon—her Gideon—will be hidden in plain sight. The idea pleases her.

She supposes what Mama said is true: that some who have gone over to the dark side make images of the object of their desire, and chant spells that draw the beloved helpless to their arms. Sophy can't see that it's all that different from the things respectable girls like Caroline do. Wiles are wiles, and whatever the method, the end is the same: the merging of two into one.

It occurs to her that the painting she is about to make, back-to-back with her portrait, will be one flesh of a sort. If this is presumption, so be it—Gideon has his experiments, and she has hers. But she can't take time to sketch as she usually does, or her excitement will ebb; she'll wake up tomorrow full of doubt and never do it at all. She takes up a brush and adds white to carmine, chooses a place where his head might go. This first stroke always stirs her: something where there was nothing, all possibilities open. The color she has mixed is too fiery for pale skin like his; she will have to blend in more white and some ochre to get close. Once the tone is right, she works quickly, building his face in layers of paint, thick, as if she were sculpting him. Cheekbones, chin, curve of brow, angle of nose. Empty statue eyes: she will do them last, she isn't ready to meet his gaze.

His mouth is very fine; her brushwork is too clumsy to shape it. Sophy follows the curve of her own lips with her little finger, dips it in paint and transfers the touch directly. On the other side of the board, her painted self burns.

TWO SESSIONS LATER, she has a likeness that pleases her. Not that it is finished. She doesn't want it to be, she will be improving it for some time. Her mind is the palette, memory mixing with her own longing to make a Gideon she can possess. She didn't know how well she knew him until she painted him, yet she's caught only the shell; it would be impossible to confine a man so deep to a single image, even if she were good enough. The eyes won't come right. No matter how she fusses, she can't infuse them with more than a cold light: a scholarly dispassion that falls far short of the soul mirror she wants. She's making yet another attempt when she hears footsteps on the stairs. She barely has time to reverse the poplar board before Sam blunders in, butting into a rafter as he straightens up.

"What do you think, Soph?" He rubs his forehead, grinning, a gesture that does double duty to soothe his bruised brow and convey astonishment. "Wonders never cease! You have a bidder!"

CHAPTER 16

WEDDING

"WEDDING" MUST HAVE STARTED AS A VERB, GIDEON thought. In the weeks since Sophy returned home, the process had gathered momentum around them, setting them spinning faster and faster as they struggled to keep their footing, to keep their wits, to keep—for a few stray moments—still.

There had been, first of all, the matter of the ring. On the Sunday after James left to retrieve Sophy, Mrs. Hedge asked Gideon whether he had a band from his "dear mother." It took him a few seconds to understand what she referred to. His mother wore a ring, but it was thin as a thread, of no more weight than the invisible father who had, in theory, presented it. The ring had been part of her hand, like her prominent veins and her nails that were always breaking. It never occurred to Gideon to remove it for a keepsake when she died. Mrs. Hedge said not to mind, she had a perfectly good ring from her grandmother, far too small for her big bones but a perfect match for Sophy's twig of a finger.

He went back to seminary with the box in his pocket. In his room he took the ring from its nest of velvet and held it to the window's light. It was almost as narrow as his mother's, but crowned with a minute diamond and incised with delicate rays around the jewel's base. Someone had taken great care with it, though it seemed to have been sized for the hand of a child.

"I am about to possess the pearl of great price," he whispered, conscious of how actorish the words sounded.

He looked at the ring for a long time, at the gold circlet and the tiny disk of sky that it enclosed, before putting it back in the box.

Sophy arrived the next day. Gideon waited with Mrs. Hedge and Micah while James helped her out of the cart. She came toward them with her head down, her face half-hidden by her bonnet. Once the usual inquiries about the journey were dispensed with, James led the horse to the barn, trailed by Micah, who was visibly eager to escape the looming momentousness of the occasion. Gideon felt like bolting himself. When he dreamed of being with Sophy, he had never imagined following this drab, predictable script. Sophy seemed as uncomfortable as he, refusing to meet his eyes and looking off to the side when he spoke to her. They might have been meeting for the first time. She had been timid then, too—moony, Mrs. Hedge had called her—but there had been freedom in it, and independence, the instinctive shying of a wild creature. Now she was merely awkward. If he could only get her alone, he thought, they could be themselves again, and the right words would come.

He didn't have to wait long. He was ushered to the parlor while Sophy went to greet the Reverend and deliver news of Sam. Gideon sat stiffly in a horsehair chair, thinking that he ought to have kept his hat so he could twirl it on his knee in the ritual manner.

Sophy came in and sat opposite him. She was wearing a simple gray dress that he hadn't seen before, and she had smoothed her hair. After an absence of weeks, Gideon was beguiled again by the modesty of her manner, her serene containment. His little nun. She would dance, but only for him.

"I don't imagine you found much time to paint with all those children to look after," he said. He was startled when she blushed.

"Not much. I began something new, but only as an exercise. It isn't fit to show."

"You're too modest about your work."

She didn't answer, and he could think of nothing else to say. It seemed possible that they would sit forever in constricted silence.

Sophy looked up suddenly, her face lively. "You don't have to!" she said. "We can go on as we are. Or not go on at all. You mustn't feel . . . compelled."

Her few words released a flood of feeling in Gideon. How little Hedge's manipulations counted when weighed against such generosity, such a pure, selfless heart! He would be fortunate to have her, under any circumstances.

"If I love anyone, I love you," he blurted. "Only you. But I wish we could run away to our own little place. I hate all this managing."

As soon as the fatal phrase was spoken, Gideon realized that he had never said it aloud—not since he was a small child, returning his mother's endearment at bedtime. He stood apart for a moment, like another person in the room, watching its effect. Sophy didn't move, but emotion suffused her skin and radiated from her eyes. It was, he thought, like shyness turned inside out. Her mole-colored cloak showing its scarlet lining.

Dropping to one knee, he swept the box from his pocket in a deliberately broad gesture, meaning to mock the convention. He realized too late that he had neglected to open it. "Will you do me the honor . . ." he began, but the rest of the words did not come.

Sophy took the box from his hand. Instead of looking inside, she held it to her heart and knelt before him, so they faced each other like two children playing. She brought her face to his and kissed him on the lips. He closed his eyes, lost in some dimly remembered sweetness, and kissed her back.

When at last they came apart, Sophy said, "We will run away. But not yet."

GIDEON HAD ASSUMED they would be married in the parlor, or even at the Reverend's bedside—a quick exchange of vows, with family looking on. Hedge was still far from well, prey to persistent discomfort that kept him confined to his room for most of the day.

But the parson had invested the wedding day with hopes he had once reserved for Heaven. He had seized on the ceremony as the occasion for his formal rebirth as head of his congregation, and it soon became clear that only a sanctified setting would do. Twice a week Gideon and Sophy came to him to be instructed in the duties of marriage, and on each visit he presented them with some new idea, as the solemnities evolved in his mind. Hedge would be seated at the head of the meetinghouse, having been enthroned before the congregation assembled. He would look on as Gideon processed down the aisle, flanked by church elders, visiting clergy, and dignitaries from the seminary. Wedding attendants and family members would follow, and last of all, the bride, on the arm of one of her brothers. With the young couple before him, the Reverend would raise himself on Micah's crutches—"as on the wings of angels," he said—and stand before his flock upright! Once the vows were spoken, he would address the newlyweds and the congregation on the new dispensation of duties, and Gideon would be ordained to the service of the church.

"Surely it would be better to keep the two rites separate," Gideon said, after being informed about the latest enhancement, "to give each one its full due. I can be ordained after we're married."

"I grant you, it is not the orthodox way. I suppose some of my colleagues will balk." Hedge was seated in his rocking chair, his leg stretched out on a footstool. The chair had been moved to his bedroom to serve as a way station on his road to ascension, and he sat in it for at least an hour each day, however poorly he was feeling. "But at times the Lord calls us to transcend custom. The ancients saw patterns in the heavens and celebrated the cycles of the sun and moon. Should we be deprived of our festal days when events converge to show us that 'all things work together for good'? In fact"— his eyes slid from Gideon to Sophy and back again—"I have been entertaining thoughts of a *double* wedding. James and Caroline have been pledged for too long. The boy's gone soft. He seems to lose all force when he deals with that young woman. I've counseled him to show some spirit and set a firm date. And if the stars should align . . ." He looked down his nose at them and winked, as if they were fellow conspirators.

Gideon thought he had used up all his anger, and found some to spare. Damn the man and his endless mixing! He would boil the lot of them in a brew of his own making until they lost all distinction. But Gideon was alarmed by Hedge's volatility, his roaming eyes. It seemed that the idleness imposed by the parson's long prostration had generated an excess of vigor that mimicked the symptoms of madness. The energy he'd once spent in constant activity was wreaking havoc with his body and his mind. Hedge talked incessantly; his hands were never still, his face was an alphabet of tics and grimaces.

"Papa, you know that won't do," Sophy said. "James knows very well that he can't command Caroline. She must agree of her own free will. And she isn't even home. She's staying with her cousin in the city, attending a finishing school."

"Her parents are indulging her. Ruining what is left of her character. Why has no one told me until now?" Hedge plucked querulously at the blanket covering his legs. "Chaos everywhere. Pacts are broken; the weak rule the strong; our money isn't worth the paper it's printed on. If I could stand on my own two legs, I could at least put my parish house in order. Keep the Evil One from our doors."

The Reverend gripped the arms of his chair, but his voice, when he spoke again, was calmer. "Sophy, would you fetch those ornaments from the wall? I think—if you two will assist me—it may be time to put them to the test."

IN HIS ROOM at seminary, his trunk already packed, Gideon read the vows that would bind him to Sophy. He had an old copy of the Book of Common Prayer; he loved the archaic spellings, the high language gemmed with thees and thous. With the ceremony less than a month away, he expected that the words would pulse with meaning. They did not. His mind sifted them with dry detachment, pulling apart and peering under, examining the text like a theological treatise.

Marriage was *an honorable estate instituted of God in Paradise*. But who would have known better than the Creator that formalities were irrelevant in a world made for a single couple? Gideon concluded, with some fellow feeling, that the first man and woman would have had no idea of how to inhabit this exclusive preserve; Adam would know only that he had been alone—all one, sufficient unto himself—and now he was joined to another.

He was cautioned against entering in *to satisfy carnal lusts and appetites, like the brute beasts that have no understanding.* Gideon thought of the girl in the schoolroom: the bovine bulk of her, her moist underlip and dull eyes. He thought of his solitary efficiencies in bed, how his hand crept to his crotch like a thief in the night. He would be done with all that when he married Sophy. But he wasn't sure what replaced the bestial urge, or how, exactly, his understanding would increase, once they were legally bound and lying side by side in the boarder's bedroom at Hedge's. He wasn't sure he would know what to do. He wished he had a friend close enough to ask. Most men seemed to know such things by instinct—or to act as if they did.

Gideon rushed through the giving and taking and having and holding without being further enlightened. These were so familiar that they offered nothing new. He stopped when he came to the one vow reserved for the groom alone. The ring was on his desk again. Sophy had returned it after she accepted him so he could give it to her on their wedding day; he had no money for a plain gold band, but, as Fanny said, who would quibble over that scrap of a jewel? Once the pledges were exchanged, Gideon would present her, as instructed, with the sliver of gold—not much, but more solid than paper money in these uncertain times—and then he would promise to worship her with his body and endow her with his worldly goods. Tantalizing, the conjunction of wealth and fleshly reverence. The hint of paganism appealed to him. It was the same quality that drew him to Catholic churches, with their naked Christs presiding over gilded altars. But worship seemed to have nothing to do with the kiss they had shared, only their lips touching, their bodies held chastely apart. He remembered his first sight of Sophy, how he had gazed at her across a field as she did her Maenad's dance. Soon he would hold close what he had seen then at a distance. He imagined falling to his knees before her—in earnest, this time—and clasping her childish hips, burying his face in her belly, teasing her breasts with his tongue. Thinking of her this way, he felt what he had never felt before: a pure, stabbing desire for her flesh. It was so intense that it pained him; he had to satisfy himself.

He was ashamed afterward, but wiser, for he had learned by way of his body the reason for the church's elaborate ritual. Lift the veil of formality and the stately phrases revealed their carnal truths. The idealized emotion of love—the "thou"— brought low, reduced to a rubbing of parts, dissipated in pure sensation. Raised up again.

In his first reading Gideon had hurried over the means of redemption. *Procreation of children*. The text listed it first among reasons for marriage, but the fusty old term shrouded reality in a carapace of leaden duty. Children were the culmination. They elevated the animal act, changed it into something sacred. His mother had this much in common with the Queen of Heaven: they both had sons they doted on. Yet Gideon, for all his obsessing over the wedding night, had given little thought to the outcome of the act. Unlike other men, he had never felt the need to make a miniature of himself. His great role had always been to *be* the child.

He got up and walked to the window. The trees outside were a tender green, but a strong wind whipped their branches, the last breath of winter. He thought of his Sundays in the study with Sophy and Micah, of the family they made. He had pretended to father Micah because Micah was grown, and not really his, but to bring a new being into the world seemed an arrogance he wasn't capable of. He tried to imagine his features and Sophy's combined, and found that the mental exercise was beyond him. His eyes, her mouth, her eyes, his nose, her ears, his chin. The two of them didn't look the least alike. The face kept mutating, and in the end resembled nothing human.

It was easier to visualize the sequestered infants he'd written about in his thesis. They came to him at night, unbidden, and they came to him now. Although no image had ever been made of them, he could see the babies clearly. The radical innocence of their faces. Their round, clear eyes, mirroring the other in perpetual astonishment. Their alertness, registering the slightest tremor in their cloistered world. The word— one or many; Phrygian, Hebrew, or tongue unknown—forming in them over time, an embryo of thought maturing slowly until ready to be born as speech. Thinking of these children, his heart raced as it did when his studies yielded a discovery. Just so it must have been in the Garden!

"I SUPPOSE YOU will want to know things," Mama says. She speaks with difficulty, pins bristling from one corner of her mouth. To herself she mutters, "The sleeves could be fuller, but they would drown you."

Sophy is distracted, feasting on her image in the glass. The dress she will be married in is the first fashionable dress she has ever owned. Mama has always scorned fashion, but for this occasion she has overcome her scruples and modified a pattern from the dressmaker, who claimed it came from Paris, France. The bodice is gently scooped, front and back, the sleeves belled just enough to widen her shoulders and show off her slim waist and the delicacy of her wrists. Mama had predicted that white would fade her. The opposite is true. The layers of fine muslin make her shine, though quietly, the light seeming to emanate from within. *Luster* is what this dress gives her. She might not aspire to be a diamond, but she can—she will—be a pearl.

The Sophy in the mirror is the one Gideon will see as she walks down the aisle. She will never match him for beauty, but her reflection testifies that she's prettier than she's ever been. In her white dress she can stand beside her husband with pride and not shame him by comparison. Later he will help her with all the tiny buttons she can't undo herself. Will the luster fade when she stands before him in her skin? Is naked easier to be than to say aloud? These are things she would like to know, but she doubts Mama is the one to ask.

"I want to know whatever you think I need to," she says.

Mama removes the pins from her mouth one by one. Her lips stay pressed—whether in exasperation or a rare moment of contemplation,

Sophy cannot tell. After a pause she says, "You've seen the animals. You know what boys are like. You must have some idea of the parts and such. What goes where."

She releases these statements in rapid-fire pellets, but her eyes are clouded. Sophy has the impression that boulders are moving in her head.

"I don't ask what you and Mr. Birdsall got up to when the Reverend and I were otherwise occupied. Whether you stopped at a kiss or went beyond. It's of no account now, with all about to be made right. But I do reproach myself for allowing you to nurse him when he was sick. I did it with a good heart, thinking to teach you charity, but I wonder if seeing him so helpless and childlike didn't stir up certain thoughts. It begins with thoughts, you know. That's what sets us apart from the beasts—though not in any way we can preen on."

"The only thoughts I had were for Mr. Birdsall to get well," Sophy says, truthfully enough. "He is a perfect gentleman."

"So he appears. But men are men." Mama sighs, philosophical. "I won't tell you it's pleasant at first, lying back and being breached, and you might as well learn now that even gentle men forget their manners in their throes. Don't be alarmed if there's bleeding, perfectly natural when you consider a path is being forged where no foot ever trod. What you must remember is that things will soon improve. And the discomfort is nothing—the merest drop in an ocean—when set against all the rest of it."

Sophy has been stealing glances at her reflection, thinking that she and Gideon will sort out this confusion of body parts and forest-clearing for themselves. But Mama's last words get her whole attention. Could this addendum be the Portal to Bliss that Caroline's cousin spoke of? It would seem that the cave of crystal is accessible even to clergymen and their wives—a revelation, to be explored later. She waits expectantly, but Mama's face is grave. She is gazing at Sophy with a brooding sympathy that solemnizes her features.

Without warning she pulls Sophy to her. Even in times of sickness, Mama has never been a woman given to physical affection. Sophy is introduced abruptly to the limp apron and the long, flattish bosoms behind it, the sharp hipbones and hammock of loose flesh slung between. Her layers of white gauze are crushed against Mama's faded calico. She is breathless, her ears ringing, so can't be sure if Mama actually says "My lamb," or if that tenderness comes back to her with the words that followed on the night of Papa's accident: *I am here to bear it with you.* At this merciless proximity, Sophy absorbs directly what Mama means by "all the rest of it." The bloody labor of childbirth, Eve's curse leveled again and again. The babies stillborn or dead in the cradle. The endless toil of serving others, with little thanks and never a thought for yourself. The special burden of the clerical wife, held to a higher standard, forever falling short. Mama wants her to know that this is what is in store once the door of delight is opened.

Mama lets her go. She straightens Sophy's dress with curt tugs to the shoulders and waist, and fluffs out the skirt. She licks her hand and slicks Sophy's hair back in place.

"Some find that a pillow under the hips eases the way," she says.

CHAPTER 17

POSSESSED

*J*AMES LEFT FOR BOSTON ON APRIL 30, A DAY OF SOFT BEAUTY, the sky a new blue and a green haze frothing the trees. His intention was to spend the night with Reuben and visit Caroline at her cousin's house the next day. He had written ahead to both, but only Caroline had replied, in a style more elegant than the one she had departed with. He managed to divine, amid expressions of artful inconsequence about the weather, the state of the Boston pavements, and her health, that Caroline would be happy to receive him, that she regretted it had been so long since they had talked. This was more communication than he'd had for weeks. James was taciturn about his expectations, but he had elected to travel with the wagon—to bring Reuben back for Sophy's wedding, he said, owning to no further hopes about his own. Still, it was obvious to the Hedges and Gideon, gathered in the front yard to see him off, how much the prospect of seeing Caroline again lifted his spirits.

On a day as lovely as this, optimism was less an attitude than an instinct. The Reverend had managed the journey from his bedroom to the front stoop on crutches, with Gideon and Sophy supporting him on either side. It was the longest distance he had walked since his accident, and the first time he'd been outdoors. The sights and smells of spring

seemed to awaken the sensualist he'd buried long ago. He raised his face
to the sun, shut his eyes, and inhaled the sweet air.

"A man wants to spread his wings on such a day," he said.

Gideon's skin prickled; he was aware that the parson's youthful self
was speaking. The horse seemed to sense the phantom presence, as animals will. The muscles of its back rippled in a delicate shudder, and it
began to trot before James could shake the reins.

MRS. HEDGE SENT Sophy and Gideon out to the field to look for fiddleheads. Both of them knew that she was trying to spare them the
instruction they were due and give them some time alone. "The Reverend needs to rest, whether he knows it or not," she said. "And the
ferns won't wait. Get them in their first youth or they'll be too tough
to cook."

Gideon was beginning to feel more like a man about to be married.
As the two of them walked side by side along the road, each holding a
handle of the basket, a farmer hailed them from a passing wagon and his
wife waved her kerchief in their direction. The world was smiling on
them for no other reason than that they were young and in love. Gideon
took off his hat with a flourish and waved back.

Sophy dropped her end of the basket, snatched the hat from his
fingers while he was still waving, and ran, veering away whenever he
reached to reclaim it. It was like trying to catch a bubble, she was always
floating out of his grasp. Her hair was coming undone, and she was
laughing, holding his sober hat above her head to tease him. The farmer
brought his horse to a halt so he and his wife could watch. A woman
with a bundle of laundry on her back shouted encouragement.

"Enough, Sophy! We're making a spectacle!" Gideon was vexed to
be made a fool of, ashamed to be short of breath. He had been spending
too much time at his desk.

"I don't care. I hate this hat. I'm going to let the wind have it."

But something she saw in his face stopped her running and made
her come to him. Her loose hair and rosy cheeks, the dwindling light in

her eyes, reminded him of the day in the sickroom when he had commanded her.

"It's only that I like to see your hair," she said. And then, "I thought
we were playing."

Her voice was so meek that the will to master stirred in him, as it
had when he was too weak to move. He wasn't weak anymore. He could
knock the hat from her hand, grab her wrist and pull her to the ground,
mock-punish her with rough kisses. Or he could do as he'd done before:
speak, and she would obey. Gideon tasted the taming words on his
tongue, liquorish and harsh. He swallowed them.

He took the hat from her and clapped it on his head, knowing that
it sat too low on his brow, like a bumpkin's. Let him be ridiculous, he
deserved it.

"I'm no good at playing," he said, still breathless. "Not much experience. Perhaps you will teach me."

Sophy knelt to pick up the basket, and stood with it under her arm.
"I never knew what play was until recently. My brothers thought it was
amusing to torment me. Mama would find me tied to a tree or blind-
folded in the pasture, long after they'd forgotten me. I was nearly grown
up before I learned."

"Who taught you?"

They were in the field before she answered. Gideon had the odd sensation of walking in the dream he'd had months before. The setting was
the same, a few early flowers showing their heads, the grasses still swaying, new green interspersed with brown stalks from the winter. But in
his dream his progress had been hindered, and now it was effortless. No
tough vines tripped him; the vegetation was so frail that he could easily
tramp it down. The expanse that had churned like a raging sea could be
crossed in five minutes at a leisurely stride, and the girl who had waved
at him from the opposite shore was by his side. When Sophy stopped
suddenly and turned to face him, he realized they were standing on the
same spot where she had danced a year ago. He felt wonder, akin to awe.
If a voice were to address them from above, or issue from a clump of
dead milkweed, he would not be surprised.

"Do you ever think about your father?" Sophy asked.

It was the last question Gideon was expecting. Its irrelevance punctured the sublimity of the moment. "Not often," he said. "He had no part in raising me. Do you think of yours?"

"I don't really believe in a father. If I had one, he's not to be spoken of." Sophy looked down with sudden concentration, as if fiddleheads had sprouted at her feet. "You asked who taught me to play. It was—is—my mother. My real one. She has been a presence in my life for a while now."

"Are you saying I'm about to enter into Holy Wedlock with a haunted woman? What do you think she does for you?"

"Urges me on. Dares me. She's far more adventuresome than I am. I don't see her, but I know when she is there. That day you first watched me . . . I was dancing because of her." Sophy hesitated, cautious. Until now the dance had been a silent compact between them. "If you haven't been visited, I don't expect you to understand."

"There isn't enough of my father to make a decent ghost," Gideon said. "My mother told me he went down in a ship before I was born, and when I was little, I used to imagine 'Lost at Sea' cut into a stone in a churchyard, all stark and solemn, and me standing before the grave with my head bowed. I suppose that was the closest I ever came to missing him. Fathers were for other boys. I went my own way, from the beginning." He considered telling her what his mother had said about his being hatched from an egg, but thought better of it.

"He is in you, whether you pay attention to him or not."

And so must yours be, whether you *believe* in him or not, Gideon thought. Sophy was meeting his eyes now, her chin lifted. That stubbornness again, rearing up when she appeared most humble. When they were married, he would have to learn how to temper it.

"I have better things to do than listen to a dead man," he said, "and so do you. We're young, Sophy! God willing, we have years ahead of us. We should be preparing for the children we'll have, the parents we'll be—not wasting our precious hours fraternizing with the departed."

Gideon realized with a chill that the words he had just spoken were not his: the pedantic, hectoring tone, the sanctimonious sentiments, belonged to Hedge. Perhaps he was the one being haunted. How often had he lamented the Reverend's hold on him? Possession by the living was far more terrifying than the shriveled mischief of the dead.

He smiled to leaven his sharpness. "If my spectral mother-in-law chooses to make my acquaintance, I'll treat her with every courtesy, but frankly, Sophy, I'd prefer she keep to herself. I have enough trouble with your living relatives!"

Gideon raised his eyes heavenward and pulled his hat down even lower, so the brim nearly touched his nose. He was gratified to see Sophy break into a grin. He had done well in his first attempt at marital diplomacy; he was growing into the role of husband even before he occupied it.

He put one arm around her waist, took her hand and held it up. "My mother gave me a dance lesson once. I was ten or eleven, she wanted me to have the social graces. But she was displeased with me for riding on her shoes and never offered again. Will you give me another chance, Sophy? The fiddleheads will accompany us."

Gideon whirled her in a wide circle, then another, heady with delight that she was following him. She was so light in his arms that her feet left the ground when he spun her. Her hair had fallen to her waist and whipped like a banner. Each time the road hove into view, he saw that they were observed, first one, then several passersby pausing in their daily business to gawk. The two of them were making a spectacle, and he did not care.

CHAPTER 18

PRACTICE

"WHO EVER HEARD OF REHEARSING A WEDDING? PAGANS may marry as often as they like, but good Christians are joined only once, and for most of us, that is enough. Cite me chapter and verse if I am wrong, Mr. Hedge."

The parson had introduced the subject in an understated manner, but was having a hard time convincing his wife, who had stationed herself in front of the kitchen fireplace with her arms folded across her chest, a fortress of refusal.

"My dear, I'm speaking of the choreography, not the vows. If this were a wedding alone, or even an ordination, no preparation would be needed. But the congruence of events, the number of people involved . . ." Hedge flapped his hands helplessly. He looked to Gideon and Sophy with pleading in his eyes.

Gideon considered whether he had witnessed the crumbling of yet another brick in the parson's foundation. Until this moment, Hedge had never been known to leave a sentence unfinished. His character, his profession, the whole bent of his being, was declarative.

"We could do with some practice ourselves," he said. "It will give us courage, won't it, Sophy?"

"And how do you intend to get the Reverend to the church with the horse and wagon gone?" Mrs. Hedge asked. "A wheelbarrow? Now that would be an inspiriting sight. The pastor carted to meetinghouse like a load of dung. There are those in the parish who would grieve to see the shepherd of their souls brought so low—and a few I could name who'd rejoice. If I didn't know you for a man of sound mind, Mr. Hedge, I'd conclude you had taken leave of your senses." She pronounced the last with weary finality, as if she had arrived at her destination after a long and trying journey.

Hedge met her gaze. "Lost my mind, have I? You should not be surprised, Fanny. I've endured many losses since the Lord chose to make me a cripple. To be ministered to when I am used to ministering. To be restricted to the compass of my bed when my influence once was felt throughout the county. To calculate my every motion and pay the price in pain. My life has become a continual warfare with my natural feelings. Each day I am forced to commit pious violence upon my pride just to get by. Do you understand, woman? Pious violence!"

Each successive phrase had been spoken with a tighter tension, a slightly escalated volume. All three of the listeners were familiar with the technique from the parson's sermons. As one, they braced themselves for the cannonade to come. But Hedge's voice dropped.

"If I have any dignity left," he said, barely audible, "a ride in a wheelbarrow would not diminish it."

IN THE END, Micah was able to borrow a cart and an old workhorse from a neighbor. He and Gideon hoisted the Reverend up the step and into his seat, where Sophy waited with his crutches. Mrs. Hedge insisted that they wrap blankets around his back and legs to cushion him. The wedding was a week away, and they were all on edge. Although the horse's plodding step came near to disguising the fact, they were going forward.

Hedge started to chatter as soon as they were underway. "In ordinary circumstances, I would never keep anything from my dear wife, but I thought it prudent not to mention the surprise awaiting us at church. She will know eventually, of course, but why burden her, when the world rests on her shoulders? Her pleasure will only be increased if we are discreet now."

"You can't mean that James is back, Papa," Sophy said. "Mama had better know that right away."

"Do you think I would withhold such news? Don't be foolish."

Gideon was sorry to see Sophy cringe, but he had to admit that Hedge's rebuke was justified. James had been due to return two days before, yet not so much as a word had come from him or Reuben. Mrs. Hedge was convinced that some dreadful fate had overtaken him in the city. "He's too trusting, that one," she kept saying. "He never was hard like his brother. What if he's thrown himself in the river for the sake of that prinking thing?" The parson insisted that James was only pleading his case with the young lady, but his calm had begun to fray as the great day approached. James had been assigned the plum role of escorting Sophy down the aisle.

Within sight of the church, the horse perked up its ears. Music was in the air, faint but distinct, riding lightly on the wind that carried it. It charmed them like panpipes, drawing them on, growing fuller and sweeter as they approached. No one spoke until they arrived at the meetinghouse door.

"It can't be," Sophy said, though there was no doubt that the melody was issuing from the same white-shingled building where she had spent most Sundays of her life.

"Handel," said Reverend Hedge, as if the selection of music, and not the astonishing fact of it, required explanation. Since the church's founding, a small choir had supplied the only music other than hymns ever heard within its walls, singing psalms a capella with a tuneless rigor that did not offend the plainness of their faith. Instruments of any kind were considered to be the devil's distractions. Let the High Church have its booming organs, the Catholics their voluptuous Masses. First

Congregational would make do with the human voice harmonizing the Word—well or badly, it hardly mattered. The Reverend had subscribed to this view himself.

Now he feigned surprise at their amazement. "What is a procession without music? I think you'll agree that our valiant little choir is not equal to the task. I didn't know where to turn, but the Lord provided."

As Gideon and Micah helped him from the cart, he told them the story. One of the retired masters at seminary had a nephew staying with him, a gifted violoncellist, trained abroad, but reduced to giving lessons for a pittance until a suitable position turned up. The young man was eager—hungry even—to play the music he loved for an audience.

"Had he been a violinist, I would have had to refuse him," Hedge said. "A fiddle wouldn't do in church, you know. But a cello is majestic. It is deep. It inspires awe in the listener."

"That's fine for us, Papa, but what about the others? They aren't used to change." Sophy slipped the crutches under his armpits, and Micah and Gideon slowly stepped away.

The parson's face contorted as his weight settled on the sticks, and he let out a breath through his lips. For a minute or two he stood in place, neither speaking nor moving, his eyes fixed in concentration. Gideon had observed this before. It was as if the pain were spreading through-out his body like mercury spilled from a vial, dispersing so he could bear it more equally. "All the more reason to jolt them out of their complacency!" he said at last, putting the force of his effort into the words.

Sophy opened the doors and the music swelled, rich and luscious. Hedge planted his crutches and swung toward it. Gideon and Micah fell in behind him, following so closely that Sophy had the impression they were levitating her father up the steps by will.

The source of the glory was not immediately apparent. It took them a moment to find the young man seated in the back balcony, all but obscured by the formidable instrument he was playing. The fellow looked more like a bank clerk than a musician, Gideon thought; yet his rapt intimacy with the cello could not be denied. He raised his bow when he saw them, but Hedge indicated with a grand gesture that he should continue.

The Reverend took a paper from his vest pocket. "The order of service," he explained. "We will have to imagine the others—I could not ask them to come twice—but we can form a little mock procession ourselves. When the day comes, we can direct our visitors with more confidence." He gazed at each of them in turn with stern fondness: the commander reviewing his loyal troops. "You know, children," he said, "I thought I would need your assistance, but I feel so strong this morning that I might attempt the aisle myself. If one of you would get that chair? My spirit will not flag, but my body might. Mr. Birdsall, you will come after me—solitary today, sir, but soon to be girded by virtue before and behind. Micah, you will take James's part and escort your sister—slowly, please, and don't forget to give her your arm. Be serious, both of you. Remember, a week from now you will be taking this walk in earnest."

The cellist, observing the scene from above, began to play Bach as Hedge started down the aisle. Of the three who waited, only Gideon knew enough about the music to identify it, but Micah and Sophy were no less lifted by its solemn joy. They stood together, constrained by a common tact from offering help as the Reverend made his laborious progress from one end of the church to the other, stopping after every few steps to gather his powers. The closer he got to the altar, the lower he slumped over his crutches, until, from the vantage point of the watchers, he resembled a suit of black clothes draped over an airing rack. Within feet of his goal he stumbled, and they started forward, but before they could go to him he righted himself. When at last he reached the chair, he stood with his back to them for long seconds before swiveling on his sticks and venturing a descent—bone by bone, it appeared—to the seat cushion. Hedge's face as he looked out over the church was slack with fatigue, but peaceful—the emotion of a man who has taken a long route home. Lacking the breath to speak, he pointed a crutch at Gideon and nodded.

"The gallows march," Gideon had described it to Sophy earlier, hoping to make her smile but also to quell his own dread. The source of his terror was not the union with Sophy but the falseness and final-ity of Hedge's whole arrangement. He did his best, now, to walk with measured step, neither so slow as to look foolish, nor so fast as to appear disrespectful. This was not easy to accomplish alone, though the music helped. He wished he could feel the way the Bach sounded: stately and profound, summoned to a sacred calling. But the sight of the parson awaiting him with a bland smile confirmed that he was advancing toward a future that another man had ordained for him. How had he allowed himself to be maneuvered so? A gibbet would at least signify an end. He was looking at the rest of his life.

At the end of the aisle Gideon stood before the throne, consciously holding his shoulders back and his head erect, as Hedge waved him to his right. The Reverend nodded again, and Micah and Sophy began to walk. Gideon's heart twisted as he watched them. They were like a couple of children, shuffling awkwardly as they strove to match their unequal strides and keep in step. Micah had folded Sophy's arm into his own and placed his big hand over her small one, as if to protect her for as long as he could. She leaned into his side, looking alternately down at her feet and ahead to her fiancé. Gideon thought he might be tempted to violence if Hedge dared to offer improving remarks, but out of the corner of his eye he could see that the Reverend was as moved as he was. Hedge beckoned the two to come closer. He leaned forward. "I promised your mother that no vows would be spoken today," he said, "but I don't think she would object if I gave you a blessing." He placed a hand on their bowed heads and spoke the benediction of Aaron, invoking the Lord's face to shine upon them and lifting up his own countenance in the Deity's stead. Then Micah stepped to the side, and Gideon took his place beside Sophy before the altar.

It was not real—not yet—but his chest was so tight that he struggled to breathe. The music had stopped in mid-phrase, and the silence gaped like physical space: an emptiness in which the two of them were marooned. He took Sophy's hands in his and stared intently into her face, repeating to himself: the pearl of great price, the pearl of great price . . .

The Reverend gripped his crutches. He pulled himself to a standing position in a single heroic contraction of muscles—the first time he had accomplished the feat on his own. "I have prepared a brief homily," he told them. His voice was thin, all his power spent on the struggle. "Pray God my memory is as durable as my legs."

He cleared his throat. "Dearly beloved friends, we are gathered here today at the peak of this burgeoning season, when nature exults all around us and abundance is bestowed without our asking, to celebrate two joyous events: the formal calling to the Lord's service of my student and amanuensis, Gideon Birdsall, and his joining in marriage with my beloved only daughter, Sophia. Little did I imagine when first I set eyes on Mr. Birdsall, a green shoot (if you will permit me to indulge the botanical metaphor), untutored in the world's ways, yet endowed with a seasoned scholar's gifts, that he would become an essential part of my work and a member of my household. Strange and wonderful are the workings of the Lord! But before I expound further on our braided history, I would ask you to consider what we mean when we speak of *celebration*. The Latin root describes 'a place much frequented,' even as our festive sanctuary is today. Look around you, my friends, and see—"

The doors swung open, disgorging not the multitudes they might have expected but Cephas Mills at full steam, followed by an ashen James.

"A wedding!" Mills exclaimed. "Well, well, well, nuptials are in the air these days. There's no getting away from 'em, Pastor." He spoke with an effusive pleasantness that might have been taken for good humor if he hadn't been shaking with rage. He was fair and short like Caroline, sanguine of complexion, his slight frame long given over to the fat she was fending off—dollops of it, seeming to vibrate with the emotion he strove to contain. The only firmness in him was his stance. His feet were planted a half-yard's width apart in the center of the aisle, his hands were on his hips, his chins were lifted to the pulpit at an angle so aggressive that his eyes retreated behind his cheeks. He was dressed like a gentleman, but looked, Gideon thought, like an Irish pugilist made daring by drink.

"Not a wedding, Cephas," Hedge protested meekly. All of them were struck by the fact that he had called Mills by his Christian name. "A practice only. We have a week to go before the happy occasion."

"Is that the new fashion then? To do a bit of drill before taking the big step? My girl's a great one for keeping up with fashion. It's a pity she wasn't informed before running off with your worthless, scheming speculator of a son. If they had only thought to *practice* first, we could have stepped in and talked some sense to her, snatched her out of ruination's way. But they've gone and made it official, Pastor, and there's not a damned thing I can do to make it right. Not that I won't try—I'm off to my lawyer when I leave here. A man with but one daughter does what he can." Something seemed to break in him then, a crack in the armor of his bluster. He swiped at his face with one fist.

Hedge looked at James, and James looked back at him. The line of sight between them was so clear and straight that Cephas Mills seemed no more than an aberration.

"Don't take it out on this one, Pastor," Mills said. "He's a decent enough fellow. He came to me direct from Boston and told me what he'd found out, and you can see for yourself what a state he is in. I do believe he loves my daughter truly, and that's to his credit. I never was in favor of the match, though. I told Caroline she could do better. 'If you want to see your life in ten years, look at the father,' I said. 'Pieties dropping from his mouth while his poor wife does all the work. It's no wonder half his congregation's gone over to the Baptists. And who's to know what's lurking under all the high and holy talk? One son a gambler, another can't get a word out, the hope and heir packed off to godforsaken Lowell in disgrace. 'Blood will tell,' I told her. 'The apple don't fall too far from the tree!'"

The Reverend had received this outpouring with stoic impassivity. Now that Mills had ceased fulminating, it appeared that he would speak. Hedge inclined toward the intruder as far as he was able, and gazed at him with the same mildness he'd shown earlier. Indeed, it struck Gideon that his glance was broad and generous, embracing Cephas Mills's trouble along with his own, and reaching beyond them both to the woes men are born to. He sighed and sank down into the chair, descending with a loose-limbed grace that seemed purposeful, his crutches falling inward as he let them go.

CHAPTER 19

WEDLOCK

THE REVEREND HAD HIS FESTIVAL OF CONVERGING EVENTS after all, Gideon reflected afterward, though not precisely as he had planned. Hedge was present only for the first of the milestones, laid out in his best black vestments on a table in the parlor. Micah worked through the night to build him a coffin of oak for his last habitation, sturdy enough to withstand the elements for many years, whatever one's view of mortal remains. He seemed comfortable in his new home, his features composed in the expression of spacious understanding that he had worn when he died. There was some discussion about whether he should be buried with his hat, or even with the crutches that had aided in his ascent to meet his Maker. Micah was the chief advocate for the crutches, and threw an uncharacteristic fit when the doctor suggested they be given to a patient of his who was crippled from rheumatism. "I m-m-made 'em for Pa," he said, clutching the sticks to his chest, "and n-n-no one else will have 'em." In the end, neither of these artifacts of worldly life accompanied the parson to his grave. His elegant fingers were folded over his Bible, with a spray of violets that Sophy had entwined to remind him of their walks in the woods.

On the day of the funeral, so many came to pay their last respects that not enough chairs could be found. Neighbors and friends, townsfolk, parishioners (including some who had left the church), seminary colleagues and fellow ministers filled the parlor to the walls and spilled into the hall. The doleful Satterfield was wedged into a corner, exuding consummated gloom like the Angel of Death, but restrained by lack of space from flapping his wings. Gideon read the Twenty-Third Psalm in Hebrew. He had thought he would be a pallbearer, along with Sam and James and Micah, but it was decided, without being overtly stated, that the absence of the fourth Hedge son would be too glaring. The Reverend was carried from his front stoop through a meadow spangled with wildflowers by a delegation of those same dignitaries who would have paraded down the aisle to celebrate his return to his pulpit.

At the churchyard, Reuben and his new bride stood apart from the mourners. Fanny refused to let them in the house. The doctor might claim that Hedge's exertions had overtaxed his heart, but the woman who knew him best had no doubt that he had died of shame. Reuben looked the same to Gideon: a dark, sardonic figure, self-possessed. Even on this occasion, he observed the gathering from a cool distance, a corner of his mouth lifted in a smirk. He kept a firm hand on his wife's elbow—a restrictive measure, perhaps, because Caroline was weeping soundlessly, great, gulping sobs that racked her like a consumptive's coughs. Gideon pitied her. He couldn't help it. She was a fatuous deceiver who had betrayed a decent man for a bad one, but he was certain that until this moment she had never counted the cost of her actions. In a sense, he thought, she knew not what she did. It wasn't innocence, exactly, but a flaw of nature. She was drowning in her own shallows.

GIDEON AND SOPHY were married three days later, on the Saturday following the funeral. A number of women in the congregation called it disrespectful, a mockery of decent mourning, and speculated about the reasons for such unholy haste. Mrs. Hedge was adamant. The Reverend had favored the match, she said; he would have wanted them to bring joy out of sorrow. And there were practical matters to be considered. Sam had to get back to his family in Lowell, and Parson Phelps, who had officiated at the Reverend's services, would need to return to Andover.

Gideon wondered privately if Fanny thought he was not sufficiently snared—that he would flee if too much time elapsed, now that the Reverend's talons of righteousness were permanently withdrawn. In her grief Sophy leaned on him, often literally: in the midst of muted frenzy as the household prepared for the funeral, she would stop and rest her head against his chest, and he would hold her. He felt at these moments that his mission in life was to be strong for her. Still, he was aware, with the reverberating awe of a man sprung from the noose, that he'd been liberated—released from his obligation to live out the role that the parson had written for him. His future was his own again, though he wasn't sure what to do with it. He had not expected that the freedom he'd longed for would leave him floundering and disoriented; in some primal way, exposed. It was as if the ceiling overhanging the earth—the firmament of Genesis—had been lifted by divine fiat, leaving only a gaping void. He hardly dared ask himself whether this was what it meant to lose a father.

The wedding resided in all their minds as the final act of the funeral: a denouement, or worse, an afterthought. They assembled in the parlor where the Reverend had so recently made his last appearance. Flowers from the funeral shed petals on the mantel and side tables. The room was empty except for the family and the minister, a meek man, resolute only in his effacement of personality. Sophy's wedding dress had been folded with care and put away in a chest—"for you might have a daughter," Mama said. The black they wore set their paleness in relief, and accented their weariness and strain. James had sunk so far into himself that he was barely present at all. He stood at his mother's left and Micah on her right: pillars of support, though a stranger intruding at that moment might conclude that Fanny was holding both of them up. Sam, off to the side, kept glancing out the window, perhaps anticipating his return to the comforts of his own unswept hearth. Gideon and Sophy had the same thought, though neither ever shared it with the other: that the wedding party looked like a clutch of bedraggled crows after a thunderstorm. The vows were read, the responses given, and it was done.

CHAPTER 20

ONE

*N*OT THE FIRST NIGHT. NOT THE FIRST WEEK, NOR THE second. The house is too quiet and they are too tired. He puts his arms around her, and she nestles into him, and they sleep. Over a month has passed—long enough to stamp a pattern. She thinks they could go on this way for years, which would be tolerable if only they didn't wake as strangers each morning, setting their feet down on opposite sides of the bed and turning away from each other as they dressed. Papa said there was no such place as Limbo, but she and Gideon seem to be residing there now. Married, yet not.

Living at home doesn't help. She wonders how it would be between them if they had done as he wanted and moved to another house or town, instead of another room. The boarder's bedroom is not a congenial place for love. It was furnished to meet the passing needs of guests, and Mama hasn't had time or heart to transform it into a nuptial chamber. The mattress sinks in the middle; the boys used to joke that it discouraged long stays. Sophy can't forget the strangers who have slept here: seminary students and visiting clergy, hard-luck parishioners, harvest help, the listless queue of schoolteachers. And who knows what snatched glances Mr. Unsworth hoarded beneath the covers, what humid thoughts he brought to bear upon the linen? It isn't to be dwelled on.

Gideon was sick in this room. She had no qualms then about lifting his nightshirt to bathe him, but would never be so bold now, though she has a right.

It is hard to put aside their single selves when the rest of the family treats them as though nothing has changed. The household is struggling to right itself after Papa's death, and they must do their part. James and Micah have taken on the heaviest burden, laboring in the barn and fields for much of the day; her little brother grows older by the minute, his shoulders already bowed. Gideon helps where he can—where they let him—but the boys tire of explaining tasks that are as elemental to them as eating. He isn't used to farmwork, or suited to it. While the parish debates his candidacy, he wanders about like a lost soul, seeking a place to attach himself.

Sophy feels a bit like a lost soul herself. Now that Papa is gone, Mama has deserted the house for the garden, which has become her occupation and solace. Sunup to sundown, in all but the worst weather, she is outside with her spade and hoe. She works her grief into the soil, talks to the ground as she won't talk to them. Some days she won't come in at noon, and Sophy brings her dinner in a basket, as if she were a farmhand. The domestic tasks that once filled Mama's days have fallen to her, who has no natural gift for them. Sorrow hasn't dulled Mama's sharp tongue. The eggs are too hard, the bread is too soft, the meat too tough. Even the boys are kinder.

Mama has shared one secret with her. Reuben sends money, gleaned from Papa's properties in the city—or so he tells them. James mustn't know. He would call it blood money and forbid them to spend it; he would fall into one of his black moods and disappear for days. Micah followed him and found out where he goes. The half-built house.

Once Gideon is ordained, he will take Papa's place in the pulpit and draw his yearly stipend. This is the expectation, the only obstacle being Deacon Mendham and two of the elders, curmudgeons who bewail Gideon's youth and inexperience and extol the virtues of the two venerable preachers who spelled for Papa while he was laid up. No one in the family thinks to ask whether Gideon wants to assume the mantle. Mama takes comfort in the thought that her son-in-law will carry on her husband's work. "It was always what he intended," she assured Gideon one night, having swept Mendham and his obsequies out the door, "though who could know you'd be called so soon?" She lifted her chin. "The gall of that Judas, asking after my health with thievery in his heart. If he tries to rob me of my widow's mite to line the pocket of that milk-face Phelps, he'll have the Reverend's anointed to contend with."

Sophy alone sees what a pall the prospect casts over Gideon. He avoids speaking of it, even to her. "I must get back to the study," he tells her. "Make some order while I can. What would the Reverend think of me if I abandoned the Lexicon?"

She knows too well what will happen. The work will draw him in, and soon he'll be lost to her, a citizen of that country he longs to return to. In the early days, when she was fresh to him, he'd invited her to come along. Now she has what she could only covet then: the two of them joined in the sight of God and man. But if the marriage doesn't take, how can she be sure the link between them will hold? A rope not tightly twined can easily be pulled apart.

ON SUNDAY, GIDEON STAYS late after meeting, at the elders' request. At table with the others, Sophy can't eat the dinner she has overcooked. The beef is tough and gristly and won't go down; the morsel she swallows sticks in her throat. She puts a napkin to her mouth and runs to the kitchen. The gray day, the dry sermon, the dregs of grief mixed with disappointment, the bleak life ahead—the mass of it coiled in a lump in the center of her chest. She heaves over a bucket, her insides clenching, and for all this effort brings up nothing but a few tears. *Sick at heart*, ladies say, fluttering their fingers over their bosoms. A flowery malaise, it sounds like, until it afflicts you.

Mama rushes in. "I knew that beef wasn't fit to eat." She grasps

Sophy's shoulder with one hand and thumps her back vigorously with the other. "Out with it, you'll feel like a new person when it's gone."

"I just need to lie down," Sophy says, pulling away. The nausea is ebbing, but her legs are shaky under her.

"Look at you—pale as a ghost and twice as wobbly." Mama claps a hand to Sophy's forehead. "No fever as yet, though one may be rising. Get to bed now, and I'll bring you a nice cup of chamomile to settle your stomach."

The tea is sweet, the hay-and-meadow taste brightened with a little honey. Sophy takes small sips, leaning back on pillows Mama plumped, tucked to her chin in the quilt Mama made. The best comfort is Mama herself, planted on the edge of the bed, blowing gusts into her cup to cool it. Sophy can't remember the last time they sat together, sharing a quiet moment. Even in the old days, Mama was never one to linger— when did she have time, forever called away to another task, another crisis?—yet, somehow, she was always there when needed. Sophy feels a twinge of guilt for favoring her own flighty mother over this solid, dependable presence. When Mama sets her cup down, she says, "Stay with me awhile. Please."

"Lonely, are you? I wouldn't be surprised if that's what ails you. I've been neglectful, moping in the garden all day and leaving you to cope with the house, and never a kind word when I come in." She picks at a loose thread in the quilt. "I believe I was jealous, Sophy, for you had your new husband to keep you company, and I'd lost mine. The Reverend used to say that some women make a banquet of their grief and choose to dine alone. I ask your pardon, daughter. I should be thinking more of others' sorrow and less of my own."

"There's nothing to forgive." Sophy's eyes fill again, the tears spilling over. Mama never calls her "daughter" to her face; the ownership goes to her heart. "It's nothing to do with you, or with missing Papa."

"Not due for your monthly, are you?" A new thought pricks. "Can you be . . . ? There's no shame in the condition, however soon it comes. I can testify, nature is no respecter of brides. With Sam, it was a matter of weeks. I'd scarcely put the last stitch in my wedding dress when I was cutting squares for nappies——"

Sophy swings her head from side to side like a child learning no, reduced to pantomime because she can't find words that Mama will understand. Mama with her faith in nature, her belief that all men are alike in their throes.

"The opposite," is all she can muster.

There is a silence as Mama holds this fragment to the light, squinting. She nods dolorously. "And what else can be expected? Rushed into marriage. Starting life in a house of mourning. Oh, Samuel, I have much to answer for, I don't deny it. But how was I to occupy my right mind when you left so sudden?"

Sophy follows Mama's gaze across the room, where, for all she knows, Papa's shade may be casting his woeful pulpit gaze over them both.

With a corner of her apron, Mama dabs at Sophy's streaked cheeks. "Enough of this. What's done can't be undone, and we'll have to make the best of it. Now, throw off those covers and wash your face and run a comb through that bird's nest before your husband comes home. It's early days, still. A little time alone might be all that's needed."

AN EXCURSION IS PLANNED——the first since Papa died. Mama and the boys are going to the village to do a few errands and call on old friends who have been kind. Gideon is quick to claim those hours for the study. He doubts he'll have time to do more than blow the dust off the pages and sweep the floor, but it's a beginning.

"I don't know why you won't go with them, Sophy," he says. "You need to look at something beside these four walls. Put some roses in your cheeks." He touches her face tenderly, his eyes already distant.

Sophy wakes early on Wednesday and plunges into her chores. By the time she waves her family off in midmorning, she has made them breakfast, packed food for their lunch, cleaned and swept, weeded the herb garden, punched the bread dough down once and covered it for its final rising. At the door she whispers to Mama, "Say a prayer for us."

The glint of mischief in Mama's eye is unsettling. "Now, Sophy," she says, "don't trouble the Lord when you can do the job yourself."

As soon as they're out of sight, Sophy rinses her face and hands at the pump, and walks quickly toward the study. The sun is hot today, summer setting in early. She cherishes these few precious weeks when outdoors is more sheltering than the house, the biting New England air turned mild, cradling the skin. Today she can't linger to bask in it. Gideon promised Mama he'd do some weeding in the vegetable garden. If he leaves early and gets to the study before she does, the opportunity will be lost.

A moment of painful suspense as she opens the door: the wood has swollen and she has to lean into it while working the knob. The room is vacant, but not empty, steeped in stillness. She has always found churches most holy when unoccupied, eternity thick in the air, and she has that feeling in this temple of thought. If Papa is anywhere, he ought to be here, but she doesn't sense his presence—not even in the widened way that people call the spirit. One of his tomes is lying open on the desk at the place Gideon left it on the night of the accident, a magnifying glass resting atop a word he was exploring. Papa was in the world when that glass was laid down. Where is he now?

It occurs to her for the first time that Papa and her mother may be reunited in Heaven, brother and sister looking down upon her as she does what she is about to do. She thinks it unlikely they'd be of one mind about it. Her mother would surely approve, even goad her on, but she has been quiet lately. A glance ceilingward reveals no cautionary words from the Reverend inscribed on the whitewash. Still, Sophy's fingers fumble with her bonnet strings, and she moves nearer to the bulk of the woodstove.

She is dressed for a day of work, so, with no stays to unlace, it goes quickly. Shoes and stockings first. Her everyday cotton dress has few buttons; the stains on the bodice need not trouble her under the circumstances. She unties a single petticoat, limp from long use. Pulls the shift over her head, peels off her stockings. Her hair is the conundrum. Should she take it down, or leave it knotted and wait for him to command her again? She has imagined this scene over and over, trying one style, then the other, working herself into a state of shameful excitement, for, either way, Gideon's response is dependably fervent. Now that she is acting out her plan, she isn't so sure of her attractions, or of him.

She reaches up to remove the pins in her hair. The cape it makes over her shoulders and breasts is a shelter of sorts. She feels shy at first— *naked*—but after a minute or two, natural to the point of pugnacity. She believes she could happily walk through the meadow and across the road wearing nothing but her ring, if only it wouldn't cause a scandal. God sees us? Let Him. He made us! Clothes are the scandal—the care they take, the fuss some folks make about them. If Gideon's Garden dispenses with cumbersome wrappings, she will go there without a second thought.

But when she hears him on the path, she shrinks into the murk behind the stove. He contends with the door, just as she did. The flood of light is briefly shocking—her arms cross over her breasts with a will of their own—but he doesn't look in her direction. His eyes go straight to the desk, and before the door creaks shut he's shuffling papers, muttering to himself, one hand harrowing his hair in a gesture she knows well. Too much to do.

She pads to the center of the room, her bare feet stirring dust. He glances over his shoulder, not sure what he heard.

"Sophy! What is this?" A pause. He seems to absorb her in stages.

She thinks he might be angry, but she doesn't look down and he doesn't look away. His eyes narrow, and it's as though someone else is studying her, a stranger she's glimpsed before, bent on taking by force what she freely offers. She walks to him slowly, keeping him at bay with steady, patient confrontation. She touches his shoulder to remind him who he is. Runs her fingers lightly down his body, tugs his shirt free of his trousers and lifts the hem to pull it over his head. The whiteness of his chest startles her. He is always pale compared to other men, but she sees now how brown his face and arms have turned, how hard the world has used him while this middle part, the heart of him, remains untouched. He raises his arms, docile as a child.

Naked, they are equals. It doesn't matter that he is more beautiful than she. In every picture she's seen of the Temptation, Adam is the handsome one, Eve mannish and muscled with rigid tresses flowing over stony breasts. Yet, there they stand on either side of the Tree, knowledge to be acquired between them. Sophy takes Gideon's hand and leads him to the rug.

PART THREE

EARTH AND AIR

CHAPTER 21

EXILE

THE SERMON FOR THE FIRST SUNDAY IN THE NEW YEAR WAS
traditionally devoted to Job. The late parson never confided his reasons,
but Gideon suspected that Hedge had meant to divert his parishioners
from whatever small measure of frivolity they'd managed to wring from
the festive season to the long, punishing winter ahead. In surrender to
this convention, Gideon sat shivering in the study on a bitter evening
in late December, hunched over the Reverend's desk with a shawl over
his shoulders, pondering the roots of endurance at an hour when he
should have been in bed. A fallen word, if there ever was one, and it
was fitting—all too bleakly suitable—that hardening was at the core of
it. Hardening of the heart, the will, the back and brain. He shaped the
syllables with his lips, feeling their effortful pull, the harnessed horse
dragging its load over cobblestones.

An hour ago he and Sophy had made love in front of the stove. She
often joined him here at the end of a long day, when he gathered what
was left of his energy to work on his sermon. It was the time they stole
for themselves. Tonight, tired as she was, she had played the coquette,
dancing around the room, tossing her hair and swishing her skirts, collapsing breathless in his lap. "Did you see how full the moon is?" she

said, nuzzling his ear. "I think it's bewitched me, I can't be still." If a less onerous subject than Job awaited him, he might have been irritated at the distraction, but he was all too willing to be seduced. He scooped her up and carried her to the rug.

"Last year we only talked of Paradise," Sophy whispered as they began, "and now we visit whenever we please. Isn't it a wonder?"

"If this were Paradise," he said sharply, "it wouldn't end."

Ashamed of himself—for being brusque with her, for succumbing in the first place—he fought too hard for his moment of rapture and proved his own words by finishing too soon. Then, compounding his sin, he'd turned his back as if the failure were hers. He knew her body well now. Too well, perhaps: he had explored its hidden niches with as much skill as he could muster, and still, the essence of Sophy eluded him. The girl who had danced in the field looked over her shoulder and darted, time after time, just out of his reach. When they made love, it was this wild, skittish creature he chased.

Even on the rare occasions when he caught her, it was never enough for him. She made her whinnying sound, and arched against him, and they locked together as one. For a single moment he wanted nothing else, knew nothing else, and then the fullness ebbed, and they came apart again. This seemed, each time, such a betrayal that he had to discipline himself to tolerate her head resting on his chest, her arm flung across him in that claiming way, the beatific look on her face as she gazed into his eyes—as though lovemaking had transported them to a higher plane, miles above the drudgery that filled their days. He didn't doubt that Sophy felt an ecstasy he only feigned. For him, the act was a tease. Why, once the peak was reached, was there only subsidence and the longing for more? Perhaps, in the Beginning, it had been different: the unity more absolute, man and woman, once joined, never falling back into their separate selves.

Now, Gideon thought, the only hope for completion was making a child. But, for all their efforts, Sophy showed no signs of pregnancy. To his eye she appeared thinner than ever, spare and boyish from her added workload. Fanny had begun to set special broths before her at dinnertime, leaves and twigs floating ominously on the surface. To build the girl up, she said.

Sophy would have stayed with him tonight, however badly he'd behaved. She often kept him company when he worked late, curling up in a chair like a drowsy cat when her eyes got too heavy for reading or mending, offering her presence and asking nothing in return. Most nights he liked her company—needed it. Quiet as she was, the sense of her, the barely audible sound of her breathing, buffered him from his own despair. He never felt more married than on these evenings, when they were together in the room they still thought of as home and she was simply there, reminding him that he was no longer alone.

On this night, even such primal comfort was an impediment. As gently as he could, he sent her back to the house, pleading the rigors of his day: he had visited Mrs. Jennings, who lost her boy to whooping cough; he needed to be alone.

"I'll call on the poor lady tomorrow and bring her some soup," Sophy promised, already practiced in the role of pastor's wife.

He stood on the stoop and watched as she picked her way along the path they'd stamped earlier in the snow, the lantern bobbing before her. The night was as clear and bright as it was cold, the stars like crystals of ice. Even without the lantern, he could have kept her in sight all the way to the door.

THE ROOM CLOSED AROUND HIM, enfolding him in its soothing dusk. It seemed to him that the inside of his mind must look like this—a haven he had once occupied readily, a space so fundamental to him that he had assumed it was a state of nature and taken its riches for granted. He rarely took refuge there now. The demands of a clergyman's life left little leisure for musing, less for meditation. A mere six months after his ordination, it was clear that he lacked Hedge's vigor and his affinity for the work. He labored over his sermons for hours, earnestly circling around the Reverend's favorite themes, and still they struck not a spark from his congregants, who occupied the pews impassively and

filed past him with a cursory nod and a murmur as he bade them good-
bye at the door. "If you could only *simplify*," Sophy begged him. "These
are laborers who want a little bread of Heaven to get them through the
week. When you explain too much, they think you're being superior."

"I suppose I ought to lament my education," he'd snapped at her.
Sophy was too kind to point out that the Reverend had also been a
learned man, but able to distill his knowledge into plain truths for ordinary folk.

With a sigh Gideon looked down at his notes. To be patient was to
endure with calmness. Delve down to the Latin and the vein of suffering
was struck: thus, the medical patient, bearing with fortitude the intimate
agonies of the flesh. Gideon thought of Job, patron saint of loss, scraping at his oozing boils with a potsherd, and then of Mrs. Jennings, the
bereaved mother he had visited that morning. "I could bear it if only he
hadn't had to suffer so," she had said again and again. Her frayed gentility, the fineness of her worn face, reminded him of his mother. He suspected, from the humbleness of the house, that she had married beneath
her. The boy had been her confidant, her consolation. "It's one thing to
lose an infant," she said, "but to have had him for nine years, and him
so promising . . . What was it all for, I keep wondering?" Gideon could
not bring himself to offer the usual words of solace. Unable to meet her
eyes, he bowed his head and watched her hands as they kneaded a damp,
grayish handkerchief with purposeful efficiency, as if she were doing the
weekly wash.

There were too many like her. The harsh cold of the last months had
taken a toll on the village's children; whooping cough and an outbreak
of scarlet fever had robbed several families of their young. Gideon was
constantly being pulled out of himself and made to address the raw needs
of others, and—lacking Hedge's conviction—he had nothing to offer
them but the stock phrases and tired justifications of his trade. How
could he preach about Job to those who had already suffered so much?
Yet this, precisely, was what the elders expected of him. He was aware of
their growing displeasure, their disappointment—had even overheard
mild-mannered Mr. Brown defending him to Deacon Mendham after

a church meeting. Once their loyalty to Hedge's memory had run its course, he had no doubt that they would find a reason to replace him.

He shuffled through the papers strewn across the desk until he found the list of sermon notes he had started weeks ago, a practice he'd learned from the parson. He had marked the few items with Roman numerals as Hedge had done: *I. The Lord's Loving Chastisement*, and *II. God's Purposes Are Higher than Ours*. Under this he had written, in a cramped, uncertain hand, *fruits of affliction?* The phrases must have had some meaning to him when he wrote them down, but now they seemed as remote from Mrs. Jennings and her grief as fragments of an ancient Chinese text. Had he really intended to answer her anguish with these non sequiturs? Not that there wasn't a precedent. When Job, broken and suffering, had asked why his life had been destroyed, God had waved a sea creature in his face.

For the first time that night, Gideon took up his pen. Where item *III* should have gone, he began to sketch a whale, realizing as he outlined its form that he wasn't sure what, really, a whale looked like, or where the blowhole was located—was it nearer the tail or the mouth, or in between? After several botched tries, his marine monster resembled a bloated goldfish, spouts erupting along its back like leaks. A creature that would awe no one.

Poor as the drawing was, the movement of his hand recalled to Gideon's mind the Hebrew letter that became a house, and how he had penetrated its façade and entered in. In the first weeks after his illness, he had been desperate to retrieve the experience; he had questioned Sophy over and over about his delirious ramblings, combing her memories for clues. But as his health improved, practical concerns dominated his thoughts, and he had stopped asking. The remnants he clung to faded, and soon he was left with nothing more than a misty impression. The deeper reality that he had glimpsed began to seem illusory to him. It struck him as pure irony that he had lived these last months in a state of normality he once would have scorned, with a wife and a profession and an acquired family. Life, the consuming mass of it, had overtaken him, and he had forgotten what he saw.

The memory came back to him now. It came back whole, in a continuous flow, as he had lived it.

Again he slid headfirst through viscous white, a slow fall such as Hedge claimed had been reserved for the angels. The ether filled his eyes and ears, erasing all his senses. In a blind panic he flailed, arching his body like a fish's, trying to right himself; then surrendered, becoming nothing but the velocity of the fall. He woke, as if from a long, deep sleep, and opened his eyes to a cutting clarity. At first it was like staring into a celestial jewel case, the world coming at him in hard, brilliant chunks. He couldn't look at it for long, but neither could he look away, and with each glimpse the scene around him became more legible. He made out a clearing, set about with flowering bushes and trees, rising to a small hill. A recognizable landscape, but superearthly: each blade of grass shining separate; the foliage throbbing with life, its green a pulsing energy; the ground beneath his feet firm but resilient, upholding him even as it sped him forward. He was perfectly at home, though he knew he had never been here before. The land seemed to open before him, ever widening, offering up its features for his delight. His vision had expanded so that he saw the whole picture and its parts: the veins of individual leaves on each tree and the harmonious vista the trees made together, some standing singly while others clustered at measured intervals, their laden branches arcing toward each other with formal grace like the arms of ballerinas. He came to the hill, and as he gazed at its gentle slope, had the notion that he should climb it, put his new powers to use by discovering what he could see from the top.

That had been his last conscious thought until he opened his eyes on that fateful afternoon to Sophy doing needlework at his bedside.

The present return was more jarring. Gideon was disoriented, unsure of where he was, or how he had arrived in a place so cold and colorless. He huddled deeper into his shawl, peering at the crude drawing before him, trying to make sense of it. A hieroglyph it seemed to be, of a creature native to these shores where he had, unaccountably, washed up. He was aware of fending off some unpleasant knowledge, to which the drawing held a clue. In a spasm of distaste he pushed the paper aside, and remembered, as his wrist swung out, that he had made it himself.

Reality flooded in on a tide of grief. He had resurrected an experience that had been dormant for months, but the passage of time had not dimmed it. The brief exposure left him torn with loss, his heart like a shackled slave in a ship's hold, keening for his motherland. He was in exile! They all were, whether they knew it or not: his Sophy, and Micah of the crippled tongue, and down-to-earth Fanny, and poor Mrs. Jennings; yes, even that Leviathan of self-righteousness, Mendham. In exile from their true home, and clinging to a forlorn hope that they would be delivered to a better place after death. Gideon had never felt the slightest call to be a missionary, but he felt it now. He had glad news to bring to his suffering flock; he had traveled to a country more real than Heaven, more accessible than they dared to dream. He must banish from his mind thoughts of how he would be received. His only obligation was to tell what he had seen. He flipped the paper over, jettisoning whale and sermon notes at once, and began to write.

We are accustomed to think of Paradise as a realm utterly foreign to our own: white light, billowing clouds to cradle the weightless feet of angels, an atmosphere bleached and floating and insubstantial. Imagine, if you can, that just the opposite is true . . .

CHAPTER 22

PREACHING PARADISE

Sophy is anxious. Gideon is happy. On a Sunday morning he is happy, and has been since he woke up, humming as he dressed for church and brushing her hair for her, as if within an hour he didn't have to stand before the congregation in his armor of stiffness and deliver the message he has labored over all week, polished phrases and closely reasoned arguments that will fly right over their heads. She wonders if he will break forth in some way. Loose his real nature at last. She has been expecting an outburst for some time, but thought it would happen privately, that she would go to the study and find a scrawled note, Gideon fled in search of the destiny she interrupted. Sometimes, Sophy imagines that he asks her to come with him. The two of them walk up the road holding hands, she in her shawl and he in his old hat, as free of possessions as the birds that careen above them. The road vanishes into the hazy distance, her imagination having failed to provide them with a destination.

They are walking up that same road now, but Mama and Micah and James are with them, forming the customary procession to church. Their blacks and grays rebuke the brilliance of the morning. Sun dazzles their eyes as it glances off the snow, and every branch and bush is sheathed in ice. The trees glitter like chandeliers in a grand ballroom. When wind agitates their branches, Sophy hears glasses clinking in pine-scented rooms where, tonight, Sabbath or no, revelers will raise cups of punch to toast the New Year. She has always nursed a secret envy of worldly folks who defy winter with warming spirits and light talk and laughter. Papa said that those who chose to celebrate the beginning of the year by addling their brains with drink were worshiping Janus, the two-faced god, whether they knew it or not. But, remembering how Papa longed for festivity at the end of his life, Sophy wonders if under the skin he was as pagan as her mother was. As she suspects herself to be.

They walk quickly because of the cold. She has to skip to keep pace with Gideon, who strides ahead like Papa used to, instead of lagging behind to brood over fine points of his sermon.

"The world is wearing all its diamonds," she says. "It doesn't know today is Sunday."

Gideon laughs and takes her arm. "Fortunate old world. I'll do my best not to depress its spirits."

AT GIDEON'S REQUEST, the choir has opened with a hymn, instead of a Psalm. It is a stirring hymn—*Glorious things of thee are spoken, Sion, city of our God*—and perhaps this accounts for the spring in Gideon's step as he processes down the aisle. He looks confident, Sophy thinks. He is always handsome, but she has observed that the men, sensing his discomfort in the role of church leader, regard his fine features as the outer sign of an inner weakness. Now that he is married, ladies who once coveted him for their daughters don't spare him the jaundiced eye. She is almost grateful for the gaggle of girls who flock together after service, watching him and whispering, lingering to babble nonsense to him at the door. Sophy doesn't mind that they ignore her, though she stands each week in her rightful place by his side. She is happy to see him admired, even by these featherbrains.

The parishioners offer the choir their usual patchwork support, some opening their mouths no wider than a penny bank, while others, like old Mrs. Campbell, whose trembling soprano has wandered athwart of the tune for years, sing louder than they ought. Just as Gideon reaches the end of the aisle and turns to face them, the second verse rings out, triumphant, filling the church:

Who can faint when such a river Ever will their thirst assuage?
Grace, which like the Lord, the giver, Never fails from age to age.

There is a moment when the congregation rallies as one, basking in the illusion that it has made a joyful noise. Sophy is among the first to follow Gideon's gaze to the tall man in the rear pew, who slipped in while they were singing and lent his powerful baritone. For a few seconds he and the choir carry the third verse on their own while the parishioners swivel their heads to stare at the newcomer.

Sophy can't blame them. Leander Solloway cuts a striking figure. He is not the common run of Ormsby schoolmaster. His height alone would set him apart in any company; he looms over Moses Apthorp, who exceeds six feet and sits in the back out of consideration. Solloway looks like a man who would be more comfortable wielding an ax in a wilderness than correcting grammar. He is bareheaded, his coarse black hair slanting untamed across his broad forehead and culminating in a full beard. He has dressed for church in a long, shapeless coat of some crudely woven cloth, under which a patterned vest can just be glimpsed, and has tied his cravat in a drooping bow. He arrived in the village only two months ago, when school commenced after the harvest, and already rumors are circulating. That he has never been seen in church is the least of them. He seems not the least disturbed by the stir he has caused, and goes on singing with full-throated vigor, his head thrown back.

Gideon moves briskly through the prayer and morning Psalm, emanating an ease he has never shown in the pulpit. And something more: a radiance she hasn't seen for months, the angel in him rampant. The change has come on too suddenly for her to trust it. Usually she gives only half an ear to the rote parts of the service, but now each word of prayer, even his peculiar choice of Scripture passage—the first chapter of Genesis, read by Elder Sims in a tone so flat as to reduce the milestones of creation to a list of morning chores—seems to mask a hidden message about his state of mind. Sophy chances a sidelong glance at her family to see if they have noticed. Mama wears the Sabbath face she has forged over years of Sundays, conveying a polite tolerance of any wisdom the minister might bring forth, however dubious, and James is gazing vacantly at the prayer book in his lap. Only Micah is alert. He senses Sophy looking at him and briefly meets her eyes.

Gideon keeps his calm until the moment arrives to deliver the sermon. Sophy hopes that no one else observes how pale and set his face has turned as he looks out over the congregation, how his hands grip the sides of the pulpit so tightly that the knuckles show white. His eyes rove over the pews from front to rear, gathering his flock as one. She knows what he sees from his high perch: a few faces uplifted in expectation; others stony, enduring the cold and discomfort; the lucky few with foot-stoves hoarding their ration of warmth, perhaps anticipating a doze. "Brothers and sisters," he begins. His voice is strong.

"Some of you may have wondered why I departed from custom to choose Genesis for the Scripture reading this morning. Granted, the Roman calendar proclaims it the first day of the new year, a time when tradition dictates that we put aside old habits and begin afresh. Yet, given the losses we have endured as a community over the last months, a passage from Job would surely have been more appropriate. We too have seen those whom we loved taken from us, we too have lifted our voices to Heaven and cried out, 'Why?' How often have I sat in your parlors, wordless, helpless to do more than share your grief, and wished that I could supply an adequate answer! To that end I have shut the door of my study many nights and submerged myself in prayer and contemplation. The response I was given, after much seeking, was as uncanny, as remarkable, as Leviathan, that mythical denizen of the sea, must have appeared to Job." He has been speaking in a natural, almost conversational way, his face frank and open, but now he pauses and takes a deep breath, summoning his forces. Sophy, aware of the heightened expectation around her, feels a hitch in her own breathing. "Brothers and sisters, I believe I was granted a vision of another world. Notice, I do not say 'next world' or 'afterworld,' but 'other,' for I have reason to believe that this place exists parallel to the world we know."

The church falls silent, the usual coughing and seat-shifting stifled all at once, as if someone dropped a cloth over a cage full of birds. Gideon glances at his notes for the first time and speaks into the stillness.

"We are accustomed to think of Paradise as a realm utterly foreign to our own: white light, billowing clouds to cradle the weightless feet of angels, an atmosphere bleached and floating and insubstantial. Imagine, if you can, that just the opposite is true. That the place we call Paradise is more *solid* than our familiar earth, the foliage more richly green, the sky a more piercing blue, the ground beneath one's feet more firm. That the air is so pure it goes to the head like celestial spirits, bringing clarity instead of confusion. But how can I describe what I saw when the very words at my disposal are fallen?

"With such a picture in our minds, it is possible, if we permit ourselves, to imagine further. To envision our lost children capering and laughing in that same emerald parkland, naming the birds and beasts even as Adam did—for learning is the play of Paradise—and exercising their fertile young minds by inventing games to amuse each other. A beloved wife sitting on a bench beneath a shade tree, observing these antics with a smile, as the infant who accompanied her out of this world babbles in her arms. A departed husband or brother absorbed in that task which gave him most satisfaction in life, whether wood-carving or verse-making or wall-building or tending the soil.

"And what can these pretty imaginings mean to us, you are asking— we who are left behind to shoulder our daily load without the help and comfort of our dear companions? Yet, I am asking you to be patient and indulge me further. Open your Bibles to the first chapter of Genesis and—those of you who are able—read a few verses."

There is a rustling as people take up their books. As Sophy opens hers, she thinks: He is bringing us back to the Word, all to the good, he won't go far astray. After a minute Gideon begins to speak again, softly, like a father telling a tale at a child's bedside.

"What does it mean to read? What is this Lordly skill that we acquire as children and take for granted ever after? Your eyes move over the page—yes, even as God's spirit moved over the waters!—and as you pass from line to line, your mind's eye re-creates the making of the world. You *look* at black figures on a white ground. You *see* the blazing colors of God's handiwork—that self-same Garden where Adam first experimented with the power of speech, where the helpmate he sought emerged full-formed from his side, where our First Parents strolled, and loved, and feasted on nature's bounty—and, alas, sinned." Gideon leans forward. He grasps the pulpit again, but this time it seems to Sophy that he would thrust the barrier aside if he could, and address his flock directly. "This world we walk through is only a text we must learn to read before we are permitted entrance to the deeper, truer story. Adam and Eve knew Paradise as a birthright and were expelled into the outer darkness. Brothers and sisters, it is the work of our lives—we who still wander in that darkness—to find our way back." His eyes shift, he hesitates. "We may discover that our departed ones have made the journey before us. Let us not think of them as lost, then, but only . . . *translated*. Removed, that is, to their first home."

Sophy has sat in an attitude of rigid attention since Gideon began to speak, looking neither left nor right. The persistent silence in the church tells her she had better keep her blinders on. She endures through the prayer and closing hymn this way, her mind whirling with trepidation. Why must he speak of outer darkness when the day is so bright? And what will they make of "translated"? Wouldn't "changed" have served as well? The little he said was too much, too revealing of his vision. He has put the whole family at risk. As Gideon recites the benediction—a part of the service that always moves her, for how can God fail to bless when He is asked so nicely?—her mouth is dry with dread of facing the crowd.

Keeping her head down, she manages to slip out of the pew before

Mama and the boys, and to avoid neighborly chatter until she arrives at Gideon's side. People shuffle by as they always do, perhaps a little quieter than usual. Sophy, nodding and smiling, tries to read their faces as they pass, knowing they are likely to save their opinions for the churchyard or the journey home. A few look bewildered, most merely blank. She begins to feel reassured. A fair number of folks probably slept through the sermon, or retreated into their thoughts. Hasn't she often done so herself? Of those who managed to stay awake, most lack the understanding to be alarmed; for them, Gideon's words amount to little more than high-flown talk of Heaven—the common grist of Sunday lessons, easier to digest before dinner than Papa's pungent evocations of Hell.

But one or two have heard. Mrs. Jennings presses Gideon's hand, her tear-filled eyes saying all. Effie Minor, a dried cob of a woman who lives alone in a tumbledown cottage, the last of her large family, stands on tiptoe and croaks, "Couldn't I just see that place as you was speaking, Parson, and them all at home there!"

Deacon Mendham has been earnestly conferring with Sims and two other elders at the back of the church. Now they make their way to the door as one body, the deacon at its head. Mendham, miming alarm, fends off Gideon's greeting. "You will forgive me if I don't take your hand, Pastor Birdsall. Your sermon has put me in fear that *doves* might fly from your sleeve. Such original interpretations! Heaven as a glorified village. Ought we to pray, then, for our souls to ascend to . . . Andover? Salvation as a conjurer's trick. You say nothing of sin or grace, nothing of moral behavior. Perhaps we may expect a mention of these venerable concepts next Sunday?"

Mendham's show of wit ignites a dry cackle in the elders. Dead leaves clinging to a dead branch, Sophy thinks. Her smile falters, but Gideon gazes steadily at the deacon. Although he doesn't speak, his calm seems to her magisterial—both lofty and compassionate. She remembers the certainty he showed that day in the sickroom when he first confided what he had seen. Fragile as he was, she had believed him, and she believes him still. Then she had been too timid to take the hand he offered, but she is a woman now, and a wife; she must prove to him that she will follow wherever he leads. She sidles closer to Gideon and lets the back of her hand touch his. The churchmen will see that they are of one mind.

"Cloak old truths in new dress, and behold, we see them new!" Leander Solloway's speaking voice is as mellifluous as his baritone raised in song. Light-footed for such a large man, he has meandered up to pay his respects and has been observing the exchange.

"Truth needs no ornament," Mendham mutters.

"And that's true, too." Solloway flashes a grin wide enough to encompass the deacon and all his minions. Sophy is momentarily dazzled by this streak of geniality, the glint of perfect white teeth in a black beard. "But you will allow, sir," he goes on, "that we fallen children are not strong enough to take our truths unadorned. Jesus, the great teacher, spoke to the people in parables."

Mendham, not a tall man, does his best to look down his nose while thrusting his chin up at the towering intruder, and pulls at his lip as if summoning a crowning reply. But the newcomer's cordiality seems to have a withering effect on him. Already he is retreating in the direction of the yard, shrinking backward, the others following alongside as if departing the presence of a king. Talk has circulated about the schoolmaster's uncommon method of imposing order in the classroom: how he tames his charges, even the unruly older boys, with a soft word and a potent glance, and has yet to make use of the switch. The woman who helps with the laundry has heard that he was a mesmerist, and assures Sophy she doesn't doubt it, for one has only to look—if one dares— into his strange "greeny" eyes. Men are more likely to credit Solloway's authority to his height and the knotted muscle of his long arms. Sophy sees now that his power lies elsewhere. He is a veritable Goliath of good nature.

With the elders gone, Solloway turns the sun of his regard fully on Gideon. "Some intuition told me to visit your church this morning, and now I know why. I was struck by your sermon, Pastor. You gave voice to my own thoughts, and expressed them with eloquent economy, hinting much and saying little. How could you do otherwise in such company? Reticence is only wisdom here." He inclines his head toward the churchyard, empty now except for her family; Sophy is chagrined at the oafish look of them, staring narrow-eyed at the newcomer like hill folk who come to town twice a year. "We must talk. I have no proper place to entertain at present—I am living in the schoolhouse, and believe me, I've set my pallet down in worse places—but I can offer you a seat by the stove and a bowl of soup, if you would not be offended."

If Mr. Solloway is such a peasant, why does he speak like a prince, Sophy wonders? Each word chiseled to its perfect shape, vowels fully rounded, consonants sharp-cut. A slight fuzzing of the *w*'s—as if, were the schoolmaster less vigilant, they would settle for being *v*'s.

"I am never offended by simplicity." Gideon's eyes seek the school-master's, and some current passes between them. Sophy notes it, and thinks that the laundress may be right after all. "But you must come to us," Gideon says, in a hearty, ministerial voice that doesn't belong to him. "My wife will tell you I am always eager for conversation. She is a fine cook. Aren't you, Sophia?"

"Ah, Sophia!" Solloway looks upon her from his great height, delight dawning on his face. As he inclines his shaggy head, she has a fancy that he will hoist her up in his arms and tickle her under the chin. Her cheeks are burning because Gideon called her by her full name, as if she were a different wife altogether, and lied about her cooking. The newcomer's scrutiny makes her blush deeper. Solloway bows low, touching his hand to his brow in a courtier's salute and bringing it to his heart. "When Mr. Wordsworth wrote 'Wisdom is oft times nearer when we stoop than when we soar,' he might have had the present case in mind. Certainly his words apply most beautifully." He winks at her. "Though I suspect Mr. Wordsworth intended a different meaning."

"Or a different object," Sophy says. Is he making a joke of her? "Those who know me can testify I am not wise at all. Even the domes-tic arts are beyond me." She is suddenly furious—at Solloway for his expression of playful amusement, at Gideon for ingratiating himself with this gangly stranger at her expense.

"Then we won't put you to the test! I will come for the pleasure of a civilized conversation. Food for the gods, and no less for my humble self." Solloway takes her free hand and Gideon's, and enfolds them between his own large mitts. His flesh is warm, as though he generates his own heat.

"Etiquette requires that I call you Pastor," he says to Gideon. "I hope one day to have the honor of calling you Friend."

He turns away while they are still absorbing this overture, leaving them to gape at the easy, loping stride that takes him straight across the churchyard to greet the Hedges, who are huddled together where they have stood this last half-hour. Mama and the boys must be frozen in place by now, Sophy thinks. Their faces are so stiff that their emotions cannot easily be calculated. Not so the temperature of the schoolmaster's smile.

CHAPTER 23

LEANDER

GIDEON WENT LATE TO BED ON TUESDAY, HAVING WRITTEN half his sermon without stopping, and dreamed of a city of minarets and golden stone baking in the sun. He woke the next morning to that same honeyed light drizzling through a gap in the curtains, the back of winter broken in some silent tussle overnight. Frost had beaded into droplets on the windowpane, and the frail young birch whose branches scraped at the glass with every gust of wind was as peaceful as a palm in an oasis. The sight of the tree gave him courage to open the latch. He stood in his nightshirt, basking in the mild, moist air. It was only the January thaw, not likely to last more than a day or two, but even a sham spring was enough to infect him with a mix of languor and restlessness.

In the kitchen he helped himself to bread and cheese, and ate standing as the dog, drunk on earthy smells long withheld, rolled and whimpered at his feet. Fanny and Sophy came in just as he finished. Wednesday was their morning for making calls to struggling families in the parish. He had watched as they approached the house, swinging their empty basket between them like a pair of schoolgirls.

Sophy tore off her bonnet and shawl and dropped them to the floor with a dramatic flourish. "You can't imagine how warm it is. Go out and enjoy it, sleepyhead."

Fanny would admit no exuberance. "I suppose those pies I put in the blanket chest will spoil, and we'll have nothing but dried apples to see us through the winter." She frowned at Gideon as if he had ordered the weather. "And how do you intend to use what is left of the day?"

"Once I finish my sermon, I'll stroll to the schoolhouse as a reward. It's time I observed the controversial Mr. Solloway in his habitat and judged his methods for myself. Meeting him at church pricked my curiosity." Until he spoke the words, Gideon hadn't formed a conscious intention to pay such a visit, but he plunged ahead as if he'd been planning one for days. "Shall we do a good deed and invite the poor bachelor to dine with us on Sunday? Save him from his solitary soup? It will be good for his body, and his soul, too. With such an incentive, he'll be bound to come to service a second time."

Sophy hung her garments on the peg. "If Mr. Solitary Sollaway is alone, then he deserves to be. You know what people say about him. I suppose he'll want to mesmerize us after dinner. Not me—I prophesy a headache."

Gideon grimaced. "You're being childish, Sophy. Have we sunk so low that we give credence to idle gossip? He seemed a pleasant enough fellow, and better educated than most around here. What do you have against him?"

"I don't know. The way he said my name—as though he owned it. He's too sure of himself, too forward. Assuming we would have him for a friend . . ." She turned away, shoulders drooping, and he saw that however she felt, she would give in.

"Those overgrown sorts may look like scarecrows, but they eat enough for an army. I wouldn't be surprised if a good number of them harbor worms." Fanny had installed herself at the loom, and she pumped the treadle for emphasis.

———

GIDEON ENDURED THE MORNING at his desk, his thoughts as scattered and feckless as they'd been concentrated the night before. The sermon was still unfinished, but it was already past noon, and he was anxious to get away before Sophy came to ask if he would join them at table. The idea of the visit had come to him with such force that it seemed crucial to carry out his plan without further interruption.

He threw on his coat and began to walk at a fast trot through the softening snow, slowing his pace when the house was safely behind him. He was genuinely curious about Solloway's methods—few of the other masters had lasted more than a year—but was reluctant to invade the classroom while school was in session. Hedge had considered such visits a pastoral duty, and relished arriving unannounced, ostensibly to catechize the students, but also to observe the teacher at work; a letter, enumerating the poor pedagogue's weaknesses and prescribing Scriptural correctives, would soon follow. Gideon had no desire to strike fear in the hearts of youth. If anything, he was terrified of young people, not individually, but en masse. He wondered what would have become of the shy, precocious boy he had been if his mother hadn't tutored him— how he would have fared in a classroom like the one he was about to enter, with pupils of all ages and backgrounds shut in together.

When the schoolhouse came in sight, he halted. The building wasn't identical to the ones his mother had taught in, but it was similar enough; he recognized the gray wood showing through peeling paint, the straight, plain flanks, the tarnished bell over the door. Here, too, the narrow windows, whose small panes would fracture the view of fields spreading out on either side. Even at this distance he could recall the smell of the rooms he had been banished to as a boy during the mill owner's visits: an effluvial bleakness of damp wool, cold ash in the stove, and year upon year of unwashed bodies in close confinement. It was possible that all schoolrooms had this odor. Scrubbing could never quite expunge it.

The girl had been so lazy that she had kicked the pail with her toe to move it along, inch by indifferent inch. She rarely troubled him now.

There was no room for her in his mind, or in his life, and since he hadn't told a living soul about her, it was as if she never existed at all. Still, Gideon was grateful for the black clothes that weighed too heavy on a day as mild as this one. They bespoke his position, the man he had become.

As he walked up the muddy path, he could hear the schoolmaster's ringing question: *Who will spin the globe today?* The response was immediate, a confusion of voices proclaiming that Annie had her turn last week, Eben's spelling had improved, Caleb had helped clean the classroom two days in a row. Gideon waited until the din subsided before knocking.

Leander Solloway opened the door himself. "Pastor Birdsall! Marvelous!" His body was too big for the miserly proportions of the doorframe; his head jutted forward to avoid grazing the top. He gazed at Gideon for a moment, his eyes bright, before turning back to his pupils. "We have a guest, ladies and gentlemen. Will you rise and give Pastor Birdsall your warmest greeting?"

The students were seated in a semicircle, with the youngest at each end and the tallest in the middle. Gideon judged that their ages ranged from six or seven to at least sixteen; a couple of the older boys had nascent beards and were almost as tall as Solloway. Yet they all rose as one, like a well-trained chorus, and parroted, "Good afternoon, Pastor Birdsall."

"Good afternoon . . . children." He could not bring himself to address this ragtag bunch as their teacher had; in his mouth the words might seem like mockery. "Please continue with your class. I am only here to observe." Solloway indicated that he should sit on a mangy velvet couch wedged into a corner.

"We are just about to begin our geography lesson—the last class of the day, and the one where we travel farthest—if . . . *Clara Hooper* will spin the globe for us and send us on our way."

Clara, a thin, freckled girl of about ten, frowning to conceal her pleasure, made her way to the center of the room, where the globe was enthroned atop a carved pedestal that looked, Gideon thought, as if it ought to hold a bust of Homer. It was a handsome globe suspended in a brass meridian, the continents discreetly colored on a background of old vellum—as fine as any Gideon had seen at college. Clara, standing at a respectful distance, stretched out her arm and applied one forefinger, a timid attempt resulting in a wobbly half-circuit, but, with her classmates urging her to "give it some go," propelled the sphere into such a frantic spin that it creaked on its axis. "Now!" Solloway commanded, and the girl shut her eyes, and with a firm touch, stopped what she had set in motion. Gently he lifted the finger she had pasted on the globe's surface. "New South Wales! Well done, Clara. You have taken us to the other side of the world, where even the weather is reversed. Yes, ladies and gentlemen, at this very moment the duckbill and the laughing kookaburra-bird sport in the summer sun, and our brother Aboriginals launch their canoes on white beaches, sweating while we shiver. How appealing it seems, does it not? Perhaps one or two of you are even sailing southward in your thoughts—but I warn you, my friends, take care how you get there!"

For the next hour Gideon listened, as enthralled as any of the children, as Solloway emoted the story of a land few had heard of and none were likely ever to see. In between kookaburra calls and terrifying descriptions of convict ships, he managed to insert nuggets of solid history: Captain Cook, the penal colonies, the Aborigines' intricate tales of how the world began. Periodically, he paused to draw out a pupil's thoughts or opinions, breaking the question down into smaller and smaller components until even the slowest student was able to offer some response. When, after glancing at the clock, he tapped the globe sharply with two fingers—as if boisterous New South Wales must be summoned home and put to bed within its outline—the entire class stayed seated, rising only gradually, one by one, and shuffling to the door. Gideon felt pity in his heart for the children; some, he knew, must walk miles to isolated farms or cottages through snow higher than their boots after spending a glorious hour in the sun. One hulking boy lingered to line the chairs neatly against a wall and sweep the floor.

"I have nothing more for you today, Lem," his teacher said, "but come early tomorrow and we'll hang some of the pictures I told you about." He put an arm around the boy's shoulders. "You'll enjoy that, won't you?"

Lem's look of gratitude was so ardent that Gideon was startled, unsure whether he ought to be moved or embarrassed. "Your acolyte?" he asked, after the boy had gone.

Solloway knelt to feed another log to the stove. "My adversary, at first. I was warned against him before I ever met him. Lem and his brother had been intimidating schoolmasters for years, with some success. My predecessor was one of several who were driven away. The boys were taught to speak with their fists; it is the only language they know. The brother is long gone, but there was Lem on my first day, sprawled in the front row, emitting great snorting yawns and tipping his chair back into the lap of the boy behind him. I knew it would do no good to rebuke him. Very softly I asked him what he liked to do. Kill chickens, he said, making a wringing motion with his hands. With those arms I took you for a wrestler, I told him, and he brightened right up: he had done some 'wrassling' with his brother. I mentioned, in the most modest way, that I had some skills in that area myself. When class was dismissed I found him waiting for me outside. I won't belabor you with brute details, Pastor. I'll just say that he had strength but no skill. I pinned him easily enough, but he thrashed in my grip like a big fish. I hurt him only as much as I had to." The teacher stood and brushed off his trousers. "He's been a lamb ever since. I treat him with affection and respect, and praise him when he does his little tasks. You've seen how devoted he is."

"And do you still speak the language of fists with him?" Gideon moved to make room for Solloway, who had settled on the couch beside him.

"I give him what I give the others, and hope he takes some of it in. Poor boy, he hasn't much of a brain left. What can one expect, when his father has been clapping him on the head since he was old enough to crawl? You would be appalled at how many of the children are disciplined in that brutal way. I do what I can—which is little enough. My knowledge is broad, but not deep. I tell them stories about the world. I try to make them understand there is something larger than the patch of earth they were born on."

"You performed wonders with the globe," Gideon said.

Solloway smiled. "A cherished possession of mine. I found it in Amsterdam and carried it across two oceans in my trunk, swaddled in a nightshirt. Never did I imagine it would end up in a country school-house, claimed by the offspring of illiterate farmers. Until I brought the globe in, they would not believe the world was round. Why should they, when their only image of the planet was flat?" He pointed to a fly-spotted map on the wall, mildew stains competing with the continents; Gideon remembered one like it in his mother's classroom. "Children of this sort—deprived from birth, taught to keep their eyes down and their ambitions low—must be *shown*. They haven't the capacity to imagine the sphere, so they must see it. Mind you, they're quite the cosmopolites now. There is no place they won't travel. The more exotic, the better."

"If only I could bring that tangibility to my sermons," Gideon said. "I do my best to describe the vivid thoughts in my mind, but I get tangled up in words. What I experience as physical becomes abstract in the telling. I suppose there's no help for it. I don't have your commanding presence, or your gift for theater. One must be born with such talents."

"You are mistaken, my friend. You exaggerate my abilities and greatly diminish your own. You are a visionary. I saw it as soon as you began to preach." The schoolmaster spoke in a low tone, his eyes fixed on Gideon's face. Although the man didn't move, Gideon had the impression that he had leaned closer, so thoroughly did his conviction fill the space between them.

"I have been granted just one gift," said Leander Solloway. "I am tinder. I spark others into flame."

CHAPTER 24

THE GUEST

HER OLD BED IS TOO SHORT. SOPHY CLINGS TO THIS
simple fact as to a mast in a storm, though the rest of her family blithely
discounts it. She told them so after dinner, when it was clear their guest
would stay, and they looked at her as if she'd lost her wits, and Mama
said, all tartness, "It will have to do, since I'm not aware of another."

The others are only too eager to accommodate him. Without asking her, Gideon offered their own bed—presumably, the only one
capacious enough to receive the visitor's extraordinary length, not to
mention his great soul!—and assured him they would be more comfortable in the sitting room, knowing full well that the settee wasn't
wide enough for two. Not to be outdone, Micah volunteered to give
up Sophy's closet of a room that he'd only recently inherited and sleep
in his old place in the attic with James, and James—silent, brooding
James—said he would be glad of another warm body on a wretched
night like this. It was left to Sophy to remind them that Papa had made
that bed to her measure, and if Micah couldn't stretch his legs out, what
would Mr. Solloway do?

Leander (he has instructed them to call him Leander) refused these
kind offers and begged to be allowed to curl up near the kitchen hearth.

"I can sleep anywhere," he said, "for I sleep deep but not long. Three or four hours at most. When I lay my head down, a wood floor is as good as a feather bed." But Mama wasn't swayed by his tales of sweet slumber in the Black Forest or on Carpathian mountain crags. She decreed that Sophy's room would be suitable for a night, making up in privacy what it lacked in size, and that a clever man like Leander would find a way to rest, even if he had to sleep sitting up.

Once all was decided, Gideon had looked out the window. "Old Man Winter is having his revenge for our taste of spring," he said. "I doubt you'll be ringing the school bell tomorrow. All the better! We'll spend the morning in the study, if we can find the path."

Now Sophy lies beside her sleeping husband in a state of wakefulness so keen she believes she can hear the snowflakes as they fall. Gideon is on his back, his head sunk in the pillow and his arms flung up; he sleeps the way Micah used to, with complete abandon, as if he'd dropped from exhaustion while running. In his nightshirt, his light hair loose around his face, he could pass for a child, which might explain her nervy vigilance. She isn't sure what she is watching for. Leander is hardly the first stranger to spend a night under this roof, and not all of them were schoolmasters. In Papa's day, drunkards and tramps sheltered here; Mama used to say that only the Lord's mercy preserved them from being murdered in their beds.

Sophy doubts that the Lord's mercy would be efficacious in Leander's case. After observing his way with her family, she has to conclude that the laundress was misled: the man is less a mesmerist than a diviner— though maybe the two are not so different. Mrs. Pitt did get his eyes right: strange and, yes, "greeny," flecked with yellow and brown and gold. He uses them to look deep into each soul he meets, and tailors his response to what he sees there. She thinks of him doubled up in her little cot, his hands cushioning his head against the backboard and his legs steepled. He says he sleeps, but she sees him with those eyes open, staring at the ceiling and savoring each of them in his thoughts. His shirt is open at the neck. The triangle of flesh—not smooth like Gideon's, but matted with black hair and tanned even in winter—is as shocking to her mind as his sudden white smile was to her senses. The last thing he said to her was, "You and I will have to try harder, Sophia."

SHE DIDN'T GO to church that morning. Someone needed to turn the meat and make sure the potatoes didn't burn, and Mama deserved to go, having done all the baking and slaved for two days to make the house ready for a guest. Sophy worked alongside her, mocking the effort they were expending on behalf of a rough man like the schoolmaster, but glad to see Mama cheerful and engaged again. The holidays had come and gone like any other day, each of them brooding on those who were absent. Preparing for Mr. Solloway's visit was a welcome distraction from a fear Sophy had kept to herself since Christmas. Micah had arranged his manger scene on the mantel and added a new donkey to the worshipful beasts, but Sophy couldn't look at the tiny knob-head Jesus sleeping in its cradle of straw. All these months she had thought of her state as temporary: the marriage still new, the child waiting until they were settled before making an appearance. On Christmas Day, she tried out the name Barren.

The house gleamed. The floors had been scrubbed and all the furniture polished, the table set with good china. Sophy was determined not to exert any undue care on her person, but sheer momentum carried her to the bedroom to change her dress and arrange her hair. Mama had given her a cameo pin for Christmas, a treasure from her own girlhood. Sophy hesitated before stabbing it through the bodice of her dress, her fingers making the decision for her. She stepped back and looked at herself in the glass. The effect of the cameo was not frivolous; it made her look older, official, as if, after months of apprenticeship, she had at last merited the emblem of wife. *Sophia*: classical, composed, carved in shell. A household goddess. If this was the woman Gideon wanted her to be for his new friend, she would act the part. She descended with measured steps to the parlor and sat with hands clasped as she had on the day of her betrothal, waiting.

She heard them before she saw them, Mr. Solloway's cadences rising above the others'. He attained the peak of the story just as they approached the door. "And then, the fellow GAVE ME HIS HAT! Swept it off his dusty head and gave it to me, as mannerly as any diplomat. By Christ, sir, he says, you need this more'n I do!" This last was delivered in country dialect, followed by the extraordinary sound of Mama's rich, unfettered laugh.

Sophy went to the hall and stood before the door, arranging her features in an expression of guarded welcome. Her mask of composure was undone when they burst in, red-cheeked from the cold, slapping their garments to shake off the snow. They looked so pleasant that her face softened into a genuine smile. Even James was animated, trading mock blows with Micah, whose Sunday jacket, like his own, bore evidence of a savage snowball fight. Mama spied the cameo pin right away, and sent Sophy one of her fleeting omniscient smirks that said, clearer than words, You've come round after all, haven't you? Gideon bent to touch his cold lips to her cheek—a mere peck, but so rare nowadays for him to display affection in public that she drew back in surprise. Despite his story, Mr. Solloway wore no hat to warm him, only a large shawl, fringed and outlandishly patterned, that all but covered his thin coat, and, in Sophy's opinion, might better have adorned a piano. He inhaled deeply.

"You say you are no cook, Mrs. Birdsall," he said, "but I can tell you that savory aromas lured us from a good quarter-mile up the road, diverting our thoughts from a very fine sermon to earthly joys ahead."

She was about to shrug off the compliment when he dug into his pocket and brought up a paper twist of molasses drops, tied at each end with red ribbon. This he presented to Mama—"I don't know about you, Mrs. Hedge, but the cold weather sharpens my sweet tooth"—who accepted the candies with a stifled gasp, as if they were winter-blooming roses. He foraged in the other pocket and produced a tin whistle, "in case anyone should feel like a tune after dinner."

There was something else. He held it out to Sophy, closed in his fist. "If you can tell me what animal I have here, it is yours," he said. He was contemplating her with the same teasing amusement that had enraged her at church.

"I've no idea, Mr. Solloway," she said, "but whatever the poor creature is, it must be dead by now."

The schoolmaster stared at her, they all stared, as the bent minute hand scraped a few grudging seconds off the face of the hall clock. Then he threw back his head and laughed. He opened his fingers. A tiny green rabbit crouched on his palm, its long ears carved flat against its back. Micah came close and gazed at it with wonder, stroking it with one finger. "M-m-marble?"

"Jade. From China. I have never been that far east myself, but a friend gave it to me when I first set sail to bring me luck." He turned to Sophy again. "It was one of the talismans I carried with me during my travels, but now that I'm settled, I have no need for Little Lapin any longer. I would be grateful if you would give him a good home."

He offered the rabbit again, and, wordless, she took it.

GIDEON SAT IN PAPA'S old place at the head of the table, the first time he had claimed that seat since Papa died. It seemed so natural to see him there that Sophy wondered if she was the only one to note the momentous fact. The sermon must have gone well, she thought. He had told her earlier that he would preach about loose speech—gossip and tale-telling, slander, casual oaths; the havoc that ephemeral words could wreak and the lasting harm they inflicted. Gradually he planned to introduce the idea of a higher language, of words as portals to a better life. Catching her worried look, he'd said, "Don't fret, my love, I'm well aware of the wolves in our midst. I will be wise as a serpent and harmless as a dove, and give Old Man Mendham his spoonful of Scripture." He was adjusting his cravat in the mirror, and over his shoulder he added, "I've learned so much from watching Leander in the classroom."

So it's Leander now, she'd thought.

Dinner passed congenially, festive after the silence that had reigned for months, everyone chattering at once. Sophy was the only one to hold back, quietly observing as she attended to others' needs; Mama, seated at the other end of the table, gave her a look of gratitude touched with new respect. The guest ate with deliberation, seeming to savor each mouthful, and declared himself fulfilled in all ways. The mesmerism he practiced was of a subtle kind, Sophy saw: He directed the conversation without appearing to take charge. A question here, a comment there: he drew each of them out, inquiring of Mama what methods she used to attain such loft in brown bread and preserve the sweetness of the squash; of James how he'd managed the farm through hard times and what changes he anticipated in the coming year. Rather than ask Micah a question, he took note of the boy's hands, "a craftsman's hands," expounding on the length of the fingers and shape of the thumb, "uniquely suited for fine work as well as gross." He hadn't seen the like since he befriended a watchmaker in Heidelberg. Unprompted, Micah spilled out the story of their long communal labor on the family clock, revealing a barbed humor he kept well hidden. He stumbled over difficult words but plunged ahead, caught up in the telling, even confronting "zodiac" head-on—for how could he leave out the tale of Sophy's thwarted design for the clock face? The incident had long since become a family joke, Mama dredging up her usual remark about having to consult Aries at dinnertime and Capricorn for supper. Leander laughed with the others, but Sophy saw that he had registered the fact that she painted. He would surely try to use it to reach her. She would have to be wise as a serpent to elude him.

Gideon suggested that dessert be served in the sitting room, to be followed by a tune, if Leander was so inclined. Sophy was about to retreat to the sanctuary of the kitchen, but Gideon grabbed her wrist. "Stay, why don't you? You've hardly said a word all evening. Leander must think you're excessively shy. Your mother can serve the cake."

She sat beside Gideon on the settee, wishing for the first time in her life that she had a piece of embroidery in her lap, a reason to keep her eyes down and her hands busy.

"What a picture you two make!" their guest exclaimed. "The very model of youthful domesticity." He had chosen Reuben's old rocker, and was sitting with his legs stretched before him on a footstool Micah had provided. "Such a perfect pair, a child of earth and a child of air.

You balance each other well. It's clear the cosmos collaborated in your union."

"And which of us is which, Mr. Solloway?" Sophy asked.

The schoolmaster did not smile, as she expected, but gazed at both of them seriously, as if her question were a deep one, requiring careful thought. After a pause he began to speak, but Mama came in with a tray and cut him off. Sophy had observed before that Mama heard only the part of a conversation that she cared to hear, and tonight she had heard a bachelor extolling domesticity. She swooped over him with a plate. "Now that you're settled, Leander, perhaps you ought to be thinking of acquiring a wife yourself. You can't live in that drafty schoolhouse forever. There comes a time in a man's life when he wants a hot dinner and a bit of comfort at the end of the day. I assure you, it's not too late. There are several ladies in the parish—worthy women, not in their first bloom, but young enough. You have only to say the word, and I'll do what I can."

Leander was momentarily flustered—an effect Mama's directness often had on folks—but he recovered himself quickly. "My dear Mrs. Hedge, only someone with your kind heart would be so concerned with a stranger's welfare," he said. "But the fact is, I can't marry. My love is too *wide* to spend on a single soul, even were I to meet one as charming and capable as Mrs. Birdsall. Many fortunate men find all they need in the woman they adore, but I call myself a pan-lover—doomed to love the world, whatever form that love might take. Here in Ormsby, I give it to my students—and perhaps a few friends." He spread his large hands and shrugged. "What can I do? It's my nature."

Mama's face closed. She went on handing out plates, but Sophy could see that she had received a shock and was trying to reconcile her guest's alarming comments with her recently acquired good opinion of him. A literal soul, she was possibly mulling over the schoolmaster's baffling affection for a cooking vessel, or weighing the brash paganism of "pan-lover" against the Christian self-giving of his thankless profession. The phrase puzzled Sophy as well. How could a single man love so generally as to encompass the whole world? Was Leander one of the new thinkers

that Papa had railed against in the pulpit—Unitarians, rogue Congrega-
tionalists, the odd Baptist—and consigned to a common fiery pit labeled
Boston Preacher? Or did he mean that he was a disciple of Pan? A picture
came to her of the goat-footed god in a forest glade, one furry leg crossed
over another, piping away as Leander lay prostrate at his cloven feet.

For a couple of minutes no one spoke, each of them conscientiously
attending to the cake. Then, unprompted, as though he had looked into
her after all and seen the image inscribed there, Leander took out his tin
whistle, blew a few tentative notes, and began to play.

Later, when the others had retired for the evening, Sophy left him
talking to Gideon and went to see about the state of the linens on her old
bed. As she shook blankets and changed sheets, the crux of her argument drummed in her head, a satisfying staccato: Too short! Anyone
can see it is too short! She was tugging at the corners of the coverlet
to smooth it when a shadow fell across the surface of the bed. Leander
stood in the low doorway, massive, his head poked forward, peering at
her with an air of distant benignity like a father admiring the contents of
his daughter's dollhouse. He had untied his cravat and draped it around
his open collar. The candle he held gave an antic life to the spurt of dark
hair on his chest and the tendons of his neck.

"If you could see where I usually sleep, you would not have gone to
all this trouble," he said.

"We would do the same for any guest."

"Gideon tells me that you are an accomplished artist. The likeness of
Mrs. Hedge in the dining room must be your work—and that fine portrait of the late Reverend in the parlor. It seemed that his eyes were peering into me as I played my little tune, reminding me that life is a serious
business. You must have been very close to your father to capture his
character so precisely. I regret I never knew him, but people speak of
him in such a vivid way that I feel as if I did."

"The portraits were meant for practice. I don't like to look at them
now; I see all their flaws. Papa and Mama were very kind to hang them
at all." Sophy took a few steps toward the door, but Leander did not
move.

"And do you still find time to paint, with all the demands on a minister's wife?" Leander lounged against the doorframe as though the conversation were only beginning. "It would be a shame if all that practice was for naught. Art ennobles life, whether we make it for our families or a wider audience. I seek out the salons wherever I travel."

"My husband's welfare is my first care. A minister's daughter is well schooled in putting the needs of others before her own." Sophy was pleased with the crisp correctness she had summoned, but felt her color rising in spite of herself. "As for the painting, it counts little in the grand scheme of things. I have only a very small talent." She moved more decisively to the door. "And now I must let you rest." She gave a last sardonic look at her old bed. "I expect you'll have interesting dreams, Mr. Solloway—if you manage to sleep at all."

Leander stepped aside, but only enough to let her by. As she passed him, their arms brushed. Her flesh shrank from the slight contact. That was when he said, "You don't take to me, I see. You and I will have to try harder, Sophia."

SHE OPENS HER EYES, certain she'd just closed them. The noise that woke her persists softly like the draggled hem of a dream, a slicing, sliding sound followed by a muffled thump. Gideon's eyelids quiver; he groans and turns over, burying his face in the pillow. This confirmation that the noise is real fills her at first with fear—how could she have relaxed her vigilance? —then with puzzled relief. Shoveling. Someone is shoveling snow in the middle of the night.

She slips out of bed, and plants her feet on the cold floor. The chill travels quickly to her legs. She steps lightly to the window, feeling her way with the smoke of her breath to guide her. The curtain stymies her, but just for a second; rather than risk pulling it aside, she ducks underneath it and wipes one frosted pane with the sleeve of her nightgown.

The sky is black and clear. It has stopped snowing. The moon has turned one cheek to the darkness, reluctant to flaunt itself on such a frigid night, but the stars are brazen and fresh snow casts its own light.

She has no trouble making out the shawl-wrapped figure wielding the shovel with a flowing rhythm like a rower crossing a broad, still lake. The path he is carving is shallow but remarkably straight, and it will end at the study.

Sophy is mesmerized, after all. She watches him, transfixed by her vantage: exposed to the night through her little porthole, a silent observer like the moon and stars. She has no fear of being seen. Not a soul knows where she is. So she believes until Leander sinks the shovel into a mound of snow and spins around. Looks right at her.

CHAPTER 25

INSIDE

GIDEON SAT OPPOSITE LEANDER ON THE FLOOR OF THE study, cross-legged, his upraised palms resting on his knees and his eyes shut. They had chosen the Hebrew letter *Daleth* for its simple shape, an upside-down *L*, and because it was said to represent a door. "We will contemplate the letter with the eye of our minds until we see it hovering between us like a visitor from another world," Leander had instructed, "and then we will ask its permission to come through." He had learned the technique from a Jewish shoemaker in Safed: a humble man, Leander said, a disciple of the mystic Abulafia, whose knowledge lifted him far above his dingy hole of a shop.

On this cold, sunny morning in early March, the door would not open for Gideon. He tried to spread a white sheet over his scattered thoughts and draw two black strokes upon it. But his eyes fluttered open with a will of their own. Instead of *Daleth* treading air—he imagined the fragile configuration trembling in place like a moth that turns to ash at a touch—he saw Leander, at ease in his pose. His back was straight, his breathing deep and even; his large hands were cupped to catch the overflow of bliss. *His* half of the letter must surely be manifest, Gideon thought pettishly. Would it appear transparent like a gauze curtain, Gideon having failed to do his part?

He paid for this lapse into cynicism with a sudden cramp in one leg, and staggered to his feet clutching his calf.

Leander opened his eyes—slowly, Gideon noted—seeming to glide into wakefulness as smoothly as he had drifted into meditation. "What is it, friend? Are we moving too fast? I should have known better than to impose such an advanced practice on you. Shall we return to our desks?"

For the past two weeks they had done trials on paper, combining and recombining Hebrew characters into arbitrary groups. The object was to banish meaning altogether, until, after long contemplation, the letters would release their potency and sing out the higher music of pure thought. Leander had thrown himself into the exercise, experimenting with the Roman and Greek alphabets as well, for, he told Gideon, "Hebrew may have been the mother tongue, but the others are her beloved children, and no doubt God speaks them all." Gideon dutifully shuffled letters as if they were playing cards, and stared at them until their contours blurred, but never came close to replicating his experience with *Beth*. His mind played tricks on him, turning the chance conjunctions into nonsense words that gabbled in his head like an idiot's talk. He railed silently against the obscure Abulafia—no doubt one of those difficult Jews of whom Reverend Hedge would have despaired. Too soon, the letters receded to the background as one worry or another nosed up to torment him.

Today, a Saturday, he was preoccupied with his situation at the church. The elders had told him they were bringing in a guest preacher to conduct tomorrow's service. The man had been one of the candidates for Gideon's pastorate: a nephew of Mendham's wife, well educated by local standards but—as the deacon pointed out when informing Gideon of his day of rest—gifted with the common touch.

"It's no use," he said to Leander, dropping into a chair, his cramp finally releasing its grip. "I can't concentrate, and even if I could, I don't believe it's possible to *stalk* revelation this way. The few glimpses I've been granted were gifts, freely given to a young man who never anticipated such wonders and scarcely knew what he'd received. I'm a different person now. My cares overwhelm me."

Leander gazed up at him. "Do you think I'm not aware of your burdens?" he said calmly. "I want only to alleviate them. If I've rushed you, it's because I was seeking a more direct route to that place we both long for. I confess, I saw us walking together through those green bowers —maybe even attempting that elusive hill. Will you forgive me for my presumption? I've driven you deeper into yourself when what you need is a dose of sun and air."

He rose in one fluent motion to his feet—Gideon marveled at how liquidly his long legs unfolded—and strode to the window, pulling open the curtain they had drawn for privacy's sake. Light, harsh and bright, cut through the room's sepia, and Gideon thought of Sophy's words at breakfast, an eerie echo of his question to his mother all those years ago: "What do you *do* in there all day?" "Carry on the Reverend's work," he'd mumbled, catching in her pinched expression the reflection of his own dissimulation. The hurt in her eyes came back to him now. His head drooped, and he rested his brow in his hands.

Leander came up behind him and clasped his shoulders. "I've never seen you so cast down. Is it Mendham and his merry men? Let them bring one of their own to preach! What is the worst that can happen? That they liberate you to pursue your own path?"

"It's everything at once," Gideon said. "The church. The Hedges' dour looks, and their infernal stoicism—as though I'm teetering on the edge of the Pit and about to drag the lot of them in with me. Sophy. Poor Sophy. She breaks my heart." At the mention of her name, his voice went ragged; he took a deep breath to steady himself. "All my life I've stood alone. No father, no siblings, no real friends. My mother raised me to be accountable to no one but myself. I thought I wanted what other men have, but now that I possess it, I find I can't bear the weight." He laughed bitterly. "It's no wonder the Lord has denied us a child. Can you imagine the kind of father I would make?"

"An extraordinary one, I think." Leander spoke quietly, but his grip on Gideon's shoulders tightened. "You and I have known each other for two months, have we not? It is no accident that we met when we did. I cannot express how it wounds me to hear you speak of yourself as alone in the world. From now on, let me be all that life has denied you. Father. Brother. Friend."

Gideon felt some vital force flow from Leander's hands through his body; he could not tell whether it was Leander's will streaming in or his own seeping out. His limbs were as weak as a child's. He tried to shift in his seat, but the long fingers dug deeper, sharpening the ache in his shoulders to separate points of pain. He remembered how Leander had described the wrestling match with his student—words he had taken lightly at the time, in the affectionate spirit in which they'd been offered. Sensing Sophy nearby, a nervous, vigilant presence, Gideon repressed the urge to cry out. Instead, he sent her silent reassurance: *Don't worry. He will only hurt me as much as he has to.*

Hours after, reviewing the events of the day in the shelter of his bed, Sophy breathing quietly beside him, he would conclude that he had not been mesmerized: a man in a trance would hardly have considered what his wife would think if she were watching. Captivation was the state he settled on. Imprisoned by fascination—and the merest touch of brute force. He could not recall what he'd said to Leander, or if he'd spoken at all. But he must have grimaced, or nodded, or given some token of assent, for the pressure had suddenly eased. Leander was beaming at him, sunny and boyish. "Shall we go for a walk, my friend? You will tell me your troubles, and I will bear them with you."

ONCE EN ROUTE, they had no choice but to move quickly. The wind lashed them and they bent to its will. Though hard snow still coated the ground, the sun was showing its strength, venturing an assault on the frozen earth. Gideon was content to let Leander do the talking. It was all he could do to match his companion's long stride. His eyes and nose leaked, and each breath of air carved a fresh pathway to his lungs, but he felt clearer than he had in weeks. The farther they walked from the village, the more manageable his troubles appeared;

even so, he indulged a superstitious dread of looking over his shoulder for fear that his spirit might turn to stone again. He was relieved that his companion seemed disposed to chat about Cambridge instead of extracting confidences about problems that Gideon had, for the moment, put behind him.

"Did you ever hear Mr. Emerson preach when you were at Harvard?" Leander asked. "I happened to be in Boston when he lectured to the Natural History Society, and was mightily impressed. A humble presence, but what a fountain of profundity! Phrase after phrase lodged in my mind. *The grammar of botany. The natural alphabet.* I had half a mind to seek him out and become to that wise and gentle man what young Lem is to me." He glanced at Gideon. "It's struck me more than once how closely his thought hews to your own."

"He had his followers, who'd flock to the North End every Sunday," Gideon said. "I suppose I might have been attracted if I'd traveled in those circles, but . . . I went my own way. And once I was at Andover, it was unthinkable. My professors had no tolerance for high-minded musings on matters of the spirit. They saw Emerson and his kind as deceivers, seducing the weak with their anemic philosophy. 'Satan's wraiths,' the Reverend used to call them." Gideon hesitated, unwilling to offend Leander. "I don't question the man's gifts, or his goodness. Still, I always felt there was something finicky about the fellows who aped him—forever doting on their precious souls, pillaging the forest to build their airy castles. They don't go deep enough, these philosophical types. They only dream as far as they can see. It's all well and good to find Heaven in a sunset, but why stop at that? I can almost sympathize with my father-in-law's demands for a more rigorous faith."

Leander halted in mid-stride. "I never did make my pilgrimage, and until this moment I never asked myself why. My scruples were not quite the same as yours. I feared to get too near to Emerson's airy castle, and discover it was made of bricks and mortar after all. Our heroes don't always stand up to close observation—nor do their beautiful ideas."

"Ideas are only semblances," Gideon said. "When I think back on my visions—if I may call them that—it's their solidity that haunts me. I try to convey that quality to my congregation, but what proof can I offer them? I can't blame them for their lack of enthusiasm."

They walked on in silence. Gideon was beginning to feel weary, and the astringent air made him thirsty; he scooped up a handful of snow and dissolved some in his mouth, ignoring the pain in his teeth. It seemed to him that they must be miles beyond the bounds of Ormsby. His pastoral visits had never taken him in this direction. The land had been partially cleared, but nature was holding its own: scraggy pine trees blocked their path every few feet, like fugitives from an upstart army. Gideon felt a twinge of misgiving when he calculated how long it had been since he'd seen smoke curling from a chimney.

"I wonder if we should head home," he said. "Otherwise, we may have to spend the night in a snow cave like the Esquimaux."

"Oh, I doubt that will be necessary," Leander said. "Look where the wind has blown us." He pointed at a structure atop a nearby rise. It appeared to be unfinished, the wood unpainted and the windows boarded over. Even in this rough state it was imposing: two stories and an attic, with a pillared entryway, peaked like a temple, flanked on either side by wings. Stark against the cloudless sky, the house had none of the aqueous ephemerality of a mirage, but Gideon was too fatigued to trust its reality. He would gladly have retraced his steps if Leander weren't already bounding toward the incline.

Slipping and sliding, they struggled up an ice-crusted path, planting their feet in ruts etched in another season by wagon wheels. Even Leander was winded when they reached the top. "Well worth the effort," he gasped. "But why here, of all places? Why not in Concord? Or Boston?" He grinned at Gideon. "I love a mystery, don't you?"

They circled around the perimeter, marveling at details of construction and the quality of the work. However improbable its setting, the house had been built to last. The frame was solid and looked to be complete, but along one side they discovered the skeleton of a porch, stretching across the width of the façade. Its floor had been laid, the boards patchily visible under a thin carpet of snow; a couple of rocks served as makeshift stairs, and its roof was only a promise, the beams widely spaced, open to the weather.

"A veranda! Our mysterious builder must have fancied himself the master of a fine plantation in the north country," Leander said. "Can't you just see him in his rocking chair with a cheroot in one hand and a glass of hard cider in the other, contemplating his domain?"

Gideon gazed at the cleared land sloping into tiers of trees, and in the distance, on another plane but not as remote as he had feared, the village. He saw someone else entirely.

"Not 'veranda.' *Piazzer*," he corrected, skimming over the *z*'s, mimicking Caroline's nasal, Yankee-inflected Italian. "This must be the house James was building for his fiancée. She was forever nattering about her grand porch, driving poor James mad with her demands. He worked on this place every spare minute he had—even at night, if there was a full moon—but I had no idea how close he'd come to finishing. I'm ashamed to say I never helped him, though all the others did. When he spoke of it, it was always 'half-built.'" He paused. "After she left, he used to spend days there. But now he won't go near it."

"Ah, yes. The tragedy."

Gideon had informed Leander of James's history weeks ago, aiming to forestall awkward moments at the dinner table. Now he judged from his friend's thoughtful expression that Leander must be as moved by the poignancy of the snow-covered porch as he was. The very landscape seemed to be suffused with elegiac sorrow: the anguish of lost love hallowed by the stately descent of the afternoon sun. He was startled when Leander clapped his hands, as though summoning a groggy student to attention.

"Well! Shall we avail ourselves of James's hospitality *in absentia*, and cross over the threshold as the avaricious young lady did not? I don't know about you, but I could use a little refreshment."

Gideon stared. "You can't mean that we should break in."

"Ought such a vulgar term apply? Strangers break in. Friends and family *visit*." Leander sighed. "We put such faith in barriers in this country. I suppose we inherit that tendency from our English forebears. In the warmer climes, a weary traveler can knock on any door and be feted like the Prodigal Son. I remember one evening in Napoli . . ." He rambled on, as he crossed the porch and tested his weight against the planks that blocked the entrance. "This is firmer than it looks, but if I can loosen the nails with my knife, I think we can pull it free."

The room they found themselves in echoed the length of the porch; a fireplace, naked without a mantel, presided over its elegant sweep. James had done a thorough job of sealing the house: once the planks had been propped back in place, the space was snug, if not warm. A thin, sweet reek of resin hung in the air. Gideon blinked as his eyes adjusted to the muted light. He thought he could sleep where he stood.

"I see you're as tired as I am," Leander said. "Let's rest first and look around later. Over here, by the hearth." He brushed sawdust away with his foot and waited for Gideon to sit before dropping down beside him. "With a little help we'll soon conjure a roaring fire." He reached under his coat and brought up a flask, passing it to his companion. "You may find it strong at first, but it is wonderfully warming in the belly."

Gideon was not used to drinking from a flask. He put his head back, took a large swallow, and choked. The Hedges' cordials were mild as milk compared to this; the liquor seared his throat and burned all the way down. Leander took the flask from him while he was still coughing, swigged, and passed it back. The gesture was so comradely that Gideon drank, and drank again, stoked by a dawning wonder. This is what men do, he thought. This is what it is to have a friend.

After finishing off the last few drops, Leander produced a cloth-wrapped hunk of bread and cheese, which he sliced deftly on his palm. He was no prophet, he insisted: only a seasoned traveler who never set off on a journey without carrying provisions on his person. "Now," he said, "I am ready to listen."

A childlike comfort stole over Gideon. His limbs were loose; honey dripped, slow and sweet, in his veins. Leander was right, as he always seemed to be. The fiery liquor had banked to mellow warmth inside him. He chewed his bread and cheese, debating which trouble he should launch into first. The words that burst out of him seemed to have nothing to do with his present state of well-being.

"I am a miserable failure as a husband," he said.

"Such a statement! You damn yourself and dismiss your partner, all in one blow. When I look at Sophia, I see a woman whose affections run deep and steady, though in a narrow bed. She is perhaps overcautious in her expression—a pastor's daughter, after all—but I have no doubt she feels more than she is free to reveal." Leander wiped his hands with the cloth and put it back in his pocket. "Of course, I haven't seen the whole of her. I've done my best to win her trust, but she keeps her reserve around me."

"I wish you could know her as she was when I first met her," Gideon said, "dancing in the meadow when she thought no one was watching. Her freedom enchanted me. I thought I was spying on a woodland sprite—so rare is it to find a true child of nature. There was an innocence about her, a frankness . . ." His eyes stung with tears again, and this time he couldn't hold them back; his emotions surged, too profuse to be contained. "If she had married a man who could love her properly, she might still be that joyful girl."

Leander moved closer and covered Gideon's hand with his own. "We tread in delicate territory, my friend. I wouldn't pry for the world, but I want you to know that you can tell me anything. If it is a matter of, shall we say, mechanics, many men have such problems. You have only to avail yourself of a few simple techniques. In the East, poets write manuals on the art of love. Here, in the Vale of Righteousness, marriages founder for lack of a little knowledge."

"It is not . . . mechanics." Gideon's pride overcame his sorrow. "I don't claim expertise, but whatever I—we—do seems to make her happy. The trouble is in me. I try to share Sophy's rapture, but the worst of it is that each time we join, I feel less for her." He turned away from Leander's level gaze to focus on a pile of planks stacked in a corner. "I saw a girl in a blue dress dancing for her own pleasure, and I wanted her—more than I have ever wanted anything in this world. Even now, when we're intimate, I close my eyes to the woman in my arms and think of that girl. It may be that I'm only capable of loving from afar."

"Earth and air," Leander murmured. "The elements meet, but do not blend. How should they combine?" His face went slack.

Gideon felt the withdrawal of the other man's attention, with some relief. The effect of the liquor had lifted slightly; he was already wondering if he'd said too much. His eyelids had begun to droop when Leander's booming voice brought him back.

"How else should a visionary love, but from afar? It's your nature to take the long view, you cannot change it. I don't believe you two are mismatched. When I saw you sitting side by side, I knew you were paired for a reason. The qualities that beguiled you are still there. But Sophy stands outside your vision now; she is knocking at the door and you've shut it in her face. You must expand your vision to include her. Imbue her with the passion that is in you."

Leander had been speaking with great energy, waving his hands about and spreading them wide to illustrate his point. Now he seemed to contract to a cylinder of intensity. "She is necessary, if anything is to happen. Don't you find it curious that the Bible tells us Adam is made of earth when it is woman who is the ground of all being? She is the one who receives the seed and grows it in her body. Without her, a vision is only an aimless fancy."

"I don't see how an infant will help me to realize my vision," Gideon said, "whatever form that might take. It will just be another responsibility, and I can't manage the ones I have."

Leander banished all impediments with another wave of his hand. "This is not the time to be timid," he said. "You and I have met! Our Eve is ripe and waiting! If we're to carve out a new kingdom, we must have as much audacity as pharoahs and kings and Holy Roman emperors."

Gideon was struck dumb. Pharoahs and emperors? New kingdom? Leander's thigh had relaxed against his, but he felt powerless to move, helplessly aware that he was alone with a very large man in an isolated place. His mother had told him to be calm and slowly inch away should he ever have the misfortune to encounter a lunatic. For several heartbeats, that warning, and the fear that he would never find his way back to the village alone, were the only coherent thoughts in his mind. Then he remembered his thesis. He had given it to Leander weeks ago, and had been intending to ask him if he'd finished it. The section dealing with the sequestered infants had been marked.

"You can't mean . . ." he said again.

"Did you think we would play with words forever? Spend our dotage sniffing out buried roots like the good Reverend? Why not take up coin collecting or spaniel breeding? Nice tame occupations for the seer who does not see." Leander was drawling, tossing the words away. "I could teach you more about the spirit of the letters. Introduce you to their numerical equivalents, initiate you into their mysteries. But it would take years, and the results would not be certain. I traveled the world seeking out the masters, studied till my brain ached, meditated till the top of my head opened, and what have I to show for it? A few tricks to amuse my students. Even the holy men sometimes fail to gain access, and few stay in that hallowed realm for long. No, my friend, if we are to live in the land you covet, we will have to re-create it ourselves. And a little child shall lead us."

Gideon reached for the flask, though he knew it was empty. "You're not suggesting that I make a child for the sole purpose of experimenting on it. Only a madman could be so cold."

"I see I'm rushing you again," Leander said. "I agree—it's too soon to think in such grandiose terms. We must proceed confidently, one step at a time. For now, your only concern should be to renew your courtship—and with such a charming object, I can't think it will be very difficult. Use your wits, my friend. Sprites are shy of men. They must be lured. When you approach Sophia, try to look beyond the construct that society calls a 'wife.' The word evokes those dreadful iron maidens that compress a woman's waist to a size nature never intended. Imagine that you are loosening the laces, one by one, releasing her from matronly armor. Perhaps . . . perhaps the marks of the boned stays are still imprinted on her delicate ribcage. Her white throat arches, her bosom expands." He touches his chest. "Two dear little birds are released to the air. She takes a full, free breath, her first in hours, a wild creature restored—and looks to you, her liberator."

Leander's voice had lulled, but now his tone turned crisp. "I suggest you give some thought to what the French call *ambiance*. Do you and Sophia have a retreat, a sanctuary that evokes thoughts of love? Women are more attuned to their surroundings than we are. Our mother Eve was the first to occupy that small red room, you know, when she was only a rib under Adam's heart."

"She used to come to the study every night. It was quite a little home for us, the only private place we had." Gideon could barely hear himself for the blood drumming in his ears.

"And she feels that I've displaced her. No wonder she is cold to me. What a cloddish old bachelor I am. You can be sure I'll be more discreet in the future."

He stood, vigorously slapping at his seat and the back of his thighs, as if to shake off any traces of regret with the clinging sawdust. "Shall we explore the rest of the house while we still have some light? Now I would guess that this imposing room was intended for a *grand salon*, or a banquet hall. Can't you see Miss Caroline admiring her *piazzer* as she picks at her dainties?"

CHAPTER 26

HABITATION FOR GHOSTS

SOPHY IS NOT SUPERSTITIOUS, BUT THIS AFTERNOON SHE TAKES
the jade rabbit out of her ring box for the first time since Leander gave
it to her. She keeps the box in a corner of her bureau drawer, tucked
under her linens. Leander's other offerings have been trussed up in a
handkerchief in the opposite corner. A turkey feather, a red-and-gold
button, a flat white stone, a speckled bird's egg—they simply appear
at her place at the table or on top of a book she is reading. She never
acknowledges the gifts and doesn't want to look at them; yet she can't
quite toss them out. Hiding them seems the best solution.

Is it bad luck to shut luck away? Pent up, does it sour like milk?
Quickly she transfers the rabbit to the palm of her hand and strokes
its ears, placating. Whoever carved the little creature put so much life
into it that it seems fidgety; she would swear to a quiver beneath her
finger. She shuts her eyes and takes a deep breath. "Please don't . . ."
she whispers, and then, "Please protect . . ." It sounds too much like
a begging prayer, and she realizes, once she begins, that she isn't sure
what to wish for.

Downstairs, someone is knocking on the door: one hesitant, two firm, right on time.

———

THEY HAVE SENT Mr. Brown instead of Mendham. There's luck in that—mercy, too—though the news he brings is all over his face. He takes off his hat and holds it to his chest, leaving wisps of gray hair standing on his pate. The sight of the three of them assembled in the hall, dressed in their Sunday clothes, must intimidate the poor man; he looks from Mama to Gideon, uncertain whom he should address.

"Come in to the parlor, why don't you, Mr. Brown," Mama says. "You might as well be comfortable."

Mr. Brown follows her in but refuses a chair, so none of them sits. He clears his throat. "Parson Birdsall," he says. "As you know, the congregation voted this morning, and I regret that it did not go your way. There were several who spoke up for you—I think your heart would have been touched by their sincere expressions—but in the end, you did not have the support, sir." He waits, anticipating a fusillade, but no one speaks. "If I may venture an opinion, your gifts are wasted in Ormsby. We're country folk here, we haven't an ear for eloquence, or much practice in indulging the imagination, but in Boston you would be among your own. You would be at home there, sir, and your young lady, too."

His eyes rest briefly on Sophy, then fasten on Mama. "Fanny—" he says. He was a friend of Papa's long before Sophy was born; Papa used to say they grew the congregation together. Mama nods and reaches out to take his hand.

Sophy is proud of her family. Even at this moment, Gideon stands straight and tall, a shining pillar. He thanks Mr. Brown for his efforts in the most gracious way, assuring him that his suggestions will be considered, that he will always be a friend. Mama exudes dignity. She is the soul of calm as she escorts Mr. Brown—rotating his hat in an agitated manner and declaring he never thought he would see this day—to the door. Then, without a glance at either of them, she stalks back to the parlor and plants herself in the middle of the settee.

Sophy sits beside her. "Mama, we all knew this might happen," she says. "It's quite a common thing for a pastor to move from one congregation to another. Remember Mr. Otis from Duxbury? And him with five children. Think of that!"

Gideon follows her in. He stands before them with shoulders sagging, looking as if he would scrape his forehead on the floor if he could. "Mrs. Hedge—Fanny—please forgive me. I tried my best, but I am not the Reverend, there's no help for it. I can only be what I am."

Mama pays them no mind. She stares stonily at the portrait of her husband over the fireplace. Contemplation has never been her natural state, and it does not become her. In the clear afternoon light Sophy sees how much she has aged since Papa died, deep lines running from cheek to chin, making her face look even longer.

"Thirty years," she says at last. "Gone. All gone. Soon you will be gone too."

JAMES AND MICAH return later in the afternoon. They had chosen to attend the crucial meeting, though the family was exempted. Micah goes straight upstairs to the attic, but James lingers.

"You've brought it on yourself," he tells Gideon. "Folks can't live on fairy tales." His dogged righteousness could almost pass for satisfaction, Sophy thinks. Since his disappointment in love, he has taken refuge in Papa's Calvinism and nourishes himself strictly on the dry biscuit of the Word, having sifted out the Reverend's leavening enthusiasm and buoyant hope. "I doubt you'll get another parish in these parts," he says. "You had better give some thought to how you'll support my sister. Maybe you can do some tutoring until you find a post."

Sophy waits in the kitchen in gathering gloom. This first day of April has delivered a light rain, and the muted tapping on the roof suits her mood. The others have retreated to their rooms. The supper hour is approaching, but no one ventures out except Micah, who ducks into the pantry without a word to her, and hurries back upstairs with the remains of yesterday's loaf tucked furtively under his arm. At half-past five there is another knock at the door.

"I hope I'm not intruding, Mrs. Birdsall," Leander says. He taps his slouch hat, releasing a small shower. "After the day you've all had, I thought you might be in need of a little restorative. I happened to have a bit of salt beef that Mrs. Pierce was kind enough to bring me for the holidays, and a few oddments left over. If you don't mind dining on the salmagundi of a bachelor's larder, I'll leave them with you." He hands Sophy a basket covered with a brightly patterned cloth that resembles one of his scarves. The unexpected weight of it almost unbalances her.

For once, Sophy is glad to see him. "Come see what Mr. Solloway has brought us!" she calls, and in a minute the hall is filled, each of them lured like mice from their holes.

Half a joint of beef, pickled cabbage from Leander's own recipe, roasted potatoes, a bottle of Madeira wine, even some coffee in a twist of paper. Sophy arranges the bounty on the table, and they discover hunger in spite of themselves. It is remarkable, she thinks, how the instinct for life persists, even when all seems at an end. They are reconstituted as a family just by the act of eating together. Gideon still occupies Papa's old place at the table. But from the moment they sit down, the family has a new head.

There never was a question of Leander leaving. Still, she is dazzled by the easeful way he assumes authority, insisting she and Mama rest while he serves, pouring the wine, getting the conversation going and fanning it when it falters. Gideon says grace, as usual, though it is clear whom they really have to thank.

"Leander, I can see why you have no need of a wife." Mama pats her lips with a napkin. "But you shouldn't have brought so much. You could have eaten for a month on what you're feeding us tonight."

"Better to enjoy it in your good company than at my desk, with a book in one hand and a knife in the other. I felt such a lifting of the spirit after escaping the meeting that nothing but a banquet would do.

I'd gladly have brought a dressed pheasant and an oyster pie, but the humble fare before you was all I had."

"If you'd stayed till the end, you would know we have no cause to celebrate," Mama says. Gideon looks first at Sophy, then down at his plate. James and Micah go on eating, the stolid clink of their knives and forks on Mama's good china the only sound in the room.

"Dear lady, allow me to differ with you. Change is always a cause for rejoicing. New life, new possibilities! I say we drink to Gideon Birdsall, one of the most extraordinary men it has been my privilege to meet in any corner of the globe. May his future be worthy of his abundant gifts, and may all our stars rise with him."

Leander raises his glass, the wine shimmering in the candlelight, and drains it by half. The other glasses are full; no one has indulged except Micah, whose cheeks, always rosy, have turned a hectic red. Now Mama drinks, pursing her lips as if funneling hot soup, and Sophy lifts her glass for Gideon's sake. She's only had a few sips of wine in her life, and never cared for more; the sour taste doesn't appeal to her. This wine is different, sweet on the tongue but a trifle sharp when swallowed: like drinking rubies, Sophy thinks. She is pleased at how easily it slides down, pleased that it tastes the way it looks. Only James abstains, keeping to his customary milk and refusing even to join in the toast.

By the time coffee is served, the atmosphere in the house has changed. The men lean back in their chairs. James lights his pipe and asks Micah if he wouldn't like a puff, now that he has acquired the vices of a man of the world. Micah obliges, aping the gentleman as he makes a show of sucking in smoke. He expels it less elegantly. "I p-p-prefer wine," he declares, when he can speak. Mama has recovered enough spirit to protest that the smell of tobacco puts her off her food, but she seems in no hurry to collect the plates and shoo the men into the parlor. Sophy reaches for Gideon's hand under the table, and is pleased when he gives it a little squeeze. The table is a raft, and they are all clinging to the edges. Knowing what uncertainties await them tomorrow, she wishes they could stay afloat forever.

Leander offers the bottle around one last time and pours the last drops into his own glass.

"You'll never guess what Gideon and I discovered on one of our rambles the other day," he says. "As handsome a house as I've seen since I came back east, marooned in the middle of a wood. Gideon had an idea that you might be the architect, James. If so, I congratulate you. I knew you were an able man, but never imagined your gifts lay in that direction."

No one mentions the house in James's presence. The last time Mama ventured to ask about his plans for it, he didn't speak for three days.

Leander takes no notice of the ice in the room. "Architecture is one of my passions, you know. I've done a bit of building myself. Gideon is the soul of reticence and would never think to ask, but I wonder— would you consider taking us along the next time you inspect the castle? I'd dearly love to see the interior."

Gideon drops Sophy's hand.

"I never go there. It has nothing to do with me anymore." James directs his words to the table. He pushes his chair back with a scraping sound.

"Never go there? Leave that fine property to the squirrels and mice, and any tramp looking to keep the rain off his head? All manner of folk roam about these days. A whole tribe of Gypsies could be encamped in your parlor, and their goats and chickens, too. Only last week a fellow came to the schoolhouse door wanting food. Filthy, a pirate's patch over one eye. I gave him what I could, though he had a distinct look of the jailhouse about him."

"Whoever finds his way in is welcome to it. The place is a burden and a curse. They'd be doing me a service if they set it on fire."

Leander shakes his head. "Destroy what you made? My friend, the house isn't to blame for the hopes invested in it. It's a thing of beauty, thanks to you. Why not look beyond dashed expectations and put it to good use? Build a new life for yourself there. Rent it or sell it. But don't let it turn into a habitation for ghosts."

"I've had enough of beauty . . ." James mutters. He stands, his pipe awkward in his hand, an artifact of an easeful moment. "The house is mine, and I'll dispose of it as I will. It's no business of yours."

He is having one of his silent fits, Sophy sees. His thoughts rage and batter him from within, and he shakes with the effort to contain them. He was never meant to be so angry, she thinks; he lacks the constitution for it. The pipe is trembling. He grips the afflicted wrist with the other hand, dumps the tobacco on his plate, and stalks out. They hear his footsteps in the hall, the front door slamming shut.

Mama reproaches Leander with her eyes before she can bring herself to speak. "What were you thinking, stirring him up so? Hasn't Gideon told you?"

Leander nods solemnly. "Better to lance a wound than let it fester. Poor boy, he holds his pain too close. He must be made to release it if he is ever to be free. Forgive me if I spoke untimely, but I thought to spare the rest of you. An outsider wields a more efficient knife, and has a thicker skin to ward off blows." He glances at Gideon out of the corner of his eye, all the while sending sympathy across the table. "Don't disturb yourself, Missus. James will come around, I'm sure of it."

Sophy feels that current again, passing between Gideon and Leander. She has sensed it more than once, and each time, the words that ignite it are tame to the point of blandness. James's condition is a sorrow, but why should a simple wish for his improvement kindle such interest? It's as if something lies beneath the words, a meaning known only to the two of them. A code she can't penetrate. She looks hard at Gideon, sending him her own message. *I am the wife! You can't have secrets from me.* His face has relaxed, now that James is gone. He seems very young at this moment, with his hair brushed back from his brow and his wide blue eyes musing aimlessly. The corners of his mouth are lifted in a private smile. Look at me, she commands him. I dare you to.

Leander is the one who meets her gaze. "Sophia," he says, speaking her name as if he always addressed her so. "If Mrs. Hedge can spare you, won't you join us in the study? Gideon and I have been having such good talks about the vision of the *artiste*. It's time we tested our theories on a practitioner."

CHAPTER 27

SMALL RED ROOM

WO SUNDAYS AGO THEY MOVED HER EASEL INTO THE study—a liberty she never dared ask of Gideon. This afternoon, at Leander's request, Sophy is rendering the room. She has told them she is no better at interiors than at capturing faces.

"My walls *will* slide into my floors, no matter how hard I try to separate them," she warned. "Perspective is quite beyond me. Outdoors is easier, the trees give me clues."

Gideon and Leander exchanged one of their smiles, and Gideon took out his little book and wrote down what she said. He does this often now, inscribing her most commonplace remarks as if they were the droppings of a sage, precious for the mere fact of who produced them. She finds it disconcerting.

"Oh, that bugaboo perspective!" Leander said. "I assure you, it's nothing but the Devil's trick. Sleight of hand, sleight of eye, it's all the same foolery—no different from the now-you-see-it-now-you-don't I divert my students with on rainy days. Forget the deceiving imp, dear girl, and paint what you see."

So she is painting away, quickly and with a broad brush, laying down thick swathes of color with a child's abandon. She isn't even trying to make it true, only to slap the images down as her eye takes them in: Papa's desk, now Gideon's, with its row of massive black tomes leaning shoulder-to-shoulder like mourners at a funeral. The engraving table squat in the center, suspended in air along with the woodstove. The braided rug—*their* rug—levitated like a magic carpet. Sophy brings these floating objects back to earth with a few stark stripes for floorboards—she ignores the blandishments of the Serpent, urging her to consider the vanishing point—and where the stripes end, ventures a bold line across and down each side. Behold the walls! The room is like the inside of a treasure box, filled with curiosities. The window is an afterthought here, an intruder in her snug little container. She fills in the white square with feathery strokes of green, a reminder of the burgeoning spring that awaits them outdoors.

When the painting is done, Sophy pushes her chair back from the easel to see what she has wrought. She can't help laughing. Her innocent eye has begotten a bad dream of a room, but she feels as tender toward her creation as a mother might feel toward a newborn with a harelip; she loves it for its flaws. Leander and Gideon have been lingering nearby, watching her work while they pretend to do other things. She has been performing for them—taking her revenge for their ogling.

They observe her. It is the price she pays for being admitted to their conversation. In their presence she feels like one of Micah's animals, admired for her oddities. They praise her for what she does poorly, and shake their heads over her better efforts. "You were thinking too much," Leander said the other day, dismissing one of her old landscapes. "Why make a slavish copy of the world when you can see it fresh?"

She can tell by the expression on their faces that she has done well this time. "Marvelous!" Leander says. "Such exuberance! You are a prodigy in reverse, Sophia. You have not lost your child's eye. You go back to go forward, and so must we all."

Gideon is more restrained. He bends and drops a kiss on her head, as if she were, in fact, the infant savant they fancy her to be. "A great improvement on the original. I think we should hang it here, and feast our eyes on its colors when these dull old walls close in on us."

Sophy stifles the pang she feels when Gideon condescends to her in front of Leander. Reminds herself that in an hour or so he will not be treating her like a child at all. "Since I've been so clever," she says, "perhaps you won't mind if I paint outdoors tomorrow. I am confident I can ruin the garden too."

THE TALK IS, MOST DAYS, worth the price of their scrutiny. Gideon stumbles at first—not a month free of parish duties, he is sluggish from having held back for so long—but soars to the heavens as his ideas take possession of him. He lives in a lucid fever now, his mind always tuned to a high pitch. This afternoon he returns to his pet subject, the Fall of Language, traveling back to the beginning to fill in what the first pages of the Bible failed to explain.

When God spoke the world into being, piece by piece, the distance between the Deity and his Creation was short and charged. (Gideon points one tense forefinger at the other, and Sophy can almost see lightning crackle between them.) Words and the things they represented were one. But ever since the Serpent stretched his twisty neck around the Tree of Knowledge and bandied words with Eve, the gap between Name and Object has been growing. Eons of subtle distortion, of abstraction, of careless speech have sundered that organic unity. As for the beasts that Adam named, these days they would be labeled in Latin and classified according to their common attributes, their singularity lost to the ruthless democracy of science. Words are only signposts now, slung around the necks of creatures whose essence they once perfectly expressed: a wholeness so profound, Gideon insists, that it is no sacrilege to liken it to the One Flesh of marriage. Remnants of this unity are everywhere, most tellingly in those rhetorical flourishes we call the figures of speech. Simile and metaphor? Good soldiers picking through the detritus of the shattered city, trying to reconstruct the ruins.

"One might even," he says carefully, gazing over her head, "extend the analogy to the act of love . . ."

Sophy looks down at her lap. How can Gideon say such things in front of a guest? He knows as well as she what they will be doing when Leander leaves.

Today, it seems, he will never go. The two of them are deep in discussion, Leander sprawled in the desk chair, Gideon pacing back and forth as he rattles on about gathering speakers of other tongues to join them in the great task of restoring language. Together they will excavate primal roots and assemble a dictionary that will give the enlightened the keys to a new Eden.

"Perhaps a few pupils, to begin with," Leander says. "Then a small school, a workshop for scholars. The Institute for the Rejuvenation of Language, or some such title. It is not too soon to think about a place."

Leander tethers Gideon's ideas to earth. His magic is the practical kind. Presto, he shrinks the heavens to the size of a house, and Gideon smiles and nods, not the least deflated. If she were to offer such common-sense suggestions, he would sigh and tell her she doesn't understand.

Suddenly, Leander is up and shrugging his coat on in haste, as if a clock chimed the hour in his head. "Be happy, children," he says at the door. Lately it is this way whenever he visits. Sophy suspects secret signals, but fends off the notion. It is unbearable to think that the schoolmaster arranges their intimacy—that he intrudes even here.

Gideon closes the curtains. He fiddles with the bolt on the door—rusty because no one ever used it until now. He lights the lamp on the desk, keeping the flame low, and scrawls on one of the papers strewn across the surface. Sophy waits, quiet, in the corner. Difficult to gauge his mood today. He isn't agitated; his movements are leisurely, he has perhaps expended himself in talking. No matter how still she tries to be, her heart always starts to jump at this moment. She knows how the mole feels when the owl circles lazily overhead.

NOT SO LONG AGO their lovemaking was soft and slow, his touch careful, as though he feared to damage her. She had been the bold one then—her mother's daughter, teasing him and showing her saucy side, but only to bring him on. At times he seemed to be somewhere else, but she told herself that this was his lofty nature: angels may condescend to fleshly pleasure, but they cannot relish it like ordinary men.

These days he is a different sort of angel. Avenging. He has a mission to complete, and in its service he becomes the lover that Solomon sang about, terrible as an army with banners. There has always been a coldness in him, but it was of the mind: a will to know, clear and pure as a block of ice. Now that same will is lodged in his body, and she is the object—or the means. They do things together that she has never heard or thought of: shaming things that stay with her all the next day as she goes about her work. If it's a child he wants, she would like to tell him that the straight path is as effectual as the twisted. Even if, for them, it isn't so.

He is smiling, a good sign. "You have a smudge of paint on your face," he says. "The first time I saw you at your easel, it was a streak of green. I remember thinking how natural it looked. Your true character showing through."

Sophy wants to ask why, exactly, her character had a botanical hue, and whether the shade has changed over time. Instead she says, "What color am I today?"

"Carmine, I think. Across one cheek, like a savage." He looks around. "No, don't wipe it away—we can use a touch of color in this drab room, don't you think?"

"I don't care how the room looks, so long as it is ours." She feels offended, as if he had criticized her dress—plain enough, Lord knows. She should at least have taken off her apron, which bears the stains of a week's cooking along with splotches of paint. Quickly she unties it and tosses it to the floor.

Gideon shrugs off his jacket, lets it drop. Without intending to, Sophy has set things in motion. Obediently she begins to undo the fastenings at her neck, but he puts his hand over hers to stop her.

"Let's pretend we're in the room you painted," he says.

She doesn't have a chance to ask what he means. He takes her by the shoulders and pushes her against a wall. Pulls up her skirts. When she cries out, he presses his mouth into hers and feeds her own words back to her. "The walls *will* slide into the floor." He says this again and again, timing it to his thrusts. Words break into pieces; only fragments reach her ear. "The walls *will* . . . walls *will* . . ." He brings her down to the floor to finish, groaning as he gives the last of what is in him.

Afterward he is too spent to leave her. Sophy puts her arms around him and strokes his back, as best she can, pitying him for his emptiness. They were lower than the beasts tonight. Her spine is a long bruise, every crevice in her body is sore. But something has been planted: she feels instantly and unaccountably strange, her juices muddled like one of Papa's homemade wines, and yet, lit from within. Mama said she always knew.

Sophy wonders whether the study might be an anteroom to this new world Gideon and Leander are always talking about: the old certainties still in place, but upended. We must go back to go forward, Leander says. Sink low to accomplish our higher purpose. Her eyes, shut all this time, open wide. Above her the ceiling spins—or is it the floor?

PART FOUR

POPULATING PARADISE

CHAPTER 28

BRICKS AND MORTAR

"A MIRACLE? HOW MANY TIMES MUST I TELL YOU? YOUR brother-in-law is a stubborn man, but not beyond reason. All I did was ask him." Leander flashed his teeth and put the water jug to his lips, his Adam's apple bobbing as he drank. All morning they had hauled debris from the upper story of James's house, shedding clothes as they worked, until the July heat drove them downstairs.

They had been laboring for weeks to make the main floor habitable: white-washing the walls, putting glass in the windows, sanding the floors. Micah had been enlisted to make doors and had promised to construct mantels for the parlor and dining room before the cold weather set in. Leander's pupil, Lem, had been hired out to a neighboring farmer, but came when he could to help his true master with heavier tasks, and to work outside. The soil was rutted and full of stones, not yet fit for planting, and, as Leander pointed out, who ever heard of an Eden without a garden?

"Now, if I were a true miracle worker," Leander said, "I could solve the problem of the nursery. I really thought the attic might do. I saw it lined with bright quilts to cheer a baby's eye, sunlight and birdsong pouring through the little window. But sound will float up, and the extremes of temperature might be too much. We mustn't risk the little one's health."

"Miracles are ordinary life for you. You'll wave your wand, and mumble a spell or two, and the answer will come to you." Gideon spoke with more confidence than he felt. Leander's mention of the baby as a creature affected by heat and cold made him uneasy.

Without a shirt his friend looked even more massive—the sort of genial giant who could conquer a small country with a toothy smile and a few deft twists of an iron girder. For such a colossus, persuading a haunted man to relax his grip on the seat and symbol of his heartbreak would be no great matter. Still, Gideon never ceased to marvel that they were at rest in the same room they'd broken into months before—this time with the assent of the builder. Landlord now: James professed indifference to the house's fate, but had allowed himself to be convinced of the virtue of collecting rent. The money, for the time being, would come from Leander. He was as vague about its origins as the Reverend had been about his business in the city. "Since you persist in calling me a magician, let me do this one trick," he'd said when Gideon protested. "Turn a pile of paper notes into a roof and walls. A home for our dream."

Leander might make light of his sorcery, but he was behind every recent marvel in Gideon's life. Even the pregnancy—for Gideon would never have been so masterful with Sophy, exercised his imagination so freely, had Leander not taught him how to see her. The schoolmaster ate the world with his eyes. Man, woman, well-favored members of the animal kingdom; Fanny's jars of quince jelly on the windowsill; the copper beech that overlooked the study; a perfect pear—Leander feasted on them all at his leisure. Pan-lover indeed! A cat may look at a king, the old saying went, but so might a king look at a cat, and use the creature for what pleasure he could take from it.

"Irrigate yourself, young Apollo." Leander offered the water jug, watching with a teasing smile as Gideon crouched on his haunches and reached out an arm. His frank appreciation had bothered Gideon at first; there had been men at Harvard who were the subject of whispers. But his friend's lingering looks were cast so widely that they were almost impersonal.

"Why do you stare at me?" he'd asked once, when they first began to work on the house.

Leander had raised his eyebrows. "Because you are beautiful," he said, as if the answer were obvious. "If it disturbs you, I'll stop."

By now Gideon was used to the scrutiny—felt, even, that he merited it. Weeks of physical labor had turned him brown and muscled. From boyhood he had regarded his body as a kind of clock case, ornamental to no purpose, important only because it enclosed the works. Now that it had seeded a child and helped to complete a house, he viewed it with new respect.

"I must speak to Micah about making a long table," Leander said. "Oval in shape to facilitate a communion of equals. When the students come, you can converse with them here. No lecturing in your school. You will be Socrates, and the table will be your sacred grove. Think of the meals we'll have! Banquets for the scholars, and intimate suppers for our little family. We'll nourish our bodies in silence, as the monks do, and our spirits will exult in the view."

Gideon drank. "I'd love to see Caroline's face if she ever learns what we've made of her salon. Micah says she was intending to play her spinet here, for a reverent audience of the cultured few." Another thought occurred to him. "What about the Hedges?" he said. "They'll want to see Sophy . . . and the baby."

The child was not quite real to him. Enthralled as he was by the fact of its existence, he had trouble picturing it in Sophy's arms, or in her womb, for that matter, for she was as slender as she had ever been. True, it was early days: she was sick most mornings, and in bed each night she pressed his hand to her belly, inviting him to marvel over a roundness he pretended to feel. But Fanny seemed satisfied, and Leander, ever the expert, assured him that in a few months he would be an extraordinary father to an extraordinary child. Gideon was no longer certain how this prophecy would translate into humble human form. It was difficult to connect the infant paragons he'd conjured while writing his thesis to the squirming, red-faced specimens who had squalled through his sermons at Sunday meeting. Not, by any leap of the imagination, first citizens of a new world.

"I am already considering how to deal with the family," Leander said. "James is no problem. I doubt he'll come within a mile of the place. Micah is already one of us; he knows the virtues of silence in his bones. But dear, talkative Mrs. Hedge . . ." He sighed. "A worthy woman whose claims should be honored. We must think of a way to keep her at a distance while reassuring her that the baby is well. A fragility, perhaps . . . a constitutional delicacy requiring isolation, something the child will grow out of in time. Sophia could display the little one in a window. Wave its tiny hand at Grandmama."

Leander flapped his fingers, widened his eyes, and blew out his lips in an expression of imbecilic delight. He doesn't even care what he looks like, Gideon thought, feeling for once like the sober adult.

"I haven't told Sophy yet," he said. "I don't know what to say to her. That she and the baby will be locked up like the princes in the Tower? That she'll be let out once in a while for *talking* meals? She'll never understand about the silence. What mother doesn't want to speak to her child?"

"It's all in how you present it," Leander said. "If you spell out the terms of the experiment, she'll think we're both mad. She'll retreat to the bosom of her family, and James will make a noise, and you and I will be lucky to escape the asylum, or worse. Little by little is the way. Let her settle into her new home. Enjoy the comforts of her own domain, and accustom herself to the rhythm of life within its walls. Then, when she is feeling safe and content, suggest an interlude of silence—only an hour to begin with, a respite from the day's tasks, a time for each of us to consult his soul. She might like to spend it painting, or in the garden with her flowers. Gradually, we will introduce the notion of sanctuary. If one hour is bliss, why not two? Why not silent dinners, a silent Sabbath?"

He had been vehement as he leaned toward Gideon, hands sketching on the air. Now he slumped back against the wall and grinned. "Gravity will be our friend. They get enormous, you know. Big as barrels. Big as houses!" He stretched his clasped hands before him, as far as he could reach. "Trust me, the last couple of months she'll be a globe unto herself, and crave nothing but a rocking chair in a quiet corner, where she can commune with her population of one. By the time she gives birth, silence will be her native habitat."

Gideon flushed. A vein of coarseness surfaced in the man now and then, breaking the flow of his polished speech. In the past he'd told himself it was only Leander's earthy temperament, but his own nature recoiled from it.

"They? I wish you wouldn't refer to Sophy as if she were a species," he said. "You're talking about my wife. The experiment is my child."

"I meant no disrespect," Leander said. "I love Sophia *because* she is yours—and the little one, too. If I was overfamiliar, forgive me."

Earlier there had been a listless breeze through the windows. Now the air was still, the atmosphere somnolent. The little flame of tension that had flickered between them wavered and extinguished itself. Leander closed his eyes and spread his hands on his thighs. Gideon was relaxed, but alert. He was thinking how lovely the bare room was at this hour, the afternoon light gilding the warm wood of the new-laid floor, enhancing its graceful proportions. If silence was a sanctuary, this serene emptiness must surely be its cathedral. A table would be an intrusion. How little anyone needed, really, to be content.

The thought was locked safely in his head, and then it burst its bars. His own voice startled him. "Do you ever think we might go on just as we are?"

Leander's eyelids lifted, but only a fraction. "As we are? I don't understand."

"I mean, live here as a family and have a little school. Keep chickens and plant vegetables. Get by as simply as we can. Micah would join us, and maybe a few like souls would drift in. Young Lem might be useful, though we would have to watch him around the chickens." Gideon tried to laugh, but his throat was very dry; he drank from the jug. "We could share ideas in the evenings, and perhaps put our thoughts together in a book. We might discover that the Eden we seek is more . . . easily attainable than we know."

"You are afraid." It was a plain truth, and, having exposed it, Leander seemed to observe it from a distance. "You can choose that path," he said, measuring his words. "Eke out your existence from day to day, until death claims you. Hide from the truths that drive you. Embrace triviality in the name of respectability. Most men live so. I tried it myself once." He paused. "I could never go that way again."

"Must you paint such a bleak picture?" But even as he spoke, Gideon was remembering the night of Hedge's accident—how he had dreamed of fleeing to a monastery to escape the mortal round of family life. "I worry that we'll go too far," he said. "If the baby were to come to harm, Sophy would never forgive me. I could never forgive myself."

Leander shook his head. "What you must think of me to have such fears! And yet, how tender, how natural is your concern. The fatherly instinct is quickening in you, even as the child quickens in Sophia."

He straightened his back against the wall and gazed at Gideon through half-closed eyes. "The most exquisite images came to me as I was meditating. Plants with huge spreading leaves like the wings of noble birds. Lush blossoms, crimson and purple, bending double the vines that bore them. And amidst this voluptuous display, the shyest little white orchid, so fresh and sweet, so modest, yet all the other blooms seemed to wait upon it. Where, in the waking world, does such exotica flourish? Only the Tropics—yet, in all my travels I never set foot in the torrid zones. I thought the day's heat must have sowed these vivid pictures in my mind. Now I see that they were our answer."

Gideon had forgotten the question by now, but whatever it might have been, tropical flora seemed an inadequate response. He had expected to be rallied, or at least reassured. Was Leander trying to distract him?

The schoolmaster stood and strode to the far end of the room. "Here we have a sweeping expanse, solid along the inner wall except for this"—he pointed to the arched doorway that led to the rest of the house—"while the outer wall is perforated with windows and the intention of French doors, all meant to overlook a south-facing porch that matches the room for length. It struck me that the porch belonged to the room. It could easily be enclosed. But how, then, to preserve the illusion of openness?"

He stopped in front of Gideon. "Glass, of course. A conservatory, where the flowers of summer can grow in all seasons. And in the center, the white orchid, the pure, delicate bloom that is the reason for it all. You see now, don't you? You have been thinking your loved ones would be hidden away in some dark prison of a room, when, in truth, they will be in Paradise! Imagine them in this ample, sunny space, with every comfort at hand. Sophia in the dead of winter tenderly nurturing her indoor garden, knowing that each plant she cultivates feeds the soul of her little one, even as her milk nourishes its body. The freedom she will have to mother as the primitive races do." Leander paused and glanced out at the porch with a musing look, perhaps anticipating the charm of the sight. "Imagine a child whose eyes have absorbed beauty from its first hour of life, who has never heard a harsh word, whose every need is answered promptly and with love. Will such a child cry? Or will it sing a song not heard since the beginning of the world?"

"All children cry, it's an instinct," Gideon said faintly. He took no pleasure in the thought of Sophy suckling the baby in a fishbowl, particularly with Leander looking on. "A conservatory is a pretty idea, but hardly practical—it would only attract prying eyes. And how can we possibly think of building one when we have so much else to do? Not to mention the cost of the glass. Perhaps next spring, after we've been settled for a while . . ."

Leander put up one hand. "Enough. You are losing the courage of your vision. Soon you'll convince yourself that what you saw was nothing but a delusion. If you have no faith, why should I? I've cast my lot with you, overcome your 'impossibilities' to bring you a child and a house, and now that fulfillment is at hand, you thank me by pelting me with pebbles. *The cost of glass?*"

He infused the words with such menace that Gideon flinched, more from shame than fear. For all his newfound strength, he was weak at the core. He would never prevail against this tree of a man who confronted him with hands on hips and legs apart. He braced himself and prepared to be bested. This time, he knew, the application of pain would not be salutary. But Leander spread his arms.

"Come," he said.

In a daze Gideon stood. The long arms drew him near and closed around him. He stood rigid, his heart knocking so wildly he was sure Leander must feel every beat of its ragged tattoo. He had never been close to a man, never skin to skin. He breathed Leander in as if his own breast were open: the rise and fall of his chest, the swell of his belly, the smell of him. His eyes filled. He had not been aware of being deprived; yet once the sobs erupted—great, gulping hiccups that seemed to start at his feet—he couldn't keep them down. His brow was resting in the cleft of Leander's throat, and Leander was stroking his head, smoothing his damp hair.

"I am here," he whispered. "I am here."

THEY LEFT THE HOUSE at half past four. The day was still noon-bright, though the heat had ebbed. The two of them strolled side by side, arms swinging freely. Gideon was drained of emotion but had no trouble matching Leander's pace. He felt as light as he had while walking through the landscape of his vision, the promise of wonders ahead.

"Sophia will be glad to see you so early," Leander said.

"I'll be glad to see her." Gideon was surprised to find that he meant it. He wished he had some offering to bring Sophy. A bouquet of wild-flowers would do, but the midsummer heat had taken its toll; the few patches of day lilies he spotted were drooping on their stalks. Never mind, she would have her flowers in good time.

Something his companion said had been tugging at Gideon since they left the house. He waited until they were within a quarter-mile of the path Leander would take to the schoolhouse before framing it into a question.

"Until today I never heard you speak a word about your past," he said. "I know nothing about you. Won't you trust me with a bit of your history?"

"It is not a question of trust, but of relevance. Why should you care what I come from, or where? We occupy the same niche in time and space. Is that not what matters?" Leander spoke easily, but Gideon detected a hint of pedantry in his tone, a querulous impatience that recalled Hedge's manner in the classroom. "I am my own first cause. I created myself, just as you did."

"Even I had a mother," Gideon said. "A father, too, though I never knew him."

Leander directed his deep gaze at the spire of the church, which had just become visible in the distance. "I could tell you about my family, about my father's profession, about my youth. But really, there is only one fact. If you know that, you know the rest."

Gideon waited, his expectation ebbing as they walked on in silence. He realized he had a great deal to learn about the absence of speech: a nullity at first, then textured with sounds; every bird cry and creaking branch, every grinding circuit of wagon wheel distinct, oddly significant.

They had arrived at the bend where they usually parted. Leander turned to him and smiled. Gideon wondered how they would say good-bye—whether they would embrace or part with a wave, as usual.

"I am a Jew," Leander said.

Gideon stared. His long study of Hebrew had led him to believe that he knew a great deal about the Chosen People, but his knowledge was academic. He had never met one.

"So now you will understand the true nature of my so-called magic," Leander said. "If the world regards you always as a son of the circumcised, you have a choice. You can live your life within the walls they have built around you, consorting only with your own kind, or you can become a shape-shifter. I didn't extricate myself all at once. It took some years, but in time I learned to pitch my tent in other men's minds. Make myself at home in their ghettos. In a space so confined, it is not long before you are intimate with unspoken needs and secret longings—often hidden from the host himself. Witness our poor James. He is tormented by the house even as he refuses to acknowledge it. There it stands, his great gift of love, a monument to betrayal and deceit. In a sense, he has transferred the idolatry he once felt for the young woman to this artfully constructed wooden box. Only now, his worship is inverted: the house must neither be seen nor spoken of, such is its potency."

They were standing in full sun. Leander swiped at a flap of dark hair that had fallen over his brow. "You cannot reason with belief; you can only work within it. I appealed to his righteousness. What kind of example did he set for his Reverend father's parish, letting a useful structure go to waste? Worse, maintaining it as a shrine to the vanity of the one who commissioned it? Mind you, I never spoke the lady's name, I referred to her only in the abstract. Would it not be better to conse-crate the place to a higher purpose? A school, perhaps. A house of study for gifted scholars, the only criterion a love of learning, the children of farmers sharing desks with the children of merchants and bankers, each paying what they can. In Boston one might find such an enlightened institution, but locally? In six months, a year, who would remember that the house hadn't always been a school? Well, he wouldn't hear me at first. He turned his back to me, muttering that the children of the poor were better off learning an honest trade, and if I was so worried about them, why didn't I improve my teaching to begin with? But he didn't walk away, and I could tell from the tautness of his shoulders that I had snagged him. I sunk the hook deeper. A respectable occupation for the apostate brother-in-law. A home for the expectant sister. Then I mentioned the rent. He is a practical man, is James. I saw him calculat-ing. Such a sum every month, and in the bargain, three fewer mouths to feed. The family homestead restored, himself in his father's place at the head of the table."

Leander snapped his fingers. "He capitulated like that. Months of resistance, of refusal—gone. He wanted to be free, poor boy, whether he knew it or not. I was only the facilitator."

As Gideon listened, he realized that Leander was right: there was only one fact, and once revealed, all other information must be siphoned through it. Though he had never met a Jew, he knew what people said about them. He had to admit that his friend fit the popular image in some respects. Swarthy, with an indefinable air of foreignness. Brash under the veneer of refinement. Clever, with the native shrewdness of the perpetual outcast. How skillfully he had manipulated James, insinuated himself into their lives, molded them all to his will as if his desires were theirs. The money he was about to spend so liberally—where had it come from? Surely not his schoolmaster's stipend. Gideon looked this leering caricature full in the face, and, with a single shaky breath, dismissed it.

"Why . . . why have you pitched your tent with us?" he asked.

Leander had been watching him all this time, keen but without expression. Gideon was sure he must have registered each stage of his thought as it made its lurching pilgrimage from common wisdom to fable.

"Even wanderers must rest sometimes," Leander said. He lifted his hand as if to wave, and ruffled Gideon's hair lightly. Then he was on his way.

CHAPTER 29

RITES OF PASSAGE

*I*T SEEMED THEY HAD BEEN MOVING FOR WEEKS, THOUGH IT was only days. Wagonload after wagonload, Micah leading the horse uphill, slipping on wet leaves as slick as ice: Leander's battered trunk, containing all his worldly goods not stored in the schoolroom; Gideon's odds and ends and his small collection of books, along with a few essential volumes of the Reverend's and the Hebrew Lexicon, toward which he felt a superstitious obligation; pots and pans, mattresses and bedding; the furniture that Mrs. Hedge had set aside for Sophy; and lastly, Sophy herself, riding in her tethered rocking chair like Cleopatra enthroned upon her barge. So many trips, such a quantity of objects, and yet, once their possessions were dispersed, the house seemed as empty as it had before. Worse than empty, Gideon thought. The settee looked lost in the vastness of the parlor, adrift in space like something left behind; the table was better suited to a game of whist than the serving of a simple dinner. He had lived for so long with Leander's verbal embellishments of their future home that the reality shocked him. Who could anticipate that a few harmless sticks of furniture could so disturb the peace?

The sky, gray all day, had darkened to full dusk by the time they finished. Leander unpacked the basket of provisions Mrs. Hedge had sent to sustain them through the transition. "The First Supper!" he trumpeted, struggling to maintain his carriage atop a spindly stool. "Brother Gideon, will you give our little family a special blessing?"

Gideon gazed at each of them in turn, hoping for inspiration. He found none. Sophy was sagging in her chair, her head drooping. He felt a sinking fear when he saw how pale she was. They had been solicitous of her condition, refusing to let her lift anything heavier than a pot; still, he wondered if the move had been too much for her. Even Micah had bridled when Leander called for a grace. He was sitting with his elbows on the table, eyeing a roasted chicken like a wolf about to pounce.

"Tomorrow," Gideon said. "We're all too tired for ceremony. Sophy needs to rest."

Fanny had made them a gift of their bedroom furniture from home. Earlier he and Micah had assembled the bedstead near the fireplace in the long room, to be joined by their old dresser, a simple pine wardrobe, and Sophy's rocker. With a flourish he'd laid down a small hooked rug, congratulating himself on creating a cozy nest in a chamber intended for public gatherings. Now he saw the room through the eyes of his weary wife. The light of their candles grazed the barren floor and wall before finding the familiar pieces, huddled together as if for comfort. Sophy sat on the edge of the bed, her back rounded like an old woman's. Gideon tried to remove her shawl, but she clutched it tighter. Leaning closer, he saw two tears sliding slowly down her cheeks.

"You mustn't be discouraged, dear one," he said. "It looks bare now, but we've only just moved in. You can't see it properly at this hour. Wait until morning."

"Mama cried when I left," Sophy said. "Mama never cries." Gideon understood that her grief was for herself, as well as for Fanny. Through all these weeks of work he had nourished a vision of the moment when he would show her the house. He had imagined her gasping as she took in the spaciousness of the rooms—her domain, as Leander called it. He had planned to save the conservatory for last, leading her out the connecting door into a blaze of light. In his mind the sun was high, the day brilliant, the glasshouse verdant with flourishing plants. He had not accounted for the time of year and the uncertainties of weather. He had not considered that this would be Sophy's first night, ever, under another roof.

Gently he urged her to lie down. He took off her shoes and stockings, wishing he had thought to light a fire; it was only the middle of October, but the night air was cold and the large room was not embracing. Sophy burrowed into the pillow, sighed, and was still. Her tears were still wet; he dried them with his thumb. He spread the shawl over her, thinking how young she looked, how small for the six-month burden she bore.

He undressed quickly and folded himself around her, drawing the quilt up over them. His arm circled her belly—that arbitrary lump that, even now, stirred no natural emotion in him. "I'll take care of you," he whispered to the lump, forcing what he could not feel. Whatever was curled inside, he was responsible for it, and he feared he had already wronged it, bartered its future for his own selfish ends.

Something blunt, like the horn of a baby goat, butted the heel of his hand.

GIDEON WOKE THE next morning with his head throbbing, the sun slicing into him as if he'd overindulged in wine. He had stayed conscious for what seemed like hours, finally surrendering to a sleep torn by dreams. The only one he could remember was the last. He and Sophy were hurrying along a road that was, and was not, the village road they knew. It was pelting rain, and he was trying to cover Sophy with a cloak—a futility because she kept stumbling and falling behind. In desperation, he grabbed her arm and dragged her along, but after a few yards she fell on her knees. She looked up at him, water streaming down her face. "It's time," she said. He managed to get her to the shelter of a tree. She collapsed against the trunk, her belly undulating beneath her skirts. He reached under and tried to pull the thing out, his hand connecting with a hard, bony appendage but unable to grasp. "Stand up!" he commanded her. "Gravity is our friend." Sure enough, two thin stalks of legs emerged; a narrow head, eyes squeezed shut and ear-leaves pasted to the skull; a slick, hairy torso followed by a pair of hind legs, still folded. When the creature was free, he set it on its feet, and, trembling, it stood.

The dregs of the dream were still with him: a mix of horror and helpless fascination that roiled his stomach and sent him running to the basin. He heaved a couple of times, but brought nothing up. He splashed some water on his face and stepped into the trousers that lay where he had dropped them. Only then did he look back at the tossed bedclothes and register that Sophy was gone. What if he had not been dreaming—if she had crept out of the house during the night, determined to go back home, and he had sensed her leaving through the fog of sleep? What if she had gotten lost, and wandered until fear and exertion brought her pains on?

The door to the conservatory was open. Gideon went through, feeling as if he was moving from one room of his dream to another. Just inside he stopped, dazzled by the sun glaring off the glass. Sophy stood with her back to him, barefoot in her chemise, brushing her hair. With each stroke, strands flew up and caught the light; it seemed to him that she was spinning her own nimbus. He took another step, and she turned. Her eyes were wide, her face rapt with a private joy he hadn't seen since her dancing days. The airy sprite was gone. She was substantial now; she reminded him of one of Botticelli's Graces, abundance swelling beneath her gossamer wrap.

"Oh, Gideon. Such a glory!" she said.

For all their grand plans, he and Leander had been far too busy building the conservatory to nurture plants to fill it. The glass had come from South Boston, and Leander had hired a small crew to help with the labor. Once the work was done, Gideon had spent hours worrying about what Sophy would make of their walls of glass. Without greenery, the haste of the construction would be evident, and how would he justify the extravagance? But, as if to compensate, nature had put on an impressive display. Beyond the clearing, a conflagration of scarlet and orange and gold flared as far as the eye could see. The glasshouse framed the spectacle; the wavy glass gave it the magical quality of a painting. Looking up to the slanted roof, he was momentarily startled by a band of sky, which seemed a brighter blue for being sequestered. In his fantasy he had been accurate about the brilliance, erring only on the season.

Gideon felt, absurdly, as if he had planned it all. He came up behind Sophy and put his arms around her. "In the winter, if you look *this* way," he said, taking her hand, pointing with it, "you can see the village. You may even be able to find the parsonage."

"In the winter," Sophy said, resting against him, "we'll be three. Can you believe it?"

The moment was so bounteous, his satisfaction so complete, that Gideon never thought to remind her they would be four.

THE AROMATIC SMOKE of bacon cooking seeped into the glasshouse. Gideon had postponed telling Sophy about Leander's origins. He suspected she'd be more interested than repelled—the Reverend's daughter, after all—but was wary of taking the risk until their new family was established. Her opinion of the man was shaky enough. Now he questioned whether it would be necessary to bring the matter up at all. Leander might declare himself a Jew in the present tense, but he had lived for so long among Gentiles that he fried pig meat like a native.

Sophy dressed quickly, declaring herself famished. Gideon's queasiness had vanished; he was hungry himself. The dining table was set for three. Someone had laid a cloth over it and put a colored leaf above each plate, a small delicacy that made them both think of Micah.

"Your brother must have risen before us," Gideon said. "I hoped he'd stay a day or two, but I suppose he's fled back to the comforts of home."

"He doesn't like to leave Mama for long." Sophy was glancing here and there, taking notice of the room's features.

Privately, Gideon thought that, furniture or no, they were more civilized here than they had been under the Reverend's roof. Looking around the sun-splashed room, he felt for the first time the pride of possession; he had never imagined living in such elegant surroundings. It was easy to imagine their lives prospering in these generous spaces; their plans, which had seemed far-fetched under Hedge's roof, flourishing beneath these lofty ceilings.

"This is a gentleman's house," Sophy said. "James would not have been happy here." Her hand strayed to the skirt of her wrinkled dress, one of two that Fanny had let out, thrown on in haste to see her through another day.

"You are the lady of the manor," he assured her.

A manservant appeared, bearing Mrs. Hedge's silver wedding tray laden with steaming dishes. Sophy gave a little cry and put her hand to her breast. Gideon stared.

"Good morning, friends. You're keeping city hours, I see, and so you should while you can. I went out early, hoping to find some nice mushrooms, and found a nice farmhouse instead, and a most obliging lady who sold me some eggs and agreed to part with a few of her fine chickens, as soon as I get wire for a coop." He set the tray on the table.

"And the lady had a pair of shears, and struck a bargain for your raven locks." Gideon was just beginning to merge the clean-shaven stranger who spoke in his friend's voice with the black-bearded man he knew. The reality of a shorn Leander seemed no less uncanny than the specter of a servant had an instant before.

"Never! I pruned my own foliage. God knows I've lived behind it long enough. I wanted to honor our new life by showing my true face to the world. The temple priests did the same." Leander patted his head. "I'm not quite a Nazirite. There's plenty left on top." He smiled at Sophy, a bit tentative. "Your brother took one look at me and ran all the way back to town. What does the lady think? Am I more handsome now?"

"I think you should have thought less of the Nazirites and more of Samson," Sophy said.

Leander winked at Gideon. "I'll have to tread carefully, with such a wit to trim me down to size."

As they ate, chatting about their plans for the day, Gideon struggled to keep his eyes on his plate and his mind on the matters at hand. Whenever he glanced at the naked face across from him, he got a small shock. The Patriarchs had been bearded, or so they were always portrayed. Yet he saw clearly now what he had only sensed before: the undefinable thing that marked Leander as an Israelite. It wasn't the features—though the nose jutted more boldly without the cushioning effect of shrubbery—but the expression that overlay them. He recognized it, but couldn't name it, quite. Skepticism, a kind of blighted humor, worldliness and weariness with the world—it was all these things and more, congealed into a cast that had hardened over time. What must it be like to know from your earliest years that you were not yourself only, but your history?

Gideon thought back to his first acquaintance with the Israelites, in the Bible stories his mother read him. They had been mythic characters, conquering Canaan, but conquered, too. Feisty rebels, at the mercy of invading armies and a moody, imperious God who vanished for long stretches, yet—how mean his young self had thought this—begrudged them their golden calf. Good companions for a fatherless child. From his boyhood, two tribes had lived side by side in him: the Hebrews in the stories and the Jews, who "kept to themselves," his mother had told him after a peddler came to the back door. They were strangers wherever they wandered, she said. Leander had qualities of both. By virtue of his height and appetites, he was biblical, but his skills were those of an exile and survivor.

"Your pupils won't recognize you," Gideon said, feeling a new trepidation for his friend. Leander had resolved to teach until the new schoolmaster arrived at the end of November.

"They expect me to astonish them. I'll tell them I said a magic word." Leander caressed his smooth chin. His eyes were larger in the new face, more gold than green in the morning light. "In a week they'll have forgotten I ever had a beard."

Sophy rose and began to collect the plates. He and Leander both bobbed up to help her. "Stay where you are," she ordered them. "I'm not infirm."

She had a slight sway now when she walked, balancing her weight from step to step like a woman carrying a basket of laundry to the river. They watched her. These days they watched her whether she painted or not, though Gideon knew that it made her shy. Was every first pregnancy such a primal fascination, he wondered? Was every firstborn the first citizen of a new world?

"We are a small tribe," Leander said, when Sophy was out of earshot, "but we are increasing."

CHAPTER 30

ANNUNCIATION

*B*ATHE IN IT, THEY TELL HER. ALSO, REST IN IT, TASTE IT, breathe it in, dream in it, listen to it, learn from it, think about it, and then, don't think about it. Apparently there are Commandments of Silence, written on air instead of stone, said air emanating from Gideon and Leander, who expend a great many words to describe the absence of sound.

They are silent on Sunday afternoons and at dinner three days a week. The sessions remind her of prayer, in all the worst ways: one might wish to set one's mind on higher things, but even in this quiet place, the hum of the world intrudes. Contemplations are tolerable, even pleasurable, as long as she fills them with reading or painting. Evening devotions are what they have always been, though she has yet to see anyone open a Bible. Now that they don't go to church, they've become their own Quaker meeting: she knits for the baby, enjoying the clack of the needles; Gideon pores over one of his tomes; Leander sits square in his chair like the Pharaoh, in one of his waking sleeps. Meals are a trial.

This Sunday, at table, they point to what they want—as the monks do, Gideon says, but she thinks, more like monkeys. Please and thank-

you pared down to the stab of a forefinger. Cider! More squash! Mastication is a cacophony, every chew and swallow and swish of the tongue
resounding. Bite into a hard crust and the crackle lingers like a curse.
Leander makes a great show of savoring his food, chewing each mouthful slowly, pretending to muse upon its qualities before he releases the
morsel to its destiny. For all his efforts to prolong the process, dinner is
over in a quarter of the time it used to be. If silence is a sanctuary, no
one chooses to shelter in it for long. Gideon says she must think of these
interludes as islands in a sea of talk, but what if the islands should spread
into continents? What if the chatter they've all bathed in since infancy
should dry up?

"One of us could read aloud while the others eat," she suggests
when speech resumes. "We could take turns. The Bible, or whatever
the reader pleases. Even the monks allow that." She would happily listen to Papa's Lexicon, let the Hebrew seep into her hungry ears and fly
straight to her brain sans impediment—only a smattering of French to
keep it company, and a few stray bits of Latin from the boys' lessons.

"But Sophy, don't you see—it wouldn't be silence." Gideon sighs
and wrings his hands as if she'd asked for lettuce from the witch's garden. Words often fail him nowadays; he looks to Leander to supply
them. She feels that he is struggling to confide in her, but can't find the
proper expression.

Leander is never at a loss. "You must give yourself to it, Sophia,"
he exhorts. "You won't reap its benefits until you do." He fixes her with
his greenest eye, all glitter gone. She's warranted the rebuke only once
before, when Micah made a sheep-face at her across the silent table
and—owing to her pent-up state—laughter spurted out. It's like being
observed through the wrong end of a spyglass, the object being to make
her small. "If you can't submit for your own sake, think of your husband! Think of your child! Measure your petty resistance against their
well-being."

"I would gladly give myself to *it*, if I knew what *it* was," she says.
"Perhaps one day you'll enlighten me." She turns to go, but not before
catching the look that passes between them. She can't help herself then.

She throws a dart over her shoulder. "Who are you to lecture me about my family's well-being? A bachelor with no family of your own. Did you think you could borrow ours?"

Sophy doesn't stay to see the effect. She marches straight to the conservatory and slams the door as hard as she can. Glass shudders all around her, the tremor resounding in her bones. The fire in the stove has burned low, but she doesn't mind. The cold is clarifying. She stands by the easel, taking an odd comfort from the sight of her breath on the panes. Her new painting repeats the view outside: a stark November landscape, black tree trunks reaching bony fingers to a pallid sky. The branches seem to be pleading. *Please, let us keep a few leaves to see us through the winter.* Or, *Please, help us shake these clingers off.*

Strange that a place so exposed should be her only refuge in this house. The transparent walls don't bother her—not even when she catches Leander looking in on his way to the woodpile. She likes being able to watch the weather, and has thought what a picture it would make if she could mark nature's changing dress day to day, week to week, the costume gradually altering at the bidding of her brush. But then, what else would she ever paint?

With both hands she strokes the mound under her apron. She feels closest to the baby in this room; she talks to it and sings to it, always in a low voice to protect their intimacy. If it is still, she knows it's listening, and if it moves, she senses a spark of will, a reminder that her tenant is restless, just as her mother used to be when she was in residence, and won't be content with such modest accommodations forever. "Sometimes I wish you could stay," she'd confided yesterday, and was answered with a flurry of kicks.

"We might as well do some painting while the light lasts," she tells it now. The baby is a good companion while she works, though each week the distance between her arms and the easel seems longer.

A knock at the door. "Sophy . . . may I come in?" Hesitant, which means nothing.

She stands tall, armoring herself with the tatters of her anger. One look at Gideon's face and she is seized with a need to apologize.

"I am sorry—" she begins.

"No, I am sorry. I should have spoken to you before. I was waiting for the right moment. I see I waited too long."

She says nothing. There are other uses for silence.

He pulls the chair away from the easel and sits, gazing bleakly at the supplicating trees. "We—Leander and I—feel that an extraordinary child deserves an extraordinary upbringing. We have made special plans for the baby. For you, too, of course."

"I'm happy to know our child will be extraordinary, but shouldn't I have been consulted?"

"We thought it best to introduce you gradually. We hoped you'd take to the silences as we do—find nourishment in them, and pass that richness on to the baby. It gives me such comfort to think of our little one inside you, nursing on sweet peace." Gideon scrutinizes her landscape as if it were a page of Aramaic. "Our aim—our *mission*—is to preserve that peace. To shield the tender new soul from pollution, once it is born into this babbling world. We're the gatekeepers, you and Leander and I. But we must be united."

Her skin goes cold. "Look at me," she says. "Tell me plain."

He turns to her. "We intend to raise the baby in an atmosphere of love and beauty, and answer its every need. But in its presence, we will—all of us—refrain from speaking. We'll listen as we've never listened before, and record every utterance, from the first cries and gurgles to the first spontaneous word. Leander has presented me with a journal—a handsome one, worthy of its contents. The boards are the color of new leaves." His face brightens. "Oh, Sophy, I dream of the day I make the first entry. Will it be a fragment of an ancient language or a tongue not heard since angels barred the gate of Eden? What an honor to be God's clerk. His amanuensis . . . I like to think the Reverend would be pleased."

"Are you saying we're not to talk to our child? How are we to communicate? Will we make signs with our hands as they do with the deaf?" It is the extremity that keeps her calm. Her voice sounds like Papa's, dry as dust, sorting out the facts of a parishioner's calamity.

A flicker of uncertainty in his eyes. He seems to weigh the possibility that she's being farcical.

"Some gesturing is inevitable," he says, "but we mustn't use our bodies as a crutch. The baby will see what we see and hear what we hear, lacking only words. It will be steeped in the sounds of nature and domesticity, as we are. Our paradise is earthly, so we can't expect to shield our little one from the hubbub of daily life. Its first words may mimic the plash of water in a basin, or the call of a bird—or a dish breaking. Few believe now that speech began as imitation, but we'll have an excellent opportunity to put that dusty old theory to the test—"

"How long?" She cuts him off.

"Until the words come. A year and a half, three at most. Leander and I are of two minds on the subject. He thinks language will evolve slowly, given the lack of a model. I'm persuaded that, in a mind so clear, speech will bubble up like a natural stream. There's much we don't know. The ancients conducted similar experiments, but their methods were more primitive."

He's speaking quickly now, caught up in his ideas. "What we envision has never been attempted before. To return to a pre-Babel condition. To create our own paradise, and let a child come to consciousness there in perfect freedom, nurtured by affectionate caretakers—but with a light hand! We must never impose, only observe. I called us gatekeepers, but our function is higher than that. We will stand in the place of the Lord in Eden, watching over our precious creation."

"And if—after a year or two or three—the words never come?" Sophy has heard of children raised in the wild, bestial creatures who walk on all fours and howl like the wolves that nurtured them.

"That won't happen. The Bible tells us God brought the beasts to Adam to see what he would call them. We can infer that the names were already in him, dormant, waiting for the proper objects to present themselves. If Adam is the model for humanity, why should our little man be different? With the three of us to entertain him, he won't lack for stimulation, and the garden room will feed his senses year-round." Gideon looks about him with a mildly puzzled air, as if the lush flora had taken it upon itself to vanish out of spite. "Leander wants to acquire a pair of peafowl to strut outside. To amuse Prince Adam, he says: every kingdom needs its court jesters. The fellow is besotted with poultry . . ."

Our little man. The baby has been an *it* until now, neither of them willing to confine it to one sex or another. Sophy tries out this new identity on her intimate companion, and sees it—him—in her arms, then teetering on squat legs as she beckons him. A presence become a person.

"You're too late," she says, not bothering to contain the note of triumph. Her emotion makes her careless. Let them try to use her boy! "He's been listening to us all these months. Do you think he doesn't know our voices? We have conversations every day, he and I. We're already quite familiar."

"Why must you always oppose me?" Gideon gets up and paces from one end of the conservatory to another. "No one is more aware than I am that we can't *achieve* perfection, we can only try to approach it. Look at this place! The greenery was supposed to be installed two months ago."

"Gideon." She is sweet reason, calling him home. "This is our baby that we waited for all these months. We don't have to put him in a glass case and study him. Only to love him. What else does a little child need? Our love will be paradise enough."

"If you had seen more of the world," he says, "you would know it is never enough."

The words are harsh, but she sees a wavering in his eyes, and she speaks to it.

"Do you remember, the day you asked me to marry you, you said you wanted to run away, just the two of us? And I said, not yet?"

"I meant from your father and his eternal managing. Our circumstances have changed."

"Have they? It seems to me we've gone from one manager to another. You open your mouth and Leander's words come out. We're a family now. It's time for us to rule our own lives."

"All very fine, but how would we live? We have no resources."

"You're a man of gifts. You will find another position—if not in a parish, then a college, or a school in the city. I don't care where we go or how humbly we live. I would be happy in a single room, if only we can start new."

"Why else are we here?" Gideon passes a hand over his forehead. "You don't see what Leander has done for us. Your dislike blinds you— and your lack of vision. He's sacrificed so much. The rent is only half of it. Do you know that he paid for this conservatory out of his inheritance?" He stops in front of her. "I suppose you have no idea of the cost of glass. He could easily have built a home of his own."

"Let him have this one, then. I won't sell my child for a roof over my head."

He is the only man she knows who turns white, not red, in the grip of anger. His whole body clenches like a fist, flesh stretched taut over bone. She steps back, her arms crossing over her belly.

After a minute he says, "You have a short memory. We were miserable a few months ago, and if we run away, we'll be miserable again. Single rooms may suffice for the lovers in romances, but try to imagine raising an infant in one. I would be away all day, trying to scrape a living, and you would be alone with the baby, doing all those chores you scorn. If you felt the urge to paint, you'd have to stifle it. Compare that to the life we have now. A fine house with more space than we need. Time to pursue our true vocations, and a generous friend to care for us. Above all, the *task*. The work we do will reverberate far beyond our family. We might begin by cultivating paradise in a—a bell jar, but what we plant here will spread into the world. Leander is convinced of it, and so am I."

We don't know anything about this man, she wants to say. Where he is from, how he came by his so-called inheritance. If we had never met Leander, we'd be an ordinary couple, coping as best we could, and what is so terrible about that? She doesn't speak because the answer has been clear since that day she first saw him across the meadow, the sun burnishing his hair.

Gideon takes her hands in his and looks into her eyes. "Trust me,

Sophy. A long time ago I asked you to come with me. Now I'm asking you again. Say you will."

He waits until she nods before letting go of her hands. At the door he says: "Say a word to Leander, won't you? Your heart would melt if you knew how fond he is of you. He doesn't expect an apology, but a little warmth would be welcome."

Their generous friend, who, a scant minute ago, was lurking outside the door, listening. She doesn't know how she knows. A sudden absence; a receding of attention that thins the air. She's had the sense before.

Sophy sinks down in her chair, exhausted. Her back aches, her legs ache. She won't work today. Her winter scene gives her a headache—dead earth, dead trees. The sky is empty. How could it be otherwise when she painted it from life? She turns the picture to the easel.

THE PAINTING COMES to her like a dream, and in the manner of dreams, she sees it first in motion. The couple in the bell jar, walking arm in arm through a forest of potted plants, red and yellow flowers climbing the glass walls like ivy. The two make their decorous way to a bench beneath an orange tree. The young man helps his lady to sit before settling at her side. They don't touch or look at each other; then one of his hands wanders to her ample skirt to rest on her stomach. His fingers spread, her hands cover his, and they are still. The view widens to the larger landscape, where November reigns in bleak contrast to the luxuriant greenery inside the jar. Skeleton trees, the breath of winter agitating the branches. Across the matte sky, a pair of wings growing larger: a swan's neck; no, a serpent's, topped by a human head. The creature hovers over the jar, shedding letters like feathers with each stately sweep of its wings. When the wings stop beating, she has her painting.

If the scene were less vivid in her mind, transferring it to canvas might be easier. She works for hours, ignoring the pain in her arms and shoulders. She puts her shock into it, her righteous anger tinged with fear. While she paints, she feels some mastery over her situation. If her hand is steady enough to wield the brush, she is not helpless, she still has her wits.

At dinner—a talking meal—Leander says, "Have I grown a second nose, Sophia? Or a third eye in the middle of my forehead?"

She doesn't take his meaning at first. She has been studying him, discreetly, she thought, trying to memorize his features so she can render them accurately. But Leander sees what other men don't. She wouldn't be surprised if that black hair slanting across his brow hides a third eye.

"You have an interesting face," she says. "Unusual."

"Ah, the artist's pitiless eye. Are you threatening to immortalize me?"

"If I tried, you wouldn't know yourself. Don't fret, I'll spare you— for the sake of family harmony."

He laughs and turns back to Gideon, but she has been warned.

She clears the table quietly. The men are still deep in conversation, and Leander has taken out his pipe, a sure sign they'll be occupied for a while. Neither seems to notice that the room has darkened. She lights a candle and places it between them; then she lights one for herself.

"Off to bed, are you? Dream well, little lady." Leander puts a match to the candle and ignites his pipe.

"I'm not tired yet. I thought I might sit in the glasshouse and watch the stars."

"Oh, Sophy, don't sit in the dark," Gideon says. "You'll catch cold. You could be reading in your own chair by the fire."

"I like it there at night," she tells him. "It's very peaceful."

"Perfectly understandable," Leander says, with a look at Gideon. "Of course you will want to be by yourself at such a time. Yourselves, I should say."

She bristles when he alludes to her pregnancy, as he often does. He has the soul of a Norseman. He invades her casually. She could say something, but she lets it pass.

———

DARKNESS HAS A DIFFERENT texture in the glasshouse than in a room with solid walls. It is luminous, even on nights like this one, when the murky weather hides the stars. Mysterious, not eerie: Sophy has hated dark rooms since she was a child, but she is never afraid here. When she sets the candle by the easel, her painting glows like a stained-glass window—that hushed light that Papa said signifies the Holy Spirit.

She begins to paint immediately, while the image is fresh in her mind. She did the wings yesterday—layers of feathers shading from white to gray, tipped with black—and the long sinuous neck, which seemed to unfurl of its own accord, with very little prompting from her brush. Faces are always a challenge. If only he still had his beard, there would be less territory to cover. She has done a few pencil sketches of him for practice: a profile which came closest to capturing his aquiline features, a three-quarter view that was less sure, and a full-face that failed entirely, suggesting an old woman who bore a rogue resemblance to Mama.

The three-quarter view will work best for her purposes; she wants to convey arrested motion, a pause in mid-flight above the couple in the glass dome.

The area is so small that it's hard for her to see. She squints into the circle of candlelight, aware that Gideon may come in at any moment and order her to bed. Even with a fine brush, it is impossible to achieve the precision of pencil, but at her level of skill, accuracy matters less than the overall impression. Painting him, she can almost love him for the angles of his face, his swooping nose and square chin. She takes some care with the eyes. How to suggest their mutability? It comes to her to make tiny gems where the irises would go: emeralds, their facets catching the light. She solves the problem of motion by lifting his hair off the brow and to one side, a black banner in a stiff wind.

Sophy leans back in her chair and considers that she's done a good night's work. The face confronts her like a genie out of a bottle, audacious: *Who are* you *to have made* me*?* This creature would dominate even if it didn't occupy the lion's share of sky. She isn't sure what to name the beast—flying serpent or dark angel—but, remembering the letters falling from its wings, she thinks she'll call the painting *Annunciation*. The message it brings to the pair below will have to wait until tomorrow.

She hears Gideon's footsteps in the bedroom, and calls out, "I'm just cleaning my brushes." She sets the picture near some older canvases stacked in a corner and covers it with a cloth, mindful that the paint is not quite dry.

Gideon is cross with her for having stayed up so late. Lying by his side, her head still buzzing with the night's work, Sophy thinks of Leander's odd words when bidding her good night. She'd scarcely noted the phrase at the time, dismissing it as one of the quaint foreign expressions he affected. Dream well, he said—as if he'd peered into her with his third eye and seen what she would do.

CHAPTER 31

VISITATION

MICAH IS DUE ON THE FIRST SATURDAY IN DECEMBER, bringing clothes and blankets for the baby, along with the cradle that rocked all the Hedge infants to sleep. When Sophy hears the wagon lumbering up the hill, she is alone in the house, a rare occurrence. A fine snow is falling, the first of the season. The men have gone to a neighboring farm to see about purchasing a horse. It is a sensible step, now that an infant is on the way, but neither is delighted at the prospect. Gideon has always relied on his feet to get around the parish, and Leander seems to find the idea of keeping a large animal intimidating; he is a city man, in Sophy's opinion, for all his tales of living rough. She hopes they'll take their time debating the merits of the beast so she can have some private moments with her brother.

Flinging a shawl over her shoulders, Sophy rushes out to meet the wagon. Stops short when she sees who is sitting beside Micah: Papa, or a simulacrum from the beyond, the unmistakable beaver hat low on his brow and his endless muffler wrapping him from neck to nose. Her first thought is that he's come back to reclaim her, but she has no time to think further for the wagon halts in front of the house, the horse snorting smoke, and Micah circles around to help the transfiguration descend, whereupon it straightens layers of wool and gingham and reveals itself to be Mama.

For Sophy, it is no less a resurrection. She throws her bulk at Mama, all but knocking her over, and buries her face in her bosom. "And you with your head uncovered," Mama says, patting her sides, appraising as she embraces. "Near eight months gone, and not enough sense to know that cold travels down through the crown." She clasps Sophy tighter and adds, in a hoarse croak, "God help the child." The sentiment, so foreign to her usual speech, lingers in the rimy air. Sophy wonders, which child?

They help Mama into the house and settle her by the hearth in the kitchen. The old bustling Mama would have refused a seat and walked briskly through each room, noting what needed doing and attacking the task on the spot. But that vigorous woman has been displaced by her own grandmother, who holds crooked fingers to the fire and declares she is frozen through. They must wait for her to thaw before coaxing off, in turn, the beaver hat, the outermost shawl, a yard or two of muffler.

"She w-would come," Micah says, "though I tried to stop her. Her chest has been stuffed for days, and you h-hear how her throat sounds."

"I don't recall getting an invitation when it was warm and pleasant," Mama mutters.

While Sophy fills the kettle for tea, Micah goes out to unload the wagon. He returns with a basket spilling over with small garments. Sophy holds them up one by one. Mama's fingers may be bent, but they have not been idle. There are new things: gowns of soft cotton and flannel, knit caps and vests and blankets, and a stack of snowy squares, finished with a care that belies their purpose. Under these, a long yellowed linen dress edged with lace that has seen three generations through their christenings, more gowns and blankets, and clothing of various sizes, all washed and pressed and preserved by Mama in a cedar chest with sprigs of lavender between.

"I g-gave it a good polish," Micah says, carrying in the cradle. When he sets it near the hearth, Sophy's eyes fill. She remembers rocking Micah in this very cradle when she was scarcely more than a baby herself. For a moment, she feels the strength and fellowship of those who endured before her: that long line of bearing women at her back, each of them anxious for the child to come, each looking ahead with joy, and also with dread. Sophy takes one of the worn gowns and lays it in the cradle, smoothing out creases as sharp as seams. Mama has been watching, half-nodding over her tea, but now she darts forward and snatches up the gown.

"Never do that!" She clutches the thin cotton to her chest as if she'd rescued it from the fire. "It's bad luck to croon over a cradle before it is filled. The Spoiler sees and interferes."

Shaken, Sophy is tempted to rebuke Mama for her superstitions. Then she remembers the three little girls Mama lost. Three porcelain dolls capped and robed in white, each laid out in her wooden box. She's rarely given them a thought until this moment, for Mama isn't one to brood over griefs past. She sees sweet pinched faces, tiny fists peeking out of ruffled sleeves.

Mama takes note of her expression. "Now come here, let's have a look at you," she says, glancing sidelong at Micah. "If the young man will take his tea elsewhere? There are rooms enough to choose from." As soon as he is gone, Mama creaks to her feet and begins to poke and prod expertly beneath Sophy's apron. "All seems in order, as far as I can tell. You're carrying low and narrow, which ought to mean a boy, though Mother Nature has fooled me more than once. A big boy for a wisp of a thing like you. You're like the woman who swallowed the cow, and I suppose you feel like her, too. I doubt you'll last till January."

A clamor in the hall. The men have returned early, in boisterous good humor from the sound of it, Leander shouting, "My kingdom for a horse!" and Gideon laughing as he never laughs with anyone else. Gideon relishes these excursions. Leander brings out a bluff, raucous side of him, as if he were made of coarser stuff. It's not enough for some men to bring angels down to earth, she thinks; they must wrestle them to the ground and rub mud in their hair, all in good fun. They tramp in, bringing the smell of snow with them, Gideon as rosy as a boy.

"Sophy, you've never seen such a nag as Leander's honest farmfrau tried to sell us——"

The sight of Mama strikes them dumb. Sophy would swear that Gideon's color fades on the spot. By now they are so caught up in their grand scheme that they can't fathom the unexpected. Mama was not planned for; therefore she cannot be here.

Leander recovers first. "Mrs. Hedge, what a delightful surprise! That slybones Micah never told us you were coming. Doesn't our Sophia look blooming? You see what good care we're taking of her."

Gideon surveys the bounty with a wincing smile. "The little one will be well provided for," he says, "thanks to you, Fanny." He pats the sleeve of a gown, self-conscious, and riffles the stack of nappies like the pages of a book. With a cautious touch he sets the cradle to rocking, staring at it fixedly as if it were a new invention. Only then does he brush a kiss on Mama's stiff cheek.

No one seems to know how to proceed after pleasantries have been exchanged. "Well, have you been shown the house yet?" Leander asks. "Let us give you the grand tour, then. It's changed quite a bit since you saw it last." He takes Mama's arm and ushers her into the next room, drawing her attention to improvements they've made. Gideon sends Sophy a long, questioning look. *Is this your doing?*

She finds Micah in the pantry. His legs are curled around the stumps of a low stool and he is snoring softly, his head pillowed against a sack of flour on a shelf. His talent for napping anywhere, on the instant, is legend in the family. She makes mouse tracks up his neck to wake him. "Silly, what are you doing in here?"

He blinks, shaking off sleep. "It's warm. M-Mama brought some food, I was putting it away."

Sophy lowers her voice. "Gideon and Leander are back so we haven't much time. Have they told you what they're planning?"

"You mean about n-n-not talking to the, the b-bah . . . ?" He cradles his arms as the word slithers away from him.

"What do you think about it?"

"It's d-d-daft."

So he has known for a while—perhaps before she did. She wonders if he grasps the peril, or if he's too young to understand that this is more than a harmless whim.

Then he says, "They th-think silence is better than medicine, that it will mend the world, maybe w-wake the dead. They think it will cure *this*." He points to his mouth. All delivered in a smooth rush, the wit bringing the fluency.

Sophy sometimes forgets how quick his mind is, how much he observes. She reaches for his hand, which feels older than the rest of him, the callused fingers rough in her palm. "Micah, I am depending on you to come as often as you can. I need someone on the outside, someone I can trust." She looks down at the mound, and his eyes follow hers. "I tell myself Gideon will come to his senses when the baby is born. Once he sees his child and holds him, he'll throw off Leander's influence. I pray we won't need help. But if we should . . ."

He nods and squeezes her hand. She never misjudges his heart. It's as good as done.

Another thought occurs to her. "Does Mama know?"

"They said not to t-t-trouble her. To keep it to myself f-for now."

"Perhaps that's best," Sophy says. "There's enough worrying her already. It hurts my heart to see her looking so ill."

IN THE GLASSHOUSE, Leander is consulting with Mama about plants. "I'm told we can start bulbs any time and get a jump on spring. Pots of earth have their own beauty, isn't it so? The city dweller sees plain brown dirt, but the gardener is already imagining a new bloom stirring beneath the surface." When Sophy comes in with Micah, he gives her a courtly little bob.

Mama dismisses this fancy talk by ignoring it. She confines her attention to the plain brown earth outside, rapidly being coated with a layer of white. "We'd best get going while we can find the road," she tells Micah. "This is a sticking snow, it doesn't look like much yet, but could be a heap by morning. Sophy, you had better pack a few things and come back with us. I thought we had a week or two, but sooner would be best. You oughtn't to be stuck in the middle of the woods in your condition."

Gideon has been quiet, hanging off to the side while Leander expounds—counting off the minutes, Sophy thinks, until their visitor is gone. Now he snaps alert and puts a husbandly arm around Sophy's shoulders. "How can you think of it, Fanny? Sophy will give birth at home, as other women do—as you must have yourself. Her home is here, with us. You have my solemn promise, we'll send for you when the time comes, and the doctor too, if needed. We have weeks to go before we need to worry."

"Arithmetic doesn't apply here," Mama says. "Babies are not obliging creatures, first ones least of all. Her pains could come on at any time, and what would you great thinkers do then? My mother was by my side for a month before Sam, and I had women at the ready for the others. It's as good as deserting her to leave her alone with a pair of men." She mutters, as if to herself, "And in December, no less. Never make it easy, Lord."

Gideon tightens his embrace. "My wife's welfare is our first concern," he says. But his voice is feebler than his grip. Sophy senses his confusion. He and Leander have been so busy plotting the baby's first months that they've given little thought to its arrival. She can hardly blame him. She's known her pains would come, but hasn't dared to dwell on them. She remembers being taken to see Micah swaddled in the cradle, and Mama on the bed: the flatness of her beneath the covers, and her depletion, the labor of her smile. If there were screams, she's forgotten; perhaps a neighbor kept her until it was over. Women of the parish suffered from their babies—died of them, too—and after church or over sewing, talked about the agonies endured, not sparing the particulars, and Mama didn't always shoo her away. That this same course will be worked in her cannot be imagined. Yet, once begun, it must be completed. She will be brought to bed soon, whether she is ready or not.

She might die. Her mother did, of her. Papa never said as much, never blamed her, though he must have thought of his only sister whenever he looked at her. How her questions must have tormented him, and how carefully he had replied, every word a cautionary tale. *What did she look like, Papa? Small, like you. Light on her feet.* Meaning, she was made for dancing, not mothering, and you had better acquire enough heft to avoid her fate. Sophy has never thought of that bedchamber—what child cares to go back that far? —but she would summon it now, if she had any idea where it was. Did her mother give birth in the shelter of the Hedge house or alone in some dingy room, whispering Papa's name to a landlady who would have sent the mewling infant to an orphanage? All she will ever know for certain is that her mother loved life, clung to it fiercely even beyond the grave. And now Sophy has killed her a second time, evicted her to make room for a new tenant.

"Even a short journey wouldn't be wise at this late stage," Leander is saying. "We can't have her jostled in the wagon. The little one might be shaken from its nest. And in such weather! No, she is better off where she is, safe and warm, with all her familiar things around her, and two loving companions to cater to her. I assure you, dear Mrs. Hedge, all the best physicians would agree."

Seeing his error, he adds, hastily, "Not that anything can compete with a woman's experience."

Micah says, "Well, then, Mama should stay here," and Mama says, "No, no, I'd only be a burden, I'd rather sleep in my own bed where I can hack and cough without risking Sophy's health," and Gideon reminds Mama that they are only a few miles away, and Leander begs everyone to keep calm and remember that birth is a part of nature, animals drop their young unattended, and so-called primitive peoples do the same, he has seen it himself . . .

They are talking about her as if she isn't here.

Sophy rests heavily against Gideon's side. If she doesn't get off her feet soon, she will surely faint. She feels light-headed, light all over, as though her soul fled early, leaving the great bulk of her to travail on its own.

CHAPTER 32

NATIVITY

IT IS NOT EASY TO FESTOON A GLASSHOUSE WITH GREENERY, but Leander and Gideon are doing their best. Leander, atop a ladder, damns his eyes and other body parts as he tries to pin bunches of juniper and holly to the wooden frames between the panes. His fingers keep fumbling, and the fragile bundles that Sophy tied with thread come apart and litter the floor. He has no right to curse, for it was his idea to garnish the conservatory as the Germans do, Christmas being two days away. "It's about time we had some vegetation in here," he said, and, as ever, the others jump to do his bidding. Gideon has arranged numerous pine boughs in numerous crocks. He has run out of containers, but Lem Quinn is still dragging in severed limbs. He reminds Sophy of an automaton which, once set to a task, must repeat it unto eternity.

"Enough now, leave a few branches to shade us in the summer," Leander tells him, and the boy turns slack at his master's mild reprimand and shuffles to a corner, scowling. He misses the thwack of the axe, Sophy guesses; also the sticky ooze of the wounded tree. Lem is a souvenir of Leander's teaching days, recently ended. He does much of the physical work about the place, and is most tolerable when occupied. She and Gideon are a little afraid of him, though Leander insists he's a gentle soul, roughened by hard use. Deprived of activity, he emanates a noxious compound of ill will and strong odor. Smells—even good ones—don't always sit well with Sophy in her present state. She is grateful for the pungent, scouring fragrance of the pine.

In the midst of all this industry, she is the potted plant, spreading where they've placed her. She spends the brightest part of each day in here, conscientiously basking for the baby's sake. Young plants don't grow well in the dark, Leander reminds her, and it stands to reason that the same applies to infants. Sophy shuts her ears to his lectures on the Romans and their solariums, but has to confess she finds the sun nourishing. They've moved her rocking chair in, and someone—Gideon, she hopes—has thought to provide a chamberpot. Gideon keeps her company when he can. He has inherited a couple of Leander's old students, sons of a dry goods merchant with aspirations beyond the village school, and three days a week he walks an hour to their house to tutor them; after months of tedious labor, he's eager to call upon his old skills. Sophy doesn't mind being alone. If Leander wanders in, she pretends to be asleep. Conversation is an effort. Her thoughts are few and sluggish. Her paintings are stacked along the back wall, safely covered. Pictures don't come to her any more, but neither do the fears and worries that plagued her only weeks ago. She has surrendered to her body. At night she lifts her gown and combs the stretched skin with her nails. This is her greatest pleasure, though never enough to sate the itching. If Lem weren't here, she would risk a swipe under her apron now.

MAMA'S THROAT HAS NOT IMPROVED, but she makes her presence known in her notes and potions. Lately she's instructed Sophy about Hardening the Nipples, and sent tincture of myrrh to toughen them for nursing. Twice a day, dutifully, Sophy lowers her chemise and bathes her breasts in the solution, marveling at their size and fullness, wondering if the baby will suck them small again or if she'll be allowed to keep them. Usually she performs this rite in private, but on a morning last week she delayed her ablutions to coincide with Gideon's. He seems oblivious to her lately, except as a vessel for the child. At times she even misses his skewed attentions in the study.

It was perhaps not the best moment. He was preparing to see his students, harried, pulling out one drawer after another in search of a shirt that could pass for clean. "We'll have to find someone to do the washing until you're able to work again. Look at this rag. You'd think I cleaned a lamp with it—" He waved a shirt at her, and she was ready, turning from the basin, breasts glistening.

He gaped and looked away, but not before she caught the raw shock in his face. "What are you doing, Sophy? Cover yourself, you'll catch cold!"

She could have offered a simple explanation. She meant to. Instead she said, "I thought you might enjoy that I'm more womanly now— seeing as the rest of me is unsightly."

He pulled a shirt over his head. "Why must you use such a word? Naturally you're more womanly now, what else would you be? You look just as you ought to, and I *enjoy* you as I always have. You must try not to be so hard on yourself. Leander says women often fall into these moods toward the end." He dropped a distracted kiss on her brow, staying well clear of the startling objects below, and went back to the dresser to root for a cravat.

HALF-PAST THREE, the sky already darkening. Gideon and Leander gather armfuls of branches for the sitting room, and Lem follows, a stroke behind. The greenery has put them in a festive mood. Leander is promising to make eggnog "with a drop of brandy to help our little mother sleep." Sophy understands, from a drowsy distance, that they are having a joke at her expense, for at this hour of the afternoon she couldn't stay awake if she wanted to; by now she's half-gone. Gideon adjusts her lap robe and he and Leander look down on her with that fond, patronizing gaze: she is another kind of prodigy now. Lem's heavy presence is felt in passing. Even his shadow must be thick.

The room is warm, too warm, but outside snow has begun to fall as it does most afternoons when the sun sinks: big, lazy flakes drifting down. What a thin skin the glass is, yet how strong, keeping out the elements and who knows what creatures of the wild, wolves, bears . . . The baby moves suddenly, sharply, and she imagines him on his knees, his fists punching at the wall of her, trying to see out. Then it is she, Sophy, peering through a window. Bars interrupt her view, but she can see the spears of pine trees marching into a brilliant white distance. The sight fills her with longing. Such a vastness out there, and less and less room inside, the air so thick with moisture she can scarcely draw it in, even if she had space for a full breath. Her arms—how long have they been pinned to her sides? In a fit of impatience she works her wedged hands out until she can grab hold of the bars and shakes them until they give way. She rises, the ground dwindling beneath her. At first it seems nothing has changed. The atmosphere is as oppressive as before, but her vision has sprung free. She is hovering above, looking down upon a mountain of a man sprawled on his side across the snow, solid as the earth he rests on but for the aperture in his middle, in which is framed . . . a woman's face. Perspective is the Devil's trick, but wonder of wonders! The world is infinitely larger than she knew, and so brazen-bright it pricks her eyes.

"Such a beatific smile. You must be dreaming of angels." Gideon breathes brandy into her face. "Are you ready to wake up and be merry with us?"

While she slept, they transformed the conservatory around her. Candles glimmer atop upright logs and on pedestals of stacked stones, their flames doubled, blearily luminous in the glass. They've moved the table in, and dressed it tastefully: a white cloth, a vase of holly with a candle on either side, three flowered china plates from some long-departed aunt, and cut-glass goblets at each place, mismatched but harmonious.

Sophy blinks, suspended between two dreams, trying to make sense of this dazzling new realm. Gideon is her only orientation, and he is flushed and grinning, his hair tumbled over his forehead. "Come see what the elves wrought."

He arranges her shawl around her and helps her to her feet. She is a little shaky, as she sometimes gets after a long sleep, and the whiff of spirits is not pleasant. Putting a hand on his arm, she moves stiffly, with a dawning sense that something has shifted inside her. A few more steps, and she knows she isn't imagining it. The mound has descended. It is a revelation at once momentous and casual, for here she is, still in one piece and in no apparent discomfort. She takes an experimental breath, and finds that the crowding she's endured for weeks is eased, the air reaching deeper down.

Gideon is looking at her anxiously. "Is everything all right?"

She pats herself to make sure. The baby is safely in residence, but no longer squeezed under her breastbone. She knows what this must mean; yet she feels lighter—buoyant even, as if a weight has been lifted off her. Eating has been a duty lately, each bite forced down only to be sent up again half-digested, but she has space now for her share of the feast.

"Oh, I'm quite comfortable," she says, smiling at him.

Leander marches in, bearing aloft one of her mixing bowls brimming with white, foaming liquid, singing, "*The eggnog in hand bring I, perfumed with spice and brand-ee-iiii . . .*" He lowers it to the table without spilling a drop, and flings out an arm as if he'd just pulled a rabbit out of a hat.

Sophy claps her hands like a child. She would like to hold herself aloof from all this, to declare her preference for the austere observances of the Hedge house, the crèche on the mantel and the Nativity story read aloud by the fire. She ought at least to bemoan the prodigal waste of candle wax. But the magical atmosphere absolves her—absolves all of them. They have been serious for too long.

Leander dips the ladle in and gives her the first cup. "Perfectly wholesome," he assures her. "Eggs and milk, with the merest whisper of spirits."

Sophy sniffs cautiously: nutmeg and cinnamon. She intends only a few sips, but once she tastes it, she must have more. It is a concoction uniquely devised for her present state. She would happily subsist on this nectar for the rest of the pregnancy, though she can taste the brandy: a subtle serpent, its insinuations lathered in cream.

The bowl is nearly empty when Leander remembers that a proper meal is waiting. This is a matter of general hilarity for the eggnog is rich and no one is hungry. They laugh harder when they see that he has stuck quills in the capon, exalting it to a dainty dish to set before a king. Medieval manners prevail; they tear off pieces of the bird without bothering to carve it, and spoon up turnip and potato direct from the serving dishes. Tonight they are free from their earnest everyday selves. Different with each other, too. For the first time since Leander and Gideon set up the household, they are treating her as a true companion, not Little Wife, nor Holy Mother, nor stubborn child. It is a great relief, after too many long, solitary winter days, to put off her reserve and laugh with them in this easy way. She feels, for the moment, glad to be part of this odd little community. Also, a fugitive fondness for the schoolmaster. Whatever else he might be, he makes a clever fool. They can dispense with the peacocks, he's all the amusement they need.

"A tune!" Leander says. Sophy has forgotten the tin whistle; he hasn't played since they moved here. He lifts the hem of the tablecloth, and she watches wide-eyed, waiting for him to whip it into the air and magick the leavings of dinner away. Instead, he opens the door and calls for Lem, who is still here, crouched in some corner of the dark house with his bread and meat. He never eats with them, though Leander has invited him. For all his crudeness he is a creature of propriety, as shy of their company as they are of his, an arrangement that, truth to tell, suits everyone. The men clear the table quickly, and, with Lem hefting the chairs, carry it back to the dining room. The boy doesn't return. She imagines him in the kitchen running his fingers around the eggnog bowl, sucking them one by one.

Emptied of temporary furnishings, the glasshouse seems capacious beyond its true dimensions, a long glinting blackness stitched with light from end to end. Leander declares he feels like a minstrel in a great hall.

"A ballroom," Sophy insists. In the novels she used to hide from Papa, there was always a ballroom.

"Well, then, we will dance." He hooks her rocking chair with one hand and drops it with a thud in its old place by the bedroom hearth.

Leander puts the tin whistle to his lips, and after a few sputters, launches into a melody that Sophy has never heard. It isn't one of the familiar carols. The notes are meandering and plaintive, rather as she imagines Gypsy music to be. A thin stream only—a whistle is no violin—yet they pull at her. She begins to sway, swishing her skirt from side to side, and her feet follow. She can't kick and spin as she once did, but her bulk is her pride, to be carried with dignity: the good ship Sophia in full sail. It is fitting that Gideon should bow before her, and call her Milady, and steer her up and down the floor, and turn her with a touch, Leander piping away until he joins them, the three of them linking hands and weaving in and out and under, dancing to the music in their heads as, one by one, the candles gutter out.

When a single flame remains, drowning in its pool of wax, they come apart. In the dark they are ghostly to one another, she and Gideon making one shade, Leander looming before them. Leander leans in close and kisses her full on the lips; then he kisses Gideon. It is a seal, a solemn imprinting.

GIDEON IS TOO FATIGUED to worry about the wisdom of their late night. He manages to pull his boots off and loosen his trousers before collapsing on the cold bed. He fans his arms back and forth over the linen to stir some warmth, moaning, "Hurry, Sophy, I need you."

It is left to her to build the fire, though they won't get much benefit from it. Shivering, leaning toward the feeble heat, she peels off her stockings. As she lifts her dress over her head, a wave of nausea hits her. She barely has time to get to the basin. The eggnog comes up, and the capon, and the remnants of their festive Yule, the laughing, the dancing, the kiss. A long, nasty business. When it's over, she crawls into bed, cradling her belly, and draws the covers over both of them, inching Gideon's arm to his own side. He slept through it all, sprawled where he dropped.

Sophy closes her eyes and composes herself as best she can. Sleeping on her back is unnatural for her; these last weeks she's reposed most nights between fitful dozing and waking. Gideon's snores erupt raggedly, jarring her anew each time, and even with a wall between, she can hear the panes in the glasshouse rattle with each gust of wind. Minutes pass, or hours. She feels a need to use the chamberpot. Tries to ignore the urge—what can be left in her?—but it is pressing.

Unwieldy as she is, it is a feat akin to levitation to stay clear of the icy rim. Sophy squats as best she can, straining but issuing only a trickle of water. After a few minutes she struggles to her feet, realizing too late that she wasn't finished after all, she's drizzling down the inside of her leg. Her fingers come away clear, and only then does her heart begin to race, her weary mind warning her of the risk of blood. No use looking for a cloth now, might as well use her shift.

As she dabs at herself, the cramp grips, clenching her from back to thighs, doubling her over. She gasps, too shocked to cry out. Tells herself it must be her bowels, it's too soon for the other. When it passes, she is afraid to lie down; she paces back and forth, hands on her back. Then she remembers the mock pains the women spoke about. Their voices rush in on her, a comforting chorus. *Not due for a week . . . came regular every five minutes . . . had me thinking I'd push my firstborn out all alone and not a soul near to help.*

Yes, she has had a false pain, and in a few minutes there'll be another, and she will wake Gideon then and tell him he must get Mama in the morning. Calm and prepared.

The fire is only embers, but she gives it a poke and lowers herself into the rocking chair. Soon she'll be nursing the baby in this very chair— a soothing thought. If they won't let her sing, is humming permitted? Will the rhythm of rocking be enough of a lullaby? Five minutes must have passed by now. She wishes for the dependable click of the hall clock; here Gideon's pocket watch is their only timepiece. Thoughts of home bring a powerful yearning for Mama. Sophy wants her with a pure infant's need—would wail for her open-mouthed if she could. Mama said she would be here to bear it with her. How angry she'd be if she knew her hoyden daughter had danced . . . *Just like you to jog the little one loose before its time* . . . but all the while she'd bustle about, doing what needed to be done . . .

Pain yanks her spine straight, the cramp sharper now and more insistent, a poker through her innards. This time she screams.

"What? What is it?" Gideon starts up from his nest of covers and gropes for the lamp. She notes through her pangs that he looks comically like other men, his face bristling with two day's growth of whiskers and hair standing up all over his head.

"Oh, no," he says. "Please God, not now, not tonight. We're not ready."

GIDEON WILL FIND that great swatches of the night are lost to memory. He is accustomed to residing in the interludes between events, those hushed, dimly lit receiving rooms where he can gather his thoughts. This night is all activity, from the moment he wakes to Sophy's cry to the relentlessly approaching consummation.

He rushes into the parlor, shouting for help. Leander comes running, wide awake and hoisting up his trousers. "She is early," he says, "but not so early that we should be alarmed." He claps Gideon on the back, as if the two of them are about to embark on a long-anticipated adventure.

His manner changes when he goes to Sophy. He kneels before her and folds her hands in his. "Now you mustn't be frightened," he tells her. "Every soul that walks in the world has entered by this route. Think of that!" He glances at her bare feet, and, without hesitating, takes them in his hands and rubs them vigorously. "Blue with cold," he says to Gideon. "Fetch some woolen stockings, would you?" Sophy accepts his attentions without protest; even, Gideon observes, with a kind of mute gratitude. He has longed for this; yet, for the first time since the three of them began to live together, he feels a needle of jealousy—of whom or what he isn't sure. A new etiquette prevails tonight, and for this, too, he isn't ready.

Lem is roused with difficulty from the mat near the kitchen hearth. The plan is for him to fetch Dr. Craddock while Leander collects Mrs.

Hedge and Micah. Sophy is seized with another cramp, and all pretense of calm goes.

"For God's sake, what if it happens while you're gone?" Gideon says, near to weeping. "How will I know what to do?"

In the end, Lem is dispatched into the night swaddled in Leander's scarves, with only a lantern to guide him. He is to walk first to the Hedges, and with family in tow, take the horse and wagon to the doctor's, all returning together. "It's a better plan," Leander declares, seeing him off. "Simpler. The sun will be up in an hour or two—though you know this land so well you could find your way blindfold, couldn't you, Lem?" The boy blinks and screws up his forehead, as if pondering the nature of the compliment.

By the time dawn arrives, bringing a blush to the blanched landscape, Sophy's pains are coming every six minutes. No one tells you it is a kind of possession, Gideon thinks. Sophy is no longer Sophy. Her face is blotched with tears and sweat, however often they sponge her. Her hair hangs. She is too hot, then chilled to the bone; hungry, but can't swallow more than a spoonful of broth. The respites aren't long enough to relieve her. No sooner does one siege end than she lives in dread of the next, her mouth contorted and her eyes pleading for help he can't give. She cries out for Fanny and begs her to hurry. She goes from bed to rocking chair and back to bed, as if she could escape her misery, and weeps when it grips her again.

Leander takes him aside. "Walk with her. I don't hold with all this lying about, it does no one any good. While you walk, talk to her. Remind her of some tender moment in your courtship. Tell her she is young and healthy, and won't remember a thing when she holds the baby in her arms."

"How can you be so sure?" Gideon says with some bitterness. Leander's confidence is beginning to grate on him. "It's not as if you've had experience."

"On the contrary, dear boy," Leander says. "I had a wife once, in another life, another age. I know enough not to panic when there's no cause."

But he turns to the window, where he has stationed himself this last half hour, watching the snow turn from gray to pink, and drums his knuckles on the sill.

GIDEON WRAPS HIS ARM about Sophy, and steers her slowly around the bedroom. She will not help him, she makes herself a dead weight, and he feels, in spite of himself, a trace of resentment. Do all women carry on so? It is not easy, under the circumstances, to make conversation. The blankness of his mind recalls the night of the Reverend's accident—the last time he was asked to talk a person through pain. If a stream of Hebrew were to gush from him now, it wouldn't be the least efficacious. But he does have a useful thought, though only one.

"Come, let's get away from this room," he tells her. "Let's go to the glasshouse and watch the day come in. The day our child will be born."

They walk into the pale, watery light of early morning. Baptismal, it seems to Gideon: the stains of last night's festivities tenderly washed away, all things made new. But Sophy is looking at the candlesticks clotted with wax, the greenery sagging from its string or fallen to the floor during their exertions.

"This place will never be the same to me," she says, very low.

"Why do you say that?"

As if he didn't know what last night's revels portended. Her paintings stacked in a corner, her easel propped against the wall. Soon her sanctuary will be a laboratory, he and Leander observing the infant and noting each advance of its consciousness, while she—what role had he assigned her? In his visions of their communal life she has been on the periphery, caring for the child's physical needs and running the house, perhaps painting in her spare time. A well-trained servant, essential but invisible. He must find a way to draw her in, as Leander told him long ago. To honor her as she deserves. She is his wife, after all—his beloved Sophy. And the fact is, servants can be treacherous: prone to gossip, disloyal. Smiling to your face while plotting mutiny in their hearts.

Sophy gasps and clutches her back, and Gideon banishes those thoughts, ashamed of his own perfidy. First get the child born, and he will make it up to her. He is about to dredge up a memory of their early days in the study when he glimpses in the distance a bulky figure trudging toward them, stamping a neat seam of footprints across the snow. In the intensity of his relief, Gideon doesn't think to question why Lem is still on foot, why he is alone.

He has carried the message all the way from the village, determined to deliver it intact, but his face is too stiff, his lips won't form the words. Leander leads him to the kitchen fireplace and puts a steaming bowl of broth in his hands, unwinding his exotic wrappings while he drinks; the boy had balked at wearing "lady clothes," even from his master, but had shed his pride along the way. With each swallow Lem makes a mewing sound in his throat, equal parts pleasure and pain. He upends the bowl over his face to catch the last drops.

"Doctor says Missus Reverend is poorly and he will come in the hour meantime ask Missus Teague failing that a neighbor." He pauses for breath. "I went to Missus Teague's, but she were at another birthing."

Sophy begins to whimper softly. Gideon can tell from the slackness of her body that she is at the end of her strength, and he has none to give her. People call on God at such times, but he has spent too many months constructing his own house and never once deferred to the Builder. It would be like crying out to a stranger. He looks to Leander, more out of habit than hope. His friend looks back, dull-eyed. Lem's news has drained the vitality out of him: his flesh hangs from his long bones.

Lem gapes at them. He is still clutching the bowl, which no one has had the presence of mind to refill. He seems dimly mystified by his reception. Gideon can almost see the thought winding its slow, impeded way through his head like a funeral procession in a snowstorm. *Did I get the message wrong?*

Leander has perhaps read the same thought. He pats the boy's shoulder. "You did well, Lem—everything that was asked of you. You're a good, faithful fellow. Now, you stay by the fire until you're warm, and go to the larder and find yourself something to eat. We must all keep our strength up."

This small show of comfort restores Leander to himself. He puts an arm around Gideon and Sophy. "We're able and intelligent, are we not? We'll see it through together. These medical men have convinced us they're indispensable, but the fact is, women have been giving birth for centuries without doctors. I'm told the Polynesians are so relaxed they have no pain. Out pops the little one, and it's back to pounding taro root for dinner . . ."

Sophy rebukes him with a groan that ends in a howl. It takes both of them to get her back to the bedroom; again Gideon wonders at her resistance, but now he thinks, She is contending, but not with us. He smooths the bedclothes and plumps her pillows; it seems easier for her to recline than lie flat. When she is settled, he stretches out beside her on top of the covers, resting his back against the oak headboard. He doesn't dare get too comfortable; in spite of his agitation, he is swimming in fatigue. Somewhere in the background Leander is feeding the fire, muttering to himself about soap and string. A moment of oblivion, all his faculties shutting down. Sophy pulls at his hand.

"He won't wait," she says, her voice high and thin, as if she's given up arguing. "He is coming now."

THE TIME IT TAKES will forever be a blur. It seems to Gideon that they are in the bed for hours, Sophy straining, alternately wringing his hand and pulling at the sheet that Leander tied to the bedpost. Even in extremity, he is struck by the strangeness of the process, the primitivism of it. If everyone in the world enters by one route, then his own mother—his cool, contained, brittle mother—must have writhed like this, reduced to her animal self. The Bible calls it a punishment, but what if Eve had resisted the fruit? Would the child have slid out effortlessly from the gate of life, singing hymns?

Leander is talking to Sophy, telling her softly what he is about to do. "Now I am just going to reach under your gown and see if I can feel the head. No need to be ashamed, we are all cut in the same pattern, and Gideon is right here. I'll be as gentle as I can, and you will let me know if I'm hurting you."

Sophy is beyond resistance. She cries out only once, when his fingers intrude. Leander keeps up a constant patter. Is his hand too cold? Can she be patient a moment longer? Yes, the head seems to be right where it should be, positioned correctly, as far as he can tell. The baby is waiting at the door and they have only to escort it over the threshold.

He directs Gideon to drape a quilt over the back of the rocking chair. "You will sit in this good, strong chair, and Sophia will sit in your lap, and you will put your arms around her and give her your support. Our ancestors were wise enough to let Mother Earth be a midwife, and we will do the same."

Gideon locks his arms under Sophy's bosom, clasps her hips between his thighs. Sensing her absorption, he has kept his distance these last weeks, telling himself it was for her own sake. Now there is no distance. When the pain takes her, her head rears back against his shoulder, her fingers dig into his knees, he feels her convulsive effort in his own body. The sound she makes comes from a deeper place. Gideon hears the anguish in it and wonders if the child is crying with her.

Leander sets the hearth stool before them and sits, his legs forking out on either side of Sophy. Without a word, he lifts her garments above her knees, peers under, reaches in. "Now bear down," he commands.

"I am," she moans. "I can't bear down any harder, I'll split in two."

"Nonsense, you're made for this. Give me one more push, and roar when you do it—like a Red Indian on the warpath. Open your lungs."

Sophy howls. She hasn't another one of those in her, Gideon thinks, holding her fast; already she sounds like a lost soul. She is so limp afterward that he wonders if she's gone, but Leander cries from beneath her skirts, "And here's the head! Gently now as we bring him in, *er kommt, er kommt*, little by little, that's the way."

It looks like some creature of the deep, crushed and slippery, covered in blood and slime. Gideon remembers the streak of red on Sophy's cheek the night it was conceived, and thinks, this is the child I deserve.

Leander holds it up, still attached to the cord, and lays it on its side on Sophy's belly, and, forgetting himself, proclaims, full of triumph, "We have got our little man!" The creature, having been announced, bawls. Not until later will Gideon reflect that the covenant of silence has already been broken.

Dr. Craddock staggers in half-frozen in time to deliver the afterbirth. Sophy has sustained some tearing, and must be kept quiet and recumbent for the first few days, and cushioned from any undue shock, but "all in all," he informs them, "better than I expected, a mercy under the circumstances." He congratulates Leander on the neat tying of the navel-string, and Gideon on his fine son.

Sophy, fresh from her own extremity, begs to know how Mama is. "We're doing all we can," Craddock assures her. "She's resting now, and so must you." He promises to give Fanny the good news about the baby on his way home.

He would be stopping there in any case, he tells Gideon and Leander, taking them aside. "Pneumonia. Mrs. Hedge is a strong woman, but if she's ill enough to let me treat her, she's very ill indeed. I've told the boys not to leave her unattended."

"Fanny will rally," Gideon whispers. "I believe she's indestructible." He realizes that he has feared her as one fears the whims of nature. If she wanted to see her grandson and babble to him in baby pidgin, she would find a way, Leander's ploys notwithstanding. He is very fond of Fanny and would never wish her dead, but he can't help thinking how much easier it would be if they were spared her good intentions.

The doctor has been up most of the night, and could reasonably expect a bite of supper, or, at the very least a celebratory dram. He is perhaps too tired to be more than mildly discountenanced when they put their fingers to their lips and usher him, firmly but graciously, to the door.

WASHED IN LARD and warm water and wrapped in flannel, the child has been deposited in the cradle. It looks up at Gideon through slits of blue, as though mindful of the serious nature of the task ahead of them. Gideon offers his forefinger, and when the waxy fingers clutch, his heart contracts. It is more mottled than the infants he had imagined, not so alabaster and symmetrical, but without a doubt the seedling of a man, perfect in its way. The purity and the clarity: he had gotten those right.

LONG AFTER THE LIGHT FADES, Sophy turns her head to gaze at him nestled in his cradle within easy reach of her arm. She thought she would feel empty when he was out of her. Instead she is filled to the brim, contentment coating her discomfort. It won't last, any more than the ecstasy of her dancing lasted, or the peak of love. In an hour or two she'll wake to a fretful wail, every part of her sore and aching, and gather him up with awkward hands, and blink back tears as he nibbles at her breasts. She'll cradle his few pounds in the crook of her arm and know that the weight of his future is hers alone to bear. None of this touches her joy. If it ends, it isn't Paradise, Gideon says, but Sophy is resting there tonight—and never has she been more alive.

WHEN SOPHY AND THE BABY are asleep, and Leander has retired to his room, Gideon takes out his green journal. By the light of a single candle, he dips his quill in ink and writes at the top of the first page, in his best script, *December 24, 1838*. He hesitates, weighing the merits of "Male infant"—scientifically correct, but clinical—against the more succinct "Boy." After a moment he writes: *Son born at ten past three o'clock in the afternoon to Gideon and Sophia Birdsall. A strong piercing cry.*

———

PART FIVE

PROTECTING PARADISE

CHAPTER 33

NAMING

THE REVEREND WILLIAM ENTWHISTLE WAS A YOUNG MAN—
no more than thirty, Gideon estimated—but he had a graybeard's comfort with platitudes. "The Lord giveth and the Lord taketh away," he said, shaking his head over the two new entries in the parish register. He had intoned the same words earlier that morning in the Hedge parlor as Fanny scowled up at him from the plain pine box she had requested, and repeated them an hour ago to the harsh scraping of ropes as she was lowered into her last resting place beside her husband.

"And what name will you give the baby?" Entwhistle asked, pen poised.

"I—we—haven't decided yet." Through the window behind the parson's head, Gideon watched as a pair of gravediggers shoveled dirt over the coffin, the turned earth a raw gash in the snow. How had they managed to carve a hole in ground this hard? "A loss like this, so soon after the birth . . . My wife has been distraught. We thought it better to wait until she was more herself."

The pastor nodded. "No need to hurry. You will let me know before the little one is baptized?"

Gideon was grateful for the tentative note. He had not returned to church since his dismissal and had dreaded meeting his successor, who must surely have been informed of his reprobate ways. But Entwhistle was nothing like his Uncle Mendham. He was a conciliator: a short, round-cheeked fellow with nervous hands that seemed always to hover in the vicinity of his chest, as if to ward off misunderstanding. Gideon had no intention of bringing his son to be christened—he had discussed the matter of infant baptism with Leander, and they had both remarked on its absurdity—but he felt that the new parson would be genuinely flattered if he did.

He walked rapidly away, glad to leave the church and its rigidities behind him. The experience hadn't been as bad as he feared. At Fanny's funeral there had been a few stiff faces, but whatever his former congregants thought of him and his apostasy, their judgments had been softened by grief. He had stood next to Micah in the Hedge parlor and collected all the heartfelt sentiments that came his way to take home to Sophy. He could truthfully tell her that Fanny had been held in greater regard even than the Reverend; that long after the house was filled a silent flock continued to gather outside, on foot and in wagons, assembled as if for a revival meeting; that the procession to the churchyard was an endless caravan, as long as anyone could remember.

He had offered this consolation, though he wasn't sure Sophy really believed that Fanny was dead. When the doctor and Micah came with the sad news—Micah's face swollen with weeping—she seemed not to take it in. "If you will just show her the baby, she'll come back," she pleaded with Craddock. "We must leave right away." They'd had to restrain her from getting out of bed.

In a sense, Sophy was right, Gideon thought now. Fanny would always come back, if given half a chance. It was her nature. An oppression had fallen upon him when he saw the coffin suspended over that narrow hole. The churchyard was a bleak, fallow place, its grounds chalky with old bones. If they had planted her in the rich soil of her garden, she would have risen in the spring, crotchety and complaining

of pain in her back, and looked around for the nearest hoe—and none
of them would have been surprised.

FOR THE FIRST WEEKS of his life, he was simply the Baby. Gideon
sat for hours each day with the journal on his lap, observing him as
he suckled and slept and woke and fretted, diligently recording the
character of each cry, taking care to distinguish what Sophy knew
by instinct: a hungry sound from a tired one, a need to be held from
a need for a fresh diaper. His experience with infants was scant. At
times, when the phantom eyebrows drew together or the forehead
wrinkled, he was sure that he was witnessing the genesis of thought.
But Sophy would lift the child to her shoulder and pat its back, or write
in the message book, "A colic," and Gideon would wonder whether, at
this early stage, the gut inevitably reigned over the mind. He had been
terrified of holding the baby at first, but now he was quite relaxed.
He loved to look into his eyes. His son seemed to recognize him, but
it was possible he was only seeing his own reflection in that pure and
depthless blue.

At supper one evening—a talking meal, for the little one was
sleeping—Sophy said, suddenly, "We can't call him the Baby forever.
It's time he had a name."

It was the middle of February, the birth and Fanny's death a little over a month behind them. Once the initial shock was absorbed,
Sophy had dealt with her loss quietly, sitting with Micah when he visited, the two of them clasping hands, wordless. Caring for the child had
been healing for her, that was clear; Gideon even fancied that the long
stretches of silent intimacy were mending her heart. She had made no
demands and voiced no protests. He was startled now to hear her speak
so assertively.

"We're just getting to know him," he said. "He'll tell us what his
name is when he's ready."

"Oh, you expect him to name himself! Isn't that asking a lot, considering we never talk to him?"

"All the more reason to wait. If the name is for our use only, I don't see the urgency. We could call him Samuel the Third, or Francis for dear Fanny, but why impose what we'll only discard?" He didn't mean to be short with her, but Sophy had a way of wringing all the vision from his ideas, and hanging them up, wrinkled and flapping, in the full sun. She was a pragmatist at heart, like the Hedges who raised her.

"A child can have more than one name," Leander said. He had seemed weary this evening, disengaged until now; Gideon wondered if the baby's crying was keeping him up at night. "The Jews give their children two, a secular name to clothe them in the world and a Hebrew name for the temple. Some even call the little one by a false name to confuse any evil spirits lurking about the nursery. What harm would it do to give our boy a temporary name? If he has his own ideas, he will let us know."

"I suppose you have some candidates in mind," Gideon said sullenly.

Leander shrugged. "You are the expert with words. Sophia?"

"A first son is usually named after his father." This offered tentatively, with none of the force Sophy had shown before. It was obvious to him that she was only saying what was expected of her.

"The last thing I want is a copy of myself," Gideon said. "If we have to give the baby a name, let it be one that hasn't been soiled by association. No hand-me-downs from the ancestral attic. None of your biblical names—I'm sick to death of Johns and Jacobs and Abrahams and Matthews. It was amusing to call him Prince Adam before he was born, but we must put these ancient stories aside and start telling one of our own. The first Adam named a new world. Our boy will have an even more daunting task—to name this broken old world anew."

Sophy started to speak, but stopped herself. After a pause Leander said, "With each child the world begins fresh—or so my mother used to say. Sentimental in most cases, but with our lad only a statement of fact. So, a brave new name for the little prince. You had better get your journal and a pen. We have a job ahead of us."

February 6, 1839

NAMING THE NAMER

L. suggests we start with function (also the matter at hand).
Thus: Name. *Heb.* Shem. *L. likes strong, solid sound, but G. feels*
meaning veers too close to character & reputation, inappropriate for
newborn. S. has no opinion. L. persists with Lat. Nomen, *nomi-*
nated or chosen. S. says sounds like "gnome."

G. plays variations on "youth" and "new." Heb. Noar, Nove.
Greek Nearos, Neos. *Lat.* Novus. *G. partial to* Neos *or* Neo —
concise, euphonious, with unfinished sound, befitting an unformed
creature. L. has no objection, but S. says more like a dog's name.

L. pursues theme of freshness with Heb. Nevet, *meaning sprout.*
S. uncooperative: "Why not call him Tansy or Bloodwort?"

Impasse. About to suggest postponing decision when baby heard
to cry. All remove to bedchamber to observe as S. nurses him.

G. to L. (after infant is asleep): "He has no personality yet. It is
difficult to name a creature so elemental."

L.: Then let us go back to the elements! Instead of words, letters.
Alpha and Omega."

Discussion follows. G. & L. agree Alpha, *arch-symbol of Begin-*
ning, eminently suitable for first child. S., dozing in chair, wakes to
raise specter of one Alpha Higgins, daughter of Arthur, late of Rev.
Hedge's parish. "A girl's name, and she was not a good girl." All
seems lost. L. intercedes: "Why not Aleph? Language of the Bible
... Rich in meaning ... Good, solid masculine sound." A silent
letter, breathy, signifying a beginning before the Beginning, God's
intent for the world before He spoke it into being. A humble letter:
could have started the Bible but left that honor to assertive Beth, who
is said to look back at Aleph in gratitude.

G (recalling first visit to Hedge's study): "S., you remember the
wooden letters. The Alphabetical Bestiary."

S.: The ox?

L: Only one of many associations. (Requests G. inscribe an
Aleph; *G. complies.) Now, to me, the diagonal resembles the line*
of life on the palm of the hand, and the strokes on either side are the
hands of God, always enfolding. What does it look like to you?

S. (deliberating): A man running. To me it looks like a man
running.

Resolved.
ALEPH
ALEPH BIRDSALL
א *BIRDSALL*

At first light the next day, they had a little ceremony. Nothing formal like a christening, Leander said. Just a simple celebration of the name.

The baby had roused them before dawn, as usual. Sophy attended to his feeding while Leander and Gideon built a fire in the conservatory stove. The door had been shut since the baby was born. During Sophy's recuperation and the child's first weeks of life they had clung to the comfort of the sheltering inner rooms. Entering the glasshouse, his arms full of logs and his cheeks burning from the wind, Gideon was struck by the stillness of the cold. The panes were all frosted, like the blocks of ice in an Eskimo hut. He shuddered. The place had always been open to light, and now it had a blind, subterranean feel. One would have to live in the Arctic to find cheer in a cave of snow.

"Aleph will think the world is white," he said to Leander.

"Not for long. He was born at just the right time. The whole pageant will unfurl before his eyes."

Gideon noticed the bottle of wine, set atop a stone pedestal. "Surely not at this hour," he said. They had shunned spirits since the Christmas feast. For Gideon it had not been a sacrifice. Even the thought of alcohol brought back the agonies of that interminable labor.

"It's a passable substitute for holy water. Besides, a little sweet wine never hurt anyone. Do you know, when a Jewish child is circumcised, a drop of wine is placed on his tongue to dull the pain of the cut?" Leander smiled placidly. "I have been thinking of suggesting the remedy to Sophia to help the little one sleep through the night."

"I wouldn't mention it now," Gideon said, "especially the part about the circumcision. You'll only stir up her fears." He kept a sober face; it was sometimes hard to know when Leander was joking.

When the room was tolerably warm, beads of moisture spreading on the glass, Gideon went to fetch Sophy and the baby. Sophy wouldn't meet his eyes. She had let it be known that a pagan rite was no substitute for a proper baptism, but he saw that she was wearing her best shawl. The baby had been swaddled in so many blankets that only his round face showed. He was getting plump; he rested his serene gaze on his mother, smacking his lips as if still savoring the morning's milk.

Leander held out his arms to welcome them. After a few weeks they had gotten used to this language of gesture. It was not quite habit—they were always checking themselves, stumbling raggedly from conversation in the parlor to mime in the nursery—but the impulse to speak had been blunted. And the new mode eased certain awkward transactions. Sophy was clamping the child to her bosom with that primitive two-armed grip she'd adopted, which reminded Gideon of monkeys, and yet Leander was able to take him from her without resistance. Sophy's face was set. Short of clutching at a fragile limb like the competitive mother in Solomon's tale, there was little she could do.

How naturally he assumes the priestly role, Gideon thought. Leander had motioned for them to stand on either side of him. He was gazing above their heads as though consulting the sages, the baby nestled casually in his arm. Perhaps he had been a rabbi in his long-ago other life, the one that contained a wife.

He had poured wine into a glass. Gideon, anticipating a ritual anointing, hoped he would take care not to sting the baby's eyes; he saw that Sophy had the same misgiving. But Leander dipped a forefinger in the wine and traced three strokes on the brow. Gideon recognized the letter's slanting spine, the vestigial arms sprouting unevenly from its sides.

Leander lifted Aleph on the palms of his hands and mouthed his name. Ignoring Sophy's gasp, he held him up for a few seconds before placing him in Gideon's arms. The baby was calm, though Gideon sensed he was puzzled at this sudden expansion of his close, milky world. The letter had dried to an indecipherable smear. Gideon felt a pang to see the clear forehead marred, even so slightly; he had an urge to wet his thumb and wipe the stain away. Was it his imagination that the face was more defined, the expression livelier? He would have liked to reflect on the mystical properties of naming and its effect on the molding of character, but a patch of damp was spreading under his hand. In haste he gave the baby to Sophy, who took him to the bedroom to do the necessary.

Leander drank from the wine in the glass, then offered it to Gideon: "One sip, to celebrate the occasion." After the two of them had finished what was left, he reached into the folds of his coat and brought out a small scroll, tied with ribbon. "A souvenir of our first great work," he said. He watched as Gideon unrolled the single sheet and read aloud,

ALEPH BEN GIDEON
Aleph, son of Gideon

"And whatsoever Adam called every living creature, that was the name thereof."

Beneath was a line of Hebrew, the characters inscribed in an ornate style that was difficult to read. Faltering, he translated,

Such shall be the covenant between me and you

He looked up, confused. The fragment seemed an odd fit for the occasion.

"There is more, much more, of course," Leander said, "but your friend is no scribe, he lacks the stamina and the skill, in this case also the space. I thought, since a boy acquires his name at the circumcision, this passage would be appropriate . . . the third covenant, you know . . . first the Sabbath, then the rainbow, then"—he scissored his fingers—"then the snip! But it is too obscure, I chose badly and ruined the whole . . . " He broke off. "I'm a bit addled these days. This ceremony has raised phantoms from the past."

"No, not at all. It's a perfect memento. Splendid. I'll keep it in my study to remind me how blessed I am to be a father."

Gideon was already feeling the effect of the wine; he was very tired and the day had hardly begun. He felt pity for Leander's rambling discomfort—a rare show in such a confident man, and more than a little unnerving—but he had no energy to cope with him now. He wanted to be alone with his son: a private communion where he could pursue the thoughts that had come to him during the ceremony.

The opportunity came in the afternoon. Leander had gone off on an errand and Sophy was busy in the kitchen. The baby had been fed recently, but was still wide awake, kicking his legs in his cocoon of blankets. Gideon took courage and lifted him out of the cradle, careful to support his head. Sophy looked up from the potatoes she was peeling and nodded. She liked to see him with Aleph.

Gideon carried the baby into the dining room and pulled a chair up to the hearth, where a fire was still clinging to life after the midday meal. He loosened Aleph's wrappings to give him more freedom, and thought he saw some slight alteration in the child's expression that might signify gratitude. How tempting it would be to have a father-son chat, to laugh with a conspirator over the fussiness of women! For a second he believed he would actually speak. He sometimes had these spasms of nostalgia in Leander's absence, when it was just the three of them, a little family like any other. *Aleph my Son.* Gideon shaped the words, searching the soft features for the change he had glimpsed that morning. The eyes were different, but he couldn't say how. It was like staring at the letter *Beth* in Hedge's study. Now you see it, now you don't.

Aleph stared back at him. He was already extraordinary, Gideon decided: few infants had such a power of concentration. Likely, the silence had done that. He moved his finger back and forth, and Aleph's eyes followed. They looked darker. It was no trick of light: the blue was less liquid, deepening to brown around the pupils, retreating from the color of his own. He had never noticed how widely spaced they were. Perhaps it was the setting that gave them their contemplative look, both dreamy and penetrating, the observed object only a conduit to wonders just beyond. There was no mistaking the imprint. Sophy's eyes.

CHAPTER 34

ALLITERATION

REE. SOPHY IS NOT PERMITTED TO SAY THE WORD, SO SHE
thinks it, hard, as she introduces Aleph to a silver maple. It is finally
warm enough to take him outside, spring having muscled through early
this year, and she imagines his fledgling senses exulting, just as hers are,
to feel the air on his cheek and smell the earth, to see the new greenery
without the barrier of glass. Gideon was hesitant, but she persisted, and
in the end curiosity got the better of him. He is right behind them with
his journal, starting at every rustle and twig snap and bird cry, ever on
guard against fugitive word-spouters who might turn up in their woods
and pollute the baby's virgin ears with a clumsy greeting or a request for
directions. They have recently been spied upon.

On Sunday, a warm bright day, she had carried Aleph into the conservatory for his morning feed, thinking how pleasant it would be for
him to dine in the sun. She was about to unbutton her dress when the
baby turned his head. At the far end of the room, two urchins were
staring in at them, their noses and hands pressed against the glass. She
had grown so used to seclusion that she froze like a deer. Aleph was
delighted. His small body quivered with excitement; he pushed against

her with his fists as he used to in the womb, and let out a shrill squeal—
a sound he had never made before. Any noise from him was a reassurance; he was a quiet child. She lifted his hand and waved it, and the
boys grinned and waved back. When Gideon came in a moment later
and hurried them back to the bedroom, the baby wailed in protest. He
seldom cries these days, except for the occasional bleat to let them know
he is wet or hungry. Leander says it is because he has everything he
needs.

Leander went out to investigate. "A couple of my pupils," he reported.
"Harmless fellows, missing their old master. I had a word with them and
they won't trouble us again."

Gideon was not convinced. "Now that they know where the Pied
Piper lives, they'll be flocking here in droves. The warm weather will
bring them out."

Sophy bends a low-hanging branch, tickles Aleph's chin with the
tender new leaves. A smile is her reward. Are trees like people to him,
creatures with faces? She sometimes wonders how Aleph sees the three
of them. The milk one. The fair one that hovers. The tall dark one.
Today she has shown him an oak, a maple, a birch. Is each a separate
phenomenon, springing up like a jack-in-the-box to astonish his eyes, or
does he join them in his mind? If so, with what glue? His mother can't
tell him, *leaf, branch, trunk*.

Gideon perches his spectacles midway down his nose and records the
leaves and the smile. All part of the process, he has assured her: a smile
is the embryo of a syllable; they have only to let it ripen and be born
as speech. Having captured the observation, he expands on it without
looking up, the crease in his forehead deepening, his mouth pursed like
an old man's. Sophy hates those spectacles, and not only because they
make him look pinched and ungenerous. They narrow his sight even as
they sharpen it. The small, round lenses magnify his own notions, and
the wide world—the wife, the blooming child, the lush foliage—fades
to a blur at the fringes.

She is showing the baby a cardinal preening on a nearby oak, imagining that *red* and *loud* will be fused for him, when an insistent tapping

disturbs the tranquility. The *BIRD* flies off—Sophy can track its reeling path *AWAY* in Aleph's eyes—and Gideon drops his book and claps his hands over the baby's ears.

It's only Micah, knocking on the glasshouse walls to get their attention. Leander must have let him in. He's as light-footed as an Indian; they never heard his step on the path. He promised weeks ago to help with the garden, but James must have kept him at home.

The sight of him blowing out his cheeks at the baby makes it easier to return to the glass box.

MICAH CAN'T GET ENOUGH of Aleph. He is fearless with him. He swings him aloft and takes him on wild flights across the room, welcomes him back with smacking kisses and belly-nuzzles. The baby adores it all; he gurgles and laughs for his uncle as for no one else.

Gideon watches these antics tensely. *M. treats baby like a toy*, he writes in the message book. *Don't worry*, Sophy answers, *you can trust his hands*. In a way, Aleph *is* a toy for her brother. Micah was the youngest, everyone's favorite, but isolated by his infirmity. She had been his only playmate, and she was four years older. She remembers how clever he was as a little child, how eager to learn. He talked early, as Mama predicted. He has been trying to catch up with himself ever since.

"You've tired him out," Sophy says, after restoring Aleph to his cradle. "Now he'll sleep all day and wake us in the middle of the night."

Micah shrugs. Speech has become such an effort for him that he no longer wastes words on trivial matters. His stuttering has gotten worse since Mama died. Sophy thinks it's the strain of being stretched between two households, each a fractured remnant of the family he once had. He is the only link between them, but however hard he tries, he can never mend what has been broken.

"We'll talk later," she says, releasing him to the garden, where Gideon and Leander are waiting. She has Micah's unexpected visit and Aleph's early nap time to thank for this rare respite. When the baby is awake, one of the men is always with her, and even when he sleeps they're never far, keeping watch to make sure she doesn't break the trust. Thus far, her transgressions have been too subtle to alarm them. Sophy spoke to her son when he was inside her, and she speaks to him now in her thoughts. Only a few short months have passed since he was bathed in her juices and lulled by the drumming of her heart. They are still close enough that he can hear her without words, but as he gets older he'll grow away from her. She must find a way to do more while she can.

Lately she's been bolder. When Gideon is lost in study or expanding on his observations in the journal, she will sometimes hold the baby close to her face and whisper in his ear, or shape an endearment with her lips and punctuate it with a kiss.

Sophy steals back to the bedroom, shutting the door behind her. Aleph has thrown off his blanket and is sleeping on his back, one arm thrown over his chest. Soon he'll be turning over, he's right on the cusp. She's restrained herself for so long that her throat closes; she manages a raspy "Ahhh" before his name emerges. "Mama," she says, pointing to her bosom as if he can see her; then, risking, "Mama loves Aleph." The baby stirs, whimpering, and her skin creeps with the certainty that someone is outside the door. She adjusts the coverlet and makes it snug around him. She had hoped to give him more, but he has three new words, at least, to add to the others that have slipped through the net. Leander's exclamation when he was born. The doctor's chatter when he examined him. The sentences they've all started, blurted out of habit before a warning finger cuts them off. Words that can't be taken back. She counts them like coins. One day Aleph will open his mouth, and out will pour treasure.

Outside the door, the house is empty and still. It hardly matters. Leander haunts her, whether he is here or not. It is impossible, now, for her to stand aloof from him. The man has pulled a baby out of her. He has a knowledge of her that Gideon never possessed, even in the days when they still made love. Leander gave her the gift of her son and probably saved her life, yet she can't thank him for it. She thinks instead, what more will you take?

———

MICAH HAS ALWAYS had a hearty appetite, but lately he eats like a starving man. He has worked his way through two bowls of stew without resting his spoon, and has designs on a third. Sophy doubts there'll be enough left in the pot for supper.

"You and James, you're managing with the cooking?" Leander asks. They all try to pose their questions in a fashion that will be easy for him to answer.

Micah shakes his head. "N-n-nocooking. W-weeatwhat'shandy, m-m-moh, momohmoh—mostlycold." Struggling up the slope, sliding down. Sometimes he never makes it to the top.

"The poor fellow is still grieving his losses. Sorrow upon sorrow. I would ask him to share a meal with us, but he would never come."

And what wiles would you work on him if he did? Sophy thinks.

"H-h-huh-huh——" Micah grabs his throat, as if he would force the word out. She knows he isn't choking, but the effect is the same. He brings up a resonant belch. Looks down at his plate, reddening, though no one is smiling.

"*Alliteratio*," Leander pronounces. Sententious, a doctor naming a malady. "Moses's curse. Also his blessing."

Gideon sends her a look across the table. Papa's dinner-table sermons on the subject of Micah's stuttering are lamentably fresh in both their minds.

"Moses flings himself at the first letter again and again, begging entrance to the word, but there it stands like the angel at the gate, waving its flaming sword whenever he comes near. With each attempt, he puts his whole soul into the struggle. Eventually his pleas reach the ear of the Almighty, who hears a prayer like an incantation, a rhythm that transfixes like a spell. 'So,' says the Holy One, 'here we have a man who loves my letters so much he can't let them go. Such a man will I send to lead my people out of Egypt.' When Moses protests that he is slow of tongue, the Lord tells him, 'My boy, you're already a magician. All you need are a few tricks to impress the elders.'"

He plants his forearms on the table and leans close to Micah. "You suffer because your tongue is slow, but we are the ones who lag behind. Words come easily to us, so we use them carelessly. We spit them out like apple pips and never look to see where they land. You value each syllable for its full worth; you test your strength against it and respect its power. When our experiment begins to bear fruit, you will be holding Aleph by the hand, striding ahead of us to the Promised Land. In fact"—he reaches two fingers to tap Micah's wrist—"I have been thinking you ought to consider moving in with us. The second floor could be yours, for now. Do the finishing work and claim it as your kingdom. You would blossom here—and I don't have to tell you that we could use your skills."

Micah chews his lip. He looks to Sophy.

"How would James manage?" she says quickly. "He is our brother. We can't leave him to cope with the house and farm by himself."

"It might be the best thing for him," Gideon says. "The church is his family now. I had the impression that Entwhistle is a little jealous of him. He's become Mendham's pet, your sainted father without the manner. If you were to leave, Micah, he'd be more likely to find the good Christian wife he should have courted to begin with, and start again." Seeing Micah's face, he added, "Not that you're a burden to him. But James is a brooder, he clings to the past. You tie him to his old life."

Sophy is startled by Gideon's quick assent. Usually he takes a while to assimilate Leander's swerves and leaps. He said once that Micah would always be part of their family, but that was before he had a son of his own.

"Micah is reaching an age where he can make decisions for himself," Leander says. "How many years are you, boy?"

"S-s-sixteen."

"Almost a man! By the time I was sixteen, I had already plotted my escape. I ran away to the nearest port to be a seaman on a merchant ship, but my father had a long arm and fetched me back." He peers at Micah under heavy lids. "When it comes to making plans, it is sometimes a great impediment to have a parent."

———

THEY HAVE THEIR MOMENT alone later in the afternoon. Lem arrives to consult with Gideon and Leander about building a stone wall around the house, and at first sight of him, Micah takes refuge in the glass-house to help Sophy with the potting. Spring is fickle in Massachusetts; they are starting some plants indoors in case the cold comes back again. She finds it satisfying to bed the wispy seedlings, pat fresh earth around them with fingers practiced at tucking in. Leander is convinced they'll sprout like Jack's beanstalk and sprint up to the ceiling by summer's end. Sophy doesn't want these babies to grow up too quickly. She hopes for cloudy days and cold spells—any whim of nature that will preserve her view.

"Would you actually come here?" She hushes her voice by instinct now. "They don't know where your loyalties lie. Keeping you near is their way of making sure of you."

Micah shakes his head. "J-J-James w-w-w. . ."

If she waits for him to expel the words banking in his throat, there'll be no time to talk. The message book is too risky. Scanning the room, she lights on her old sketchbook, stowed in a corner alongside her paint-ings. The last used page is filled with her failed sketches of Leander. She turns it over quickly. One way or another, he is always watching.

Micah writes with his wrist curved inward, fencing the letters in as he shapes them. *James will never let me go. Thinks y'r house is curs't.*

"How cursed?" Sophy asks.

Some folks at meeting say L. keeps you all Mezmerized. Ask where is Sophy? Baby never baptized. Gossips talk Devil worship. Stupid women but James listens.

Sophy's eyes sting. These are the people she grew up with. Papa's congregation, the wayward sheep he chastised on Sunday. She has always been a trifle strange in their sight—she will own that—but still the Reverend's daughter, secure under the Hedge mantle. Now they suspect her of dancing with the Devil?

"Leander is often in the village, and Gideon goes there to teach. Is it really so odd to keep a newborn at home during the winter?"

Folks fear what they don't see. Come to meeting. I'll bring you myself.

"You know they won't let me take the baby. I can't leave him, he's too young."

But she is blinking tears now at the thought of sitting beside Micah in the wagon, wheels jouncing under them as the horse picks its way over rough road, the trees thinning to meadow as they approach the village. *Come to meeting*, he writes, as if she could put on her bonnet and waltz through the door. How many months have they kept her in this house, confined her to their company? She and Aleph might as well be prisoners. The idea shocks, as if another mouth had spoken it. Absurd to fling such a term at a woman living in a fine house with her husband and son, comfortably secluded. But what other name for those who aren't free to leave?

She's thought of escape before, but always as a distant possibility, an extreme remedy should the sickness turn mortal. For the first time she wonders, where would we go?

"Does James . . . ask about us?" She trusts Micah to tease out the other questions embedded in this one. Does he look upon me still as his sister? If I turned up at his door with Aleph, would he take us in?

Micah writes: *Asking is not James's way. He thunders about school Leander promised, believes himself fooled. "House sewn in corruption, corrupts all within." Gideon & Leander are giv'n over, but you are family, w'ld save you and baby if he c'ld.*

She smiles at "sewn in"—a more apt description of their circumstances than he knows. "I must be fallen very low if James thinks I need saving. I'm not sure I could bear being the Prodigal Sister. It would be too grim to be grateful for my brother's charity and put on my church face every day at home—or what passes for home without Mama." True as far as it goes, though it's her own mother's fate she's thinking of. "If I have to choose between jails, maybe I'm better off where I am. But I'll go if I must, for Aleph's sake."

He starts to write, bearing down so hard that the lead in the pencil breaks. He tosses it aside. "N-n-n-never go back, Sophy! Nojoy. No JOY!"

She understands, finally, what he swallows each day in patient silence. An ocean of words and thoughts, phrase after phrase gulped whole like Jonah, alive but undigested. The steady trickle of condescension from those who presume his mind is as slow as his speech. Grief and more grief, his parents dead in quick succession, his sister in jeopardy, the lively household of his childhood reduced to a rigid overseer who used to be his favorite brother. The daily bread of solitude that sustained him all the years of his growing up pinched to loneliness.

Sophy opens her arms and he comes to her, just as he did when he was small. He is tall and large-boned like Mama, but thin for his frame—nowhere near the girth of a man, whatever Leander says. His wing bones are as sharp as elbows, she can feel his ribs. His big, tousled head flops over her shoulder, too heavy for its slender stalk. A body like this—how much can it hold before it breaks?

CHAPTER 35

LAYING STONE

*O*NE ON TWO, TWO ON ONE. THE METHOD FOR BUILDING A stone wall was as elemental as the material. Leander would not stop trilling about the simplicity and economy of the process, the generous New England soil that spewed up stout rocks each winter, to be collected and stacked in orderly piles around the cleared land. "Such a marvelous efficiency on nature's part to give us the means to protect our gardens." He had even made a rhyme of it, which he persisted in singing in a booming bass: "ONE on two, TWO on one, pile the stones 'til our wall be DONE!"—rather, Gideon thought, as if he and Micah and Lem and his brother, passing rocks from hand to hand, were Nubian slaves chained at the ankle. If only the relentless rhythm had a numbing effect, it would be tolerable, but pain grooved deeper in his back and shoulders with each bend-and-lift, and the hinges of his arms felt as brittle as a marionette's. He would be as lame as a man twice his age by the time they finished.

Poor Micah could fare even worse. His hands were made to work with wood, an accommodating medium with none of the obduracy of stone. Sophy soaked them in warm water each night and dressed the scrapes and blisters, pleading with him to leave the labor to the Quinns, who were, she said, built like bears. Micah was always back the next day—goaded by the brothers' smirks, Gideon guessed. Lem and Walt, who had few opportunities to look down on others, had conferred between themselves and decided he was backward.

"At the pace we're going, it will take a year to circle the property," Gideon complained. It was noon, a cloudless day in June, and he and Leander were sitting under a tree, refreshing themselves with the buttermilk Sophy had brought. "And to what end? We can't possibly build high enough to keep anyone out."

Sightings had increased since the weather warmed. Groups of men had been seen at the border of the property at dusk, keeping a silent vigil. They were too old to be students; Gideon thought he recognized a couple of them from church. When Leander strode out in his forthright way and hailed them with a wave, they scattered like marbles, disappearing into the woods at the side of the road. Leander never admitted to fear, but the wall had been his idea: a gesture, effortful and perhaps empty, but something they could do.

"Any wall can be scaled," Leander said, "even if it's as thick and high as Jericho's. But a wall is more than its dimensions. It marks the boundary between what is ours and what is theirs. A stranger comes upon an unprotected house and thinks nothing of knocking on the door. He sees a wall and thinks, 'Is it worth my while to storm the gates?'"

"A picket fence would've had the same effect and been kinder to our backs."

Gideon was in a sour mood. A week ago the dry goods merchant had informed him that he would be sending his sons to a "real school" in Leominster come September. Gideon had tried to reason with the man, exaggerating the strides that the boys had made under his tutelage and confiding his hope that they would be among the first pupils to shine at his own academy. He had scarcely given a thought to this temple of learning since they'd moved in, but found that in extremity he could conjure its Athenian ideals as glibly as Leander. The merchant was unmoved. Gideon suspected that gossip circulating in the village had reached his ear.

Leander mopped his brow with the tail of his shirt. "Stone has qualities one wants about one's house. The permanence of it, the stability. The way it grows underground, so slowly, layer by layer, taking its infinite time. If you think about it, there is a kinship between stones and speech." He had spoken dreamily, communing with himself, but now he stroked Gideon's knee. "You've done enough for today. Go back to your real work. It isn't wise to leave our Sophia alone for too long."

Gideon trudged toward the house, turning his aching shoulders to his friend's ruminations. Leander, with his limitless vitality, might muse on the nature of stones while hefting them, but Gideon's head felt most days like a toolbox overturned, a jumble of functional objects. No sooner was one project finished than another reared up to sap their time and energy. The long walk to and from his pupils' home had been a holiday for him, a time to unleash his thoughts from practical matters and let them roam where they pleased. He was so rarely out in the world now that he'd indulged in a bit of castle-building, imagining himself traveling to other, larger towns; even lecturing at the Athenaeum as his Harvard classmates gazed at him from the front row, aglow with admiration. He would miss those contemplative walks more than the tutoring and the money.

Gideon turned the knob slowly. Just inside he paused, aware of a breathy whisper, like a blown curtain brushing a sill. He strained his ear toward it for a few seconds, trying to discern words. He could not be sure. The sound was too thin. He walked toward it on the balls of his feet, following it down the hall toward the kitchen. The door, usually left open during the summer, was closed. His hearing had grown acute since they'd been practicing silence—painfully so. He listened with such intensity that he sometimes heard things that weren't there, muffled noises or fragments of talk that faded when he came near. This was low and indistinct, but persistent, and the cadence was unmistakable.

Sophy was at the table, packing a basket for their lunch as Aleph watched from a blanket on the floor. She started when he opened the door, but turned to face him calmly. If she was discomposed, she did not show it. He was the one who was overcome, his breath shallow, his hands trembling with the desire to take hold of her and shake the truth out of her. For Aleph's sake, he reined himself in. She held out a handful of tiny greenish plums—the first fruits of a young tree they'd started in the glasshouse. He popped one in his mouth, wincing at the tartness. In the message book he scrawled, *Ripped untimely*, and spat out the pit.

I couldn't resist, she wrote. "*Will you watch A. while I bring the bears their lunch?*"

Tending to Aleph soothed him. The baby was a solid weight in his arms, not doughy like other infants but no longer fragile. Half a year in the world, there was a bright quickness about his son that reminded Gideon of Sophy as she used to be. He had an intelligent look: a high forehead fringed with streaks of brown hair that Sophy combed down from the crown, and round dark eyes that darted hungrily like a bird's. His stare was formidable; Leander shrank from it in mock alarm, declaring himself known and judged, and even Gideon wilted before such fathomless astonishment.

Gideon strolled from room to room, carrying the baby face-front on a seat of his arm, mindful that for Aleph it was a journey of sorts. In the bedroom they made their daily stop before the mirror. Gideon hoped to catch the crystalline moment that the *I* met the other in its reflection, and recognized itself. Aleph loved to see the baby in the glass. Thus far he had uttered an "e-e-e-e" and an "ahhhh"—duly recorded, though Sophy had laughed—and on one halcyon morning had combined the two into something resembling an exclamation. Today he arched forward, as usual, and reached his little arms, but made no sound. Gideon wondered if Aleph was losing interest. However far he stretched, he could never come close enough to touch his mirror friend.

After his morning labors, Gideon had been glad to retreat to the coolness of the house. Still, stepping into the fragrant heat of the glasshouse was a pleasant surprise. The plants were flourishing in their raised beds and Sophy's rosebushes were in bloom, the stalks growing taller by the day. The runt of a plum tree that they'd nurtured as an experiment was bearing fruit. Emboldened, Leander promised an orange tree for next summer. True, it wasn't the lush jungle his friend had envisioned, but a sweeter and more modest place, a New England Eden. More to his liking, though he would never say so to Leander.

He set Aleph down on Fanny's patched quilt with the woolly lamb Sophy had made. Sighing, he sank into his rocking chair as into a tub of warm water, and, stretching out his legs, opened his journal. His last entry, coming after pages of scrupulously described eee's, ahhhs, and ooohs, had a somewhat forced tone.

Aleph has yet to "bite down" on a syllable. The sounds he makes issue from his throat & pass directly out of his mouth, bypassing lips and tongue. They are open, moist, & full of air, not shaped in any way. Yet their variety is remarkable: he squeals, sighs, huffs, pants, hoots; lately I would swear that I have heard him croon, no doubt aping his mother's thoughtless humming (she claims she is not aware). It is too early to say what these utterances signify, but it is worth-while to ponder the nature of Vowels.

He dipped his pen and continued. *Who is to say that our Ancestors did not speak thus? They for whom all was provided, who knew nothing of fear or want, who walked hand in hand with Nature?* A pause, mulling a difficulty with Scriptural purists. *It may be that the "names" Adam gave the beasts were spontaneous cries of wonder and delight as each fanciful creature presented itself; that his pronouncement upon discovering his helpmate was, in truth, an ululation. That the hard-edged consonants that chop throat-song into "words" are a phenomenon of a more rigorous age—*

Micah burst in, followed by Sophy, her apron in hand. Both were gesturing for him to come, Sophy mouthing a phrase he couldn't decipher. Gideon didn't bother to stifle his annoyance. He had been about to expound on infancy as a remnant of the Paradisal era, and to launch from there into interesting speculations about the stages of life. His thoughts had been flowing freely—could not youth be said to embody those first fumbling days outside the Garden gates?—and now life had interrupted again.

Aleph had fallen asleep with his thumb in his mouth, one cheek resting on the lamb. He never stirred when Sophy gently moved the toy and stroked his back. She stood, whispering that it would be best to leave him; Micah would stay behind to watch.

In the hall she said, "The parson is here. Leander is showing him the wall."

HIS UNCLE MENDHAM might think he had the common touch, but William Entwhistle was not at ease in the company of a certain kind of man. This was evident to Gideon from the way he crushed his hat to his chest and averted his eyes from the ruddy torsos of the Quinns, who had been so seldom to church that they didn't know enough to put their shirts on for the parson. Leander loomed over him, standing too close as he explained the fine points of wall-building. "Yes, ah, yes," Entwhistle kept saying, leaning back until he threatened to topple over. His relief at seeing Gideon was palpable. He came toward him with hand outstretched.

"I opened the Register this morning, and saw that it had been six months since the, ah, sad and joyful events. I've wondered how your wife is getting on, and the little one. I ask after you at meeting, but Micah is reticent." He looked around him. "Quite an estate you have here. Extensive! I had no idea from James . . ." He stopped abruptly, as if he had revealed too much.

"The place keeps us occupied from morning to night," Gideon said, "but somehow we thrive."

There was an awkward lapse, Gideon agonizing whether to do the proper thing and invite the visitor in, and receiving no help from Leander, who was on the other side of the wall, admiring the parson's handsome horse and carriage. He was about to divert Entwhistle with the garden when Sophy appeared in the doorway. Gideon stared. In the few minutes since he'd left the house, she had changed her dress and arranged her hair. Keeping so much to themselves, they had all gotten lax, and he'd grown used to seeing her day after day in the same shapeless dress she'd worn while pregnant, her hair straggling down her back in the frayed plait she'd slept on. He'd forgotten how the neatness of her small person had pleased him once, how perfect she had been in her own simple way, his mild gray dove.

The parson seemed equally struck. He hastened toward the house, Gideon and Leander trailing in his wake. "Mrs. Birdsall! At long last! What a privilege to meet the daughter of such esteemed parents."

Though he pronounced himself satisfied just to make her acquaintance, Sophy insisted he take tea. There were still no chairs in the parlor, so they sat in the dining room around the table, which she had embellished with flowers, a bowl of blackberries, and a fresh loaf of bread; delicacies like cakes and pies had fallen by the wayside months ago. Entwhistle tore off pieces of his slice and buttered each fragment with fastidious care. The talk, too, was small and careful: snippets of weather, repairs to the church, the lasting legacy of Reverend and Mrs. Hedge. He has come on a mission, Gideon thought, but isn't bold enough to jump in.

When the tea was almost gone, Entwhistle asked, "And how is young—Gideon Junior, is it?"

"We call him Aleph," Gideon said. "He's well, thank God, and growing like a weed. Napping at the moment."

"Good as gold," Leander added.

"Aleph . . ." The parson moved his lips, treading backward through a snarl of ancient languages acquired during his studies. "Ah, yes. If names are destiny, I suppose he'll be a Hebrew scholar like his grandfather. And his father, of course." But it was Sophy he was looking at. "Mrs. Birdsall, it is not my way to impose doctrine on others. None of us has the whole of the truth, the Lord arranged it so. But I can't help but feel that your parents would rest easier if you would bring your son to be baptized. James is not a confiding man—at least not to me—but he has mentioned the matter several times. Trust me, it would do a great deal of good—and not only for the child."

"We're hardly the only ones who question the practice," Gideon said, interceding smoothly. He had anticipated the conversation. "I don't believe that sprinkling water on a baby's head binds him to the church. When Aleph is old enough to reason, he'll decide for himself what path—"

Leander broke in. "The pastor is trying to tell us that more is at stake than theology. We should hear him out."

Entwhistle seemed as startled as Gideon by the unexpected support. He took courage from it. "You must understand, the people in this village are not bad souls, but they are narrow and superstitious. They judge the world by what they know. When someone chooses to live outside their circle, a few talk, and the talk spreads, and all too often hardens into gossip. I'm sorry to say that your little household is the subject of a particularly vicious slander."

This much had been rehearsed. The parson took a steadying breath and pushed on. "There are rumors that you worship strange gods, and . . . cohabit as the pagans do. That Mrs. Birdsall is mesmerized and kept against her will, and the baby . . . the baby is subjected to devilish rites. Some even say"—He faltered, turning his cup in his hands—"forgive me, they say that you *use* his blood . . ."

"To season our soups. To add flavor to our bread." Leander threw back his head and laughed. He tried to stifle the hilarity with a napkin to his mouth, and another torrent shook him.

The others watched him, stunned. Gideon recalled another occasion when he had questioned Leander's sanity. Sophy put her hand to her cheek.

"I wish it were a laughing matter, Mr. Solloway," Entwhistle said, finally.

"Dear, brave Mr. Entwhistle, I, too." Subsiding, Leander wiped his eyes. "One expects such barbarities in Europe, but that the tentacles reach to our artless little village . . . I hadn't bargained for the scope, the *sophistication!*" Then, taking one of his sharp turns toward the practical: "You've told us what we must do, but there is something you can do for us. See our Aleph for yourself and judge whether we mistreat him." He glanced at Sophy. "Sleeping, is he? We'll all be very quiet."

Gideon led the parson on a winding route through the house, making sure he saw the grandest rooms. He knew that Entwhistle, with his well-made clothes and air of refinement, would look beyond their bareness and appreciate the elegant lines. Passing quickly through bedroom musk, thankful for the closed curtains, he opened the door to the conservatory.

It had been perhaps an hour since Gideon left the glasshouse, but the pale morning light had ripened to gold in the noon sun, and he would swear that the plants were taller, that buds tightly furled minutes earlier had burst into flower. Micah, the only witness to the miracle, was dozing in a corner. And in the midst of this fecundity, just as Leander had foreseen, the sweetest bloom, his son. They stood around the quilt, charmed by the picture the baby made on his bed of colorful scraps. Aleph had been sleeping on his stomach, but now he stirred and, turning over, opened his eyes to his mother and smiled. Gideon hoped Entwhistle noticed how full his cheeks were, and how rosy.

The parson put his hands to his heart. "Lovely!" he breathed.

Gideon and Leander walked out with the pastor as he took his leave. Leander was effusive in his thanks, but also urgent. "All we ask is that you tell them what you saw. We live in simple harmony here, and enjoy our own society, and do no one any harm. Seclusion isn't a crime."

"I'll do better than that. I'll preach a sermon on it." Entwhistle patted the horse's nose. "But you will give some thought to baptism? Mine is not the strongest voice."

LATE THAT NIGHT, Gideon rose from a restless bed and went back to the glasshouse. In the dark he picked his way among plants until he found the rocking chair. The air was pleasantly cool, and the slumbering greenery breathed out a mineral smell, more of earth than leaf. He sat for a while, letting the quiet enfold him, calm for the first time in hours. He had been angry since the parson's visit, and his anger had made him impatient—with Sophy for her treachery, born of weakness and yet to be dealt with; with Leander for his infernal optimism. Even Aleph had grated on him, wide awake after his long nap and refusing to go to sleep. All their work—what had it come to? Leander pleading with the parson to intercede for them with his flock of Philistines. Himself begging the merchant for the privilege of educating his lumpish sons.

Once, not long ago, there had been a naïve young man who'd compared the text he translated to a wall, and confessed his longing to penetrate it. How flattered he had been by his teacher's attention, how eager to confide in the great man, how unprepared when the question came slamming down on him like an iron gate. *Tell me, Mr. Birdsall, what is the purpose of a wall?*

It came to him that Hedge had not stopped him. He had persevered, and he had broken through. He was not so young anymore—certainly not so innocent—but there was no doubt that he was on the other side of the wall: a new settler in the country he'd glimpsed through chinks between stones. A foreigner still, not yet fluent in the language nor acquainted with all its ways, but a citizen, with a citizen's rights. He had overcome Hedge's moral certitude and his tidy Calvinist exclusions. He would not be evicted now.

If the Reverend were to ask him that same question today, he would have a ready answer. "To discourage intruders, to be sure. But the real purpose of a wall is to keep Paradise intact."

His purpose also. Closing his eyes, Gideon gave himself over to his new resolution, the swell of it filling his breast and spilling into the room and the sleeping house beyond. In the darkness his own borders seemed to dissolve. He felt immense, invincible. The pettiness that oppressed him earlier—what power did it have against such a will as his?

But when glass shattered behind him, once, twice, he pitched forward as if holes had opened in the back of his head.

CHAPTER 36

FORTRESS

GUNSHOT IS HER FIRST THOUGHT. THE BLASTS OF NOISE, one after another, followed by silence, then the baby's broken crying. She flings herself at the crib, lifts Aleph and clutches him to her. He's wet and frightened, though otherwise unharmed. Gideon is not in bed. She puts the baby back in his crib, still weeping, and lights a candle, her fingers cold and deliberate. The door to the glasshouse is unlatched. Before she can open it, she feels a hand on her shoulder.

Leander, armed with a lamp and a stout log. He motions for her to stay where she is, but she follows him in.

Gideon is sitting in the rocking chair in a litter of glass. He is so still that Sophy runs to him, certain he must be injured, or worse. He squints when Leander lowers the lamp to his face, but gives no other sign that he sees them.

Leander does a quick scan of the damage. "Only a couple of panes gone. Not bad, considering the artillery we provided." Kneeling, he picks two small rocks from among the shards. "They have some wit, these devils. They use our own defense against us."

———

ALEPH SENSES THAT SOMETHING is amiss. He screams and reaches for her whenever she tries to settle him. Sophy walks with him from one end of the bedroom to the other, and back again, bone-weary but alert to every sound. Gideon and Leander are out patrolling the grounds. After perhaps an hour she hears them come in and walk toward Leander's room at the other end of the house, conferring in low tones. Toward morning, asleep on her feet, the baby an inert weight on her shoulder, she lays her burden down on the bed and curls up beside him.

Sun drizzling through a gap in the curtains wakes her. Aleph is still sleeping; he hardly stirs when she moves him to his crib. Even in the shut and darkened room, summer is heavy in the air, defying the window seal and cutting the staleness of the bedclothes. Sophy knows perfectly well that the events of last night were no dream, but a childish belief possesses her as she opens the door to the conservatory. On a summer morning—if it is still morning—anything can be undone, everything is possible.

The damaged areas have already been fitted with boards. Oddly symmetrical, they look like sightless eyes in a comely face as all around them clear panes show off the beauties of the day. Someone has swept up the shattered glass. If it weren't for the parson's warning, she might be tempted to dismiss this as a prank, a bit of costly mischief, to be taken up with parents or, at worst, the magistrate.

Sophy latches the conservatory door behind her and tiptoes past the crib. The central rooms are peaceful, somnolent in the sun slanting through the long windows. Not a sound in the house, and she hears nothing outside. After months of being observed, she's developed a sense of presence: Gideon's has a different texture than Leander's. There is a vacancy now that beckons like an invitation. Is it possible they have left her alone with Aleph?

She ought to be nervous after last night, but this sudden respite brings her to a full stop in the middle of the parlor. She could be cautious, feed Aleph a few phrases with his breakfast, bring him outside and risk recriminations if the men come back too soon. Vandals, Sophy! Lurking in the bushes, behind the trees! If you haven't a care for yourself, think of the child!

Or she could bolt. Leave with Aleph and, keeping to the woods along the road, make her way to town, or stop at a house along the way. She is still the Reverend's daughter; someone will take them in until she can get word to Micah. Now that the idea is in her mind, she feels that she might actually reduce this enormity to simple steps: put one foot in front of another, grab the baby and a little food, and go. As she approaches the kitchen, she remembers what Mama always said when they were small and hanging back from some errand out of fear: What is the worst that could happen? A moot question in those days, when Mama was always there, a citadel of common sense, to come back to if things went wrong. But she has no time to dwell on misgivings. Intent on her purpose, she can't immediately comprehend the sight of Gideon in a chair by the hearth, greeting her with a serene smile.

"You must be walking in your sleep, Sophy. You're staring as if you've seen a ghost."

He has shaved and slicked his hair back and looks as fresh-faced as a schoolboy, except for the dark shadows under his eyes. A different man from last night, she would think, if it weren't for the rifle across his knees.

"Aleph still sleeping? I came in earlier and the two of you were lost to the world. You looked so comfortable, I didn't want to wake you. Leander's gone to town to inform the sheriff, for all the good it will do."

"For the Lord's sake, Gideon," she says. "Where did you find that?"

"Our friend is endlessly resourceful. He told me he got the gun when he first came to Ormsby, to shoot varmints with. Apparently the schoolhouse had rats. I had to beg a lesson, never having touched one. It's really quite a simple mechanism. I believe I could use it with some confidence."

"You would put a bullet in someone? You're not a man for killing."

"I didn't think I could, at first—not so much as a squirrel or a rabbit. When Leander showed me how to aim it, my hands were shaking. There we stood in the pink dawn of a tender morning, and braced against my shoulder, none too steady, was this awkward object fashioned to kill. I hadn't slept or eaten, and I don't mind telling you the thing unnerved me. But when I thought of all that was at stake, I knew I had to make friends with the old soldier. All morning I've been sitting with him, hearing his stories." His fingers caress the stock. "We're intimates now. We have an understanding. He'll help me protect what is mine."

Sophy can tell at a glance that this old soldier never saw a battlefield; Reuben had one like it to shoot small game. It isn't the gun she fears, but Gideon's grip on it, and his eyes. She says evenly, "What do you think you're protecting?"

"How can you ask me? Our home. The life we've made here. After last night, do you have any doubt we're under attack?"

"The house isn't ours," Sophy says. "And the life we have here is no life at all. We see no one, we hide like fugitives, and because we hide, they suspect us. Is this the Paradise you'd raise your son in? An armed camp?"

"The armed camp is out there." A bold assertion, but Gideon's voice is barely audible. He shifts in his chair, keeping both hands on the gun. "I suppose you think it would be a kindness to send our innocent lamb to live among the savages and learn their ways."

"I think this is the only world there is, and we're meant to make the best of it until we pass on to a better one. Your Paradise is a dream. A *fever* dream. I've had enough, Gideon. I've abided all these months, out of love for you. I've prayed for you to see reason. But I won't stand by any longer while you sacrifice Aleph to your notions."

"My notions. Mental trinkets, you mean, that rattle round my brain. Such a racket they make as my little wife waits for me to come to my senses." Gideon shakes his head slowly. "The real amusement—the amazement—is what I made of you. Holding you up as a superior being. A child of nature, a pure mind. I confided in you—told you things I told no one else. Who better than a wood nymph to comprehend another world?" A bark of laughter. "I was the innocent. What did I know of women? No more than I knew about guns! A more experienced man would have seen you for what you are, if he bothered to give a second glance. A common country girl whose mind is as small as the town she was raised in. As stunted as—as—"

He stands suddenly and with elaborate care props the rifle against the hearth. Advances toward her. Takes a breast in each hand. "I wonder what we'll do with you when we have no more use for these. The boy will be weaned one day. Poor old milk-cow, what then?" He tightens his grip, and she cries out. Two damp circles spread on the front of her dress.

"Do you think I don't know that you betray me?" he says, very low. "I hear you talking to Aleph. I hear you!"

The door slams and Leander's footsteps reverberate in the hall. He strides into the kitchen, mopping his brow with a kerchief. "So! Daniel has returned from the lion's den, still in one piece." His eyes move from Gideon to Sophy, and back again. "All well here?"

Aleph begins to wail for his morning meal, and the quiet house fills with noise.

CHAPTER 37

QUESTIONS

AUGUST. A DRY SPELL, THE EARTH PARCHED, FOLIAGE DROOP-ing. Leander diverts himself from deeper worries to fret about the state of the well and the garden. The wall struts bravely across the front of the property and straggles off to nothing at the sides: Lem and his brother have left without warning to help a farmer with his harvest. Heat lounges in the house like a shiftless uncle. Twice, birds have plummeted down the chimney and run Sophy ragged from room to room, eluding the swipes of her broom. Mosquitoes plague them at night: Gideon scratches in his sleep, Aleph whimpers under his gauze tent. The weather imposes its own stasis. Day after day, under siege or no, they go on.

After a brief respite—the parson, Micah reported, had preached on tolerance—human wildlife has been spotted at all hours, ogling them from the road. Gideon claims he can hear voices after midnight, loud enough to wake him, though no one else is disturbed. "They sit on the wall, arrogant as jays," he says, "planning how to torment us. I thought I heard James last night." It does no good to remind him that James won't come near the house. Logic only makes him more avid. He spends half his waking hours hunched in a corner of the wall—"like a statue in a niche," Leander says—with the rifle and his journal. Glancing out the window, Sophy has seen him bent over his book, writing with fierce concentration. She wonders what he can possibly be recording. He has little time for Aleph now.

"One of us should always be on guard," he tells Leander. "Day and night, like a ship's watch."

"How would we manage that, with only two of us and someone always needed in the house?" Leander inclines his head slightly toward Sophy. "Don't expect me to volunteer for duty night after night. I've spent enough hours of my life staring at the stars." But he assures Gideon that he sleeps with one eye open. "A useful habit from my years of living rough."

Gideon is militant even when unconscious. He keeps the rifle at his bedside, standing at attention against the wall. Fast asleep, he throws an arm over Sophy, trapping her ankle with his foot or clutching her nightgown in his fist. She doesn't mistake this possessiveness for affection, but chooses to call it need. He reaches for her at night because the two of them are still one flesh, and no one—not the interloper who lives with them, not the stranger Gideon has become—can sunder them. The ugliness that passed between them is etched on her, yet she can't bring herself to hate him, or fear him as she fears Leander. Since their confrontation they circle one another stiffly, never locking eyes. When she opens her dress to nurse the baby, he looks away. It is a matter of faith to Sophy that the face he hides shows the same raw pain she saw that morning, when Leander burst in. At his core, he can still feel shame.

On nights when she lies awake, restless in his grip but wary of disturbing him, Gideon's sermon about Paradise comes back to her with a force she never felt in church. There is a world parallel to our own, and in that world she and Gideon are the young couple they were when they courted, advancing gracefully in time. Gideon teaches at the seminary, and she keeps house and paints when she can, and at night she slips into his study and dances for him, and they live for each other and their son. It seems so familiar, that world; so tantalizingly near. Some mornings, waking from an hour of snatched sleep, she believes they've lived there all along.

IN THIS WORLD, Sophy is making plans for her departure. Visitors are discouraged—Gideon is in a nervous state, apt to shoot before he thinks—but Micah still comes, and they find a few moments to themselves. On his last visit, he brought some news. James has developed a sudden interest in his nephew—his nephew's soul, to be exact. The poor little pagan is half a Hedge, and entitled to the full measure of salvation through baptism. He's made it his personal quest, Micah says; he talks of little else. Their welfare is not James's only concern. He is convinced that the presence of his sister and her son in the house is staying the hand of Judgment. To allow the Lord free rein, Sophy and Aleph are to be plucked from their unclean surroundings and resettled among the righteous. In a few weeks James intends to take the coach to Dedham to see a banker about a loan to keep the farm going. While he is gone, he will leave the horse and wagon for Micah.

"Why doesn't he come get us himself?" Sophy asked. "He puts the whole burden on his little brother. It isn't right."

"Y-you know why. He w-won't even cash the rent checks, Sophy! Throws them in the f-fire while the farm goes to ruin."

"And once Aleph's soul is seen to, will he bring us home?"

"M-maybe. Or board you in t-town. Place isn't fit for pigs."

To calm herself, Sophy makes lists of essentials in her sketchbook, adding two items for every one she crosses out: Mama's brooch weighs nothing, the jade rabbit will bring them luck, Aleph won't sleep without his lamb. Today she thinks of her paintings, baking under a cloth in the conservatory. She can't take them with her, but should at least pack them securely and see that they're stored in a safe place until Micah can bring them to her. In the trunk, she finds an old blanket that Mama wrapped dishes in, and some twine. She feels a pang of conscience for her neglected children. They deserve to await Armageddon in a cooler spot.

———

IF ELSEWHERE THE HEAT OPPRESSES, in the glasshouse it transports. Once she closes the door behind her, she could be in a perfumed isle, or Spain. Short, scorching New England summers are all she's ever known. The glasshouse reminds her that there are places in the world where people bask in moist, fragrant air all year round, where they move through life unhurried. It is difficult for Sophy to remember that this tropical zone used to be her studio and Gideon's laboratory. In August, only the plants are diligent.

Warm as it is, she turns cold at the sight of her paintings lined up along the back wall with their secret sides exposed. Leander is sitting cross-legged before the display, lost in contemplation. He seems not the least alarmed at her intrusion. He unfolds to his full height and bows from the waist.

"Sophia, my congratulations. What marvels! The flowers of a singular mind. I've always said to Gideon, leave her to herself, away from the proprieties of the Academy, and she'll do wonders. You pretend to dabble, but in your quiet way, you've grown into a true *artiste*." He points to the painting of the flying serpent. "You've caught me, dear lady. That wicked eye of yours has pinned me to the board. I admit, the motif is a little startling. I've heard of Jews with horns, but wings? An innovation!"

"What right have you?" She is trembling. "Is there no end to your arrogance?"

He holds up a pacifying hand. "I meant no harm. I wondered what was under the cloth, that is all. Why do you hide your work? It should be seen."

"My pictures weren't intended for your eyes, or any other's. Could you not leave me this one last thing? You've taken everything else."

Her sense of violation is overwhelming. Against her will she starts to cry, ugly coughing sobs.

"Sophia. Sophy, please." Leander raises his arms as if to comfort her; lets them drop. "What have I taken that I haven't given back thrice over? My money, my time, the house that shelters us, this pretty room you paint in. All that I have is yours."

"The price is too high. You've destroyed my family—left me with nothing. Because of you Gideon persists in this foolishness. He deprives his own son!" Her voice spirals up and up. Aleph is sleeping on the other side of the wall. Let him wake, let him hear. "Give Gideon back to me and you can keep the rest."

"He isn't mine to give, or yours to possess." Leander is quiet in measure to her shrillness. "Neither of us owns him, but he needs us both. These seers who live in their exalted minds—the world makes short work of them. Without us to brace him, he would try, and fail, and compromise, and flounder, and one day he would not get up. You and I, we make it possible for him to exist. To be his splendid self."

Her cheeks flame. "That is a wife's job."

"A wife might do the trick for an average fellow. Our Gideon is more complicated. What you call foolishness is the breath of life to him. Madness would be more accurate, for once the obsession takes hold, it has no end. First the words, then the roots, then the letters, then the mystical numbers, each box promising revelation but opening to a smaller box. I had a touch of the malady once, and I can testify—some never find their way back."

"You don't share his affliction? I'm not surprised. You seem a very worldly man. Maybe you'll explain what you want with my poor deluded husband."

"My temperament inoculates me. The curiosity is still with me, but the zeal—that's long gone." Leander gives a little shrug, dismissing his youthful passion. "You accuse me of possessing Gideon, demonizing him. I assure you, my powers are strictly mundane. I put his gifts to practical use. Keep him anchored on our sad old planet. Some women would thank me." He has been pinioning Sophy with his eyes, as usual, but now his gaze sweeps the length of the glass room: the flourishing plants, the green world outside. "I wonder if you appreciate how unique our situation is. Such a pure, wholesome experiment. I find it endlessly interesting. We are plowing virgin fields."

The image undoes her; she can see it. She says, faintly, "You destroy my child for your entertainment."

He shakes his head—more in astonishment, it seems, than in denial. In the moment it takes him to answer, she realizes she's stung him.

"I love Aleph, too, can't you see that? Do you think a man like me—a *worldly* man, as you quaintly put it—has no tender feelings? Show me a father who is more devoted to the son of his flesh than I am to our little one. If harm comes to him—to any of you—through me, may it be on my head!"

Vows resound, Sophy thinks. If spoken loud enough, they could shatter glass.

When he speaks again, his voice is level. "You paint me as the serpent hanging over the innocent young couple, casting a shadow over their lives. But it was never bliss, was it? There was trouble long before I came. Gideon was restless and discontented, and you were, shall we say, confused. Am I wrong?"

"We weren't perfect, but we were a family. Now I don't know what we are."

"Still a family! A stronger one, if only you would allow yourself to see. To accept." Leander takes a step toward her. "When I first met you, I saw a couple who were at odds by nature. Charming, yes, this union of earth and air, but the attraction that drew you to each other also worked against you. Forgive me for speaking candidly, but I believe your barrenness was a symptom of an elemental antipathy." He advances another step. "I undertook to be your alchemist. Fortunately, I have some acquaintance with the art. The result? Our beautiful boy."

Sophy would move away, but she is rooted to the spot. "You have no part in Aleph."

"Have I not? It seems inevitable that fate called upon me to bring him into the world." His white grin. "Naturally, I was terrified at the time."

Have I not? The foreign inflection, the old world coiling about her simple country ways. The shrewdness, which reminds her of how much she doesn't know.

"Who are you?" Three plain words to counter his. She puts what is left of her strength into them.

Leander reaches for her rocking chair, spins it around to face her and sits heavily. "Who I am, you ought to know. But you are really asking who I was. What if I were to tell you that I was born in Germany, in a town called Kassel; that my father was respectable and despaired of me, and my mother was rich and doted on me; that I had a wife I tolerated, and a child I dearly loved . . . and they died. That some men are content with the families they are born to and the life they inherit, and others travel the world seeking their true kin. Would you know me any better?"

"You were married?" She would like to ask him about the child. She had caught him once bent over Aleph's cradle, tracing the baby's face with his finger, his touch lingering and delicate. Now she wonders if another child's face was written there. But sympathy is a luxury she can't afford.

"It was arranged," he says curtly, and looks away.

Sophy begins to grasp his method. Answer a question with a question. "You travel the world and you end up in Ormsby? With the likes of us?"

"You are remarkable, both of you. The serendipity of finding you here, of all places—it's enough to make an old cynic like me believe in destiny." Leander tilts back in the chair and cocks his head, studying her from a new angle. His eyes are hooded like the serpent's in her painting, but there is a need in them that she's never seen.

"You ought to try to care for me a little, Sophia," he says. "We could help each other. We're cut from the same cloth, you and I. Earthy folk who find their satisfaction in earthy pleasures. Do you know the old story about Lilith, Adam's first wife? She was made of dust, just as he was—quite literally his other half. She could fly, they say . . ."

It has been a long time since anyone looked at Sophy with desire. The shock of it disturbs her rhythm, addles her. From the day she met Leander Solloway, she has called him Enemy and Adversary. Papa used those names to cloak the Devil. Sophy wields them to cover Leander's nakedness. Living side by side, they keep a careful distance, but she has known his nature since his first visit, when he lounged in the doorway of her old room as though he had a right to be there, at home in his body as Gideon never was. That night, lying beside her husband, she'd closed her eyes and spied on the stranger who was sleeping in her bed. Come so close she could see the grain of his skin.

She is tired. Months of resistance have worn her down, and the future is bleak at best. How much simpler it would be to show him the gratitude he's earned. Fulfill the bargain that the desperate make in fairy tales: You preserved my life and my son's; you own us now. A silent giving-in. Her head resting on his chest. His arms drawing her close, wrapping her in the circle of his wide love. She can feel the pull of him, the heat of him, even as she fends him off.

"I suppose it's your mother's money that has kept us all these months?" she says. "I hope she would have approved of our glasshouse. Was her fortune very vast?"

Leander continues to gaze at her for a few seconds, as if she hadn't spoken. Then, putting his weight on the arms of the rocker, he hoists his long body out of the low seat. "She liked a garden, my mother did. Gardens reminded her of the country house she grew up in." His tone is thoughtful, without a trace of mockery. "Her fortune was comfortable, not vast. I've drawn on my portion when I needed to and put some back along the way. But our little household has drained me dry. I tell you frankly, I'm almost at the end of my resources. I don't know what we will do when the cold comes."

As he passes her on the way to the door, his eyes rest briefly on the blanket and twine. He glances once again at the impromptu exhibit against the wall. "Perhaps we'll chain you to your easel, Sophia. These might be worth something."

CHAPTER 38

———

LEAVING

HERE IS A MOON. THERE HAS ALWAYS BEEN A MOON, BUT ITS
appearance on this night is a courtesy, if not a grace. It could have been
shrouded in clouds. It could have been a sliver, with limited candle-
power. That it is three-quarters full and shedding light on Sophy as she
makes her way up the road with Aleph in her arms must surely be due
to special intercession. Mama must be arranging the celestial calendar,
Papa has possibly won an argument with God.

She and Micah contrived the plan, but the first part has fallen to her
alone. It is too risky for him to bring the horse and wagon near the
house; the clatter would be heard half a mile away. All you have to do
is leave, Micah told her: slip out with Aleph while the others are asleep
and walk straight till the road forks. If you're frightened, think of me
waiting for you.

A simple stroll, he made it seem. These past few weeks she has been
calculating each step, rehearsing every obstacle in advance. Gideon's
long hours of watchfulness could work in her favor; voices and visions
might poison his dreams, but lately he sleeps like the dead. If she could
extricate herself from the house without waking him, she would have
a chance. Should the worst happen, she could contrive some excuse—

assuming he gave her time, given the state of his nerves and the nearness of the gun. Her mind averted from this extremity. She meant what she said, he is not a man for killing. Still, he had hinted at the consequences of betrayal. Told her she was expendable.

Leander sleeps in a small room off the kitchen, near the rear entrance—if he sleeps at all. Sophy took him at his word when he claimed to keep one eye trained on the ceiling. He is well situated to monitor their comings and goings. His magic might be mundane, but she couldn't shake the feeling that he knew what she would do before she knew it herself. Aleph was the other question. He might wake crying when she lifted him, or snuggle against her and go on sleeping. Her best hope was that he'd disturbed their rest before. Gideon and Leander were both accustomed to her nocturnal pacing as she soothed the baby.

Then there were the doors, fastened with primitive latches since the trouble started; Leander secured them each night before retiring. And the weather, which, halfway through September, had shaken off summer without stepping firmly into fall. If the cold blew in, if the clouds were thick, if it rained, how would she keep the baby warm and quiet, how would she see a foot ahead of her? The passage from her bed to the bend in the road where Micah was to meet them seemed as fraught with peril as Odysseus's journey across the sea, and as endless.

THE DAY BEGAN in ordinary fashion, as momentous days often do. Up at dawn to attend to Aleph and settle him back in his crib for another hour; he'd need the rest, poor mite. Gideon was snoring gently; he had rolled over when she left the bed, his vigilance relaxed as morning approached.

Sophy had one errand to accomplish, and she wanted to do it before breakfast. With Micah's help, she had wrapped and tied her paintings as planned, with some vague idea of preserving her claim to them. But where to hide them in a house as open and bare as this one? She had poked around the wasteland of sawdust-strewn rooms upstairs and crept down in defeat. She had wedged the bulky package into the back of her shallow wardrobe, but her few dresses provided little cover, and the doors kept swinging open. In the end she settled for an obvious solution. Hidden, not quite in plain sight.

The parlor was a grand space designed for formal gatherings, now more a crossroads than a room. Though each of them passed through numerous times a day, there was no reason to linger; its one piece of furniture, the settee, had been moved to the dining room. Leander, who was forever rhapsodizing about Spain, called the sun-splashed expanse their inner courtyard: "A lemon tree, a stone bench, and we could be in *Sevilla*!" Against a wall, where lovers might have communed on the bench, was the trunk Mama had packed for them, empty now except for the remnants of their move. A cumbersome thing with curling paper lining, it had been ignored for so long that no one talked any more of hauling it upstairs. Sophy put the paintings inside, along with the cloth bag she had filled for the journey, and covered them as best she could. She had not dared to check on them since.

This morning the lid creaked when she raised it—a modest complaint, but, to her strained senses, loud enough to open Leander's other eye. The package was awkward to lift from the depths of the trunk, heavier than she remembered, and her hands shook so that she almost dropped it. With the paintings clutched to her bosom and the bag over her arm, she struggled, first to unlatch the front door, then to push it open. Rarely used, it seemed to have absorbed the inhabitants' perpetual distrust of outsiders.

There was a rhododendron bush by the pillared porch, a wild, overgrown shrub that had yet to produce a flower. Sophy set the package behind it, flat against the house under the shelter of the portico roof. She concealed the traveling bag in the bed of earth and leaves around the roots, as near to the stairs as she dared; a hundred times she'd imagined bending to retrieve it in the dark while carrying the baby.

The paintings would have to wait for Micah to pick up on another day. Better to leave them outside, they'd decided: the weather was less a risk than the door shut in his face. Sophy knew she might not see them again. Leander could discover the package and turn its contents to profit, a view of Eden for a bag of flour; Gideon could destroy them in a rage. So be it. One day, if life permitted, she would make others. But, whatever their fate, she was purely glad that these trifling works of her hand had been liberated. It was as though they were harbingers, making their way into the world before her.

The weather was promising: sunny and brisk, the breeze strong enough to send leaves flying. Already the rich mulch of fall was in the air, summer's parched leavings turning to gold. Sophy wondered idly why the first hints of decay were so stirring to the senses, why the heart quickened in full knowledge that the long winter lay ahead. It struck her suddenly that almost a year had passed since they moved into the house. The rain came back to her, and Mama weeping at the farmhouse door. The ride in the rocking chair, hugging her belly to protect the baby as the wagon jounced on the wet road. Crying herself to sleep in her strange room. Wandering into the glasshouse at first light and being dazzled by a world ablaze. And now, at the start of another autumn, Mama was gone and Aleph was nine months in the world and she was moving again.

Leander hailed her from the road, a sack over his shoulder. So fixed was her image of him listening in his room that Sophy was at first disoriented, as if he'd conjured a *doppelganger* to confuse her.

"The mistress at her front door! I was feeling a little winded, but the sight of you spurred me on." Panting, he dropped the bulging sack at her feet. "I woke this morning with apple pie on the brain. Walked all the way to Haskell's place without a bite of breakfast and raised the old man from his bed. My zeal got the better of me—I picked too many and forgot I had to carry them." He loosened the strings of the sack and the apples rolled and settled, a few tumbling to the ground. "I don't suppose you'd deliver some of these beauties to their just reward?"

"I'll make a pie," she said, "if that's what you're asking."

"No more, no less, dear lady. One day, you know, we'll have an orchard of our own." He lifted his face to the sun and breathed deep. "Do you love this season as much as I do?"

"It's my favorite, I think—though why rot should be so appealing is a mystery."

Leander shrugged. "Most men believe life begins in spring. For me, the sap always rises in autumn. A chilly morning, a whiff of woodsmoke, and I get the most powerful urge to move on. Year after year it shook me loose and drove me here and there, as if I had no more substance than one of these brittle leaves. I'd be drifting still, if I didn't keep it down by force. Perhaps you feel the same?" Squinting, he gazed at the house, dwelling briefly on the bush. "Next spring it will flower," he said. "I hear the little one crying. Shall we use the visitor's entrance?"

He followed her up the stairs, and held the door open as she went inside.

PIE IS A GREAT HARMONIZER: the rolling-out of dough, the slicing and sugaring, the crimping of the crown. In need of an extra measure of calm, Sophy made two. The aroma of baking lured the men to the kitchen. Leander declared that the fragrance was a meal in itself; he wouldn't sully such perfection by reducing it to the gross processes of mastication and digestion. "More for the rest of us then," Gideon said. They ate the first pie warm and bubbling at noon. The silence was for once contented, the men cutting slice after slice and eating slivers off their knives like peasants. Sophy mashed a bit of apple with her spoon and put it on her finger for Aleph to suck. Gideon looked her full in the face and smiled for the first time in weeks. It was an effort for her to smile back. Did he think that a moment of sweetness could heal the rift between them?

On another night, after an afternoon as tranquil as this one, she might have slept. Instead, she lay folded in Gideon's arms for what seemed like hours, her muscles tense and her brain as jumpy as a cat's. He was holding her spoon fashion, as he used to—a token, perhaps, of the softening of his feelings—but it was all she could do to bear the weight of his arm over her, his breath stirring her hair. Around midnight, she'd told Micah, though there was no way to tell the hour; the tick of the pocket watch would have alerted him, and how would she read the numerals? The darkness thickened by degrees, the muted hum of night noise overspread the house. Twice she was poised to move when she thought she heard a floorboard creaking, the weight of a step. At last, unable to bear it any longer, she began to shift her body toward the edge of the bed. Gideon tightened his hold, grunting. When she slipped free of his arm, he shuddered, his eyes fluttering open. "The baby," she whispered. He seemed to try to rouse himself, but sank back into sleep as she tucked the covers around him, her warmth still in them, her touch tender.

The dark gleam of the rifle drew her eye. The old soldier is sleeping at his post, it came to her. He'll be shot in the morning.

The refrain beat in her head with a nursery lilt. *Shot in the morning* as she dropped her dress over her shift, put on her shoes and shawl. *Shot in the morning* as she gathered up the baby, nested his bedclothes around him, stood still for a pulsing moment until he settled against her. *Shot in the morning* as she looked one last time at Gideon, threw him a kiss, closed the bedroom door behind her. Sleep smoothed out the marks of his overtaxed mind, restored his pure beauty. In spite of all, it was a wrench to abandon him.

The house was still. A ghostly phosphorescence hung in the parlor windows and spread its pale light over the inner courtyard, an illumination that could only come from stars. No candlelight seeped from under Leander's door. She stole down the front hall—a disembodied feeling, as if the flesh-and-blood Sophy were dreaming the scene in her bed— grateful for the solidity of Aleph in her arms. At the door, her hand met a smooth surface. It took her a moment to realize that the latch was still undone. Leander, who diligently checked all the doors each night, had somehow overlooked the one they'd passed through that morning. A twist of the knob, and Sophy walked out through the front entrance like a guest.

———

NIGHT SPREADING AROUND HER, impenetrable after the mottled dark of the house. The sheer infinity of space turns her to stone ; if it weren't for the baby, she would rush back inside. Gradually, her eyes begin to discern shapes. The darker mass of the bush, where, after some groping, her fingers close on Mama's sturdy homespun: a miracle, it seems, a relic of a lost world. The wall, slumping to scattered piles of rock, and a wheelbarrow filled with more rocks, abandoned by the Quinns. The narrow, rutted road that will lead her away. Over all, spilling its merciful silver, the moon.

Even on a night as clear as this, the forest presses in on either side of the path. Sophy keeps up a steady pace for Aleph's sake, though her instinct is to run. How many evenings has she tried to make peace with her captivity, courting sleep with thoughts of wolves and foxes and wild dogs and bears, *out there?* Predatory creatures looking for a meal, and now she has no walls to hide behind, and not even a stick to fend them off. These fears she can keep a rein on. A country girl, she has anticipated rustlings and eerie cries, dark shapes slinking across her path. Harder to banish is the sense that she is observed—that same feeling she's had so often in the house. She doesn't know which she dreads more: the anonymous vandals waiting to do their damage, happy to expend some malice on a helpless woman, or Leander, who sees what other men don't. At any moment he might materialize from a cluster of trees. *Off for a midnight ramble, Sophia?*

The only antidote is to keep her mind on what she is walking toward. James has arranged for the three of them to stay at the parsonage until his return from Dedham. He's instructed Entwhistle to proceed with the baptism as soon as possible, Micah says. No need to wait for Sunday meeting, or for James himself.

At the bottom of the hill, the road widens. The wind picks up; they are walking through the coldest part of the night. The baby burrows into her and bleats a thin cry, a sound so forlorn that it pierces her heart.

She wonders if she is taking Aleph from the only Eden he will ever know, a haven of sunny silence and light dancing on glass; a place he will revisit in dreams and wake up desolate, filled with vague longing. She gives him a finger to suck and rocks him awkwardly in one arm, wishing she could stop to nurse him, to take a rest herself. He's no longer a feather to carry, and the bag is heavier than she thought. Micah says the junction is no great distance, but he is young and strong and unencumbered.

Each step is an act of will. The house is long since gone from view. Her worries had been spent on leaving it, with none spared for the rest of the journey. Now the doubts creep in and nip her with their sharp teeth, and she is too weak to contend with them. If she were to sink down under a tree, Micah would look for her. She knows that. But what if the old horse should go lame, or collapse on the road, or bolt and throw Micah from the wagon? What if he's prevented from coming at all? James is a man of iron convictions, but even he can change his mind. What if he's decided that his sister and her son are weeds in God's garden, destined to be disposed of from the beginning of time? Or that Sophy is the property of her husband and must live with the consequences of her choice? And if he chooses to exercise his crabbed charity, what can she hope for but years of servitude, the fallen sister earning her repentance and her keep? A grimmer version of the life her mother might have lived if Sophy hadn't released her by being born. If, if, if . . . .

When she hears the pounding of hooves, she assumes it must be a stranger and withdraws to the shelter of a tree. The wagon rattles past her and would have continued up the road if Aleph hadn't commenced to wail in earnest—as though, she will think later, he knew his future was at stake.

Micah takes her bag, and helps her into the seat by his side. "I was w-w-worried the j-j-junction might be too far," he says.

"You came at the right time," she tells him.

And with this slight exchange Sophy realizes that they are having a conversation in the presence of the baby. The spell of silence has been broken, the experiment is over. Whatever lies ahead, she has done the essential thing, and only good can result. For Gideon, too, she believes. He will be angry at first, but he will come back to her and Aleph eventually, and together they will go on with their lives. She does not spare a thought for Leander, whose power—whose very substance—seems to ebb as they leave the house behind. They've already reached the bend in the road. The woods have thinned, and meadow stretches out on either side. Off to the right, a cottage, smoke wisping from the crooked chimney. The straggling beginnings of the village, here a farmhouse, there a field of cornstalks, here a flock of sleeping sheep, squat and still as gravestones in the moonlight. Aleph takes it all in with wide eyes. He has forgotten he is hungry, but she offers him the breast anyway, and serenades him while he drinks, the one tune she can remember, the night air having driven all others from her head. "Baa, baa, black sheep, have you any wool . . ."

THE PARSONAGE IS a gracious old house not far from the village center. Mendham has done well by his nephew; other parsons supplied their own accommodations. Pastor Entwhistle greets them at the door in his cap, a capacious robe, and slippers that turn up at the toes. It must have been after twelve when Sophy left, for it's past two now; they've kept the poor man up most of the night. Still, his concern is for them. Would they have some sandwiches? A little sherry to help them sleep? He regards Aleph—wide awake and reeking—with tender trepidation. "And the little fellow, what can I get for him? Does he, ah, chew yet? You'll excuse my ignorance."

The sitting room smells pleasantly of wax polish and dried herbs and flowers that effuse their faint spice from china bowls—"a hobby of mine," the parson tells her. "I confess it only to you." The fragrance is familiar to Sophy from Mama's mixtures, though hers were never so artfully arranged. The house glows with order and comfort, a settled domesticity that seems forever out of reach. Never more than now, when she can't see far enough ahead to know where they will sleep next week. It seems foolish to mourn the loss of a tranquility she's never coveted; still, the thought pulls a sigh out of her. Mr. Entwhistle, all repentance for his chattiness, shows her to the room he has set aside for his mother's visits. At the door he says, "When James returns, we will appeal to him. I am sure he will do what is needed. What is right." He looks down, the candle illuminating his plain face; he is the homeliest item in his house, Sophy thinks. "I would gladly have you here, but my, ah, position constrains me. You are a parson's daughter. You will understand. If I had a wife, people would call it hospitality, but, as it is, they would talk. They have such minds . . ." He shakes his head and scurries down the hall.

Flowered curtains, a maple four-poster, a white counterpane resting like a fallen cloud on a high, plump mattress. Their disheveled selves are an intrusion here, but Sophy is too tired to care. She draws back the counterpane to change Aleph, washes his face and hands in the basin and then her own. The bed is as enveloping as it looks. She snuffs the candle and folds her son to her, hoping that her closeness and the dusky warmth will soothe him back to sleep. She can see the shine of his eyes; he begins to play with his fingers—a good sign—and to croon one of his tuneless songs. Sophy drifts off to it, the single note repeated over and over, softer and softer until it fades into the dark: *baaa, baaaa, baaaaa . . .*

CHAPTER 39

RAKING ASHES

SOMEWHERE BENEATH HER SLEEP A SUBDUED COMMOTION. Voices, hurried footsteps in the hall, Micah shaking her shoulder, light slicing through the parting in the curtains. The next thing she knows is Aleph fussing at her side, tugging at her shift in search of his breakfast.

The house is silent. Bread and preserves and a covered jug of milk have been laid out on a table in the dining room, along with a place setting for one. No note that she can find. The clock on the mantel reads a quarter-to-ten, a sinful hour to be starting the day. She looks outside, but both the carriage and the wagon are gone. If Micah left with the parson, he should have let her know; he has no right to go off, given all they have to decide. She tells the baby so, and is gratified that he listens so attentively. She senses that Aleph is anxious too, and a little lost, waking up in this strange place with all his familiar landmarks vanished. After eating, she carries him from room to room, introducing him to the house, telling him the names of things. She finds the room where Micah slept, his pack on the floor, the bedclothes tossed carelessly; it's no wonder he's fallen into bad habits, living with James. The door to the parson's bedroom is open, and she is surprised to see that his bed, too, is unmade.

Sun is pouring into the sitting room. She perches gingerly on a silk-covered settee with the baby in her lap, thinks better of it, and sets Aleph on the Turkish carpet to give him some freedom; lately he has shown signs that he is ready to crawl. The parsonage, which last night seemed a bastion of comfort and security, strikes her today as too neat, too finicky in its perfections. She has the urge to mar it in some way, to upset a bowl of potpourri, as the parson called it, or dent a cushion, or etch a careless scratch on the buffed surface of the table. Then she is ashamed. Why should she begrudge the good man his retreat from the troubles he ministers to all day?

Aleph hasn't stirred from where she sat him. He keeps his eyes on her, as if she might disappear. "Shall we learn a new song?" she says. "Shall we learn 'Mary had a little lamb?'" She begins to sing, her voice falsely bright. He claps his hands over his ears and rocks back and forth, a sound coming out of him that she has never heard, more a moan than a cry. Sophy has a vision of what his world must have been before: a harmony of sounds and shapes, continuous, blended into a single fabric that she has cut to pieces with her words. All in the name of saving him for society, of making him fit to live like other men. She tells herself that she did what she had to—the only thing she could—but when she picks him up and holds him close, she is quelling her own guilt as much as his distress.

The clatter of wheels in the yard comes as a relief. "Your Uncle Micah is back!" she tells Aleph, and speeds him to the door to the dissonant chiming of the house clocks striking twelve, not quite in unison: a celebratory sound, the music of normalcy restored. The parson comes in, alone. He is covered with grime from head to foot, his eyes rimmed in white circles behind his spectacles.

"Has something happened to my brother?" she asks, when she can speak.

"Micah is fine. He stayed to help . . ." The parson's voice is hoarse. He glances at Aleph, then spreads his soot-blackened hands helplessly. "Sophia—ah, Mrs. Birdsall—I think it would be best if you sit down while I tell you what I know."

———

NO ONE KNEW when the fire started. A nearby farmer, up before five to milk his cows, was the first to notice the smoke and flames. By the time the alarm was sounded in the village and sufficient volunteers had struggled up the hill with their buckets, the house was a torch, its occupants likely beyond saving. There were those who settled for standing back to watch the spectacle, the glass walls buckling and falling in, liquefying to streaks of festive color in the blaze. But a small core of stalwarts went to the well again and again to fill their buckets, futile as the exercise seemed. Micah would have flung himself into the midst of it. They had to haul him away and wrestle him down, and when he saw there was no hope, he kicked and cried, inconsolable. Even after the blaze was contained, he refused to leave, though the parson had pleaded with him. Someone might be trapped inside, still alive. He wouldn't give up until he was sure.

"We can always hope," the parson concludes, "but we must be realistic and prepare for the worst." He steeples his smudged fingers. "The Lord does not send us more than we can endure."

Sophy doesn't cry. She is by now well acquainted with grief. She knows that it begins as disbelief, a numbness creeping up the body like the poison Socrates drank, freezing the vitals as it makes its slow, cold progress to the heart.

"I should never have left Gideon," she says. "Even a night was too much. If I had been there, I would have saved him."

She can't bear that he died by fire. His beauty has always been touched with holiness for her. That it should be ravaged and consumed by an impersonal force seems a depravity, a corruption of all that is good.

"Thank God you did leave," Entwhistle says. "I hate to think what would have happened if you and the baby had stayed in that house last night. You put your child first, and you were right to do so."

Aleph has been twisting in her lap, fiddling with her buttons and whining for his lunch. Apart from anchoring him with one hand, she has hardly been conscious of him. The parson's words remind her that her son will never know his father, that Gideon will be first an absence in Aleph's life, then a blurred memory fading to a print on his senses, then not even that. It is this that brings her, finally, to tears.

The parson is very wise. He lets her cry; he doesn't impose solace on her, or besiege her with pieties as wave after wave of grief washes over her. He gives her a little brandy and watches while she chokes it down. When she has wept herself dry, she takes the baby to the bedroom to nurse, and lies down beside him after he's had his fill, stroking his back. Sleep seems impossible, but it engulfs her. She dreams that she and Gideon are sitting by the stove in Papa's study, and there is a knock on the door, and Micah comes in with a boy straddling his shoulders who is Aleph and not Aleph, bright-eyed and apple-cheeked but blond like Gideon. Micah says, I think he's hungry, can we keep him? and Gideon says, We must test him to see if he talks, and Sophy says, I made a pot of soup, and there is a simple, happy feeling, as if she has solved everything.

Voices filter in. Sophy huddles in the shadow land between sleep and waking, eyes shut, clinging to her dream.

She hears the parson: "Right in here." Then another voice: "Straight and steady, that's the way, careful as you turn, mind the wall . . ." Dr. Craddock, unmistakable; she couldn't forget his voice if she wanted to.

The baby is gone. No wonder, it's half-past four, he must have awakened long ago. But who is taking care of him? She gets out of bed and splashes water on her swollen face. At the door, she stands for a moment, head bowed. If she tried to pray, the words would choke her worse than the brandy, but she tells the Lord that she has reached her limit.

The door opens before she turns the knob. Micah, black as a chimney sweep, and behind him the parson, with Aleph in his arms. Entwhistle is radiant. Sophy knows the expression. Any preacher's daughter would. It is the look that true believers get when the world, for once, aligns with their hopes.

They've put Gideon in the room next door and laid him on a sheet until they can clean him. The doctor is listening to his chest through an ear trumpet. He stands when Sophy comes in. "Now, Mrs. Birdsall, miracle or no miracle, we are not free and clear. He's inhaled a deal of smoke. His lungs don't sound good, and you can see from the look of him, he's halfway to the next world already. But I've treated this fellow before, and I'll tell you something about him. He sinks very low, but he always comes back."

After Craddock leaves, Sophy chases the rest of them out and bathes Gideon herself. The water in the basin is warm, the towels are thick, the parson has supplied a sponge. She washes the grit from his hair and face, cleans out his nose and ears, squeezes water on his neck and arms and takes pains with the fingers of each hand, not forgetting the nails. She washes his chest and belly and groin. They are whiter than the rest of him. She proceeds down to his toes, and turns him over, just as Mama taught her when they nursed him at home. The water is gray now, but she squeezes and scrubs and pats dry, and with each part of him that she cleans she feels a thrill of triumph because she has reclaimed it from the fire.

MICAH WAS READY to quit. He had gotten as close as he could to the smoldering ruin, searched every inch of cleared land, up to the wall and beyond. He was sitting on the slope at a little distance from where the conservatory used to be, gazing out at the woodland and trying to collect his thoughts, when something snagged his eye. A shape that didn't belong. He thought at first it was a piece of the roof. He willed himself to take a closer look; he didn't have much strength left in him, and the day had held nothing but discouragement. Within a few feet he recognized the plaid of the blanket they had wrapped so carefully around the paintings and the twine he'd knotted himself. If he had not discovered the package, with its suggestion of having been dropped in flight, he never would have ventured into the woods. He didn't have to go far. Perhaps fifty feet in, in a kind of cradle formed by the joined root systems of two ancient oaks, he found Gideon, "sleeping as peaceful as if he was in his own bed."

"What regard Mr. Birdsall must have for you, that he put himself in peril to rescue your paintings," the parson exults, still cresting on the froth of grace. "If only every husband loved his wife so well!"

Sophy smiles, but says nothing. She knows that Gideon would never have given a thought to her pictures. His journal, yes—he would have braved the flames twice over for his lifework. That the book hasn't been found tells her someone else carried him to safety, and took time to stop for her paintings on the way out of the burning house. Was it only yesterday that she hid them behind the bush and looked up to see Leander on the road? She has resisted gratitude for so long that even now—her husband saved, her work preserved—it comes hard to her, disguised in questions. *What do you mean by it?* she wants to ask. *Why would you not stay and play the hero?* Gratification is easier. She is flattered—shamefully so—that a man of the world, a citizen of many cities, judged her efforts worth the risk. There are those who would call her prideful, and worse, for rejoicing in her trivial art at a time like this. She would be hard-pressed to defend herself, except to plead that she has no other skills. She is a terrible seamstress, a middling cook, an indifferent housekeeper. The paintings are what she has to offer. Her value in her own eyes is bound up in them.

Gideon hovers for a couple of days. Sophy, mindful of the doctor's assessment, fears that having advanced so far on the journey, he has decided to go on ahead after all. But on the third day he comes back to her, rasping and coughing, the smoke still trapped in his chest. When he can summon enough breath to speak, he has little to tell them. He went to bed that night as usual. He has no memory of the fire, no memory of the forest. For him, the disaster never happened, which is, perhaps, a mercy. He seems to rest in the present and what it contains: Sophy and Micah and the baby; Dr. Craddock, and the obliging parson, whose charity they've strained past the limit.

He doesn't ask about Leander. Finally she says, as much for her sake as his, "We don't know yet what became of our friend. They are looking for him." Gideon bobs his head to show he's heard, and turns his face to the wall. Sophy wonders if, during his long sleep, Leander vanished too, and the whole life they made in the house.

———

MR. LEACH, THE SHERIFF, comes to the parsonage to see them. Instead of waiting in the hall, he follows the housekeeper to the sick-room, where Sophy is sitting at Gideon's bedside, nursing the baby. He doesn't trouble to look away as she adjusts her clothing. He asks Gideon a couple of perfunctory questions, nodding as if the scant response were anticipated, and requests to see Sophy alone. Leach is a lanky, shambling man whose joints lock together with alarming suddenness when called to action. In the sitting room he waits solicitously while Sophy settles on the couch, but declines to join her.

"Now, Mrs. Birdsall, ma'am, it falls to me to ask what others will be wondering. How did you happen to leave the house with your young one on the very night it burned? Some might surmise that you knew what would happen."

No preamble. Not a soft word to spare.

"You were told about the . . . incidents," Sophy says. "My husband had more courage than I did. He wanted to wait out the siege, but I was afraid for the baby, and I left when I could." She looks down at her hands, twined in her lap. "I never thought they would go this far."

"And Mr. Solloway—did he think of leaving too? He's a man who's moved around some."

"Mr. Solloway was devoted to us," she says low. "Dedicated."

"It's an unusual sort of household, if you'll pardon me for being so frank. Two men, unrelated, and yourself and the baby. I'm not saying what happened to you is right—far from it—but there's no keeping folks from speculating." He sounds affable, rambling, like the old men spitting tobacco on the courthouse steps, but his eyes bore into her.

"I can't help the ugliness in people. Why talk about it now? There's nothing more they can do to us. I have my husband and my son, and I'm thankful for that." Sophy is abashed to find that her cheeks are wet; she has prided herself on her control.

The sheriff offers his handkerchief and a pat on the shoulder, but that night he tells his wife, "I wouldn't be surprised if that woman knows more than she's letting on."

"I've known Sophy Hedge since she was born," says Mrs. Leach. "She always was an odd sort of girl, but there's no malice in her. Not that I believe she's capable, but if she had anything to do with that fire, you can be sure she was driven to it. Leave it be, Joseph."

A DELEGATION FROM the village searches the ruins, Micah in attendance to make sure it's done right. Lem and his brother are members of the party. An atmosphere of grim festivity prevails. Several of Leander's former pupils speculate on what state Mr. Solloway will likely be in, whether his remains are imbued with his fabled mysterious powers, what piece of him they will break off for a talisman. They rake ashes, look behind the burned carcasses of furniture, open wardrobe doors and bureau drawers on the chance he might be hiding inside. They pry open the trunk in his room and find, under a few books and well-worn garments, the globe that graced their schoolroom, all the places they have traveled intact. Of their teacher, not an atom of bone or bit of charred cloth is found. The sheriff says it is very rare for a body to leave no trace.

Rumors spring up immediately, as if to compensate for the lack of a corpse. Leander set the fire himself to cover the effects of a spell gone wrong, a botched experiment, a murderous plot. He levitated through the ceiling to escape the law, or took on the shape of a black bird to elude the Devil (this from the sexton's wife, who should know better), or spoke the secret name of God and spontaneously combusted.

In Sophy's opinion, Lem Quinn is the only one who approaches the truth. Lem says, simply, "He'll be back."

PASTOR ENTWHISTLE INSISTS that some effort be made to contact Leander's family and inform them of the possibility of his death. "Castle," Sophy tells him. "In Germany." "Ah, *Kassel*," he says. "Homeland of the good Brothers Grimm. Very appropriate for Mr. Solloway." She tells him about the mother and the father and the wife, but has no names to give him. With hesitation, she reveals what Gideon confided in her: that Leander was of the tribe of Israel. "Excellent!" Mr. Entwhistle says, brightening. "That is information I can use."

THE PARSON DEVOTES his Sunday sermon to the effects of gossip, the noxious waste of breath that has inflicted substantial damage on a family with deep roots in the parish. The daughter of their beloved pastor. The scholarly young man who led their congregation a few months past. Mr. Solloway, a stranger among them but one who taught their children with ardor and imagination. The shame of it! Micah, the only member of the offended family in attendance, reports that Mr. Entwhistle, though not a natural thunderer like Papa, seized the pulpit as the Reverend used to and whipped his mild voice to a shrill pitch. "We will not tolerate vipers in our midst! If any of you has a weight on his conscience, let him have the courage to come forward. For the health of this congregation! For the sake of his own soul!"

To no one's surprise but the parson's, not a single soul confesses, either at meeting or in the privacy of his study. There is talk of an investigation, but without a proven fatality to drive it, a decision is made to wait until the property owner returns. James arrives home a few days after the fire. As Sheriff Leach recounts the conversation, he is indifferent to the house's fate and the loss of income it represents.

"Unclean profits," he told the sheriff. "The schoolmaster turned my head with his talk of a school for the poor. I should have known no good could come out of bad."

"But in the interest of justice—" Leach persisted. Ormsby is a small town; the last hanging was five years ago. This makes a change from the usual run of drunken carousing and petty theft.

"Whoever burned the place down did the Lord's work. And that's an end to it." He spun on his heels and left without a thank-you or good-bye.

The sheriff has his suspicions. Popular opinion may vilify an outsider like Solloway, but Leach is convinced that the blame lies closer to home. The Hedges haven't been right since the Reverend passed, the girl disappearing into that strange household and James gone peculiar; for all the God talk, he wouldn't be the first to twist his religion to unholy ends. Stone-throwers and glass houses, a story older than time. Leach makes it known that he is keeping his ears open, but can't generate much interest in the destruction of a property that no one cares about. A colleague he brings in to sniff out signs of mischief is of the opinion that the trouble started with the stove in the conservatory. Installed all wrong, he says—the work of amateurs who took a bright idea too far—but even well-constructed greenhouses are a folly. "Fire-traps, the lot of them. Some damned fool decides he wants oranges in December and ends up burning down his house." Presented with this blessedly sound logic, the sheriff decides to take his wife's advice and let the matter rest until further evidence presents itself. Soon enough, the whispers die down. Arson or no, the townsfolk have moved on to fresher scandals.

SOPHY EMBRACES HER brother and holds him for as long as he lets her. She rests against him, remembering how his solidity once gave her comfort. Somewhere in this fortress is the James she knew. The yielding she waits for never comes. She can feel in the tightness of his body how he barricades himself, as if the merest expression of feeling would collapse the temple of sanctity that he has built with such care—built to last, as he built his house. He mumbles that he is glad to find her well, and backs away.

The parson lingers in the hall, his head poked forward in confessional mode. Under the sad circumstances, they've had to postpone the baptism, but how fortuitous that the proud uncle will now be able to attend the blessed event. James looks blank for a second, then gives a curt nod. He thanks the parson stiffly for his kindness to his family and offers to reimburse him for any expenses incurred. It is well known in the parish that he considers Entwhistle too lax, an improvement over his brother-in-law but not fit to occupy the pulpit of Reverend Hedge.

"Where is Micah?" James asks Sophy.

"In the sitting room, with someone you will want to meet."

Aleph is riding on Micah's shoulder. When James comes in, Micah swings the baby down and holds him against his chest with one arm.

"Well," James says. "He's a big fellow, isn't he?" The sort of thing, Sophy thinks, that childless men always say in the presence of infants. James approaches, cautious, and pats the baby's head. Meets him stare for stare. His face softens, and for a tremulous moment it seems that he will smile. He meant to have children once, she reminds herself: lots of them, and not so long ago. But the face he turns to Sophy is stern. "He is all Hedge," he pronounces solemnly. "He looks like Pa around the eyes."

No one has ever said so, but she doesn't dispute him. Thank God she's done one thing right. "Won't you say hello to Gideon?" she says. "He has good days and bad days, but he was sitting up this morning."

Sophy thinks she has never seen an expression alter so quickly. That haunted look he used to get when his pain was fresh, just before he went into a rage. She trades glances with Micah. What brought this on? James has surely been informed that Gideon survived the fire. If his spirit is too stingy to rejoice, he should at least be thankful that his sister wasn't left a widow. She watches as he masters his unruly emotions, roping them in by force of will.

"No . . . not today," he says. "I've hardly been home. I have a hundred things to see to. Cal Toomey's been stopping by, but you know him, he will only do so much." He darts a look at Micah. "I suppose you'll all be coming back to stay. I had better get the rooms ready. Micah will tell you, I've let the housekeeping slide since Ma died."

"If we stay, it will only be until Gideon is stronger and we have a place to go. We're bound to be a burden on you, with the farm so small." Micah has told Sophy that James has neglected more than the house— that some months the two of them have barely enough to get by. "I wouldn't trouble you," she adds, "but we can't impose on Mr. Entwhistle any longer."

"You're family. Ma would have wanted it." James sighs, his shoulders already slumping under the weight of them. "We will all do our part, and trust God to provide."

He does not say, I'll be glad of your company, or, The farm will always be your home, or, The place is too big for Micah and me, or, I'll get to know my nephew better. He says none of these things, and their absence hangs heavy in the air. Sophy is torn between longing for the James she knew and anger at this sorry replacement, who sits like a lump of matter, twirling his hat in his hands, measuring the minutes until he can be alone with his misery. Micah is accurate: No joy.

"I think we should s-stay for a f-few days w-while you v-visit with James. W-we'll go together. It's time James got on with his life!" This last delivered in a rush, cutting into the silence with the force of a commandment.

Even James is startled. He blinks, an aperture in his stoical mask. "You'd leave home?"

"It's n-not home anymore. You're b-better off without me."

"But Micah, where would we go?" Sophy asks. "How would we manage with the baby? With Gideon?"

"We won't f-find out if we don't start."

PART SIX

BREAKING THE SILENCE

CHAPTER 40

DASH

OPHY WILL LOOK BACK ON THIS TIME AS A SINGLE STROKE
separating the two parts of her life, but in truth, she leaves the old life in
stages. Her brothers are stops along the road.

They stay a week with James: long enough to say a proper good-
bye, not so long that he gets used to them. He has kept to his word and
prepared a room for them, a refuge from encroaching squalor. Once
Gideon is made comfortable there, James has little to do with him,
spending most of his time in the fields with Micah. Gideon seems content to rest quietly and take his meals on a tray. He is still weak, unready
for the strains of company. Sophy can't rid herself of the feeling that he
is half in another world, not wholly returned from his journey.

She passes the days cleaning as she has never cleaned, assail-
ing floors and cobwebbed corners in a fury, punishing the blackened
kitchen hearth and chastising the kettle that Mama used to shine every
day. She never says a word to James, though each piece of furniture she
polishes is a rebuke. Papa's chair, how could you? Mama's carved sideboard that she cherished. The clock has stopped. She wipes the glass on
both sides and gently dusts the face, respecting the flowers she painted

under duress, the gloomy Scripture that Papa chose. The innards she leaves to Micah, who should have set them right before.

James seems confounded by her efforts. He walks from room to room with a stunned air, as if cleanliness were a conjurer's trick, accomplished with a wand instead of hours of patient labor. Sophy would like to believe he takes a message from it, but she can't be sure. His eyes shift away whenever she looks at him. Aleph is the only one who warrants a full glance. James stares and stares at his nephew, and as he looks, his face loses its aspect of inward brooding and becomes open and clear.

Micah has been working at James's side, keeping a farmhand's hours, sunup to sundown. At supper on the fifth day, he asks James if he will lend them the coach fare to Lowell to visit with Sam and his family. The three of them are sitting at one end of the long table: the raveled remnant of Tribe Hedge. In the silence that follows, Sophy hears the ghostly clamor of family dinners past.

"O-only a l-l-loan," Micah says. "P-p-payyou . . ." He leaves it there, ragged, a page torn in two.

James wipes his mouth. "Take Mercy and the wagon," he says, as if he were offering the salt. "She isn't much good to me, not worth the oats I feed her, but she'll get you as far as Lowell. If I'm going to invest in a new horse, I might as well have a new buggy too."

ON THE MORNING of their departure, Gideon asks Sophy to bring him to the study. There is a throb of life in his voice, and such pleading in his eyes that she counts it worth the risk. He hasn't walked any distance since the fire. It is a beautiful October day, the sky a brilliant blue, the trees in their glory. A year ago, on a day that could be a twin of this one, Gideon had put his arms around her in the glasshouse and they had shared a moment of perfect happiness, thinking of the child to come. As she helps him dress, it strikes her that he's coming back to the world like a babe, new and naked, every stitch he puts on borrowed from James and the parson. He stands slowly, and she drapes his arm over her shoulders and clasps him around the back. Thin as he is, she has to lock her feet to the floor to keep from buckling under his weight. Papa's crutches are long gone, but she wishes for them now.

Once, the journey across the side yard took two minutes door-to-door. When Gideon was too long at his books, she used to imagine taking a flying leap, landing on the windowsill near his desk and flapping her arms like an obstreperous crow. Now they hobble along like a pair of ancients, and with each shambling step he leans on her more heavily. She struggles to turn the key in the rusty lock.

Not a soul has been here since they left. Unlike the house, the study is orderly, everything in its place, preserved under a thick coat of dust. The atmosphere closes around them: paper and paste and moldering leather, the vapor that old books breathe out. Amber air, thick and somnolent, the past trapped in it. The books that Gideon left behind are stacked on Papa's three-sided desk, his chair at an angle as if a weary scholar had just risen to stretch his legs. Off to the side, the table where Gideon labored on the Hebrew Lexicon in the days when he was Papa's amanuensis. The woodstove where she brewed tea and warmed leftovers snatched from the pantry: make-believe mother of their pretend family. The mat in front of the stove, where she and Gideon made love. Made Aleph. Their whole history is in this room, and for a moment it seems no time has passed.

Gideon feels it too. The dust makes him cough, but he stands straighter, relieving her of some of his weight, his young self flowing back into him. She leads him to Papa's chair. He sits with a deep sigh, as if he's finally come home, and rests both hands on the desk. Sophy stands behind him, as she has so often before, gazing at the back of his head. His hair is as bright as the day she first saw him; gold, they say, is purified in fire. Where he is traveling she can't follow, but she knows she must let him go.

THE HORSE IS NOT as decrepit as James let on. She pulls them and their worldly goods along at a brisk trot and they arrive at Sam's before supper. The two older girls answer the door, and greet them with squeals and hugs. Alice and Annie have sprouted up—improved with age, Sophy thinks; Alice has a pert profile and a glint in her eye that reminds her of Sam-That-Was. His present incarnation is fatter than ever, but welcoming in his way. He is a man who takes what life sends him, and if it happens to be three family members with a wailing infant, homeless and in need of basic necessities, so much the better.

As he leads them to the kitchen, Sophy realizes that they have left one chaos for another. The house is as cluttered and unkempt as it was during her last visit, but this disorder is, at least, the result of an excess of life. They find Lucy scraping potatoes, more or less, tossing them into the pot striped with peel as little Edith tugs at her skirts. She puts the knife aside to greet them, unruffled, maybe even relieved to see her old helper. Sophy remembers, belatedly, that on this visit there will be no escaping to the attic. No sooner does she surrender Aleph to be kissed than she is on duty, separating the toddler from the knife, diverting the child's attention from the bubbling pot.

Lucy's girth has also increased. "We are in danger of becoming a matriarchy," Sam says, without resentment.

Aleph is the great attraction. Boys are a novelty in this house. The girls cluster around while she changes his diaper, giggling and pointing. "Look at his dear little handle!" Annie says. And then, as if this append-age endowed him with precocity, "Does he talk?" Aleph fixes his dark eyes on Sophy. She knows he is overwhelmed by all the changes, lost in this new world that is too much to learn. It will be all right, she tells him in their silent language.

By the time supper is finished, it's apparent that it won't be. Gideon could hardly eat for coughing; he is tense and exhausted, worn-out from the road. By parceling out the girls between the parental bedroom and a tiny spare room, Sam and Lucy manage to clear a space for the three of them to pass the night. Poor Micah is relegated to a chair and blanket in the parlor. The girls are already whining, fighting over toys and pillows. Nobody is in good humor.

"You ought to go to Reuben's," Sam tells her, weary over a pile of bedding. "He's got more rooms than he knows what to do with, and no one to fill them. He's as rich as Croesus."

"How can we? James would take it as a betrayal. He gave me some money before we left."

James had thrust the roll into her hand as she was saying her good-byes, about to step into the wagon. "For you and Micah," he said. "Ma saved more than I thought." He added, with an odd vehemence, meeting her eyes for once, "It's owed you." The words were ordinary enough, but she'd puzzled over them all the way to Lowell.

"It's time he got over that foolishness. What's past is past," says Sam, ever the pragmatist. "Reuben is still our brother, even if James disowns him. Besides, if you're going to make your way in the world, you'll need all the help you can get."

Sleepless in the narrow bed with the baby wedged between them, listening to Gideon's labored breathing, Sophy recalls what Mr. Brown said about Boston, the day he came to tell Gideon he was no longer wanted at the church. How, in the city, he would be among people who would appreciate him. His own kind.

SOPHY'S FIRST THOUGHT, upon approaching Reuben's house on Beacon Street, is that no Hedge was ever meant to live this way. Papa would have scorned such extravagance as sinful; Mama would have clicked her tongue. The brick façade is intimidating enough, cloistered behind a filigreed iron gate. For those who have the temerity to breach this first barrier, stone lions guard the columned entrance. People on the street glance with disapproval at their road-worn horse and wagon, their looks saying plainly, Tradesman's entrance is around the back. Sophy has girded herself for Caroline and her airs, but a maid in a starched cap and apron answers the door, her manner as crisp as her uniform. They wait in the hall while the Master and Madam are summoned. Yellow light floods the entry, though it is early evening, dusk outside. Sophy clasps Aleph to her; he is her protection from the grand staircase, the dwarfing height of the ceiling. She tries to connect this magnificence with the Reuben she carries in her mind: canny but rough, a sharp country boy. How did he propel himself from horse races at the fairground and card games in smoky taverns to such a state?

Reuben and Caroline descend on opposite sides of the stairway, Reuben stepping ahead as his wife manages her gown. He has a hard glitter now, but his fine clothes haven't civilized him. Sophy recognizes the swagger, the crooked smile that turns anything he says into a mockery.

"At long last! I never thought I would see family in this hall. I don't count Sam, who is not saddled with convictions. It's enough to make a man feel sentimental." He busses Sophy on one cheek, claps Micah's shoulder, nods at Gideon and pumps his hand. "And who is this?" Before Sophy can protest, he has plucked Aleph from her arms, tossed him into the air, and caught him neatly. The baby is too astonished to cry. Even Uncle Micah isn't so bold.

"It's just as well we don't have little ones," Caroline says, speaking up for the first time. "Reuben would surely kill them before their first birthday."

She is older, or perhaps only stiffer. Her famous tumbling curls are sugar icing, her cheek powdered to waxen smoothness, her waist cinched. Her taffeta dress whispers when she moves, a discreet sound like the gossip of servants.

"Sam promised he would send a note," Sophy says. "I hope it reached you?"

Reuben speaks for his wife. "No, but no matter. There's plenty of time to kill the fatted calf. Dear, would you inform cook we'll dine early tonight? These folks look as if they could do with a decent meal."

"Usually we are never at table before eight," Caroline says weakly. "But under the circumstances . . ."

THE DINING ROOM is large, and a pair of enormous gilt-framed mirrors on facing walls magnifies its grandeur. "Florentine," Reuben says.

"Got 'em at auction. I was neck and neck with a slick fellow from New York. I won." He has already taken Sophy and Micah on a house tour and given them the provenance of other conquests. For her part, Sophy believes she would eat with more enjoyment if her confusion over the forks was not thrown back at her from the glass. The food is sumptuous; Micah hasn't lifted his face from his plate, and even Gideon shows an appetite. If Caroline is chagrined to entertain such unfashionable guests, Reuben is in high good humor, raising his glass again and again. Perhaps it's simply that their company makes the table livelier. Sophy can imagine what it must be like when just the two of them dine, he seated at one end, she at the other, twelve feet of gleaming mahogany between them.

They are in a pleasant stupor, nursing coffee rich with cream, when Reuben recovers his bluntness. "Where do you intend to go when you run out of kin to visit?"

He addresses the question to Micah, without a glance at Gideon. Her little brother has always been a pet among the Hedges, indulged with fondness, loved and protected by all. Now, as Gideon recedes, he has become the man of her family. Young as he is, there is no one else.

"W-w-we thought of heading n-n-north. I-I want to s-s-start a shop. F-for my furniture, and the like."

Sophy is agog at his poise, the ready ease of his reply. They have never talked about a shop. Their whole bent has been simply to get away, to travel until a destination revealed itself. North is only a direction.

Reuben reaches behind him for a leather box on the sideboard. He opens the monogrammed lid, removes a cigar and offers one to Micah, who shakes his head. "So, you fancy yourself a masterhand. What d'you call it? An artisan. You and Sophy are cut from the same cloth."

"S-soph is the artist. I j-just like to m-m-make things."

Reuben takes a luxuriant puff, sends a plume of smoke across the table to his wife. Her nostrils pinch in disgust, but only for a second before she resumes her mask. All evening Sophy has been pondering Caroline's immobility, wondering what became of the arch, flighty creature who was always in motion, sipping first from one flower, then another. If that girl is alive at all, she is buried very deep, somewhere behind the eyes.

"Now I admire that," Reuben says. "I don't make things myself. Not directly, if you know what I mean. Pa sat on his investments. I keep them moving. Oh, I'm plenty industrious, but what I do strikes most folks as a kind of hocus-pocus. See a man here, see a man there, shake a few hands, twist an arm if I must, and . . ." He waves, scribbling smoke about the room, inviting them all to marvel at the abundance that came from nothing. "I'm thinking you should stay awhile. We can't have you wandering into the north country in the middle of winter, can we? I might have some work for you here."

Sophy, with a glance at Caroline, is about to demur. Reuben cuts her off with another wave.

"I'm in need of a chair for my library. A nice high-backed rocker like you used to make at home. I've got chairs a-plenty and each one has a pedigree, but they're murder to a man's back, no good for having a smoke in at the end of a long day. It's no wonder our ancestors were always in a temper, riding off to war at the first opportunity." He taps ash onto his plate. "And while you're occupied, the artist can do me a service, if she's willing. She can paint me a portrait of my lady wife to go over this mantel. You see how empty it looks, there, above her head."

Caroline's mask does not alter, but two pink spots appear in the porcelain of her cheeks and her eyes mist over. Sophy feels a twinge of disgust for her brother. His pleasure in the torment is so open and casual; he savors his wife's humiliation along with his port, and thinks no more of it than if he were teasing a dog.

"I haven't lifted a brush for months," she tells him. "A beautiful woman like Caroline deserves a true artist to do her justice. I'm sure there are many painters in this city who would be honored to have her sit for them."

It is an odd thing to watch a face bloom. Caroline lifts her chin. "Nonsense, Sophy," she says, with a touch of her old coquetry. "You'll do fine. What chats we'll have, we sisters! It will be like old times."

———

MONEY IS ITS OWN MAGIC. Easel, paints, and canvas appear, all first-quality. "Do a good job and I'll see that you have something better to travel in than that old rattletrap of a wagon," Reuben says. "How well you paint decides how well you ride."

Caroline plans an excursion to the Art Gallery at the Athenaeum—to get ideas for costumes and poses, she says. More likely, she hopes a bit of expertise will rub off on her country relation. She loans Sophy a dress for the occasion, one of her plainer frocks. Sophy feels like a dressmaker's dummy, pins everywhere; still, it is great fun to play the lady for the afternoon. She sweeps through the doors of the great mansion on Pearl Street as if she belongs there but can't repress a gasp when they enter the Gallery. Her scant knowledge of the Art called Fine comes from Papa; she's seen few examples for herself. She wonders now why Papa ever indulged her, for how could her father's God—a practical Yankee craftsman, if there ever was one—surpass the cold perfection of these sculptures, the richness and scale of the paintings? It seems, on first sight, that the flower of civilization must be contained in this long room. There is a high beauty here, but it is purely of this world, and the hunger it kindles in Sophy is earthly. *I want to make this. I will never make this. Let me try.* Caroline keeps nudging her, making remarks behind her hand. "Have you ever seen so many pictures of old men? Oh, here's Venus! Wouldn't Reuben like it if I dressed like her!" Sophy scarcely hears, having long ago succumbed to awe. She ought to be casting a critical eye, observing technique, and all she can do is take the paintings in whole. It seems the height of ingratitude to dissect such sublimity.

In the carriage on the way home, Caroline says: "It's no use taking you anywhere, Sophy. You're such a dreamer. I don't believe you were paying attention at all."

AFTER A CIRCUIT of the house, she and Caroline are quick to choose a sunny corner of the music room as the perfect background. Selecting a gown takes an entire day. Frock after billowy frock is heaped on the canopy bed, and Caroline must model each one, and Sophy must offer her opinion, and pass judgment on this neckline and that sleeve, whether this style fulfills Caroline's dire suspicions and makes her look plump. Sophy soon loses all power of discernment, but eventually truth is revealed in the form of a simple blue satin trimmed with lace. Both agree that the gown must not overwhelm the subject, that the blue is the exact color of Caroline's eyes.

Aleph, though a favorite of the housemaids, will stay in the room while Sophy works. Caroline calls him her dark-eyed Spanish boy and adores him from a sanitary distance. "I have such a heart for children," she confides to Sophy, "but I can't risk having one of my own. My nerves wouldn't stand it."

Each morning after breakfast they retire to the music room. Sophy has dissuaded Caroline from sitting at the pianoforte, pleading her own ineptitude and the strain of the pose, and Caroline has graciously settled for a sheet of music in one hand. Sophy is surprised at how natural it feels to paint again. She had expected days of struggle, reluctant fingers wielding a clumsy brush, but she'd swear she's more fluent than before, as if dormancy only sharpened her powers. The sketching goes quickly, and soon she is absorbed in the task. While she paints, Caroline talks, never pausing for a reply. Though the motions of her mouth change her face, Sophy doesn't ask her to stop. The lineament of Caroline is in the pencil sketch. Her words do what the paint does: add flesh to the bones.

Your brother is a harsh man. I don't say it to hurt you, but I am quite broken. You can see the strain I'm under. It's aged me, I know it has . . .

Paint the brittle surface, but let the old Caroline show through. Both are true. Smooth the brow and that little sack under the chin. Bring up the blush beneath the powder, blur the lines around the mouth to coax a rose from a pinched bud. Loosen those curls, give them a little freedom to wander.

Papa wouldn't see me for the longest while, but we are reconciled now. He knows how I suffer. If it weren't for him and dear Mama, I would go mad. I have no society here. The ladies are very uppish and treat me like a country bumpkin though I live better than they do. Reuben is generous, I'll say that for him. But there's no love in it. It's all show.

Get the sheen of the satin, the richness. Give the bosom its own sheen, but subtle; her breasts haven't aged, she still has them to barter with. Hands are difficult, make the lace trim a little longer. Do these stick figures look like musical notes? Do later.

Sophy, I have no right to ask, but . . . how is James? Not a day goes by that I don't think of him. I am very sorry. I would tell him so if it would do any good. I was a silly girl, what did I know of love? I deserve my misery. I'm resigned to it. Oh, Sophy, if he knew how my heart breaks he would pity me. Do you think he would?

Leave the eyes as they are. She's earned them.

THE AFTERNOONS ARE for Gideon. On sunny days she and Micah take him for excursions in Reuben's carriage, up Beacon Hill and around the Common. Sophy tries to tempt him with Lyceum lectures, bookstores, the Athenaeum, but he shows little enthusiasm. One bright Saturday she plots with Micah to bring him to Cambridge, hoping that the sight of his college will spark memories of the promising young scholar. She plans to tell him when they arrive that a classmate of his, Joshua Sturgis, is lecturing at the Divinity School.

The journey is their longest since arriving in Boston. The December landscape has its own stark beauty, and Sophy is exhilarated to be in the country again. She wishes she could ride in front with Micah, feel the wind sting her cheeks. Gideon gazes out the window with a pleasant, neutral expression. He has seemed a little more engaged today, and she imagines that he will be as excited to see his old haunts as she is to view them for the first time.

When they reach the bridge, he stares down at the murky Charles. "Cambridge? Why are you taking me here?"

"I thought you would enjoy seeing Harvard again. You used to speak of it so often, and Papa said—"

"If you had told me, I would have spared you the trip. It's a part of the past. I have no sentiment about it." He had raised his voice, and now he starts to cough, putting a hand to his chest as he searches for his handkerchief.

For once, she lets him struggle on his own. "Since you don't care about the college, or much else, Micah and I will take a little tour ourselves. Reverend Sturgis is speaking today. You've mentioned him, I think? Perhaps you can sit in an alcove while we listen to his talk. I've no mind for theology, but I like to improve myself."

They are silent until Harvard College comes into sight, the red-brick buildings set back on the green (which in this season doesn't merit the name), looking just as they do in the painting Papa made. Papa had enclosed the scene in an oval with valedictory scrolls sprouting from the borders. Sophy is momentarily startled to see how far this citadel of learning actually extends, the field of knowledge vaster than she had ever dreamed as a child.

Gideon reaches for her hand. "Sophy, you do so much for me, you always have. You deserve better. But there's so little of me left. It's painful for me to be among men like Sturgis, who cut a figure in the world. What have I to offer? A broken man who's failed at everything."

"You're young, Gideon! You still have your good mind. If only you would take advantage of the riches here, you might be inspired to work again. Why shouldn't your greatest accomplishments be before you?" She looks away as she exhorts him, afraid of what his eyes will tell her. "Come for a walk with us. A short one. Show us where you lived and studied."

Sophy and Micah stand close on either side of him, letting him set the pace. She thinks of Papa on his crutches, strong young Gideon alert to catch him if he fell. Now he walks slowly, gazing around him with a dazed expression, a ghost at his own funeral. Sophy wonders if he's pondering the same thing she is: What became of the driven young man with his armload of books, plotting his future as he rushed to his next class? She prods him with questions and he points out his dormitory, the halls where he studied Greek and ancient history, the notorious Rebellion Tree where the effigy of President Quincy was hanged in '34. If he is remote, she is carried away, imagining what a banquet it would be to study at such a place. When Gideon spoke of Harvard, it was often to tell tales on his fellow students, spoiled ingrates who squandered their days and nights drinking and carousing, harassing their tutors for having the impertinence to teach them. But Sophy is thinking that she must find a way to send Aleph here.

The Divinity School is outside the Yard, further than he should walk. "If we're to be in time for Mr. Sturgis . . ." she begins.

"I'm tired." Gideon's grip on her arm is firm. "I've enjoyed this, but I'm ready to go back now."

THE PORTRAIT IS FINISHED. Caroline is pleased with the result. She gazes at her image, widening her eyes and puckering her lips in the *moue* of feigned surprise that she wears before the looking glass.

"You've *seen* me, Sophy," she says. "You've painted my soul."

This is a semblance of the truth, not the whole. In painting Caroline, Sophy has learned much about the painting of faces in general. Capture the features with some accuracy, but refine where possible. Look behind the eyes to discern how the person sees herself, how she wishes to be seen, what she longs for that life has denied her. Seek the balance between flattery and revelation. It is a narrow ledge to teeter on: more precarious than landscapes; more exacting, if less satisfying, than the paintings she spins out of her own fancy. A skill she can put to use, if she has to.

What does Caroline long for, more than attention and admiration, more even than love? Dignity. Looking at the portrait, Sophy thinks, I've given her that.

Caroline has devoted a great deal of thought to the unveiling. "Jepson will hang the picture this afternoon—all in secret, of course. I'll be sitting in my usual place tonight, wearing the blue gown. Can you imagine Reuben's expression when he sees two of me?" Sophy has to remind her that the paint is only just dry; that, in any case, a painting can't be hung without a frame. By way of compromise, they decide to set the easel near Caroline's chair and cover the painting with a cloth.

"I suppose it will be more theatrical," Caroline says. "Isn't that what they do with statues?"

By dinnertime she has worked herself into a frenzy of nerves, bolting out of the chair again and again to correct the angle of the easel, questioning the drapery—the ivory shawl looks foolish, but where to find a sheet small enough?—and the wisdom of wearing the dress she was painted in. Sophy tries to soothe her, but she is nervous, too. If Reuben is a true son of Mama and Papa, there must be some kindness in him. She says a silent prayer that it will show itself tonight.

He strides in, trailed by Gideon and Micah. He smells of the city, of tobacco and hair oil, wool-clad men in close rooms. "What have we here? A bust of Washington? Someone's shy old auntie?"

Sophy wills herself to be calm. She had intended to make a little presentation at meal's end, when Reuben was mellow with brandy. A few deferential remarks, the shawl swept off with a flourish to give Caroline her moment of drama. But Caroline won't last that long. She has composed herself with care, but she's taut with the effort, near to trembling. A brusque word will undo her.

Better to be quick about it. Sophy rises, and, without a word, uncovers the painting. Clutching the shawl awkwardly she returns to her seat.

No one speaks at first. Then Gideon says, "Very fine, Sophy. A remarkable likeness."

"B-best you've ever done!" Micah flushes, as though he's heaped praise on himself.

"Any merit is due to Caroline," Sophy says. "She was the perfect subject."

The lady in question has not stirred. Her agitation has ebbed; her bosom rises and falls gently. She seems to have sunk into a reverie, indifferent to their praise, oblivious even to Reuben's narrow, assessing gaze. Sophy wonders if her soul has passed into the painting after all. Mama's cautions may have been sound: this capturing of images is a more literal business than she bargained for, and not to be undertaken lightly.

Reuben's eyes rove from the painting to Caroline, and back again. Sophy guesses it has been some time since he troubled to look at her.

He turns to Sophy, chin in hand, and nods. "You had better do one of me, too, Sis. My wife will be lonely staring at a bare wall."

IT IS MARCH BEFORE they get away. She has painted Reuben, and the pug dog Caroline acquired, and a pastoral scene for the drawing room. Micah has made a handsome rocking chair and an ingenious ladder that slides along the top of the shelves in the library, should Reuben ever feel moved to read the books he purchased with the house. Aleph has left his first birthday behind, and is already walking. He is his own small person now, an adventurous spirit, refusing to be confined to the room Caroline designated as the nursery. He's learned a few words, and flaunts them incessantly; Gideon wonders if it is too early to introduce him to Latin.

Reuben has offered to find them decent lodgings in Boston. "You could do well here," he says. "Why run off when you've made a good start?" But not one of them wants to stay in the city. For all the comforts, it has been a hard winter. Gideon fell ill after Christmas with a cold that settled in his chest, and Aleph sickened soon after. Sophy, worn out with nursing, feared that neither would see his next birthday. Micah blames it on the sooty city air, the crowds breathing in the foulness and spreading it around. He draws Sophy's attention to the gray snow: "If we stay here much longer, our insides will look like that." Though, of all of them, he is the most miserable, Sophy misses the country herself. Reuben has been true to his word and purchased them a carriage so capacious that—she tells herself—they could almost live in it. They may have to. The money in her purse won't last forever.

THE WEEK BEFORE they are to leave, one of the maids presents her with a letter. It is addressed to her, but has come by way of Sam, who sent it on to Reuben. Parson Entwhistle's handwriting is neat with little flourishes, like the man himself. He asks after her family's health and well-being, trusts that they are prospering wherever the Lord has led them. *How empty my house seemed after your departure! The quietness I had cherished rebuked me. You may think your long visit was a burden, but I never doubted I was entertaining "angels unawares."*

He encloses a letter he has received, after a number of fruitless inquiries, from Rabbi Goldenblum of the synagogue in Kassel. The paper is thin and crisp like parchment, the looping script so antiquated that Sophy at first mistakes the formal English for German. She manages to decipher that the rabbi knew of no Leander Solloway, but was acquainted with one Leopold Solomon, son of Immanuel, a banker whose estimable family had been pillars of the synagogue for generations. The younger Solomon, though gifted, was afflicted with a mercurial temperament, dabbling in finance and the study of medicine but persisting in neither. His father arranged an early marriage, hoping to stabilize him, but, alas, his wife perished after a few years, and his little son did not long survive her. In the wake of this loss, the young man ceased attending synagogue and resumed a youthful infatuation with the occult—"a quest for the forbidden that, since the time of our First Parents, has never had a happy end." Father and son were soon permanently estranged. Leopold left Kassel, all ties cut, and has not been heard from since. Both parents are dead; there was a sister, much older, who married and settled in Hamburg years ago. "I do not know if young Solomon is the person you seek," the rabbi concluded, "but some men wear many faces, and Leopold was one of those."

Mr. Entwhistle writes: *Whatever the fate of our Mr. Solloway, it is a great pity for anyone to be so alone in the world.*

PART SEVEN

AFTERLIFE

CHAPTER 41

WORKING FROM LIFE

FACES, SCATTERED ALONG THE KNOBBY SHORELINE OF NEW England. Oil or watercolor. Paid for with coins or paper. Bartered for meals and lodging, children's garments, the attentions of a doctor when Gideon is poorly. A week here, a fortnight there, a month elsewhere.

In Marblehead, triplets: three little beans in matching pinafores. She does what she can to distinguish them, giving one a shiny apple, another a flower, the third an open book. "Now I can tell them apart!" the Mama exclaims, as if they came equipped with these emblems in life.

In Salem, a minister, his wife, five children, and ancient mother, with deceased paterfamilias glowering from a frame on the wall. It takes over a month, and not a smile among them.

In Gloucester, a young salt in a sailor suit, pet parrot on his shoulder.

In Ipswich, newlyweds who pose on either side of a table displaying their most important acquisition, a brass-and-marble lamp lavished with crystal drops. "Could you put in a bit of the carpet for the same price?" the wife wants to know.

In Newburyport, a baby on the eve of its burial. She is reluctant, but the mother pleads so, she can't say no. She paints the eyes open, as requested.

In Portsmouth, New Hampshire, a peacock of a fellow who swells his chest and thrusts a hand in his jacket like Napoleon. Though he says the portrait is for his fiancée, his eye is always wandering to the ruby stickpin that adorns his cravat, a beauty that draws his tender glances, the furtive caresses of his thumb. Can one be adulterous with objects? Sophy makes the jewel as red and glaring as a devil's mark, and hopes the lady will be warned.

Portsmouth is the first place they think of staying. It's a handsome town with sturdy brick buildings lining the main streets, the legacy of several ruinous fires. "Enough" is the word Sophy uses most often when presenting the idea to Gideon and Micah. Large enough, but not too large. Far enough from where they started, but not so far that they can never go home. Prosperous enough that folks will pay to be immortalized. And—her best argument—fine furniture is made here. Traveling from town to town, Micah brings in a few extra dollars making frames for her paintings. In Portsmouth he can apprentice himself to a cabinetmaker, learn the trade, one day have a shop of his own.

They are standing on the wharf, four inlanders looking out at the Atlantic on a humid day in July, savoring the breeze that lifts their hair and pastes her skirt to her legs. Sophy knows already that they will never live far from the ocean, yet she fears the sea as much as she is drawn to it. Fears it with a proper awe, as Papa said she must fear God, but more so, for she can't buy its mercy by being good. It will swallow what she loves without a thought. Aleph would jump right in if she didn't keep a tight hold on his hand; he is straining toward the water now, excited by the gulls, the boats, the endless slapping of the waves. All boys want to run away to sea, but hers won't end up a sailor if she can help it.

Her worry for Gideon is different, though its end is the same. He stares at the water with glazed attention, like a man hypnotized, ready to jump on command. He's too quiet these days, too compliant, never protesting when their lodgings are less than ideal or when they move on yet again. His will, once so strong, seems to have expired, a casualty of the fire. Or the purpose that I stole from him, she thinks. He waits, without urgency, to be overtaken by a greater force, if not man then nature. Her free arm is looped through his. She almost lost him once. She won't let the ocean take him without a fight.

Still, she says, "We could make a life here, don't you think?"

"One place is as good as another," Gideon says.

Micah has been silent all this time, watching Aleph watch the gulls. "T-t-too many here doing what I do. I w-want to be on my own—not working under some p-p-puffed-up fellow who gives me orders. I s-say we go on."

He is rarely so emphatic. He's more certain of himself now, Sophy realizes. He's grown into his opinions, as a man must. Portsmouth is a good place, but for them not good enough.

They move north toward Maine. The state, proclaimed as such for a scant twenty years, seems to her rough-carved out of wilderness and half civilized, Indian names cohabiting with the English. The pine trees are thick and dark, and cast long, pointed shadows. Even in broad daylight there is a hush, a sense of presences concealed and waiting. Massachusetts, with its tamed land diced neatly into farms and village greens, is very far away.

But there are towns, and they are revelations, the houses nestled cozily in the immensity that surrounds them, the ocean lapping at the edges of their domesticity. In Kennebunk Port they board with a sailmaker's wife. Sophy paints her in profile, looking out her window toward the shed where her husband works, "keepin' an eye on 'im one way or t'other," as the woman says.

Portland, Camden, Belfast. Wherever they stay, Micah makes his way to the shipyard. Levelheaded as he is, the sea air intoxicates him. He talks of working for a shipwright, furnishing boats instead of houses, making wooden parts rather than chairs.

"I thought you didn't want to be an apprentice," she says.

This is different, he tells her. He has watched the men work, seen how easy they are with one another. He searches for the word, stumbles over it when he finds it. *Camaraderie.* Maybe this is what he needs,

Sophy thinks: to do a man's work among men, plying his skills without his tongue getting in the way.

In Blue Hill, a village that reminds her of Ormsby, the innkeeper says, "I hear they're looking for joiners over to Castine."

THEY HAVE LIVED HERE for five years. The elder Hedges would have called it an extended visit. The four of them call it home. Castine is a town of useful beauty, seasoned by the salt sea. Ships are built and fitted and sailed here, fish are caught and preserved and sold. It is a shire town, housing both a courthouse and its logical outcome, a jail. A prosperous town without being pompous. The occupants of the pristine white mansions lining Court and Main streets are as likely to be shipowners and shipbuilders as lawyers: hardworking men not born to wealth. Sophy has painted them in stately solitude, in their parlors or alongside their boats, and in the company of their wives and children and dogs. For an extra fee she will embed miniature vistas in the background of her portraits: a busy wharf glimpsed through a window, and in the distance a toy boat bobbing on symmetrical waves; the village Common with courthouse in view (this for a judge). She has achieved some small reputation, here and in the surrounding towns. Folks who have never dreamed of being painted put on their best clothes and sit still for the lady artist. Not only her sex but her smallness works in her favor. The roughest men are always the most impressed: she cherishes the memory of a burly stonemason who kept stroking his beard and muttering, "Well, I'll be!" as his likeness emerged on the canvas. She travels from town to town in the cart she bartered for painting the local doctor and his wife, often alone now, though in the old days, when he was too young to study, Aleph would come with her.

He is six-going-on-seven, tall and serious, a boy of few words though he knows many. He says what he has to say, stops to consider, speaks again if called for. Around town he has a reputation for being thoughtful beyond his years. Sophy can't be sure what he remembers but is certain that the silence of his first year is as much a part of him as his blood and bones. The hesitations don't concern her, for his mind is agile: Gideon began to teach him Latin at five and has just started him on Hebrew. Aleph is quick to learn, but his strongest natural bent is mathematical. He is good at sums—does them in his head for fun. They all marvel at it, though no one can imagine where such a rogue talent came from. Sophy suspects he caught more than a cold at Reuben's, that some spirit of mercantilism infected him during their weeks in Boston. They are already making use of his gift. Between the two of them, Sophy and Micah make a decent living, yet neither has a head for business. Each month Sophy gives Aleph the book she keeps of her commissions, and earnestly, bending close over the pages with a death grip on his pencil, he adds up the proceeds.

He is a regular boy in other ways, impatient with Gideon's gentle tutoring and longing to be off on his own adventures. They rent a small house on High Street, equidistant from the two poles of his existence, the wharves and the lighthouse. He loves to go to the shipyard to watch Micah work, but the dock is an even greater attraction, with ships disembarking from Cádiz and Liverpool and Le Havre. One summer afternoon he came home in a state of ecstasy, wearing a red cap that one of the French sailors had given him.

"You have no business talking to those rough men!" Gideon scolded. "You're not to go there again."

"They speak *French*! You told me I must learn French," Aleph said, sniffling. Sophy was amused that he knew his father so well.

The lighthouse is farther up the road they live on, but might as well be on an island, moored as it is on a tongue of land jutting out from a pasture. Once High Street ends, it's a long, solitary walk to get there, with only a couple of bleak farmhouses along the way. The place has a particular romance for Aleph; he says the beacon lights up his dreams. Micah took him there earlier in the summer and Aleph talked about the excursion for days: how the keeper lived all by himself in a round room at the top of a winding staircase, and manned his great lamp day and night. He had all sorts of questions. When did the man sleep? Did the gulls bring him food?

"I'd like to do that," he said, adding, like a little philosopher, "It would be a good life."

"Oh, I think you'd be lonely," Sophy said quickly. "All by yourself up there, staring at the ocean day after day and no one to talk to."

"I'd get a wife! She could read to me and cook for me. Micah says keepers can have wives." He walked away then, as if the matter was settled.

A few days later, she arrived home from Blue Hill to find Gideon pacing back and forth, agitated. He had tutored Aleph in the morning, as usual, and after making them something to eat had dozed for a while. When he woke, the boy had disappeared. "I went to town, to the wharves, the yard. Micah hasn't seen him. Nobody has seen him. For all I know, he could be stowed away in the hold of some ship. I warned him about those sailors . . ." He broke off, coughing. Sophy made tea to calm him, chiding him for walking so far. She knew where Aleph had gone.

Although the day was warm, she walked rapidly, quickened by a gnawing worry that had little to do with a small boy turning off a lonely road and following cart tracks through tall grass. Her son had started life with disadvantages that turned his childish fancy into a prophet's warning. He mustn't end up in an isolated room, staring at the horizon and communing with his thoughts. He mustn't fall back into silence. She had not rescued him for that.

Shading her eyes, she saw Aleph coming toward her, his gait lopsided, favoring his left leg. Sophy lifted her skirt and ran, calling his name. He picked up his pace and hobbled straight into her arms. His face was streaked with dirt and tears, and the knee of one trouser leg was torn, but he was full of the wonderful thing that had happened. The lighthouse keeper had waved at him from a window! Smiled at him like the man in the moon!

That night, after Aleph was in bed, she said to Gideon, "He is ready to go to the village school."

"Ready? He'd be so far advanced, the teacher wouldn't know what to make of him. A boy who speaks Hebrew and Latin, who is gifted at numbers—you'd trust his mind to a country schoolmistress? I've heard tales about the lady. One of those narrow souls who'd break a boy's spirit for his own good. She wields a mean switch, they say."

"If she touches my boy, she'll have me to contend with. You'll always be his teacher, Gideon, I promise you that. But there are things we can't give him. He needs to be with other children now. It's time."

He seemed to be considering, but the light was already fading from his eyes. "If you think it best," he said quietly.

One more thing she had taken from him. His only remaining purpose, all that was left of his vision: the education of his son. The shame Sophy had held back earlier washed over her. Gideon was her husband, however altered. Shouldn't her first loyalty be to him? As she'd watched Aleph walking toward her, a thought had entered her mind, stifled as soon as it formed: He mustn't become his father. Above all, not that.

AUTUMN COMES EARLY to Maine. It is Sophy's favorite season in Castine, its beauties so abundant that she calls it her season of justification. Gideon was uncommonly cheerful this morning; the crisp air has restored some of his energy. He left early with Aleph to visit the school and cultivate the good graces of the fearsome Miss Dilworth, who'll rule over the boy from next week on. Afterward they'll walk down to the yard to see Micah and stop at the baker's for a treat—"to celebrate your last days as a free man," Gideon said, sounding like a boy himself.

As he was getting ready to leave, she dared to ask him the question that was always in her mind, but never voiced. "Gideon, are you happy?"

His brow clouded. "I suppose I'm as content as a useless person can be. Why do you ask?"

"You are stronger now. You could do a little tutoring. Judge Ward has a son, and I know others who'd be interested." She hesitated. "You could write a book."

He looked at her. "What on earth would I write about?"

Aleph burst in then, with his jacket crookedly buttoned and his necktie flapping around his collar, and she was saved from answering.

A day as lovely as this one makes Sophy defiant. She pleads her case point by point. The air bright and clear, with a salty tang that thrills the blood. *Was it more invigorating to breathe in your Paradise?* The pure blue of the sky reflected in the waters of the Bay; the patches of coppery seaweed, the islands set like jewels in a silver sea. *The colors you saw, that green you made so much of—were they more vivid than these?* Against this sky, the whitewashed houses, the Indian paint of the foliage, the brass weather vane atop the church spire gleaming in the sun. *The new world you walked through—were its edges sharper there? Were its contrasts more surprising to the eye, its harmonies more subtly blended?*

She wants to wave the evidence in Gideon's face, prove to him that this life they've made is rich and full, tolerable in its imperfections, lovable for its quiet joys. But Paradise is a worm that eats at the brain. At moments of earthly happiness there is always a nagging tug of doubt. If she'd had the courage to take his hand that day in the sickroom, where might they be residing now? What kind of man might Gideon have become if left to pursue his vision? She will never know if she has chosen the best of all worlds, or only Portsmouth, not good enough.

WHILE HER FAMILY is gone, Sophy plans to spend a few hours in the room she set aside for a studio. Until now she's used it mostly for finishing work and storage; she is an artist-for-hire, and the real labor of painting is done in her patron's houses. But Micah is weary of the shipyard and has been talking of expanding the space, adding a shed where he can make furniture again. They'll have an atelier; she will paint and he will carve, and folks will come to them.

The room is south-facing, the sunniest in the house, home to chests and broken chairs that Aleph can hide behind, or erect as battlements in the epic war he's conducting between his tin soldiers and the chessmen Micah made for him. Sophy steps carefully to avoid upsetting the armies; a week ago she knocked over a whole line of troops, and the General made a great fuss. A truce this morning, the floor is clear.

She isn't sure if she'll paint today, but it is pleasant to contemplate a clean workspace of her own. She could have a couch for patrons, make a painted backdrop for posing, even hire a model. She could stack her prepared canvases against this wall—and here she finds the armies, lined up neatly on either side of a bulky package bound in twine. Aleph has balanced a soldier and a chessman on top, staring at each other across a plaid divide. Spies? she wonders nonsensically. One-to-one combat?

Five years, and she hasn't opened it. Long enough to render it invisible, another dusty relic that she'll attend to one of these days. If the contents are harmless, what is she afraid of? The vapors of the past rising up to envelop her as soon as she cuts the twine, spreading through the house, polluting the family's hard-won tranquility? More likely, she'll find a few faded images, cracked and flaking from neglect.

She returns the soldiers to their allies, and goes to find her scissors.

Folding back the blanket, she lifts the paintings out one by one and arranges them in a semicircle on the floor. They're in better shape than she expected, but so few, really; a pittance, compared to what she's done these last few years. A couple of early landscapes—why had she bothered to keep them? The only one worth saving is *The Naming of the Animals*; her Adam is a flesh-colored blotch, though the baboon has an innocent charm. The double-sided portraits of herself and Gideon make her blush, not for the original reason. Can she ever have painted so crudely? The paint looks as if it were slapped on like clay, obscuring Gideon's fine features. Her angelic philosopher is as florid and full-cheeked as a butcher's boy! As for the callow young woman—she's no better than she ought to be, as Mama used to say. She passes quickly over her childish picture of the study—one of Gideon's favorites, but tainted by the memory of what they did that day. Some things don't bear revisiting.

The stark winter scene, her state of mind reflected in the begging branches. But on the back is the couple in the bell jar, a painting she can be proud of. The flying serpent is beautifully done. Leander to the life. Sophy has never doubted that he is somewhere in this world, inhabiting another name, another set of clothes, a different profession. His wings still shadow her. His eyes graze each picture she paints. His voice, with its haughty flick of German, its amused precision, is still in her head.

Among themselves, they never speak of him. It is as if, in regard to the man they knew as Leander Solloway, the compact of silence prevails. Sophy wonders if he haunts the others as he haunts her. When Gideon withdraws into himself, brooding, his eyes far away, she imagines that he is pining for his old friend, mourning for what might have been. Micah is younger and more apt to put away the past. Perhaps, in his view, he has gone farther than Moses ever did—entered the Promised Land after all.

Though, in the course of her busy days she has no time for Leander, he invades her dreams at night, ever a man of insinuation, coming at her sidewise, burrowing into her need. He enjoys her, simply and silently, exploring her with his hands and mouth, waking her sleeping parts, and for a moment she is alive in her body as she used to be when she danced, and when it is over . . . it is over. Leander is gone, and she has no regrets.

She had called the painting *Annunciation*, but for all its polish, it isn't finished. The words she meant to inscribe on the serpent's wings have never revealed themselves. It would be easy enough to copy some Hebrew characters from Gideon's books, but this seems like cheating. What good are letters that don't spell a message?

Sophy closes her eyes. "I suppose you fancy yourself my muse. If you have something to tell me, Mr. Solloway, say it now. Plain English will do, thank you."

The sound of her own breathing. Noises from the street drift in, muted, as if the world had held back as long as it could so as not to spoil her hopes. The silence is eloquent. The paintings are the only message she will ever have from this most talkative of men. He has done his part. The rest he leaves to her.

HER EASEL IS by the window, the chair at an angle, beckoning her. She brings the only drawing she'd saved, a hasty sketch of her strange dream on the night Aleph was born. She had asked for her sketchbook while she was still confined to bed, fearful that the details would slip away. The mountain of a man; the woman peering out of his middle, contemplating the world outside through bars of bone. She always meant to make a painting of the Pregnant Adam, but never had time, and now she isn't sure she has the capacity. Portraits are a great discipline, but working from life fences in the imagination. The subject is always there, before her, demanding, *Make the best of me.* She can infuse; she no longer invents. How to recover that playfulness? Shake off her hard-won skills and romp in Eden?

Sophy sets the sketch aside. One day, perhaps. The image is old, part of the past; it doesn't stir her now. There is a moment she would rather capture, though whether it can be rendered in paint is doubtful. What does the woman see in that first instant—before she is Eve, before she is anyone—when she is delivered from her long hibernation into the world of light? Oil is too heavy and plodding, she would have to use watercolor and bring it off like a magic trick, instant translation, her hand as quick as her eye. Lacking new eyes herself, she would have to sink so deep into Eve that she saw through hers. An impossible feat. She's a humble picture-maker, no magician. But even as she takes refuge in this thought, images are coming to her. Pastels. A mix of colors raining down, the sky like a turbulent sea. In the foreground, a small, huddled figure, a mermaid out of her element, marooned on the forest floor.

She pins a fresh sheet of paper to the easel and confronts the white.

AFTER SUPPER THEY gather in the parlor for the evening reading. Sophy has been working her way through Sir Walter Scott; she is well into *Ivanhoe*, and Aleph and Micah are hanging on her every word. She has just opened the book when Aleph stands and clasps his hands behind his back. He has an air of fierce seriousness, as if called upon to recite in class.

"I have something to tell you," he says. "I have a new name."

Gideon snaps to attention. "You don't like your name? It belongs to you. No one else has one like it."

"It won't do for school."

Aleph has been told the story of his name many times. He is well acquainted with the ox and the Beginning before the Beginning. But they're all aware that the name has been a trouble to him. People can't get their mouths around it; they trim it to fit what is familiar. He's been called Alva, Adolph, Alfred, even, when he was still in skirts, Olive. Worst of all is Alf. Aleph is a stoical boy, but he can't abide Alf.

"You have a perfect right to choose your name," Gideon says, leaning forward. "Will you . . . will you tell us what it is?"

They look at one another, Sophy and Gideon and Micah. There isn't a sound in the room. Breath is suspended, the flame in the hearth stops dancing, the hands of the clock freeze, for who knows what power time will wield in a new world?

"Tom."

The quiet syllable, flat on the air.

Gideon rubs the dent in his nose where his spectacles rest. He puts his knuckles to his eyes and rubs with such vigor that Sophy thinks he must be stanching tears, but when he takes his hands away, his eyes are dry. He smiles, a slow smile, and opens his arms to his son. "Tom! Now that is a very fine name."

ACKNOWLEDGMENTS

I AM INDEBTED TO THE NATIONAL ENDOWMENT FOR THE ARTS for vital support during the making of this book and to the Bread Loaf Writers' Conference for a fellowship.

I'm grateful to all who read portions of the novel, but I owe abiding thanks to two faithful readers who read chapters as I wrote them and offered abundant wisdom along the way. Kate Blackwell's acute insights and sensitive perceptions always instructed and inspired; our conversations about our work have leavened the solitude of the desk. Sandy Cohen has given me the benefit of her painter's eye and sharp mind, and has proved to be as adept in the editorial realm as in matters of the law. When the draft was done, Lynn Auld Schwartz interrupted her busy writing life to read the whole thing and give helpful analysis. Chris Hale's comments on early chapters helped to set the course, and Victoria Hobson's meticulous close reading unearthed details I might have overlooked. I am thankful for members of our small writing community, Ann Jensen, Vicki Meade, Paula Novash, Laura Oliver, Lynn Schwartz, Christe Spiers, and Heather Wolf, who have given encouragement and support, and greatly enriched my life in Annapolis.

The sober volumes of advice for young ladies that Sophy contemplates reading in Chapter 4 are lined up on my desk thanks to Ann Jensen, who plundered her family archive for primary sources and her bookshelves for research material. I've enjoyed our talks about the challenges of writing historical fiction.

Several years ago, on a visit to the Farnsworth Art Museum in Rockland, Maine, I saw an early-nineteenth-century landscape of the village of Blue Hill, each of its sparse buildings lovingly rendered, and in the lower right corner a man in a tall hat waving a stick at a serpent, chasing the Devil out of town. The artist was the Rev. Jonathan Fisher, a polymath parson who knew several languages and had invented his own coded alphabet. Fisher was the inspiration for the Rev. Samuel Hedge, another stern Calvinist besotted with language. Although Rev. Hedge is a fictional character, I've endowed him with Fisher's love of Hebrew and borrowed Fisher's Alphabetical Bestiary and his reversible engraving table to furnish his study.

The definition of "baboon" that provokes Gideon's contempt in the prologue is an actual quote from a book I found on a secondhand shelf years ago, *A Dictionary of English Etymology*, by Hensleigh Wedgwood, published in 1878.

Leander Solloway's comments on Moses's stuttering in the chapter "Alliteration" were inspired by ideas in Joel Rosenberg's fascinating essay, "A Treatise on the Making of Hebrew Letters," in *The Jewish Catalog*, edited by Siegel, Strassfeld, and Strassfeld, 1973.

Information for Gideon's thesis about the historical quest for the first language was found in *The First Word: The Search for the Origins of Language*, by Christine Kenneally, 2007, and *World of Words: The Personalities of Language*, by Gary Jennings, 1984.

I am deeply grateful to my editor, Amy Cherry, for her valuable feedback, sound guidance, and skillful nurturing of the book in all its stages. If patience is a kind of faith, hers carried me through. My long-time agent, Wendy Weil, passed away suddenly two years ago. Two emails that she wrote me the week before she died remain on my desk, tokens of her presence.

There is no way to adequately thank my husband Stewart for his constant love and support. The characters in this book have inhabited his life as well, and we've had some lovely moments discussing them over a glass of wine. My daughter Sara is my tech guru, and I thank her for connecting her Luddite mom to the modern world and only occasionally rolling her eyes.

Finally, I would like to remember with love Ed and Jean Ryden, cousins who made art all their lives, who long ago sent me a small check and told me to keep writing.